The START *of* SUMMER

Alison Walsh has worked in publishing and literary journalism for a number of years. She wrote a popular and humorous column on family life for the *Irish Independent* for some years, and this was followed by a memoir on motherhood, *In My Mother's Shoes*, which became a number-one Irish bestseller in 2010. She is a regular contributor to the *Sunday Independent* books pages.

The Start of Summer is her fourth novel.

Alison lives in Dublin with her husband and three children.

Follow her on Twitter @authoralison or visit her website at www.alisonwalsh.net

ALSO BY ALISON WALSH

All That I Leave Behind
The House on Seaview Road
The Weekend Dad

Alison WALSH

The START of SUMMER

HACHETTE
BOOKS
IRELAND

First published in Ireland in 2019 by
HACHETTE BOOKS IRELAND
First published in paperback in 2020

1

Cataloguing in Publication Data is available from the British Library

ISBN 978 1 4736 6079 3

Typeset in Mrs Eaves by redrattledesign.com

Printed and bound in Great Britain by Clays Ltd, Elcograf S.p.A.

Hachette Books Ireland policy is to use papers that are natural, renewable and
recyclable products and made from wood grown in sustainable forests. The logging and
manufacturing processes are expected to conform to the environmental regulations of
the country of origin.

Hachette Books Ireland
8 Castlecourt Centre
Castleknock
Dublin 15, Ireland

A division of Hachette UK Ltd
Carmelite House, 50 Victoria Embankment, EC4Y 0DZ

www.hachettebooksireland.ie

To Colm, as ever, and to Cliona and Rory

1

Elise

They're there again, the three women, sitting out of the baking heat under the weeping willow on a tartan picnic rug, a wicker basket between them. With their buggies, they form a tight circle and I wonder why one of them doesn't have a buggy or a pram, but then I see that she's one of those mums who 'wears' her baby all the time. The midwives said it was the best way to develop a bond with your baby, but I can't, ever since I put my back out lifting a box from the car when we moved to our new house in Rathgar. Gray — he's my hubby — told me to lift from the knees and not to strain my back, but would I listen? I've always been stubborn like that. Honestly, I felt so guilty about not being able to carry her around much, as if I was depriving her, which is why I chose the Silver Cross — in pink, of course, because Chloe's a girl — call me old fashioned! Besides, pink's my favourite colour.

I want to give Chloe the best of everything because she's my world. I've totally fallen in love with her and, honestly, if you asked me to lie down in front of a train for her, I would. I can't believe how fierce I am about her: like a lioness with her cub on one of those nature shows that Gray loves so much. They'd kill anyone who got between them and their baby, and so would I. I'm the luckiest girl in the world to have Chloe: she's made my life complete. I suppose it's the best thing about marriage, isn't it, having a baby? At least, it is in my world. I'd never, ever say that to Gray of course. He might take it the wrong way.

The tall, tanned one is very striking, like something out of a Scandinavian TV drama, with her white-blonde hair and her strong features, like they've been chiselled out of granite. She has the kind of nose you might be tempted to fix, but it would look all wrong then, with those cheekbones. I wonder if she's the leader because she's waving her arms around, telling some story, and the other two are looking on, nodding, before they all laugh at whatever it is Scandi has said. The second one looks like a catalogue mum, with her pretty sundress and her highlighted hair, tied back in a ponytail, her delicate features all freshly scrubbed and as clean as a whistle. How I wish I looked like that without make-up. Honestly, I have to trowel it on these days, like ready-mix concrete: a big lump of concealer under each eye to hide the bags (that's what staying up half the night feeding will do to you) and a ton of tinted moisturiser because it has an SPF, and I have very delicate skin. Gray says that it's all the fake tan I use, and I have to laugh because of the amount he pinches when he's got a show on: he's a personal trainer and he's into bodybuilding, so he really slaps it on. Honestly, he looks like a mahogany sideboard — we both get such a laugh out of it. I think laughter really holds a relationship together.

The third girl is a bit mousy, to be honest, with her pale skin and that dull brown hair, and it's not helped by her baggy stripy T-shirt and leggings. God, she must be roasting in them. I've lived in shorts this summer and I plan to keep it that way. Denim cut-offs and a vest top when no one's looking, and a linen pair with a shirt for when I have an audience — which isn't often, I can tell you. Still, I'm determined not to be downhearted because I know that negative talk is a shortcut to feeling down.

I notice that the pretty catalogue mum is reaching into a wicker basket and pulling out a package wrapped in tinfoil, opening it and offering it around. So, she must be the organiser, I think. There's always one in any group. Normally, it's me because I like to have everything in order. What is it Ma used to say? 'A place for everything and everything in its place.' Well, that's me!

Mousy — let's call her that — says, 'Oh, gorgeous,' taking something from Pretty and I can't help feeling that she's trying too hard to be liked. I can see that because I was that soldier!

I really want to go over to them and find room in that little circle of theirs for me. To be honest, they look as if they don't want company, but I think if I don't talk to another adult human today, I'll go out of my mind.

It's not that I don't like being a mum – I do – but, God, the loneliness. Gray says that it'll get better when I find my feet in Rathgar, but quite honestly, I'm not sure. I thought we'd made it when we bought the place: never in my life would I have thought that I'd live there, in a big, solid red-brick with a gravel drive and a climbing rose above the front porch. If Ma and Da could see me now, I often think – even though they're both long gone. When I think of all ten of us bursting out of that little house – it's no wonder we can hardly stand the sight of each other now, when it was dog-eat-dog for so long, scrapping and squabbling over every little thing.

I don't think I really fit in in Rathgar, though. I want to, but I stick out like a sore thumb. For a start, everyone else on the road is about eighty, and they don't seem all that friendly. The elderly man next door is a reverend, and he gets very cross every time Gray parks the car on the path outside his house. If he's even six inches across the reverend's driveway, he gets yelled at about driving 'bloody tractors'. Gray laughs, of course, because he's really easy-going, but it drives me mad.

Anyway, there's only so much of being on my own all day

that I can take, in spite of the giant TV in the corner and the Sky, and Chloe of course — I could stare at her little face all day, but she's not exactly chatty. So when I see the women, I want to cheer, to jump up and down and yell, 'Be my friends!' I'm not sure how to approach them, though, so I do another circuit on the grass, passing by the little group in the process. I have to tug Poppy's lead to pull her along: she has to inspect every last inch of grass and, for a Maltese, she has a bark that would make your ears bleed, but she's very sweet really — if you're not another dog, a man with a bag or a hat, or an old lady with a walking stick. Gray calls her 'Jaws', but he loves her really.

Now, Mousy is saying something so softly, the others have to lean into hear her. Pretty puts a hand on her arm, nodding away, and Scandi tilts her head to one side, nodding too, a smile on her face. They look so ... intimate, so close, and I feel a jolt in my heart when I see them. Then Scandi looks up and sees me, and I suddenly realise that all three of them are looking at me. I give a silly little wave, cursing myself, then Scandi gets up and comes towards me. For a second, I debate making a run for it, but then I remind myself that I haven't done anything wrong, so I just wait, hand on the handle of the Silver Cross.

'Hi,' she says brightly.

'Hi,' I reply. I'm waiting for her to tell me that the grass is out of bounds or something, but instead, she bends down to pat Poppy, who gives a little growl. 'Sorry,' I say. 'She's just a bit temperamental.' That's an understatement: I've seen her attach herself to a man's trouser leg and refuse to let go, even when I emptied a bottle of water over her. I'm so embarrassed, but I needn't have worried because Scandi leans back and gives a big laugh.

'You have some growl for a dog of your size,' she says to Poppy. 'But you're kinda cute.'

'I'm really sorry,' I say again. 'She's a total embarrassment.' Then I remind myself not to begin a friendship by apologising. Gray says that I have the right to take up space on the planet and to stop constantly saying sorry, but it's a habit at this stage – after so many years, it's ingrained. 'My husband bought her for me as an engagement present. I'd have been happy with a big, fat diamond, but ...' My voice trails away as I will myself to shut up – but to my relief, I see that she's laughing again.

'I love that,' she says. 'A killer dog for an engagement present. Very funny.'

I hadn't realised that it was a joke – I really would have preferred a bigger engagement ring, but Gray was just getting his business going at that stage and he couldn't afford it – but I laugh along with her.

'So ...' she says. 'I've seen you in the park a few times.'

'Oh, yes, I love it here,' I say. 'It's such an oasis. I'm new to the area and it's the one place I can get to easily. Everything seems such a major expedition with a baby.'

'I know,' she says easily, peering into the pram. 'It took me four hours to get out of the house this morning.' Poppy gives another growl, but she ignores her completely. 'Aww, look, Tommy, isn't she cute?' She dandles her own baby in front of Chloe and, to be honest, I'd rather she didn't because the little one doesn't look all that clean, but of course, I say, 'Thanks, yours is lovely too.' He isn't lovely, really, with his mismatched T-shirt and shorts, his grubby little feet, but it's funny how we all think our baby is the cutest, isn't it? I love dressing Chloe up in her little pink dresses and matching headbands, even though the poor little thing is bald as a coot!

'Thanks, they love a good compliment – don't you, pet?' And she pops a kiss on the baby's head. Who's 'they'? I wonder. Then she says, 'Would you like to join us? It's nice and shady where we are.'

I look at her for a moment, wondering if she's joking. I've been here before, making a fool of myself when I think someone's invited me somewhere and getting all silly about it, before I realise that they didn't mean it or they meant someone else – never me.

'Are you sure?' I say. 'I mean, it'd be great because it's so hot and I feel like I haven't spoken to another adult in about a year—' I stop dead then. For God's sake, I chide myself, will you ever shut up?

But Scandi just laughs. 'I know exactly what you mean. Come on over and have a glass of lemonade. Gracie's made enough to slake the thirst of an army.' She turns and walks over to the other two, me following behind, the wheels of the Silver Cross bumping across the grass. 'Make a bit of room there, girls, will you?' she says.

Mousy moves back, brushing the tartan picnic rug with her hand, giving me a small smile. She looks friendly enough, but Pretty's face is closed and she's sitting bolt upright, the way Poppy does when she's about to strike. She doesn't make an effort to move until Scandi says to her, 'Push up, Gracie!'

In response, Gracie shifts about half an inch to the left and I go to sit down. Fake it till you make it, Elise, I think, as I extend a hand to Mousy. 'Hi, I'm Elise.'

'Jane,' Mousy half-whispers, taking my hand in hers, then, after a hesitation that makes me say something quite rude in my head, Gracie offers me a limp handshake, which I respond to with a firm grip, the way Da taught me. A limp handshake is the sign of an untrustworthy character, he always said.

'And I'm Lina,' Scandi says, reaching out and squeezing my hand firmly with hers. I like Lina, I think. She's straightforward.

'I can't believe my luck, finding you all like this,' I say. 'I can't tell you how much I've needed some adult company over the past couple of months. Sometimes, I think I'm going a bit mad for lack of conversation!' I hope they don't think that means that I don't love Chloe — she's everything to me — but it's true. When Gray comes home after a day at the gym or out in the park doing his personal training of celebs — because they like people to snap them working out, would you believe — I nearly talk the hind leg off him. He says he wouldn't have it any other way, but sometimes I see him eyeing the telly, wondering if he can watch Man United in the Champions League to escape my nattering. Honestly, that man is like an open book.

Jane tilts her head to one side, smiling sadly. 'I know what you mean. Sometimes I feel that there's no one else in the world besides me and Owen, and he's not exactly a conversationalist.' Gracie gives her a curious look but says nothing, and I wonder what that's about. Jane reaches into the pram and pats the little feet of her baby – a big bruiser of a boy who is kicking vigorously – as if she's apologising to him, and she gives me that small, sad smile again.

'I think the main thing is to get out and meet other mums for support and friendship. I find that they're the only ones who really understand,' I say.

'I know,' Lina agrees. 'It's like being part of some club. The thing is, the initiation rite involves at least twenty-four hours of excruciating pain, blood and guts, not to mention the tears and the begging for drugs. It's not exactly the Masons or the local golf club. Imagine if you had to go through labour to join – wouldn't that be funny?'

'Some golf club,' Jane says. 'I'm not sure I'd want to be a member.'

'Well, it'd be a great deal less exclusive than your average club,' Lina says. 'Maybe that'd be a good thing. No more rich old men in golfing jumpers.' At this, she looks slyly at Gracie.

'Golf clubs are exclusive for a reason,' Gracie says.

'And what's that reason?' Lina leans forward now, on the attack, and Gracie leans slightly back. Poppy starts growling again and I have to give her a little tap on the nose to shut her up.

'The reason is, Lina, to make contacts and have a good social network,' Gracie says frostily. 'My dad found it very important for his business.'

'Safe from the plebs – I get it.' Lina is laughing, but I've a feeling she doesn't think Gracie is very funny. I'll bet these two fight all the time. They have the look of two women who want to dominate. But there can only be one alpha in the pack, I know.

There's a moment's deathly silence while Gracie fingers the tiny diamond on a chain around her neck and Jane looks dreamily into the distance. Lina has stopped laughing now and there's a muscle working in her jaw. Uh-oh.

'So, where did you all meet?' I ask.

The tension is broken, as Jane says, 'Antenatal classes,' and gives a little eye-roll, while the others burst into laughter.

'What is it? What did I say?' I ask, mystified.

'Ah, it's nothing,' Lina says, reaching over and patting me on the hand. 'Excuse us, Elise, we're not normally this rude. Allow me to elaborate. We all booked this private antenatal class because, Lord knows, the public ones weren't good enough for us ...' Gracie clutches her necklace again at this, which must be her signal of disapproval. 'They were run by this complete nutcase called Oona, who believed in shamanic rituals and herbal purges to purify the soul. I have no idea why she was certified to run antenatal classes, unless giving birth in a clearing in the jungle is your thing.' There is laughter at this.

'Do you remember the day she did childbirth?' Gracie says.

'OMG,' Lina says. 'Will I ever forget it? She had this plastic pelvis and a doll, and she re-enacted the whole process, from contractions to the birth, complete with moaning and groaning.'

'I thought Jake would pass out.' Gracie smiles. She eyes Jane when she says this, and Jane blushes and looks at the ground.

'I know!' Lina says. 'I used to think I was missing something, not having an other half, but let me tell you, I was never so glad to be by myself. Do you remember Sandra's partner, Dennis? He collapsed on the sofa and Oona had to revive him with one of her weird concoctions.'

'That's men for you,' Gracie says. 'No backbone whatsoever.' She gives a little giggle to show she doesn't really mean it, but I see the way she quickly squeezes Jane's hand, and I wonder what the story is there.

'Is Jake your husband?' I ask Gracie.

There's a moment's hesitation and I curse myself inside for asking my usual nosey question, but Gracie says, 'No,' then, quietly, 'we only met a year and a half ago and we were just going out for a few months when I fell pregnant. It all happened so quickly that we never really got around to it. We seem to be doing everything backwards,' she adds ruefully.

Now, it's Jane's turn to squeeze Gracie's hand. 'I think that's very sensible when you don't know each other that well. Having a baby is stressful enough without a wedding on top of it. Sometimes, I wish I'd waited. It should be mandatory these days.'

I look around to see who is going to soothe Jane, reassure her that it'll all be fine, but instead, there's another embarrassed silence. Even chatty Lina is quiet. Meanwhile, my mind is spinning. I didn't book antenatal classes privately – maybe I should have?

I have to say, I'm surprised that Gracie isn't married, though. She looks like the type that would have the big splash with three days in some stately home in west Cork.

'I got married in the Maldives,' I say into the silence. 'It was a great way of getting away from all the stress.' The word 'stress' was an understatement. If I had a penny for all the rows it caused in my family. My two younger sisters, Siobhan and Margaret, nearly tore each other's hair out in their fight to be bridesmaids and Paddy, the eldest boy, sulked for weeks when we didn't ask him to be best man. Gray was right. It was the only thing to do, to get away from the whole lot of them and leave them to fight it out. The only person from my family who ended up coming was Sharon, but then, she's always been above all of that stuff, stuck in her books, making something of herself. She's a barrister now, which is a miracle, when the only place she had to study was a cubby-hole on the landing. She was my only bridesmaid, and Gray's brother, Shaun, was his best man, and if we both felt a bit sad about that, we knew we were doing the right thing.

'The Maldives,' Jane says breathlessly. 'What was it like?'

'Oh, it was magical,' I say. 'Just so easy, you know? No

shoes, just really casual, flowers in your hair, that kind of thing. We all went to this gorgeous restaurant after for a barbecue, and honestly, it was the nicest day I've ever had. No meringue dress, no endless posing for photos, no bagpipes or speeches. Look,' I say, scrolling through my phone to show her a photo of Gray and me on the beach, holding hands, the blue sea behind us.

'Oh, wow,' Jane says quietly. 'I kind of wish I'd gone for something like that — I did the whole meringue ... it was for my mam and dad, really.'

'Oh, I'm sorry,' I say. 'I didn't mean to put my foot in it.' Jane sits back and blinks, and Gracie gives me a dagger stare. How was I to know? I think, wanting the ground to open up and swallow me whole.

But then Lina looks at the photo and says, 'Jeez, Elise, is that your husband? What a hunk!' There's more laughter then, as Lina demands to have another look and says she wants a copy so she can pin it on her wall and then she says she's objectifying him, which makes them all roar. Honestly, Lina's very funny.

When the laughter dies down, Lina says, 'Well, I propose a toast. Has everyone got a full glass?' She looks at me and I shrug. I haven't been offered anything.

Gracie looks as if she's swallowed something unpleasant, but she opens up her wicker hamper and takes out a pretty glass bottle with a china stopper in it and a plastic wine glass, which she hands to me, filling it with the cloudy, fizzy lemonade. It tastes lovely — tart and sweet at the same time

– and I wonder how she had time to make it with a baby around.

'It's delicious,' I say, lifting my glass to touch theirs. 'I'd love the recipe if you have it.'

Her eyes fix on mine for a second, then she gives a smile. 'Of course.' But she doesn't volunteer anything further. Well, be like that, I think.

'Here's to our newest arrival,' Lina says, clinking her plastic glass against mine, her lovely, strong features creasing into a smile.

'Yes, welcome, Elise,' Jane adds, clinking her glass against mine in turn, and, after a hesitation that is so long it's a bit obvious, eventually Gracie joins in.

'Hear, hear,' Lina says, taking a big swig. 'Ah, that's more like it. All it's missing is a drop of vodka.'

'I'll remember to bring that next time.' Gracie smiles.

'Here's to a summer to remember,' Jane suddenly says, immediately putting a hand over her mouth, as if she'd said the wrong thing, but Gracie puts an arm around her and gives her a little hug.

'It will be, Jane – one way or another,' she adds.

I'm really not sure what she means by that, but I'll ignore it. Overthinking is a bit of a weakness of mine: I read things into situations and I get myself tied up in all kinds of knots. This time will be different. I say, cheerfully, 'I'll drink to that!' I raise my glass to theirs, the plastic giving a soft 'thunk' as I tap each of their glasses.

A summer to remember. Honestly, I can't believe my luck.

Lina

God, what are those two like? Lina thought, as she walked home from the park in the evening sun, Tommy in a sling in front of her, little head bobbing. Gracie was unbearable, with her silly statements, her certainties delivered with that bashful expression on her face, as if she didn't really mean them, which she totally did. And the way she'd behaved when Lina had brought the new girl over to them to say hello — like a Victorian lady in need of smelling salts. Well, serve her right that they had a new member of the gang. It might teach her to be a bit more tolerant. And as for Jane ... she was nice, Lina knew, but did she have to just go along with everything? Could she not speak up for herself once in a while? Conventional, that's what her mother would have called them. There truly was nothing worse than conventionality to Mama. She used to make a game of it when Lina was little, pointing out the housewives with their dumpy skirts and sensible shoes, clomping up the streets of Enniscorthy, mouths tight with disapproval. One of these hated women would go by, scarf tucked under her chin, eyes darting sideways as she walked past as if they were both wild animals, and then Inge would point and say loudly, 'See? That's the kind of woman you must never, ever be. Their only expectation in life is to look after their stupid, lazy husbands.'

These women didn't understand what Inge was saying, because she always insisted that she and Lina only spoke her native German to each other, even when they were in public — as if they didn't stand out enough in that little town — but their shoulders would stiffen as they walked towards the butcher's or Mr Gleeson's fruit and veg shop, and Lina would look after them and wish that she belonged to some other, nicer mother. At the same time, she did feel sorry for them, with their string bags and their tightly belted coats. They couldn't possibly be happy, she thought, with all of their 'shopping and praying', as Mama put it, but she couldn't help wondering if they were lonely, like she and Mama were. She used to see them in her mind's eye, sitting around the dinner table, Mum, Dad, all of those children they had, fighting over the last roast potato, and she'd feel a slight fluttering in her chest.

Mama and she would sit on either side of a cracked Formica-topped table and eat brown rice, which tasted of cardboard, that Mama had to order from a health food shop in Dublin, and they would talk about whatever topic had been selected for conversation that morning. Mama didn't like shallow, easy stuff like telly: she preferred to talk about dismantling the patriarchy, beating the sexist Irish men at their own game, whatever that meant. Lina remembered not being sure about it because of the lack of sexist Irish men in their own lives. Or any men, for that matter. Lina's dad was, Mama told her, a 'sperm donor' and not part of their lives. Maybe that's why she'd gone the same way, she thought, selecting a sperm donor of her very own: Seamus, who spent his entire days monitoring other people's depravity on the video-sharing website they both worked for but whom Lina had selected because he was reasonably intelligent, as a couple of conversations with him at the water cooler had informed her and a long chat at the Christmas party, the two of them the worse for Alan from accounts' lethal Christmas cocktail. Seamus was 'nice', she supposed, but she'd really picked him because, even though he was a year older than her, he looked like a teenager, a bit unfocused, a bit easy-going, and she'd reckoned he'd be unlikely to protest when she told him about the results of their one-night stand.

She'd known that selecting a real, live man instead of an anonymous donor at a clinic could get complicated, but she'd wanted to be able to see what she was getting, so to speak, to be able to look her son or daughter in the eye eighteen years from now and tell them that, yes, their father had been, if not a fine human being, at least a recognisable one. Seamus had seemed to fit the bill perfectly — and he had the added bonus of being sane, in spite of his job, and he'd laughed at a couple of her jokes. Appearances could be deceptive though, Lina thought now as she wandered into Mr Abdallah's corner shop, selecting two red onions and two bright-red peppers, wondering whether if she made a double helping of fried rice it might do her for tomorrow's lunch as well. She hadn't been expecting him to be quite so persistent.

As she selected a three-pack of tuna, because one came free, her phone buzzed. She sighed, debating whether or not to look at it: she couldn't bear it if it was Gracie with one of her cheery messages. She always had to follow every meeting with a 'you guys' text, full of exclamation marks, telling them how much she valued their friendship, and if that wasn't bad enough, she'd attach some stomach-churning bit of 'mummy wisdom' at the bottom. Sure enough, there it was: *Sometimes the smallest things take up the most room in your heart.* Yuck. Besides, all Gracie really wanted was to remind them who was in charge of their little group — still. Maybe it was no bad thing that the group had a new member — might shake things up a little, Lina thought, shoving the phone back in her trouser pocket. Perhaps Gracie was just jealous. Elise certainly looked glamorous: those smart linen shorts and that shirt that was clearly designer, not to mention the hair. Mind you, what about Elise's bejewelled nails, Lina thought, trying to walk past a giant packet of Custard Creams that only cost sixty-five cent. No, she told herself, that sixty-five cent might come in handy. She still had five days to go before the best day of the week — when her maternity benefit would appear in her bank account. If she had any money left over after the rent and the six-to-twelve-month clothes that Tommy needed, as well as actual food for the week, she'd buy them as a treat. Thank God for the savings she'd somehow managed to squirrel away when she was working. Her boss, Jeff, in Download wasn't exactly generous, but that's what a dodgy contract got you. Welcome to the flexible economy, Lina thought grimly.

'How is my favourite child today?' Mr Abdallah seemed to lie in wait for Tommy, making sure that he was on the shop floor, stacking shelves with jars of spices and odd-looking crisps, so that he could pull himself into a standing position, groaning about his knees, and pretend to be astonished to see them both there. As if a day could pass without a trip to Mr Abdallah, Lina thought, as he pinched Tommy's little cheeks and exclaimed that he'd never seen a more beautiful child. He would purse his lips and make funny noises and would be rewarded with a gummy smile. 'A child sent from heaven,' he would say, shuffling in his black plastic sandals behind the counter, barking something in Urdu at his son, who would be leaning against the cigarette display case, eyes glued to his phone.

Mr Abdallah was small, with a completely bald, round head, like a bowling ball, and deep lines, like the furrows in a field, etched into his forehead and extending from the outer corners of his eyes. His uniform of choice, a short-sleeved check shirt worn loose over khaki cargo pants, did not disguise his stomach, nor his shortness of stature. By contrast, his son was movie-star handsome, a tall greyhound of a man with a mane of thick, black hair and huge brown eyes. He seemed to be completely unaware of his good looks, regarding with bored disdain the local girls who would come in and cluster around the magazine rack, giggling.

Now, Mr Abdallah packaged up her peppers and onions and the cans of tuna, adding a couple of peaches and a large bar of chocolate into the paper bag at the end, almost as if it was an afterthought. How was it he knew that she'd want something exactly like that? she thought. Something chocolatey and sugary to console herself. He must be a mind-reader. But ever since he'd discovered, to his horror, that Lina had no husband, he considered it his mission to look after her – if she'd said she had leprosy, he could hardly have looked more alarmed. Lina smiled at the memory now, as she said thanks and made small talk, agreeing with him that it was indeed a hot summer. Of course, she'd never mentioned Seamus and his role in things – she had a feeling Mr Abdallah wouldn't understand.

None of what Seamus was now doing was part of the plan, Lina thought, as the lights turned green and she shuffled across the road, and she wasn't sure what to do about it. 'But Tommy needs a dad,' he'd said the last time they'd met at a café in town, four weeks before. He'd insisted on the meeting, calling and texting her every day since Tommy's birth in March. It was a complete nuisance, particularly as she'd made it very clear to him, when she'd told him the 'surprise' news a little more than a year earlier, that his services were no longer required — but there was something about his tone, something plaintive, that had lifted him out of the 'stalker' class and into something else, which Lina couldn't quite put her finger on.

They'd met at a hipster joint near the cathedral: a big lofty place with lots of exposed pipes and lightbulbs on bits of string. The staff had been nonchalant, placing piles of avocado on toast in front of them, then shuffling off in their board shorts and Hawaiian T-shirts to make more shakshouka or something equally trendy.

'No, they don't need a dad,' Lina had said, nicely but firmly.

'Who's "they"?' Seamus had asked. 'Do I have another child lurking under the table that you haven't told me about?' With this, he had lifted the recycled paper tablecloth and made an exaggerated mime of looking under the table.

Lina had rolled her eyes to heaven. 'I'm raising her — *them* — to be gender neutral.'

'Right,' Seamus had said, a small smile flickering on his face.

'Is there something wrong with that?' she'd snapped.

'Nope. I think it's admirable, actually.'

'Oh.' Lina had been wrong-footed for a moment.

'Yeah, I'd say it takes guts,' he'd added, 'to break the gender mould like that, you know, so that she's — they're — not just doing what's expected of them, but what they truly want, free of notions of whether something is what a man or a woman might do. It's quite revolutionary, when you think about it.'

'It is? I mean, it is,' Lina had agreed, wondering how different Tommy's life would be from hers if she truly lived it like that. What had been a bit of a whim when Tommy had been born suddenly seemed more complicated now, and Lina thought about what it might be like for her at school with the other boys and girls and how she might present herself to the world — and what the world might have to say about it.

'Would you like to hold them?' Lina had offered.

'Can I?' He'd looked so ecstatic that Lina had felt a bit sorry for him, before she'd reminded herself that this was all he would do, even if their child looked uncomfortably like him, with her dark-chocolate-coloured hair and eyes. Tommy was hers and she was just lending them to Seamus. She had unclipped the sling, which was a bit of a production given all of the loops and clips, and they had both looked at their daughter, curled up as if in a little walnut shell, knees up to her tummy.

'She — they — suck their thumb,' he'd said. 'I used to suck my thumb.'

'So did I,' Lina had said pointedly. She hadn't, as far as she could remember, but she'd wanted to make sure he got the message. He'd seemed to understand because he sat back on the uncomfortable wooden bench, exiting her personal space, hands resting on his knees, waiting.

Lina had lifted Tommy out of the sling, and as she did so, the baby's eyes had opened wide in surprise. Her arms had shot outwards, her hands like starfish, fingers spread wide, as Lina had placed a hand under her little warm bottom and said, 'Make a circle with your arms.'

'I know,' he'd said, 'I have five brothers and sisters,' and he'd taken Tommy gently, placing her bottom on his knee, cradling her with his left arm. They had both looked at her as she sat there for a moment, and Lina had waited for her face to screw up in distaste and for her to cry, but instead, she had kicked excitedly and shot out an arm, patting Seamus on the chest. Lina had felt as if she'd been betrayed.

'Ouch, you'll strangle me,' he had said, as they'd grabbed hold of the silver chain around his neck. As his voice rumbled in her ear, Tommy had turned her head to look at him, her face splitting into a grin. She'd started to 'talk' to him then, in the cute little way she'd begun to do recently, a series of little moans and grumbles, and he had talked back, telling her that, yes, what she had to say was very interesting, very illuminating indeed.

Lina had watched them both and she'd wanted to pull Tommy back into her arms, to grab them and yell, 'She's mine!' at the top of her voice. But instead, she had just sat there, immobile, letting this man talk to her child. His child.

Tommy had saved her then by suddenly letting out an ear-splitting roar, and she had reached out her arms, Seamus placing the wailing bundle gratefully into them. 'They need a feed,' Lina had said.

'Oh, do you need to go somewhere ...?'

'No, unless you object to a woman breastfeeding in public.'

'No, no ...' His voice had railed away at the challenge and he had examined a bit of exposed piping on the wall with unusual interest as she had opened the clasps on her bra and Tommy had latched on enthusiastically.

There had been a silence, broken only by the background clatter of cutlery and the hiss of the coffee machine. Then Lina had looked over at him and had seen that there were tears in his eyes. Oh, God. That was the problem with romantic connections, Mama had always told her: they get messy. It's far better to avoid them, she'd said.

'Look, I'm sorry you're upset, but none of this was planned,' she had lied, as he'd stirred a teaspoon sadly around and around in his coffee.

He could have challenged her, she knew, but instead he'd just nodded softly, looking like a beaten dog. 'It's just ... I could have helped ... or something. I *can* help.'

'I'm fine on my own.'

'I can see that,' he'd said. 'You're a really good mum, I can tell.'

'Thanks,' Lina had said, softening. 'I like it,' she had added in a near-whisper, realising as she had said the words that they were true.

'That's good.' He had tapped the spoon nervously against the side of his cup, clearing his throat and saying, 'So, how was the birth?'

'Fine,' she'd snapped. Why did he want to know that — it was none of his business. But then she got the beaten-dog routine again, so she had muttered, 'Terrible.'

'Oh. How?'

'Do you really want to know?' Lina had said wryly.

In reply, he'd looked eager, boyish. 'Of course I want to know. I'm—' He'd shaken his head. 'Shoot.'

Where would she even begin? Lina had thought. At the never-ending contractions stage, or with the cancellation of her independent midwife because Tommy was breech, and the flushing down the toilet of all the dreams she'd had of a home birth in the bath, just a few candles lighting the space as the midwife helped her to bring her baby into the world? Instead, she'd ended up lying on a trolley, the lights of the hospital corridor speeding by above her head, as she was hurled towards theatre. They'd crashed into another trolley halfway down the corridor, a high-speed explosion of jangling steel and swearing as one doctor had yelled at another and she'd clung to the trolley, a shaft of pain across her middle so sudden and intense it felt as if she'd been cut in two. 'It was like the magic trick,' she had found herself telling Seamus. 'You know, where they saw the lady in half and her torso and head appear in one box and her legs in another.'

He had given a short laugh, looking at her as if he wasn't sure if she was joking, so she had pretended to be entirely serious, but then he'd nodded and made a soft clucking noise of sympathy and she had found herself telling him the truth, no jokes this time — about going into theatre, about the blinding white lights and the *bip-bip* of the monitors and the clanging of instruments as they'd lifted her off the trolley, 'nice and easy now', and onto the table.

'They put up this kind of curtain at my waist then,' she'd told Seamus, 'and there was a lot of sucking, as if they were squelching around in a bog.' She'd had to smile at this bit. 'And then, there she was.' Lina had been so caught up in the memory that she forgot to use the correct pronoun.

'There she was,' he'd echoed. 'What did she look like?'

'A sort of bluey-purple colour, with a coating of cream.' She'd laughed.

'Oh, yeah,' Seamus had said. 'It's the vernix. They're covered with it in the womb.' Then he had blushed, as if he'd been caught out saying the wrong thing.

'No, that's right,' Lina had said. 'And her little arms were up around her face, as if she was trying to shield it, and her eyes were closed tight. She didn't open them for twenty-four hours and I was terrified that maybe she didn't have any eyes.' She'd smiled at the memory.

'So, she was perfect then,' Seamus had said. He had been doing that tapping thing against his cup again and she'd wanted to reach out and snatch the spoon out of his hand.

'She was perfect,' she'd agreed.

'Who did you have as a birth partner?' He hadn't looked up from his cup as he asked the question, but had continued tapping.

'Oh, I didn't have one.'

'You went through all of that alone?' He'd looked at her incredulously.

'Of course,' Lina had said. 'Why wouldn't I?'

'Oh, no reason,' Seamus had said.

He'd asked her then if he could be 'part of Tommy's life'. He could help, he'd said eagerly. He could give her a bottle every now and then, to which Lina had found herself barking, 'They're exclusively breastfed.'

'Well, take them for walks then, so you could get some rest,' he'd offered. 'Or I could do the shopping with them, you know, you could show me how to operate that thing,' and he'd nodded at the sling. They had both looked down as Tommy finished feeding, trying to lift her head to look at the fascinating stranger. She'd squinted at him, trying to focus, settling eventually on Seamus's bright-red T-shirt with the pattern of rubber ducks on it, staring at it in fascination.

'They like your T-shirt,' Lina had said.

'They have good taste.' He'd smiled. 'Mum still can't believe I don't wear a suit to work. "Sure, what kind of a job is that, Seamus, when you don't wear a suit!"'

'My mother would have said you were a tool of the capitalist patriarchy,' Lina had said. 'She said that suits were the ultimate sell-out, that they made us all subservient to the superstructure.'

'Wow, and I thought it was just a suit.' Seamus had laughed.

'I know, she's very dogmatic,' Lina had said, not adding that she agreed with her. 'Look, I'll think about it, OK?'

'That's all I can ask,' Seamus had said, hands held up in a gesture of surrender.

Now, Lina took the long way home, past the DIY store and the little off-licence on the corner, thinking about Seamus and that meeting, about the look of wonder on his face when he'd seen his daughter. She knew that legally he didn't have any rights because they weren't married, and even the thought of the word made Lina feel queasy, but she had to give it to him: he'd been subtle about it, not too pushy, so she might be more likely to give in.

The thought of going home made her feel suddenly depressed, as if all the air was being squeezed out of her. She hated her flat, above a locksmith's on the main road, but it was cheap because the bathroom was on the landing. The landlady, Liz, who reeked of cigarette smoke and wore too much foundation, had told her that it was a 'private bathroom', for her use only, as if it were some kind of gift she was personally giving Lina. Bloody cheek, Lina thought now as she rounded the corner, the blast of fumes from a bus making her eyes water. And the oven didn't work. Still, at least she could cook everything on the two-ring stove. She was very good at that because Mama had done the same thing, making a series of chickpea stews on one ring, brown rice on the other. Lina still liked chickpea stew, but brown rice made her stomach heave.

Her flat was a staging post, she'd told herself, between one life and another. It and her crappy job were just temporary, while she got her comedy career off the ground. And then the temporary had become permanent, which was entirely her choice, she thought now as she pressed the button on the pedestrian crossing, watching as a man in a grey tracksuit leapt out in front of the traffic to a blur of screeching tyres, horns and swearing. She'd wanted to have Tommy, after all, even though she'd been warned that it would signal the end of her comedy career, such as it was. Maybe that was life, Lina thought now, as she rummaged in her bag for the keys to her flat door: a series of temporary arrangements that gradually hardened around you, like a shell.

She pulled her key out of her bag, the little leprechaun keyring swinging in her hand, and turned in to the gate of the shabby Victorian terraced house that was home, kicking aside a pile of McDonald's wrappers that the wind had blown into the dusty, broken path that led up to the front door, with its thick coating of dust and dirt. She didn't look up until the last second because she was examining the faded black-and-white tiles, wondering if a maid had once cleaned them when this home was a grander place, but when she did, her hand shot to her throat and she dropped the paper bag onto the tiles, bending down then to fuss over it and pick the veg and chocolate bar up. 'I'm sorry, I—'

Her mother stood there, waiting, while Lina scrabbled around on the ground until finally, she stood up, a mess of dirty paper and battered vegetables in her arms.

'Aren't you going to embrace your mother?'

Lina looked down at the baby, at her full arms, then leaned forward and tilted her head to one side, while her mother kissed that cheek, then the other, her mouth making a soft *mwa* sound as she did so. Lina inhaled a mix of beeswax and must, and her stomach flipped. She stood back and looked at her mother's soft face, as round as a drop of water suspended from a tap and the same silvery colour. Her mother was short, with a puff of grey-blonde hair around her face, and small, brown eyes hidden behind red-tinted glasses, which made her look like an alien. She blinked at Lina now with that familiar expectant expression on her face and Lina felt her shoulders tense.

'So!' she said. 'This is a surprise. Come on in!' There was a pause, then Lina said, 'Ehh, can you just help me with the key?' It was jammed in between a pepper and a now-battered peach, and she tried to lean back while her mother pulled it out and held it up, examining the leprechaun sceptically. Lina opened her mouth to explain, but then shook her head. Her mother waited.

'Can you open it?' Lina said.

'*Ich werde sehen*,' her mother said solemnly and pushed the key into the door, wiggling it for a bit. '*Etwa so?*' She turned it to the left.

'Yes, that's right,' Lina said, ignoring the German. If she spoke German now, all hope would be lost. Her mother would gain the upper hand, just as she always had. 'Great!' she exclaimed as the door opened to reveal a dank hall carpet with a scatter of junk mail across it. 'I'm at the top of the stairs on the left,' she said, urging her mother upwards into the gloom while she closed the door, leaned against it and shut her eyes for a few moments. What the fuck are you doing here? she thought. I haven't seen you in three years and, now, here you bloody well are.

3

Jane

As she walked home from the park, Jane tried to hold onto the golden afternoon inside, to remember the hot sun on her back, to see the patterns of the willow leaves on the grass, to hear the laughter of the girls, the clucking and fussing over their babies. It was harder than usual, though, and she wondered if that was because of the new arrival. She was certainly something, with her big pink pram and those fierce eyebrows above the sunglasses, with their great big Versace printed on the bridge in silver letters, perched on top of her head. Though her fake tan had been badly applied so that it gathered around her wrists and ankles in dark-brown splodges, which was a bit odd considering the amount she evidently spent on her appearance. Any other time, Jane would have enjoyed mulling over what it all meant: Lina's mischievous welcoming of the obvious cuckoo into their nest; Gracie's clear distaste for the poor girl.

But Jane found that she couldn't quite concentrate on any of it because she was focusing so hard on walking home as slowly as possible. She could have taken the bus, or even a taxi — she lived three miles away after all — but the drowsy walk through the hot city streets calmed her, prepared her for that feeling of tightness in her chest, of shortness of breath, that increased as she got closer to home, rounding the corner into the leafy cul-de-sac and to the pristine red-painted front door of her suburban home.

The first time Mark, her husband, had hit her, a month before, Jane hadn't seen it coming. Literally — because she'd had her back turned, bending over the rose bushes with a set of pruning shears, trying to get at a tricky shoot near the bottom. She'd just caught it in between the pincers of the shears, registering a feeling of satisfaction as she'd pressed the blades together, when she'd felt it, like a shunt from a car: a sharp blow to the back of her head, propelling her forward onto the thorny, dry branches, one of them stabbing her in the chest as she'd fallen half onto the bush, half on the ground, with the label that she'd attached to her favourite rose inches from her eye. 'English Miss', it was called: a lovely soft pink with a heady scent.

I must have fallen, she'd thought, scrambling up to her

knees, a long line of vivid red down her arm, but then she'd turned and he'd been standing over her. She'd smiled at him, had gone to say hello, her stupid brain still stuck in first gear, when he'd kicked her, this time in the soft flesh above her hip. He'd been wearing his office shoes, shiny black brogues that she polished every morning and put away every evening, pushing a wooden shoe tree into them before placing them underneath his chair in the bedroom, the next day's suit laid out neatly on top.

That shoe needs a polish, she'd thought, as she'd lain on the dry, stony clay of her flower bed, Owen howling in his pram. I really must get around to it.

Ever since 'the incident', as he'd called it the next day, he'd been nice to her, so nice that she'd begun to wonder if it had all been a figment of her imagination. The whole thing had the quality of a dream, and she'd been so tired, after all. Owen had had a tummy bug while Mark had been away at a three-day conference in London, and she'd spent all of that time in a daze of fatigue, walking up and down the stairs to Owen's nursery for yet another change of clothes, spending each night pacing the landing while Owen roared, thanking God that at least he wasn't disturbing Mark's sleep. She'd been so exhausted that she hadn't had time to go to the organic supermarket to get the chicken breasts Mark liked and she'd got the farmed stuff instead. He'd noticed, of course. He noticed everything. The day after the incident, she'd gone early to the farmer's market to get the best Connemara lamb, because it was tender, and had bought it and a big bunch of rosemary and some new potatoes. The bag had been heavy and she hadn't been able to bend over to pick it up, so the man had had to come around the counter and lift it up for her, his face full of concern. 'You all right, love?'

'Oh, I'm fine,' Jane had said. 'Thank you. Just a tummy ache.' It *was* a tummy ache, she'd supposed, as she'd lugged the bag in one hand and held Owen in the other arm — just not the kind caused by indigestion or food poisoning. This one had made her kidneys ache: a long, low pain that made her gasp every now and again.

She'd gone home and had lain on the bed, with Owen gurgling away beside her. She'd set her alarm for three o'clock in the afternoon, so she'd be sure to wake up in time to put on the dinner. Not that she'd felt like sleeping. She'd spent the days and weeks since Owen's birth in a haze of fatigue, but then she'd felt wide awake, a sense of hyper-awareness filling her, pushing through every vein so she felt as if she'd been electrocuted. Wired and buzzing, she had looked around the bedroom at the magnolia paint, the brightly painted windowsills and the expensive blinds that she'd had made specially by some lady in Wicklow, and she'd thought how nice it all looked. A lovely home, with bay windows at the front and a view of the playing fields from the back bedroom window, through which she could hear the *thock* of tennis balls, the rumble of skateboards in the skate park, the barking of dogs. Owen loved to go to the park and look at the dogs. She'd put him on her knee and he'd wave his arms and legs in excitement as a dog came towards them. Once, one of them had licked him enthusiastically before Jane had had the time to whip her son away and he'd collapsed with laughter.

Such a nice home. Such a nice life, she'd thought. Maybe if she just concentrated on that, she'd be able to push all the rest of it away. After all, she was good at that kind of thing. And, she'd reasoned, Mark was what she deserved. What was it Dad used to say? 'You've made your bed, now you'll have to lie in it.' Funny how his sayings stuck in Jane's head, even though she'd only set eyes on her father twice in the last fifteen years.

She'd just been checking the lamb, when she'd sensed his heavy presence in the kitchen, the way the atmosphere seemed to thicken when he entered the room. Her shoulders had tensed, and she hadn't turned around.

'Jane?' he'd said softly.

She'd closed her eyes tight and braced herself, wondering if she could defend herself with the wooden spoon in her hand — 'hit him a belt', as Mam had put it when she used to use the same implement on Jane and her sister. Mam had certainly been able to inflict some damage. Jane had wondered if she might be capable of the same herself.

'Do you think you might turn around?'

Jane had gripped the wooden spoon in her hand and turned. She'd been folded in on herself, hunched over, as if waiting for the blow. Instead, she'd seen her husband hiding behind an enormous bouquet of red roses. Her heart had sunk.

'They're for you,' he'd said unhelpfully.

'I don't want them,' Jane had found herself saying.

'I know, and I don't blame you,' he'd said, coming towards her. Jane had leaned back over the cooker. 'It's OK,' he'd said as he put the bouquet down on the counter. 'It's fine. C'mere,' and he'd pulled her towards him. He had smelled of expensive men's fragrance and the medical soap he liked to use in the shower. Jane had stiffened as he'd stroked her hair and kissed her softly on the cheek. She had hoped he'd finish soon because she'd thought she might retch. The moment had seemed to go on forever, until eventually he'd said, 'I owe you an apology. For the incident.'

'"The incident"?' Had he really called it that — like a garda taking a statement. It was so sanitised, so stripped of any real meaning.

'Yes. I don't know what came over me, Jane. I was tired and hungry, and I'd spent three days slaving at the conference, and when I came home, dinner wasn't ready and you were out in the garden instead and I just—'

She couldn't help it. 'Men don't hit their wives because they've spent too long at a conference, Mark.' Her voice had sounded louder than usual, and sharp — Owen looked up from his little nest of cushions on the floor and his cloth book, his eyes moving from her to Mark and back again. He'd begun a fretful whine.

'I know,' Mark had said, a look of irritation flashing briefly across his features, as Owen's cries had become more urgent, before he assembled them into something more suitable. 'I know,' he'd said again. 'There's no excuse for it – it was an aberration, pure and simple. It won't happen again. I promise. Please, Jane,' he had said then, looking at her imploringly. 'Please say you'll forgive me.'

Jane had felt the thoughts spinning through her head. If she walked away, what would she have? She had no job because Mark had suggested she give up her teaching post at St Attracta's when Owen was born and she'd gone along with it, eager to spend as much time as possible with her baby, to give him everything she had. She had no money to call her own because they had a joint account and Mark kept a very careful eye on it. She'd be like one of those women she heard about on the radio all the time, who flees a bad marriage only to end up in a hotel room with three children and her entire life around her in bin bags. Was Jane that kind of woman? Was that who she was? Or was this the price she'd have to pay for this new life of hers – a life of respectability, a life that looked just right? If that was the case, she'd thought, as Mark had made his nightly gin and tonic and poured her a glass of chilled white wine, she'd pay it. She had no other choice. It wasn't as if she could just run home to Mam and Dad. Not after the way she'd left, all those years before. She was all out of options.

'Why don't we go away some time?' he'd said over dinner. They'd sat on either side of the dining-room table, the lamb between them, Owen in his baby chair beside Jane, and they'd talked about Mark's job and the litigation course he'd be attending in two weeks and whether he might be up for promotion later in the autumn, and she had had that sense again of two separate worlds: the one that everyone could see, of a husband and wife and baby, sitting around a dining-room table, and the other world, filled with darkness.

She was stalling for time, Jane thought as she pushed the trolley around the supermarket now, along with everyone else in their shorts and T-shirts after the baking-hot afternoon. She did actually need things for dinner, but she also knew that it would delay her return by a blissful half an hour. It was one of the things she'd begun to do since 'the incident', that and the way she'd become a watcher, standing on the sidelines of conversations, alert to every twitch, every change in mood or tempo, anticipating trouble before it arrived, heading it off at the pass. She was good at it because she'd had a lot of practice, but now, she wondered what the girls would have made of the 'old' Jane. Once, a long time before, she'd been different: she'd begun to bloom, to become fully herself, but look where that had got her.

She'd ended up in a psychiatric hospital, sitting in a yellow-painted room every Tuesday with a nice lady called Phyllis, whom they were too polite to call a psychiatrist.

She'd been a broken person, a toy without a head or an arm that you'd sweep up into the bin after an afternoon's play. Trash, that's what she'd been. 'Unworthy of God's love' — that's how Dad had put it. Jane and Phyllis had sat there in that room, picking over the pieces of her life — laying them out, examining them, picking them up and putting them back down again — until she'd emerged, six weeks later, with them reassembled into a different kind of whole, one that was no more true to her than the original had been, but which worked in a slightly different way, a way that got her through.

'Are you being yourself, do you think?' Phyllis had asked her once. 'And if not, does that serve you well?'

Of course it does, Jane thought now, as she picked up a pack of hideously expensive sirloin steak. It serves me better now than ever — that's how I met and married Mark, because of that ability; that's how I managed to maintain the fiction of a relationship with Mam and Dad, by making them think that I was sorry, by pretending that everything that had happened was just a dream. That's how I manage to keep things with Mark on an even keel, even though I think that sometimes the effort will kill me.

Which is why I can see it in that woman, Elise, Jane thought now as she queued at the till. She's a watcher too, in her own way. And she's better at it than I am, Jane thought, with a tinge of envy, handing the woman at the till the money for the food, putting the expensive items into her canvas shopper.

The woman counted the notes and coins that Jane gave her, clearing her throat before saying. 'I think you're fifty cent short.'

'What? Oh, sorry,' Jane said, patting her pockets, rummaging in the little tray at the bottom of Owen's pram, even though she knew she didn't have another cent. Mark gave her just enough to cover the shopping and not a penny more. 'You can't be trusted not to spend it,' he'd said, his face splitting into what he obviously thought was a grin, but which looked more like a grimace. She looked at the package of shallots and wondered if she could buy loose ones and save fifty cent that way. She couldn't go home without the steak, that was for sure. She looked over her shoulder and saw a big line of people behind her. A man with a red face stuck his head out and said, 'Get a move on, love, there's a queue.'

'Yes, sorry,' Jane said. She couldn't move, paralysed by indecision. If she bought cheaper onions instead of shallots, would Mark notice? Or maybe she could nip a bit of rosemary out of Mrs Callaghan's garden when she was passing — she had a lovely hedge of it just begging to be picked. Maybe she could do without a steak and have a couple of sausages instead. That was it, she thought. And then a hand reached out and put fifty cent into the cashier's hand. The cashier looked at it doubtfully, then said, 'Thank you,' and put it into the drawer.

Jane coughed nervously. 'Ehm, could I have the receipt?'

'Jesus Christ!' a loud voice said behind her as the girl

handed Jane her receipt. Head bowed, Jane put the few items into her bag and only then did she turn to the person who'd given her the money. She was surprised to see that it was a young girl, tall, with pale skin and long, mid-brown hair, nodding her head in time to the music that must have been coming through her giant gold headphones.

'Thanks,' Jane said.

The girl took off the headphones and said, 'What?'

'Thanks – for the money. I don't know why I was short. I thought I had it all worked out. You saved me,' she added, giving a small smile.

''Sno bother.' The girl shrugged. 'Mum only sent me out for two tomatoes, and she never looks at the change.'

Lucky you, Jane wanted to say to her. My husband counts out every penny and checks it against the receipt. But I won't tell you that because you don't need to know that life can be like that – not yet anyway.

She checked her watch when she left the supermarket, the man with the red cheeks muttering behind her about getting a bloody move on, stupid cow. Shit. Almost six o'clock – she *would* have to hurry. Then her phone buzzed in her pocket. It was an elderly clamshell model, and the only thing it could do was send and receive texts because Jane had dropped it once and it had stopped taking calls. Mark had spent quite a lot of time debating whether to spend money on a new one, so that he could always 'reach' her, as he called his numerous check-ins during the day, or to simply text, which he didn't like. In the end, he'd settled for keeping his money, and Jane hadn't been able to suppress a shiver of glee. She'd decided not to tell him that she could still make calls; that would be her little secret.

Home late. Board meeting. Jane felt her stomach unclench, her breathing steady. She decided to take the long route home, feeling the sun on the back of her neck, enjoying a little bit of people-watching, wondering what it might be like to feel like this every day.

Later that night, she lay in bed beside her husband, listening to the foxes howl at the bottom of the garden. She tried to calm her mind, to tell herself that it would be fine and all would be well, but she couldn't, so she did what she always did nowadays when she couldn't sleep. She pictured Mark, tied to a chair, her best silk scarf in his mouth. His eyes were wide and he was making muffled sounds behind the scarf as she lifted the knife over his head, ready to plunge it in. It made her feel both elated and relaxed, and she generally drifted off afterwards. She knew that it was wrong, but so what? As Phyllis used to say, all those years ago, 'They're just impulses, Jane. They're only dangerous if you act on them.' She'd been nice enough not to say that acting on her impulses was what had helped Jane into St Dympna's in the first place.

If she could act on those impulses once, she'd thought with a feeling she understood as fear, but later realised was excitement, she could do it again.

4

Gracie

Gracie hovered outside the red-brick building for a while, waiting. There was no reason for her not to go inside, but something made her hesitate. The stupid sling that Lina had given her was digging into her neck and Gracie lifted the straps a bit to stretch, leaning back to take the weight off, then bending forward a little. She had a pain in the small of her back that refused to go away, and she winced now as she felt the pinch of it. She wished she'd brought Jasper's travel system, a combination of car seat and pram that, even though Jake said it looked like the Starship Enterprise, was so much easier to use. Click and go, what could be simpler?

The sling, on the other hand, was a nightmare, one of those ridiculous trapeze things with a ton of straps and Gracie had had to get Jake to help her with it that morning, which was very trying because he'd been laughing so much. They'd rolled Jasper up like a kind of sausage, but when she'd tried to attach him to her front, she'd been missing a shoulder strap and she'd had to start again. She had found herself getting more and more annoyed as Jake had pretended to wrap Jasper up like a mummy, so that only his eyes showed. 'He'll smother,' she'd said sharply, as Jake had guffawed. It wasn't funny — and it wasn't funny when Jake had hung him upside down in it either. It wasn't as if she hadn't known Jake was a joker — it was what she'd liked about him when they'd first met, because everyone told her that she took everything far too seriously — but now, after a grand total of eighteen months together, it was beginning to grate. She had a child already, she'd thought as Jake had paraded around the bedroom in his underpants, Jasper attached to him, upside down, in the sling. She did not need another one.

The sling had been one of a set Lina was testing for a friend in west Cork who made organic slings out of bamboo. Gracie thought that making things with bamboo was completely ridiculous, but it wasn't as tough as she'd expected. In fact, the sling was really quite soft, so soft she'd lifted it up and brushed it against her cheek. She'd taken it when Lina offered it to her, and promised that she'd give it a whirl — and that she'd even do a mini campaign for it while she was on maternity leave. Today was the first time she'd worn it, though, and she was regretting it. Life was difficult enough without wrestling with this every morning, despite Lina's insistence that it was 'easy-peasy' and there was even a way you could loosen it so you could breastfeed. Gracie didn't want to loosen it to breastfeed. She hadn't told the girls, but she'd more or less given up on that. She hadn't been very good at it anyway, she'd told herself. It just didn't come naturally to her.

Maybe it was because of Miriam, she thought now, as she settled herself against the railings across the street from Cutlery, but then she could hardly blame the Polish night nanny, because Miriam had always tried to wake her up to feed Jasper, looming over her in the bed as Gracie tried to pull herself out of the deep sleep that she'd fallen into. 'The baby,' Miriam would say when Gracie's eyes had opened, as if that were necessary. As if she'd be expecting something else.

Gracie would take the baby into her arms and let Miriam help her to undo the hooks on her feeding bra and she would attach Jasper to her, where he would suck as if his life depended on it while her toes curled in pain. Every suck would send an electric prod right through her and she would have to grip the side of the bed, teeth clenched. How could something this natural be so excruciating? she'd wondered, as Miriam had stood over her, watching. She'd wanted to yell at the woman, to throw the TV remote control at her, but instead, she'd manage a smile, flicking on the TV and saying, 'You make yourself a cup of tea. I'll drop him down when I've finished.' Jake would have taken up his usual position on the sofa in the games room, where he now slept almost every night, 'seeing as I'm not needed'. He was joking, Gracie thought now, even if it was true: he *was* kind of in the way, although Gracie did miss waking up to his soft, cuddly body. Who'd have thought she'd ever find a beer belly attractive – but it was one of the things she loved about Jake. He was squishy and warm and safe.

Miriam would always hesitate after she'd handed Jasper over, her hands, with their sallow skin, clasped in front of her, long blonde hair pulled back from her shoulders. Her eyes would search Gracie's and Gracie wondered if she was looking for a sign of weakness, so she'd feign interest in sign-language gardening programmes, which were the only thing on the telly at 3 a.m., and wave Miriam off, waiting until she was out of the room to let the tears roll down her face.

She remembered once passing out while feeding Jasper. She knew she hadn't fallen asleep because the pain had been too insistent. It was more of a blackness into which she'd fallen, waking up with a start to find herself sitting bolt upright in bed, the pillows stuffed behind her in the way Miriam liked to do them, so that they jabbed Gracie in the small of her back. The TV remote had slid out of her hand and was resting on the duvet beside her, but there had been no sign of Jasper.

Gracie's heart had begun to thump as she'd thrown the covers off and run over to the Moses basket, to find it empty. He's gone, she'd thought. She'd found herself patting the duvet to see if he might be there, lurking in its folds, then had looked under the Moses basket stand. She'd gone over to the changing table, peering down to see if he might be lying there, wiggling his arms and legs the way he liked to. 'He's gone,' she'd repeated to herself. For a moment, she'd just stood there in the middle of the room, and she had imagined herself in a place where there was no Jasper, in a life without him. It was only the tiniest glimpse, a millisecond where she tried to remember who she had been before Jasper, but she just hadn't been able catch hold of it. It was gone.

She'd whirled around then, in a panic, before bolting down the stairs in the too-small Daffy Duck T-shirt Jake had bought her on a trip to Disney World the previous year when she was five months pregnant. A 'minimoon', he'd called it. She hadn't been able to go on many of the rides because of her pregnancy, and as they'd lain together in bed in Sneezy's Magic Palace every night for a week, she'd wondered if it was an omen.

She'd run into the kitchen, with its shiny grey cupboards and white Corian worktop. It had been empty. She'd found herself opening the back door, the blackness of the night spilling in to the room. Topsy, that awful, smelly dog of Jake's, had lifted his head from his basket and looked at her blankly before settling back down again, and for a single moment, Gracie had wondered if Jasper might be in there with him, hidden underneath his long black coat.

Then she'd heard the faint murmur of the downstairs television, the huge-screen one in the living room, and she'd walked towards it, turning the handle of the door and peeking in.

Jasper had been lying propped up on Jake's outsize beanbag, which Miriam had carefully arranged around him, his eyes taking in the vivid colours of the snooker table on the TV screen in front of him, the bright colours of the balls on the green baize. As the player leaned over, then took a shot, the gentle clack of the balls had made Jasper give a little shimmy of excitement, his arms waving in the air.

'Snooker's his favourite.' Miriam's voice had been soft and yet it had broken into the silence like gunshot. Gracie had looked over to see her sitting in semi-darkness on the sofa behind Jasper, her hands folded on her lap.

'Is it?' she'd said, kneeling down in front of Jasper, taking a little fist in her hand. His fingers had wrapped around the side of her hand in a grip that was surprisingly firm for a two-month-old. 'I didn't think they could see anything at his age.'

'They can't focus, but they can see colours and they can hear sounds,' Miriam had said, in her immaculate English. As if on cue, Jasper's eyes had slid to the side and he'd tried to turn his head in the direction of Miriam's voice, giving a little cry. 'Oh, poor baby,' Gracie had cooed, lifting him up from the beanbag, pressing him to her, feeling the softness of his hair tickle her nose. He'd begun to wriggle then, banging his head off her shoulder and giving a series of little wails. Gracie had felt the panic clutching her gut, like a hand squeezing her insides, and she'd begun to dance up and down, before remembering that she wasn't wearing any knickers. 'Shush, shush,' she'd said, as he'd begun to wail even louder.

'Here.' Miriam's voice had been soft as she took him from Gracie. It was as if she'd turned off a tap, as Jasper's wails had simply stopped and became soft hiccups instead as he'd leaned his head against Miriam's chest. Miriam had looked at Gracie carefully before stroking his hair, murmuring something in her own language as his eyelids had drooped.

Miriam was gone by the end of that week. She'd been replaced two months ago by Sunny, a tall Filipina with strong shoulders and big hands and feet, who looked as if she should be manning a milking stall, not changing a baby on a Danish-design changing table in suburban Dublin. She was deft and firm, lifting Jasper's legs as she might a newborn calf's, sliding the nappy under them, sprinkling his bottom with talc and fastening the little Velcro fasteners with one hand. When she burped him, it was with a series of insistent taps that echoed in his chest and would produce a satisfying belch promptly, whereupon he would be laid down in the Moses basket, feet touching the bottom, and a cellular blanket would be placed tightly around his lower half. He would have no choice but to sleep — Sunny had commanded it.

'She could run an army,' Jake had said, when he'd seen her in action. He hadn't understood why Miriam had been asked to leave — Gracie had made something up about her being a bit too interested in her jewellery, willing herself not to blush with shame as she did so — but he knew better than to challenge Gracie. 'It's your money, love,' he'd said quietly, when she'd told him that they'd need a nanny for daytimes now that Jasper was a bit older, even though it was more expensive. 'But I can do the feeds, you know, if that's what you're worried about.'

She'd looked at him then, at his slick of yellow-blond curls, the stains on the T-shirt he hadn't changed in a week, his shorts, which he never bloody zipped up properly, and she'd resisted the urge to say the words that were circling in her head, words like 'teenager' and 'slacker'. Instead, she'd found herself patting his hand. 'You're very good, but you need your sleep.' For whatever it is you do, she'd added in her head. 'Besides, I saved the money for it. I put it aside.'

She hadn't meant it to sound like an accusation, but how could it be any other way? She was working, and Jake wasn't because he'd been made redundant six weeks after they'd met. He was developing a YouTube channel, he'd told her. Something in entertainment, giving people a summary of the scariest bits of movies so they wouldn't have to watch them. Were people really that squeamish nowadays, Gracie thought, that they couldn't watch a scary movie from beginning to end? Clearly they must be because he had ten thousand subscribers, he'd told her, which was good, she thought. She'd have to take a look at it to see if Jake could optimise it a bit more. He really needed to monetise it or he'd be earning nothing forever.

'Better get on with it,' she said to Jasper now. 'Our finances depend on it.' She sucked in a deep breath and walked across the street and through the entrance of the large Victorian building that was home to Cutlery, the media and marketing agency for which she worked and which she loved, in spite of its silly name. Tracey, the receptionist, jumped up and squealed as soon as she saw Gracie, running around the enormous reception desk to exclaim over Jasper's beauty. 'Oh, he's *sooo* cute,' she said, bending down to kiss him, brushing his face with her bright-yellow straightened hair. Gracie wanted to stop her, to ask her if she was aware just how many germs were lurking in her saliva and her hair, but instead, she just gave a little pretend laugh and agreed that Jasper was perfect in his bamboo sling, with the clothes she'd picked out for him that morning: a pair of miniature red corduroy jeans and the cutest little denim jacket, with a white T-shirt underneath. It was really not practical, Gracie thought, to dress him in anything other than a babygro because he'd only throw up on it, but he had to look good for his first visit to Mummy's office.

After five minutes of polite chat, she gave Tracey a cheery wave and walked up the flight of stairs to the floor on which she worked, listening to the hollow clicking of computer keys and the buzz of phone conversations coming from the many workstations in the open-plan space. She felt a pang when she thought of everyone inside, being productive, getting on with their busy days, just like she used to. She hovered for a moment at the entrance, before deciding to see Toni first, turning and walking up another short flight of stairs to a narrow landing on which was one single door, now closed.

Before knocking, Gracie glanced at the typewritten notice on Toni's office door. 'Welcome to a sexism-free office! If you are a male chauvinist pig, you've come to the wrong place.' Toni had a whole series of these notices, printed with feminist slogans on them, which she'd leave in prominent places. She'd really embraced feminism and equality at Cutlery Media and Marketing, and at the last AGM, before Gracie had gone on maternity leave, she'd announced her ten-point 'Feminist Manifesto', which she'd made them all memorise. Gracie thought it was very impressive: in fact, it was one of the things that had drawn her to Cutlery. There was also Toni herself, of course, the first female CEO of a communications agency in the city, and who was a real trailblazer for women in the business, empowering them to truly be themselves, to see how far they could go and what they were capable of. Sure, the hours were long and Toni would often ring Gracie on Saturday and Sunday afternoons with 'an amazing idea that you just have to hear', but her ideas really were amazing, as a rule, and anyway, creativity couldn't be confined to the hours of nine to five, Monday to Friday.

Gracie had felt her shoulders drop the minute she'd set foot inside the door on her first day at work, not much more than a year before, the tension just melting away. She'd come from Fitzgerald Onwin, or 'Fuck Off', as it was known in the business thanks to Mike Fitzgerald, a black-clad, horn-rimmed-glasses-wearing thug, a tight cap of dyed blond hair on his head, which had earned him the nickname 'The Stormtrooper'. Gracie had found Mike physically scary, with his red face and shouty directions, accompanied by lots of swear words. She hadn't been brought up like that at all: Mum and Dad didn't do swearing under any circumstances. Gracie could only imagine what would happen in Milford Golf Club if Dad let out a stream of cursing the way Mike did — and worse still, Mike used the 'c' word and there was no excuse for that at all. Gracie found it, and Mike, highly offensive, but she'd put her head down and got on with the job, knowing that if she stuck it out for a couple of years, she'd be able to move on, which she did, two years to the day on which she had walked in the door of that hellhole. Mike had given her a €200 voucher for a department store, a completely unwanted kiss on the cheek that strayed a little too close to the lips and a speech that told her she had the nicest legs in media. After two bloody years, that was it.

On her first day at Cutlery, Circe, Toni's assistant, had been waiting just inside the door to meet her and show her to her desk, which had been decorated with a large bouquet of expensive-looking yellow roses, a bottle of champagne and a witty postcard of two ladies in stripy swimming costumes, with 'Welcome! See you in mine at 5.30' scrawled on the back. When Gracie had given Circe a questioning look, she'd smiled. 'Oh, Toni thinks everyone should get flowers. She's like that – you'll see,' and she'd beamed at Gracie from behind her directional glasses. 'Let me know if you need anything. Anything at all, that's what I'm here for.' And then she'd given Gracie a hug. Gracie hadn't been ready for it and had instinctively leaned back in her seat, but Circe had grabbed her so firmly that she'd found herself pressed against the woman's large bosom. 'There!' Circe had announced, shoving her hands back into her navy tunic. 'Hope you feel loved!'

'I sure do,' Gracie had said faintly.

Gracie had had butterflies in her tummy that whole day, constantly examining her mobile to see what time it was while a procession of friendly people had come up to her to welcome her to the 'gang'. There were more than a few hugs and, after a while, Gracie found herself enjoying them. She had even attempted to put her arms around Gar from accounts, a big red-haired young man with bright-pink cheeks, a professional Corkman, who never missed an opportunity to express his 'Corkness' and to remind them what a superior place the city was, and he'd been delighted. 'You're getting the hang of it, girl!' he'd laughed, holding his hand up in the air. Gracie had enthusiastically slapped it, wondering what Dad would make of this display. As if swearing wasn't bad enough — a high five would finish him off.

Dad never hugged: the most he'd ever done, when Gracie had got six honours in the Leaving Cert, had been a soft pat on the shoulder and a 'well done'; Mum followed his lead, confining herself to a nod of the head or a pursed lip if she disapproved of something Gracie had done. She wondered what they'd think of Cutlery, a little office with a nice view, where everyone hugged everyone else and where they stayed late, sharing order-in wood-fired pizza and the beers that Gar kept in a little fridge under his desk. Then her computer had pinged. 'Come right in!' Toni's note had said. Toni had got up from behind that huge desk of hers and come towards her, a vision in cashmere, arms outstretched. Her hug had been gentle and expensively perfumed and Gracie had wanted to stay in it, to feel Toni's heart beating behind the lovely soft wool. Her mum had never hugged her, so to be embraced by another woman in that way had made Gracie's scalp prickle. When Toni had released her, Gracie had felt bereft. Toni had gone on to explain to Gracie that Cutlery was a truly inclusive workplace, where the rights of everyone, male and female, were respected and where each person got a fair shake, an equal opportunity to make their mark.

'There's no need for macho posturing around here,' Toni had said. 'Not when everyone brings so much to the party without it.' She'd tilted her head to one side then, in that way she had, like a bird. She'd also told Gracie that she knew she'd be an account director within a year. 'I can just tell that you have the right mindset,' she'd said. 'I'll bet you're super-organised.'

'How did you know?' Gracie had said. The two of them had shared a complicit laugh. And when, six weeks later, Gracie had knocked on Toni's door and told her that she was pregnant and that it was a terrible shock but she promised that she'd be back at her desk within weeks of giving birth and would work her socks off before going on just the tiniest bit of maternity leave, Toni had shushed her, pulling her into that lovely perfumed embrace. 'Gracie, I hope you know by now that I'm not that kind of person and this is not that kind of agency,' she'd murmured into Gracie's hair. 'Your being a mum will make no difference whatsoever to the way you are seen here at Cutlery,' she said seriously. 'In fact, it'll be an advantage because you'll come back harder and more focused and more ready to get things done than ever — isn't that right?'

'That's right,' Gracie had breathed, tears in her eyes. She couldn't believe how great Toni was being about this whole thing.

'So, this is good news, and anyone who says different will get a telling off from me!'

Gracie had giggled nervously along with her boss. But

Toni had been as good as her word, inviting Gracie to every product meeting or media planning session, introducing her to clients as her 'wonderwoman of an account executive'. She'd even organised a baby shower for Gracie, with gender-neutral yellow balloons, cake, non-alcoholic champagne and expensive presents.

As she opened Toni's office door now, Gracie shivered. She wasn't sure if it was from excitement or something else.

'Hi!' Gracie said brightly.

Toni was sitting behind her enormous desk – an irony, because she was a very, very small woman, tiny, in fact, and extremely thin, her arms and legs like twigs, her blue eyes huge in her face, which made her look like a small, furry animal – a lemur, perhaps. Her auburn hair was the only thing that didn't obey Toni's precise, tidy aesthetic, being instead a bit frizzy, and inclined to stick out above her petite ears.

When she saw Gracie she said nothing, just got up and came around her desk, arms outstretched. Gracie slid into Toni's embrace, allowing her bony arms to encircle her, resting her head against the thin wall of Toni's chest, even though it was actually a bit uncomfortable with Jasper sandwiched between them. Then Toni held her at arm's length and Gracie noticed that there were tears in her eyes. 'Well, would you just look at this lovely baby boy,' she breathed, placing a tender hand on Jasper's head. 'Oh,

Gracie, he's just beautiful. Well done, you. Well done,'
and she clapped her hands together.

Gracie felt a lump in her throat. She wanted to feel Toni
hugging her again, but she knew that she couldn't ask her
— Toni wasn't her mother. As she had this thought, Gracie
wondered what it might be like to have Toni for a mum —
she could imagine them having long chats on the phone
every day, swapping gossip and recipes, talking about
baby-care routines, with Toni wistfully recalling incidents
from Gracie's own childhood. As she had this thought,
Gracie realised that that's what she wanted from her own
mum, instead of the texts she got every Tuesday morning.
Baby OK? To which she'd reply, *Great. Talk soon.* And then,
with a mixture of guilt and relief, she'd forget about her
mother for another week.

'Sit, sit,' Toni said, pulling out one of the red-felt-
covered square cubes that sat underneath her desk and
motioning for Gracie to sit down. It wasn't easy with a baby
in a sling, so Gracie had to perch right on the edge of it,
leaning forward, Jasper's legs dangling down into space as
she hovered, neck straining. Seeing her discomfort, Toni
said, 'My goodness, what an idiot I am,' and she laughed
as she went behind her desk and dragged her large leather
chair out from behind it.

'There's no need,' Gracie said weakly, watching Toni's
tiny arms trying to pull the heavy chair along.

'Of course there is!' Toni's face reddened as she dragged
the chair around, bending down to pull a lighting flex out

of the way, then huffing and puffing as she managed to push it to Gracie. 'That's better,' she said, holding out her arms and manoeuvring Gracie onto the comfy leather seat. 'A seat fit for a new mum!' she pronounced cheerfully, taking her own seat on the tiny red cube. It suited her: she looked like Miss Muffet sitting on her tuffet, Gracie thought, trying to smother a giggle.

'So,' Toni said. 'Tell me everything. I want to hear it all!'

'I'm sure you don't!' Gracie smiled, but when Toni gave her an earnest look, she said, 'Oh, you do. So ...' She found herself recalling the whole thing, telling Toni everything from the first contraction, which had happened while Jake and she were in Eddie Rocket's burger joint, of all places, having stopped off on their way home from the cinema because Jake had an 'insatiable desire' for garlic fries. Gracie made Toni laugh when she told her that Jake had spent the next twenty-four hours breathing garlic fumes over her and the consultant, even though Gracie hadn't found it funny at all. She told Toni that her consultant had turned up in his golfing gear, having been out on the 'back nine' when the midwife had obeyed Gracie's barked command to call him, sloping off to the phone, her face like thunder. She told Toni about the bliss of the epidural, and then her fear and panic when it wore off and she realised that she was going to have to push her baby out into the world and actually feel it in the process. The thought had terrified her so much that she'd refused to push, holding her breath until her face was practically purple, until the midwife had threatened her with an episiotomy, waving an instrument at her that looked like something from a mediaeval torture chamber. She noted that Toni giggled at this bit, putting a hand over her mouth to stop herself. 'It's OK,' she said. 'It was kind of funny.'

Toni tilted her head to one side, then reached out and took Gracie's hands in hers. 'My goodness, Gracie, but you are such a warrior. I salute you, and so does every other woman, whether she's gone through childbirth or not.' There was just the tiniest pause and Gracie wondered if she should say something, acknowledge that she knew Toni didn't have children herself, but then Toni added, 'Because we women are just amazing. Three cheers for us!' and she gave a little laugh, squeezing Gracie's hands in hers.

'Thanks, Toni, that means a lot,' Gracie said. She'd never felt like a warrior before. She'd felt like an obedient good girl, highlighter pen at the ready for underlining key points in her textbook, gym uniform pressed for school netball matches, exam questions thoroughly prepared for during her college years, a succession of polite, clean-cut boyfriends through the front door of her family home — that is, until she'd found Jake, which, she supposed, was the only out-of-character thing she'd ever done. And now, simply because she'd had a baby, she was a warrior, an object of admiration and awe to other women. She found her shoulders lifting, her chest puffing out as much as it could given that a surprisingly heavy baby was lying on top of it.

'Now,' she said crisply, hoping that Toni would note her businesslike tone. 'I want to talk to you about coming back because Jasper's four months old now and I'm beginning to think that maybe ...'

Her words trailed off when Toni leaned forward and looked her fiercely in the eye. 'Maybe nothing, Gracie. Even warriors need time to recover after battle. None of us is superwoman, you know. I want you to take as much time as you need, and when you're ready, Cutlery will be waiting for you. We won't be going away!' she said gaily. 'And now, no more talk of work. We'll do a Grand Tour of the office and introduce everyone to Cutlery's newest arrival.' She walked over to her desk and lifted the phone. 'Circe? Are you all set? Great!' And before she could say another word, Circe was on top of her, enveloping her in her enormous bosom, exclaiming over how gorgeous Jasper was. He'd woken now and treated them all to a gummy smile and Gracie found herself being lifted out of her comfy chair and swept down the stairs and through the office, to a chorus of *awws* and high-fives and more hugs.

Finally, Jasper was taken off her and carried down the corridor to the production department by Gar, who said he had just the present for him, and Gracie found herself temporarily empty-armed, standing in the middle of the open-plan area. Trying not to be too obvious, she peered at her desk out of the corner of her eye, her nest in Cutlery. She couldn't suppress a little gasp. Her clipboards were gone, replaced with a series of sophisticated-looking prints, and the daisy pottery jug that she'd made in art class when she was thirteen, which she had taken to every job and in which she liked to put her pens, was now a very sleek-looking designer pen holder, with one red, one blue and one black pen in it — the expensive Japanese ones. And sitting on her seat, tapping away on a MacBook Air, looking very intent and serious, was her maternity cover, Atiyah, a tall, elegant black woman with a direct manner and a certain intensity that Gracie had found a bit unnerving the first time they'd met, two weeks before Gracie's maternity leave. Gracie could still remember, with a shiver, asking Atiyah where she came from on her first day of training. Atiyah had replied, 'Ballymun'.

'Oh, I meant where did you originally come from?'

'Ballymun,' Atiyah had repeated, fixing Gracie with a stare. Gracie could still remember the hot feeling on her cheeks as she'd blabbered on to Atiyah about having been to Ballymun for a conference once, which wasn't even true. She'd never been to Ballymun in her life. For a whole day after, she'd felt at sea in her own feelings, alternating between mortification and then anger: how was she to know that Atiyah had been born and brought up in Ballymun? She was African as far as Gracie could see. Surely it was an understandable mistake.

Now, she hesitated for a moment, then went over. 'Hi, Atiyah, how's it going?'

Atiyah didn't stop typing for a few seconds, then slowly turned in her direction. 'Hi, Gracie. Congratulations.' She didn't get up to hug Gracie or to congratulate her about Jasper the way everyone else had done and Gracie felt herself shrink a little.

'How are you finding the work? I hope you're not too overloaded. I could hardly keep up with it all,' and she gave a nervous laugh.

Atiyah gave a brief smile. 'It's fine. All good.' Gracie was sure it was 'all good' because Atiyah had seemed to be very much in charge from the beginning, looking a tiny bit bored as Gracie had shown her her filing system, with its colour-coded entries for each client. She'd also made a couple of sharp comments, which Gracie had felt were unwise, in creative meetings. She'd put a hand on Atiyah's arm to urge her to be quiet, but Atiyah had just ploughed on, asking Dom from the art department if he'd tried photoshopping the ad for King Fido posh dog food to highlight the less attractive dogs. 'You know, so you're not doing the obvious. Most owners don't have show dogs — they just have mutts — so why not show them pets like theirs happily eating the dog food, so it's seen as more attainable and not an unaffordable luxury?'

Gracie had held her breath because Dom was a bit unpredictable, prone to outbursts of bad language if he felt misunderstood, but instead he just nodded, his beanie hat bobbing on his head, and said, 'Good idea, whoever you are. Like it.'

Gracie had felt the ground shift slightly under her. Dom had never told her that he liked any of her ideas. Not once. She also knew that she wasn't really an ideas person. She was great at getting things done and making the client feel special, but she knew that she wasn't creative with a capital 'C'. Still, she understood that Toni and Cutlery valued her for her other qualities — but seeing Atiyah here, tapping away, doing her job, made her feel suddenly like the only girl not invited to the party. She looked around the office and saw everyone working at their desks, in their busy lives, with all of the stuff they had to be doing and she felt as if she were watching them all through a window, pressing her nose against the glass. Where do I belong? she thought, standing there, arms empty. Which world is mine now?

She felt a sudden need to find Jasper and, with a small wave to Atiyah, who didn't wave back, she bolted off down the corridor in search of Gar. She found him in the kitchen with Jasper on his hip, surrounded by a group of people all waving and clapping at Jasper, who was getting over-excited, kicking his legs and arms out. He won't sleep a wink later, Gracie thought. And what *was* he wearing? As she got closer, she noticed it was a miniature Cork GAA jersey, in the brightest of red, with his name on the back. It was hideous, Gracie thought, but she pinned a smile to her face as Gar said, 'How are ya, girl? Jesus, you've a fine little lad here, so you have.'

'Thanks, Gar, and what a thoughtful gift!' Gracie said. 'It's so cute!'

'Up the Dubs,' Dave from production shouted and everyone laughed. Gracie took the opportunity to get Jasper to pretend wave goodbye to everyone and said she'd pay another visit very soon, then she wandered out of the kitchen, down the corridor and past Toni's office, feeling like a ghost. She hesitated outside Toni's closed door but decided not to go in again. She'd talk to Toni about coming back another time.

5

Elise

I can't sleep. I just keep tossing and turning in bed. I try to read the book the lady in the library recommended, but it's really hard work. I look at the cover and the old-fashioned illustration of a really tubby baby climbing a set of steps. *The Child, the Family and the Outside World* by D.W. Winnicott. It's full of theories about attachment bonds and the mother—baby relationship and, honestly, it really puts me on edge. I got it because I thought it would give me something half-intelligent to say to the girls at the next mothers' meeting, but instead, it just makes me think I must be doing a really bad job with Chloe. What on earth would Ma think if she could see me reading it? 'I reared eight children without a manual!' she'd say. Besides, what would a man know about this kind of thing? Women are much better – more natural about looking after children.

I tut loudly as I turn the page, confronted by yet another word I don't understand, and of course, Gray wakes up, which he never does because he sleeps like a log. It must be all the exercise. He's so lucky. The minute his head hits the pillow, he's gone, but the slightest little thing keeps me awake. It's not fair, I sometimes think, but at least it means it's easier to get up when Chloe wakes. I know that Gray would love to help, but I was determined to breastfeed, in spite of two infections that kept me glued to the bed for a few days, but it was worth it. Chloe is thriving and it's all down to me. It might be tough going sometimes, but that's life. Besides, I get Gray to do the nappy changes, so everyone's a winner!

'What's wrong, love?' he says. His voice is thick with sleep and he opens one eye as he turns towards me.

'Would it sound really stupid if I said I was a bag of nerves?' I reply.

He rubs his eyes and runs a hand through his thick auburn hair. I love Gray's hair – it's so healthy. Not like mine, which I need to spend a fortune on every four weeks just to keep it looking half-normal. One of the doctors told me that the hormones would make it fall out, but instead it's turned into this awful frizz. Ailish, the girl who does my hair, tried to get me to have one of those sixteen-week blow-dries the last time I went, but they take loads of maintenance, and where on earth would I get the time?

'What are you nervous about?' Gray asks with a yawn.

'About the mummies' circle,' I snap. 'It's on tomorrow afternoon. Honestly, do you ever listen?' I felt bad the minute the words were out of my mouth. 'Sorry, babe. I didn't mean it. It's just, I'm going a bit doolally.' The expression was one of Da's, I remember, and it used to make us crack up, all sitting around the kitchen table, trying to scoff our dinners as quickly as possible so they wouldn't get eaten by the person sitting beside us. It was do or die in my house, kill or be killed — but Da could always make us laugh with his little expressions. I really miss him. Da was my hero. He held us all together, and when he went, so did our reasons to see each other. Someone once said that the only thing siblings have in common is that they have the same parents: they're so right.

'Ah, love.' Gray sits up and puts a big, muscular arm around me. I like Gray's arms because I feel safe inside them. He really works on them, too, so they're muscly, but I'd be lying if I said I really liked that about them. I could never, ever tell him, but I prefer softer, more slender arms, with less beef. But Gray's training is his passion, as well as his business, and I try to support him in any way I can because I know how much it means to him — not to mention that it's his business that pays for all the nice things we have. My job is to look after Gray and Chloe and I'm happy with that.

'I want to make the right impression, that's all. I don't want to let myself down by saying something stupid,' I tell him, resting my head on his shoulder.

'Now, why would you say anything stupid?' Gray says, squeezing me gently.

'Because sometimes I *am* stupid,' I say softly. 'These women are so educated – I can tell – and I've nothing to say: at least, nothing they'd want to hear.' It's true – in spite of my new reading material. I was terrible at school. I wasn't thick, I know, but I just couldn't seem to concentrate. Sharon was brilliant at the books, but I just couldn't get the stuff into my head. I was always fidgeting and looking out the window: it was as if I was in a hurry to go somewhere, to get on with life. As soon as I left school, I was off to work and I loved it, even though Ma said she'd love to see me go to college, like Sharon. She wanted us all to better ourselves. I didn't understand it at the time, but I do now. I'd give anything for Chloe to be a doctor when she grows up, or a barrister, like her Auntie Sharon – something really impressive.

'Ah, love,' he says, sitting up in bed. 'You're being far too hard on yourself.'

I nod as if he is right, but honestly, I don't think I'm being hard *enough* on myself. When I came back from the park last week, after that first meeting, I took a long, hard look at myself in the mirror in my bedroom to see what kind of image I was projecting to the others. I went top to toe, not sparing myself anything. I'd tamed the frizz on my head, but my tan had faded unevenly, so I had great big patches on my collarbone that looked like dirt. I couldn't believe I'd gone out looking like that. My clothes looked OK, I suppose, but they'd want to, for what they cost me — Corinne in Daphne's Boutique has made a few bob out of me in the last couple of years — but there's definitely room for improvement. A *lot* of improvement.

'Thanks, love,' I say to Gray now, kissing his hand. 'I just really want this to work, you know? All I've ever wanted are good friends and I just keep scaring them away — there must be something wrong with me,' I say sadly. It's true: someone in work once said I had 'foot-in-mouth' disease, which wasn't very nice. They didn't think I was in the room, but I'd just gone to the photocopier around the corner and I could hear every word. Ever since, I've really tried to watch what I say, to think before I blurt out the first thing that's in my head.

'Will you listen to yourself?' Grey interrupts my thoughts. 'How do you think you bagged a fella like me? You're the best woman I know, Elise — you just need to believe in yourself. That you're perfect as you are.'

'I just need to believe in myself,' I repeat, feeling a bit better now that Gray has reminded me that, somehow, I'd managed to snap him up, so I can't be that bad.

'That's the trick. Try an affirmation. I tell all my clients to try them. Something like, "All I seek is already within me."'

I turn my head to face him, expecting his lovely, handsome face to be split by a big grin, but he looks pretty serious.

'Ah, love,' I say, 'I don't think I can say that. It sounds mad.'

'It might sound mad, but if you try it often enough, you'll begin to believe it. Honest.'

'Do you use affirmations?'

'Of course. Every day, I stand in front of the bathroom mirror and I say, "My body is perfect the way it is."'

'It *is* perfect,' I say, a bit puzzled.

'It wasn't always, pet, remember?'

I do remember. Gray told me on our very first date, in Dublin Zoo, of all places. I'd been a bit surprised when he'd suggested the zoo, to be honest, but it was great. You can't take yourself too seriously when you're both looking at a hippopotamus's rear end! We clicked immediately, from the second we locked eyes on each other outside the tiger enclosure, and from that moment on, we were never apart. I think it's because we're best friends, as well as husband and wife. I love Gray's ambition and his work ethic, and he loves my 'warm heart and sense of humour', so he's told me! I also love his honesty. Besides, it was do or die at that point: I had to put the rest of it behind me because I wanted to make Ma and Da proud, to show them that I was normal, not a 'freak' as they'd put it. 'It's not natural,' Ma had told me the time she'd caught me and that girl from the travel agent's where I worked. Fiona. The irony was, Ma and Da were both dead by the time me and Gray got married two years ago, so I could have done what

I wanted, but I wouldn't be without him now. I know he'll never let me down.

'I find out something new about you every day,' I say, popping a kiss on his lovely straight nose. He gives me a flash of his pearly whites and shrugs. 'Go back to sleep, love. You have to be up early,' I say. 'I'm feeling much better now, so I'm sure I'll nod off any minute.'

He gives me another tight squeeze and turns over in the bed and, of course, within about ten seconds, he's snoring away. Meanwhile, I lie awake until the birds start their early-morning chattering and the sky turns that lovely pale blue. Chloe stirs then for her morning feed, and as I get up, I make myself repeat, 'I am a worthy person. I have the right to take up space on the planet,' over and over again. I can't say it's made much difference, but it's early days.

The morning just seems to drag and I can't shake the cloudiness in my brain after my sleepless night, but I force myself into the shower, with Chloe sitting in her baby seat in the bathroom where she can see me. She gets very upset if I move out of sight and her little eyes follow me everywhere. It's cute, even if it's a bit overwhelming at times, to have someone who depends on you so completely. Anyway, after hopping in and out of the shower several times to readjust her soother and to reassure her that I am still there, I manage to wash and then put her down for her morning nap, while I grab some precious time at the mirror, trying on then rejecting everything in my wardrobe. I just have to create the right impression, I tell myself, eventually settling for a nice pink T-shirt, because pink always gives me confidence, and, when Chloe wakes from her nap, putting on her lovely and very expensive Baby Dior pink smock that Gray's sister Debs gave her for her christening, because she felt guilty about missing the wedding. She left the price tag on and I nearly fainted at the expense, but I have to admit, it looks the business. It's supposed to be for special occasions, but my first proper outing to the park is definitely a special occasion! Chloe looks gorgeous in the little dress with its cute embroidered ducks along the collar.

I pop her into her pram and then I debate whether or not to bring Poppy along. She doesn't exactly make the best impression, but she gives me that sad-eyed look, so I give in. That little dog might be a bit temperamental, but she really knows how to melt my heart. I put her best pink collar on, the one with the Swarovski crystals, and with one final look in the mirror, off I go, my heart thumping in my chest.

I decide to take the long way down to the park to give me more time to calm down, which is lucky, really, because I pass the gourmet doughnut shop and the smell wafting out the door is to die for. I stop dead, unable to resist. I go inside and buy a whole box of six for the girls. I know that they're sinfully unhealthy, but there's nothing wrong with a bit of overindulgence every now and again – and besides, I want to give them a little treat, to say 'thank you' for inviting me into the group.

As we get near the park, I can feel the blood pounding in my ears. The green area in front of the bandstand is heaving with picnic rugs and buggies and Poppy growls as she catches sight of a bichon sniffing the grass. I scan the crowds, afraid for a second that they're not here, which is almost better than if they are, in a funny way. Eventually, I spot them under the trees, and even though I want to run over to them, I hesitate. Then I remember one of my affirmations from last night: 'I am a worthy person. I have the right to take up space on the planet.' It's true, I think. I *do* have the right, so I put my best foot forward and walk over to them, pram bouncing across the grass. 'Hi, everyone!' I give a half-smile and a little wave, announcing my presence. Lina gives a little squeal and stands up, kissing me first on one cheek, then the other – so sophisticated!

'I thought you weren't coming back – that we'd frightened you off the last time. We can be a bit much as a group,' she says.

'Ha-ha, no,' I reply, cringing at my silly laugh. 'Wouldn't have missed it for the world.'

There's a moment's silence, and I wonder what I've said wrong, before Jane pats a spot beside her on the picnic rug, 'Sit down here, Elise.'

'Great!' I say, but getting Chloe out of the Silver Cross is such a production, between the little harness that keeps her in place and the bright-pink cover and the parasol, not to mention Poppy, who won't stop barking. I'm dying to stick my foot out and nudge her to be quiet, the way I do at home, but think I'd better not, seeing as we're in company. Instead, I try to ignore her, even though her little bark is making my ears bleed. I dread to think what the others must make of it. Eventually, I shout, 'Will you shut up!' Poppy does that cringing thing, her little ears tight into her head and I'm mortified. The others must think I'm a monster. Still, at least she stops the bloody barking.

Cheeks bright red, I squeeze in beside Jane, who remains sitting where she was, a little too close to me, but it kind of feels nice. Safe. I smile at her warmly and she gives me that little half-smile back. I'm not sure if that means she likes me or she hates me. It's hard to tell.

'You're here just in time for the debate, Elise. We were talking about how boring babies are.' Lina laughs, lifting Tommy into the air, which makes him gurgle with excitement. 'Just a feeding and pooping machine, aren't you, my love?' she says to Tommy.

'Oh, she's not,' Jane giggles, then corrects herself in her reedy voice, 'Sorry, "they". I had no idea it would all be such a chore — one nappy change after another, one feed after another, one little nap, over and over again. I know that every day is a new one for Owen, and I try to remember that while I'm thinking quite the opposite, then I feel guilty about it.'

You mean, Tommy is a *girl*, I think. Well, you could have knocked me down with a feather! And what's with the 'they'? I'm dying to ask, but it might not go down well.

'Guilt, the *raison d'être* of the mum,' Lina says and we all laugh. I make sure to look at Lina when I say, 'Don't start me on guilt! If I so much as leave her nappy on for an extra half-hour, or she gets bored or hungry, I feel that I have to apologise to her.'

'We're overthinking it,' Gracie cuts in. 'Babies' needs are really simple at this age. Feeding, sleeping, clean bottom, Bob's your uncle. There really isn't that much going on in their little minds at this point, I can assure you.'

Of course, then I had to go and put my foot in it. 'Oh, I think there is,' I say. 'I was reading this really interesting book on child development by Winnicott — have you heard of him? He's this amazing child psychologist and he said that babies are doing really complex work right from birth. If you think of all the coordination they do every day and then the development of their eyesight and their understanding of you as their mum ...' My half-reading of the book last night now suddenly feels like I'm showing off, trying to make myself sound better than them, rather than contributing to the conversation.

Then Mousy Jane chips in. 'I read it in college. He's the man who thought of the concept of the "good enough" parent. I wish I could feel good enough.' She sighs wistfully.

He said that? I mustn't have read that bit, I think — and anyway, there's no such thing as 'good enough'. It has to be just right or nothing.

Gracie pats her on the arm. 'You are, pet. Cut yourself some slack.'

'Exactly!' Lina says. 'We mums need to stop setting

ourselves impossible standards and then giving ourselves a hard time if we don't meet them. It's bad enough as it is without that weight on our shoulders.'

I like Lina, but honestly, when I look at Tommy, I can't help wondering if her mum sets herself high enough standards. She, or they, or whatever she's called, looks untidy and a tiny bit grubby, which must mean that Lina doesn't wash the child a lot. She sure does feed Tommy, though. I've only met them twice and each time I have, Tommy's been hanging out of Lina's breast. I'm all for breastfeeding, but not for public displays like that. I didn't go out for the first eight weeks of Chloe's life because I was afraid of being in Tesco and needing to feed her.

I rack my brains to say something that doesn't sound judgemental. 'I find that if I just follow the baby's rhythm, it's a bit easier. It takes a bit of getting used to, but I try to get into her little world, to see things as she must see them, learning everything for the first time. It must be such an amazing world for her — sometimes it's like I'm seeing it all myself for the first time!'

'Well, thank you for that,' Gracie says flatly. My cheeks go bright red with embarrassment. Jane and Lina exchange a glance and I want the ground to open up and swallow me. Then Lina slaps her thighs. 'Right, enough "mother talk", let's eat!' and she pulls a giant packet of Custard Creams out of her rucksack. 'Sorry, girls, this is all I could afford.'

Jane doesn't offer anything, just shifts awkwardly beside me. She doesn't look poor, but then, appearances can be deceptive. Of course, Queen Gracie turns to her giant hamper and lifts out a series of weird-looking things in Tupperware boxes. 'Now, let me see,' she says. 'Seaweed bites, protein balls, wasabi peas ...' They sound absolutely horrible, but I know that I need to get into her good books.

'How do you find the time to make these lovely things, on top of everything else? You must be superwoman!'

I've said the right thing, I realise, when she gives a little shake of her head and a soft giggle. 'Hardly. I just try really hard to be organised because it makes me feel on top of things – that I'm still in control and life hasn't slid into complete chaos.'

'I know what you mean,' I say. 'I find that a routine is the only thing that keeps me going sometimes. Order is so important for babies, I think. They like things to be really streamlined – that way they feel safe and secure.' I'm rewarded by the first genuine smile from Gracie and I feel like cheering.

Lina gives a short bark of laughter. 'God, well, Tommy must feel that she's in mortal danger all the time because I just can't do routine. I go where the wind takes me – it's how I was brought up. Mama taught me that routines were for the bourgeois and the conventional – people who didn't know how to live any other way.' She rolls her eyes to heaven at this. 'I suppose we slip into the way we were parented when we become parents ourselves.'

'Oh, I don't know,' Jane suddenly says. 'My dad was terribly strict, and I like to think I'm trying to find another way. I think you either react against the way you were brought up, or you re-enact it. I'm working really hard on reacting ...' and she gives a soft laugh.

Well, that's interesting, I think. I hadn't expected this plain, pale woman with her mid-brown hair twisted into a plait and her dumpy, sensible clothes to actually have opinions. 'Well, I think you're very brave to chart your own course like that,' I say warmly, wondering what Ma would make of all this talk. Her mothering was all about the heart — about big hugs and a cream cake when you were miserable, and the wooden spoon when you were bold, not debates about child development.

I've said the right thing once more, though, because Jane's cheeks flush with pleasure. 'And your baby's gorgeous — aren't you?' I add, chucking his little red cheek. Jesus, he really is enormous, I think, looking at the huge rolls of fat on his thighs. He must eat like a Sumo wrestler. I desperately want to laugh then, so I have to cough really loudly to cover it up.

'Oh, I've just remembered the doughnuts!' I say suddenly. I get up and rummage in the basket under the pram, taking out the cardboard box filled with the lovely gooey treats. That's more like it, I think, opening the lid and placing them gently on the picnic blanket. 'I hope you don't mind. I just couldn't resist them — there's something about breastfeeding that makes me crave sugar.'

'Me too — I can't get through a day without a biccy or two, or three,' Lina says happily, reaching into the box and taking a pink iced doughnut, eyeing it with glee. She takes a huge bite, her teeth sinking into the bright, shiny icing, her eyes closing with pleasure. 'God, that's orgasmic,' she says, mouth full, spraying crumbs everywhere. It's disgusting, quite honestly, but she's obviously enjoying herself. 'I cannot tell you how delicious dirty food is. Yum,' she adds, her mouth full.

'Truly orgasmic ...' Jane giggles, as she bites into a chocolate one. 'Who was it who said chocolate is better than sex?' she adds, blushing as soon as she's said it and putting a hand over her mouth.

Only Gracie doesn't help herself, looking at the doughnuts with a curled lip. 'No, thank you,' she says, as if she'd be sick. 'I wish I could eat that kind of thing, but if I did, I'd just pile on the pounds. I find that I have to be really careful what I eat.'

There's another silence, while Jane looks miserably down at her hips, but then Lina bursts out laughing. 'You don't know what you're missing, Gracie. I think we should have doughnuts at every meeting from now on,' and she reaches out and helps herself to another one – a chocolate-and-peanut-butter combination that even I could resist because it's so rich. She pushes Poppy, who's sniffing it eagerly, out of the way. 'All mine, bud,' she tells her, and of course, Poppy growls at her. I don't think she likes Lina, which is surprising. Poppy normally has the same instincts about people as me.

Lina takes a huge bite and makes more *um-yum* noises. Gracie's face is a picture. Then she turns to Jane. 'Listen, did you find that shop OK? I wondered if it was still there.'

'Oh, yeah, I did, thanks,' Jane says. 'The man was really helpful and Mark was pleased, so that's good.'

'Disaster averted then,' Gracie says, smiling kindly.

'You could say that,' Jane answers softly.

I look at Lina to see if she knows what they're talking about, but she just shrugs. Honestly, I think it's a bit rude to have a private conversation like that in a group. Couldn't they wait?

After Lina has finished, giving a cheerful burp, followed by a 'whoops', the party seems to break up, everyone somehow knowing that it's time to go home. I have to confess, I'm a bit sad because I was beginning to settle in nicely, but I helped Gracie to put away her horrible food – it was the least I could do, after producing the doughnuts!

'Here, have the seaweed bites,' she says, handing me a tinfoil package. 'They're really umami.'

What does that mean? I wonder, taking them anyway because I don't want to seem rude. Maybe Poppy could eat them, but then, she's got a very delicate digestive system. The amount of time and money I've spent in the vet's with that pooch, I think, as I pack them away at the bottom of the pram, before helping Jane to put Owen back in his buggy, for which she gives me a watery smile.

'I think I'm going your way,' I say to Lina, as she gives

the group a little wave and makes to walk across the grass to the bottom gate of the park.

She's a bit surprised – 'Do you live near the South Circular Road?' she says. God no, I want to say – I live in Rathgar, where a red-brick is a red-brick and no messing about it, but I just mutter something about needing to buy some spices from one of the Indian stores I've seen on my way into town. Gray would have a conniption if I cooked anything spicy, but I have a hunch that Lina might be that kind of person – and sure enough, she says she'll show me the best place to buy genuine Indian food. 'The mangos are to die for. "Alphonso", they're called. They cost a fortune, so Mr Abdallah, he's the owner, saves the bruised ones for me, but still – they make life worthwhile. And, as my boss was too mean to pay for maternity leave, I have to mind the pennies,' she says as we walk down the hill. The pavement is narrow and we have to go in single file because of the Silver Cross taking up so much room, so she has to turn her head all the time to talk to me.

'Oh, what do you do?' I yell over the din of a passing ambulance, siren blasting. God, it's noisy around here. I suddenly long for the peace of my leafy street, where the only noise comes from the pigeons that roost on my neighbour's roof. I've made Gray get one of those fake birds of prey off Amazon to scare them – there's no way I'm having those flying rats ruin my front drive.

'Well, by day I work for a video-sharing site and by night

I'm a comedian. Well, a wannabe. I'm not very good,' she adds.

I want to walk alongside her now, so that we can have a proper conversation. I think eye contact is so important when you're building a relationship, but I have to content myself with just yelling, 'I'm sure you are,' at her, as we walk over the bridge, the traffic humming beside us. 'You're naturally very funny. I can tell. What kind of material do you write?'

'Well,' she throws over her shoulder, 'it used to be long stories about going out and getting drunk and doing stupid things, like meeting awful men, but that's not exactly relevant any more.' There's a pause. 'I'm actually writing new material at the moment,' she says shyly. 'I'd really like to bring a show to Edinburgh some day. It'll be called *Motherworld* ... but it's just a silly dream and, besides, who'd find motherhood interesting apart from us?'

'Don't be silly,' I say. 'I think it's a brilliant idea — a universal subject and you can really see the funny side of it. Go for it!'

'Do you think so? Well, thanks, Elise.'

'What does your partner think of it?'

'Oh, I haven't got one. I mean, he was there at the beginning, so to speak, but I'm a single mum.'

'Oh, wow. That takes guts,' I say. Honestly, I am not a fan of single mothers — I saw far too much of their dodgy offspring when I was growing up for that. If there were fewer single mums, there would be fewer social problems, I think. But then, I realise that I'm being a bit harsh. Maybe I'm nervous about people who are different because I've chosen to go the other way: to be the same, to fit in. My decisions are hardly Lina's fault.

'Yeah, well, I was brought up by a single mum, so I don't know any better, I suppose,' she says. Is it just me, or is her tone different? Maybe she spotted something in my response when she talked about being a single mum. I honestly don't mean to give that impression. It's just not for me, that's all — at least, that's what I've told myself. We've reached the Indian shop at this point, a store with a bright-red sign above it that says 'halal', the final 'l' tilting to one side, boxes of exotic-looking fruit and veg filling the window. It looks very foreign, like everything else in this neighbourhood. I think it's quite exciting, really — even though Rathgar is clean and leafy, it's certainly not exciting!

Lina's baby begins to fuss now, so she jigs up and down to soothe it, or them — I've forgotten. 'Listen, my mum's visiting at the moment, so I'd better get back to see what awful dinner she's cooked for me. So ... see you, Elise. Happy shopping!' and she nods towards the shop behind her.

The pavement is wider here and we're facing each other, me behind my giant pram, Lina just standing there, hands on her hips, bouncing her little one gently up and down in the sling. She has such a lovely face, bright and open, huge grey eyes under that thatch of white-blonde hair. I can tell that she doesn't care a whit about her appearance, but she's just a natural beauty. I'm a bit envious, to be honest, thinking of the amount of time and money I've spent on myself.

We could hardly look more different, and yet I sense that we have a real connection. Maybe it's just my imagination working overtime, particularly after my single-mum blunder, but I think she might actually like me and the thought makes me feel a bit giddy. 'Listen, I hope this doesn't sound out of turn, but my husband, Gray, moves in media circles — he has a few contacts. Maybe he might know of some leads in the comedy world. I mean, it might go nowhere at all ... but ...'

It's partly true: Gray has media clients that he trains in the park at five o'clock in the morning: sweaty, paunchy middle-aged men trying to be twenty years younger. Still, one of them might be useful, even if Gray has warned me absolutely not to tap them for anything because it's bad for business — but sure, what's wrong with offering? She probably won't be interested anyway.

But I'm rewarded with a beam that splits her lovely face. 'Wow, that'd be great, Elise. It's very kind of you.'

'Oh, it's nothing at all,' I say lightly. 'It's a tough world and we all need a leg up every now and again.'

'Thanks, Elise. Really,' and she leans forward. For a second, I think she's going to kiss me and I can't help it — I lean in, my lips puckering, but then she pats my arm

instead and I blush bright red. You fool, I chastise myself
— you've misread the moment. Again.

I'm all action now. 'Well, see you next Tuesday for
more doughnuts!' I've rescued the situation in the nick of
time. Not like with Fiona at the travel agent's. That was
a hasty farewell, I can tell you. Besides, I think now as I
wave goodbye and pretend to walk in the door of the Indian
shop, turning and walking back out again as soon as I see
Lina disappear around the corner, I'm good at beginnings:
it's usually later, when things change, that I can't manage,
when I have to reveal the real me. But then, I'm not really
sure if I know who the real me is any more. I wonder if
that's why I really want these women to be my friends:
maybe it's more than just new-mum loneliness, it's about
feeling like a whole person, like I belong. If I have to make
a few promises to get there, well so be it. I need it, and this
time, I'm going to get it.

6

Lina

'**M**y husband has slept with my best friend. Should I leave him?' the voice blared out of the television as Lina made her way to the kitchen for her morning coffee, Tommy on her hip. Normally, nothing kept Lina from her coffee, but now there was a shape between her and the kitchen door and a pair of legs stretched up towards the ceiling. Her mother was lying on the ratty fake-fur coat she always had with her, summer and winter, legs in the air. She was lifting these up and down in a scissors movement, counting in German as she did so, the sound half-drowned out by the two women

88

on the TV screen, who were now pulling each other's hair and yelling insults.

Oh, Jesus, Lina thought. And she must be deaf, judging by the volume of the television. 'Mama?'

Her mother's eyes opened and she blinked at Lina, upside down. Lina thought she might be trying to smile, but it looked strange, more like a grimace.

'*Ja*?'

'Can I just ...? Lina indicated the kitchen and, with a sigh, her mother lowered her legs to the floor. As she did, Lina marvelled at how bony they were, like the legs of a little chicken, and her bottom was tiny, skin hanging off her hips. It suddenly came to her that her mother was old. Of course she was – she was nearly seventy, Lina thought, shuffling into the kitchen and putting a filter into the plastic coffee drainer, balancing it on top of the teapot and putting the kettle on to boil.

'What were you doing?' she asked politely.

'Pilates,' her mother replied. 'It helps with my arthritis.' With this, she mimed an aching hip, grimacing and limping up and down the living room. 'The doctor says it's the worst he's ever seen. He thinks that soon I will need a hip replacing.'

'Really?' Lina said tiredly.

'*Ja*,' her mother said, bending forward and clutching her hip, giving Lina her best pained expression. 'The agonies I go through ...' There was a chorus of beeps from the television set and Lina closed her eyes for a second. Please God, let me wake up and find my mother magically disappeared, gone in a puff of smoke, back home to Wexford, never to return. But when she opened them again, her mother was standing beside her, blinking behind those strange red-tinted glasses. No luck then, Lina thought, taking the filter off the pot and giving it a little stir, eyes fixed on the thick, dark-brown liquid. Ah, coffee, she thought, pouring some into her favourite mug. '*Mama — ein bisschen Kaffee?*' She said the words in German without thinking, cursing herself as she did so, but her mother just shook her head. 'My doctor says it's very bad for the bones.'

Of course it bloody well is, Lina thought, taking a big swig, feeling it course through her veins. It might be bad for the bones, but it sure tasted good. She looked up at Jeremy Kyle, then over at her mother. 'Mama, why are you watching this?'

'Oh, he's very funny,' her mother said. 'There's always … how do you say it, a "punch-up" too. It makes me laugh — and there are the issues of the day.'

'There are?' Lina said faintly, wondering what had happened to documentaries about Faust, and the entire works of Goethe being read over the breakfast table. Her mother had, as she never ceased to remind Lina, grown up with the finer things in life, in a little town in southern Germany, full of the 'fattened bourgeoisie', as she called them. It had certainly given her notions, Lina thought. Maybe her mother had softened in her old age. Unlikely, but possible.

'How did you sleep, Mama?' she half-shouted over the sound of one woman calling another a whore and a slag. She'd offered her mother her bed, hoping she'd say no, and she had, but Lina felt bad about that now. She's old, and you let her sleep on the pull-out sofa, she chastised herself, shuffling Tommy onto the other hip so that she could put two slices of bread into the toaster without Tommy diving at them and shoving her hand in, which she'd done the last time. 'No toasted hand this time, Baba,' she said softly as Tommy took a swipe at the bread. Instead, Lina broke off a bit of crust and gave it to her daughter to gum, which she did enthusiastically.

'Do you know that gluten is one of the major causes of dietary distress in children under five?' her mother said, eyeing Tommy.

'Watching Jeremy Kyle is likely to do them more harm than a piece of sourdough,' Lina said sharply. 'Can we turn it off?'

Her mother shrugged, walking into the living room and taking the remote control, flicking it at the television uselessly. 'You have to point,' Lina yelled.

'I am pointing, look,' her mother said, aiming the remote at the TV and pressing, as if she were zapping an alien.

'Here,' Lina said, taking the remote from her mother's hand, more roughly than she should have, and shoving it in the direction of the TV, which shut up obligingly. The silence rang in Lina's ears as she put Tommy into her little high chair beside the table then went to get her coffee. Christ, she would kill the woman.

Her mother came back into the kitchen. 'The answer to your question is, yes, I did sleep well, but I think the toilet is broken.'

'Did you pull the chain twice like I showed you?'

'*Ja, ja,*' her mother replied.

'It's temperamental. I'll check it later.'

Her mother looked at her carefully from behind her red lenses, and Lina could see the thoughts forming, the questions about how she'd ended up here, in a grotty flat on the South Circular Road. Don't you remember, she wanted to say to her, the first place we lived in, with the mould that grew on the bathroom ceiling, the big mushroom behind the toilet cistern, or the cottage with no running water and an outhouse? Lina could remember winter nights, bolting from the safety of the kitchen across the crunchy, frosty grass to the little shed with the loo in it and the flush a roar of gurgling water so loud that Lina would have to cover her ears, before running back to the house.

Life with Mama had been improvised, a constant succession of temporary situations, of places that would do until something better came along, which it never really seemed to. Mama was always in search of perfection and, of course, nowhere really measured up. It couldn't possibly because what Mama wanted couldn't be found in real life.

Lina looked around her own shabby flat, with the worn carpet through which the underlay could be seen and the battered, chipped dark-brown furniture, and thought, Maybe I'm repeating my mother's life — one improvisation after another. Maybe in time, Tommy will come to resent me, to find me completely unbearable, so much so that they have to hide from me for three years. Three years without a single word from me, Lina thought, wondering, for the first time, what that might have felt like to her mother.

'Would you like waffles, Mama? I have a waffle iron, would you believe,' Lina said, bending down to the cupboard under the sink and extracting the heavy waffle grill. 'I found it in the flea market.' It wasn't sophisticated, being two separate heavy iron plates with interlocking handles, but Lina supposed it must work. She'd never actually used it, in spite of her German heritage.

Her mother nodded. 'Waffles, yes, but I will make them.' And then she proceeded to whip eggs and milk, sugar and flour, requesting vanilla essence, which Lina managed to find at the back of a cupboard, and some butter, which she melted and drizzled into the batter before pouring some mixture onto the hot iron and putting the lid down firmly. There was silence in the kitchen while they both waited for the waffles to cook, before Mama muttered something to herself in German, lifting the lid to reveal a perfect golden-brown waffle.

'We need jam,' Lina said suddenly. 'Wait, I'll get some downstairs,' and she put Tommy on her hip, not trusting her mother with a baby and a hot waffle iron, and went around the corner to Mr Abdallah's, picking up a jar of apricot jam and waving it in the direction of Mr Handsome, his son, mouthing the words, 'I'll be back later to pay,' then going back upstairs, where her mother was placing a plate piled high with waffles onto the table. Beside it was the ancient lustre-ware teapot from the back of the china cabinet that took pride of place under the living-room window, full of cracked and broken cups and saucers. At the sight of the golden tower of sugary perfection, Tommy began to dribble. 'You're too young for waffles,' Lina teased them, relenting and giving them a tiny corner when they wailed in frustration.

They smothered the waffles with the jam, Mama nodding in satisfaction as she covered each mouthful with a mountain of apricot. Lina resisted the temptation to lecture her about all the gluten and sugar because they were too delicious and the moment was too pleasant to spoil. 'Do you remember when you used to make these for me every day after school?'

'Yes,' her mother agreed sadly. 'It was when there was no money for meat or fish. I used to pretend it was a big thing, to be allowed to eat waffles for our supper, like a big party, when the truth was that I couldn't afford to feed you.'

'Well,' Lina said magnanimously, 'I didn't notice. I just loved the waffles.'

'Simon had to tell me, you know,' Mama said, taking another waffle off the pile and putting it on her plate, smothering it in butter, then jam. Jesus, she'll get diabetes if she goes on like that, Lina thought, wondering if the jam had been such a good idea.

'Had to tell you what?' Lina said, even though she knew what. Simon was the organic fruit farmer down the road from the little cottage Mama lived in now. At ten years, it was the longest she'd lived anywhere and Simon had become a good friend to them both. He also held a torch for Mama, which was a complete waste of time, if nice to see. Lina had written to him to let him know about Tommy, telling herself that it was just a courtesy, while hoping he'd find a way to tell Mama so she didn't have to. He clearly had, and she felt a stab of guilt at letting him do something that was her responsibility.

Her mother didn't talk for a moment, lifting a corner of waffle off the plate and putting it into her mouth and chewing. She'd had dentures fitted and as she bit down into the waffle, she resembled a horse. Lina had to look the other way. '*Dass du eine Mutter geworden bist,*' she said after what seemed a lifetime's mastication. '*Warum, Lina? Warum hast du es mir nicht gesagt?*' Her words, of accusation, of reproach, were delivered with her usual precision, but her mother's eyes seemed to fill behind her awful glasses.

'I didn't tell you about Tommy because I wanted to be like you,' Lina replied, careful to speak in English so that she could remain in control of the conversation. 'You did everything by yourself, so why couldn't I?' It wasn't really the truth: the truth was that Lina didn't want Tommy to be infected with the virus of her mother, with the idea that there was only one way to live, one way to be in the world, and that was her mother's way. Everyone else's was wrong.

Everyone else was stupid or bourgeois or conventional, afflicted with dullness, conformity, while only she, with her insatiable reading of books that she agreed with and her refusal to pollute herself with American TV shows, was living the right life. Lina could still remember her lecture about the capitalist patriarchy that followed an episode of *Baywatch* that she'd innocently mentioned having seen at Darina's. Her mother's voice had shaken with anger, as she'd denounced Pamela Anderson as a pair of boobs on legs and the Hoff as a brainless bit of American muscle. It would have been funny had her mother not forbidden her from seeing Darina from then on.

You suffocated me, she felt like saying to her mother. You sucked all the air out of the room and left me with nothing — but here, in my crummy flat, I can finally breathe. I can sit at my laptop for twenty minutes every afternoon, when Tommy sleeps, and I can write jokes and rewrite jokes, and play them out and tell myself that they're not funny and then that they're hilarious, then not funny again. Twenty minutes is all I have, but it's freedom. And then, you turn up.

'I would have liked to help with the baby,' her mother was saying. 'I gave birth to you alone, of course, and that was my choice, but I didn't think you'd be able to manage. You're too ... sensitive, too easily crushed. You must have had help?'

Jesus. 'No, I did not have help,' Lina said, between gritted teeth, 'unless you count the midwife.' Oona, queen of natural childbirth at the antenatal classes, had been all on for coming to the hospital, promising to act as Lina's advocate — 'so you can get the birth that you want' — but Lina had politely declined, due to the fact that Oona was half mad.

'I just wondered, that's all. As a child you were very ... squeamish, that's the word, and easily upset. You refused to go to school until you were almost seven because you were afraid of that old nun, whatwashername? Sister Bonaventure.' She pronounced it '*Bonaventoor*'. 'The poor woman had to die before you'd go in the door of the place.'

'Yes, well, I'm thirty-two now, so think I'm able for a nun or two and the birth went just fine, thanks for asking.' Lina lied, hoping her mother would notice her sarcasm and was gratified when she saw Inge's knife hover over a waffle for a few seconds before she continued to spread butter and then jam onto it.

'Fine,' she eventually said. 'I shouldn't have given an opinion as you so obviously are in charge of your life.'

'I am, but thanks,' Lina said more softly. 'Mama, why have you come to visit? Why now? I mean, it's not that you're not welcome, of course you are,' she lied. 'It's just, I was wondering ...'

'Can't a mother visit her daughter? Isn't that normal, when she's had a baby, that her mother takes care of her? Is that so bad?' Her mother's hand shook as she rattled the knife against the plate, and she began to rummage in her handbag for a tissue, whipping one out and blowing her nose with an exaggerated honk that made Tommy's eyes widen, before she let out a long giggle. 'It's not funny,' Inge said, before giving a short laugh.

'Mama, what is it? What's the matter?'

At this, her mother collapsed. 'Oh, I have nothing, Lina, can't you see? That bastard has thrown me out of my own home and I'm on the street with only the clothes I'm sitting down in, and the lady in the social office told me that I can't have any money because I should be looking for work, but who'd give an old woman like me a job?'

It's the clothes you're standing up in, Lina thought wearily. 'Hang on, who threw you out – John?' John was the farmer who had rented Inge's cottage to her.

'Yes, John. He has sold the land for one of these nasty blocks of apartments, the bastard capitalist pig, and I must leave. So, I have nowhere to go. All my friends are gone and I don't want to ask Simon because he has a new girlfriend and I don't think she likes me ...'

I wouldn't exactly blame her, Lina thought. Poor Mama – even Simon had given up on her, a man whose adoration she had always taken completely for granted, until it was too late. 'I don't suppose you have any savings, do you?'

Her mother shook her head. Of course not. Saving was for the bourgeoisie – the entitled, who expect to live long and comfortable lives, playing golf and going on holiday. Instead you turn up on my doorstep, penniless and homeless, expecting me to bail you out. Who's the child here, Mama?

'Mama, I don't have anything. I'm on maternity benefit,

which is basically the dole, and I'm trying to write for a living. I can barely feed myself and clothe Tommy, not to mind anyone else.' She knew that she sounded mean, but it was the truth, and besides, there was no way she'd take her mother in. No way. She'd sooner die than put up with Inge. She really would.

In response, her mother bent her head and sniffed, hands playing with the tissue, squeezing it between her fingers, wringing it while the silence grew. Look at me, her gestures seemed to say. A poor little old lady. A homeless poor little old lady.

Lina sighed. 'How long do you think you'll need to stay?'

Her mother's head snapped up. 'A week or two? Just until I sort myself. I will live very quietly, as you know, Lina. I promise not to say a word.'

I very much doubt you'll live quietly, Lina thought sourly. And as to your promise not to say a word, I'd give it ten minutes.

'Can you babysit?'

'*Ja. Natürlich*. I love babies,' and she reached out and chucked Tommy under the chin. Tommy looked at her grandmother doubtfully, then at Lina. I know, Lina thought – me too, but let's give it a chance. I can't throw her out on the street, can I?

'OK, well, if you can mind Tommy for a couple of hours every morning, you can stay, but no telling me what to do, please?'

'I promise. *Ich verspreche es, mein Liebling*.'

Oh, God.

'Mama?'

'Yes?'

'If there was anything else, you'd tell me, wouldn't you?'

Inge had been concentrating on picking up waffle crumbs from her plate with a damp finger, but at Lina's question, her head snapped up, eyes bright with suspicion. 'What else would there be – is being homeless and penniless not enough?'

Your choices, Mama, Lina thought sadly. All your choices, and now, somehow, it's all down to me. And then another thought – and I'm not entirely sure I believe you.

'I don't think that is very healthy,' Mama was saying as they stood at the counter in Mr Abdallah's, watching him stuff a large pack of iced biscuits into her plastic bag on top of the onions and coriander she'd bought. He'd refused to take any money for the jam. 'Do you not think you will gain still more weight?' And she looked at Lina's hips.

'He likes to help, Mama. You're not obliged to eat any of it,' Lina said crisply.

'I was just saying, why not give you some fruit or vegetables instead of just sugar?'

Says the woman who has just eaten her bodyweight in sugary waffles with extra apricot jam, Lina thought.

'Indian people love sweets, I suppose,' her mother said loudly.

'He's *not* Indian,' Lina hissed.

'Well, he's brown,' her mother replied. 'How do I know where he's from?'

Sweet Jesus, Lina thought, chattering to Mr Abdallah in her loudest voice to drown out her mother's racist comments. That was the thing about Mama — for all her espousing of New Age ideas, she could still behave in the entitled manner in which she'd clearly been brought up.

'So this is Tommy's granny?' Mr Abdallah said, clasping his hands across his heart. 'You look so like your daughter! So young!' He chuckled.

Mama looked suitably regal in response. 'Thank you,' she said solemnly, even though she and Lina looked nothing alike. Where Lina was tall and big-boned, with her thatch of blonde hair, Mama was tiny, fragile and dark. When she was a teenager, Lina had often thought of how she could physically overpower her mother if she wanted to — if she was that way inclined, which she wasn't. If anything, Mama's delicacy had made Lina more careful, tiptoeing around real conflict, using humour instead of anger to get out of awkward situations, and this was a tactic she had taken into her adult life. Seamus had said it to her once, when she'd told him about her pregnancy and had cracked a joke in the process: 'You know, not everything's funny, Lina. Some things you have to take a bit seriously.'

She'd tuned out of Mama and Mr Abdallah, and when she tuned back in, he was saying, 'I'm so glad to see you with her — I worried about her, all alone, you know. It's not good to be alone in the world ...' I'm not, Lina felt like saying. I have Tommy and she – I mean, they – are all I need.

'No.' Mama shook her head sadly. 'It is not. That's why I have moved to be closer to her, so I can help.' Her mother ignored the look Lina was giving her.

'Oh, very good for you. I can see you are a mother who truly loves her daughter.' He sighed wistfully.

'*Ja*, if only she appreciated that,' her mother said darkly.

'Ah, but the young; they never respect their parents. They think we are, what – "old farts", with our silly opinions and our old-fashioned views. Look at my son,' Mr Abdallah said, rolling his eyes and nodding his head towards his gorgeous offspring, who was talking into his mobile in low, urgent tones. 'Does he have any respect for the old man? No.'

'I know exactly what you mean,' Inge said, warming to her theme, glaring at Lina. 'They have no appreciation for our sacrifice, for everything we— what?' she said, as Lina picked up the bags and interrupted.

'Mama, it's time for our outing to the park. I thought we'd have a picnic. Thanks, Mr Abdallah!' she said, ushering her mother out the door.

'I didn't know Indians could be so cultured,' her mother exclaimed as they left, in her loudest stage whisper.

'For the last time, he's not Indian!' Lina said. 'He's from Pakistan.'

'Well, there's no need to shout,' her mother muttered. 'Can't a woman have a chat in a shop with the owner without you causing a fuss? Honestly, Lina, you're not a teenager any more.'

I will kill you before these two weeks are out, Lina thought. I really will.

The two of them walked home in silence, her mother shuffling along now, all traces of her earlier Pilates energy seeming to have deserted her. She seemed smaller out here on the street with the people milling past, a little old lady in a too-warm coat and a pair of sandals with a broken strap. 'Is your hip bothering you?' Lina said softly.

'I have learned to live with the pain,' her mother said, looking miffed.

'Maybe we should get someone to look at it while you're here. There's a nice doctor down the road — and he's cheap. I'll make an appointment.' Lina was trying to mollify Inge now, feeling suddenly sorry for her. It was a weakness, she knew, but her mother always could tug at her heartstrings, even when she thought she couldn't bear her for another second.

'Whatever you like,' Inge said snootily, lifting her head up and shuffling slightly more quickly along the road. Lina noticed that she was lifting her left leg slightly, like a pirate limping on his wooden stump, and she couldn't resist a smile.

They reached the door of Lina's flat and she rummaged in her handbag for the key, her phone beeping at the same time. She pulled it out of her pocket and stared at the words on the bright screen, heart thumping.

'*Was?*' Inge said.

'I have a meeting with Mack McCarthy,' Lina said faintly.

'Who?'

'He's a top agent — he represents some of the best comedians in the country. He's having a party to open a new comedy club in town and I have an invite. *Me*. Jesus H. Christ, I'll never be ready.' Lina pushed the phone back into her pocket before taking it out again, scanning the lines for any chance that she'd misread them.

Hi, Lina. So, I spoke to Gray and he spoke to Mack McCarthy, who he takes for kickboxing on Tuesdays and Thursdays and, anyway, Mack says if you want to turn up at this party at Number 28, he'll give you 'five minutes'. Doesn't sound much to me, but hope it's better than nothing! Break a leg! Elise xxx. There were a few smiley emojis after the text, one with tears flowing from its eyes, which was just about how Lina was feeling. Five minutes, she thought. Now, what could I do in five minutes to really blow Mack McCarthy away?

She stared at the text again. *Break a leg* — she'd probably have a heart attack first, Lina thought. She'd met Elise twice and Elise had done this for her — how great was that! She wanted to hug her, if only she knew where she lived. She looked at the text one more time, while her mother tutted and asked her if she'd open the door because she needed 'that terrible bathroom'. She wondered where Elise had got her number — Lina hadn't given it to her, as far as she could remember. She recalled expert highlights, designer clothes, a posh buggy. She wasn't Lina's kind of person and yet Elise had done what she'd promised. Lina didn't know how she'd thank her.

7

Jane

I'll have to watch the time, Jane thought as she noticed the number 25B bus coming down the hill. She'd been surprised to get Gracie's text, inviting her to coffee in Rathmines just a day after the mothers' meeting. Jane only ever met Gracie and the others on Tuesdays, and the only reason Mark let her go then was because Gracie knew him from Oona's class, so any objections on his part would be noticed, even if Gracie would be far too polite to actually say anything. Getting out for a simple coffee had involved a lie about taking Owen for his vaccinations and a promise to buy line-caught salmon in the fishmonger's for dinner.

She ran to the bus stop, Owen squealing in delight as his

chariot picked up speed. It made Jane laugh and remember pushing Helen, her baby sister, around the block to Mrs Davoren's shop while Mam rested – one of the few times she could ever remember Mam resting. As she'd get to the top of the steep hill leading to the little country shop, she'd let go of the handles of the pram and watch it gather speed as it rolled, then sped downwards towards the crossroads. She'd time it so that she had to sprint to catch up with it, her arms reaching for the big, cream handle, the pram remaining just out of reach, Helen's face contorted in glee as the pram whizzed down, her big sister following at breakneck speed. Why do we do these things, Jane thought as she hailed the bus and waited for the door to open and the step to come down to allow her to push Owen's buggy on. Why do we take risks like that, when disaster lies around the corner?

The thought made her fumble the change and the bus driver tutted as she scrabbled around in her purse for twenty cent, eventually saying, 'It's grand, love. Leave it.'

'Thanks,' Jane said, mortified and relieved. She wasn't entirely sure she had the twenty cent. When she pushed Owen's buggy into the alcove and applied the brake, she opened her purse and examined the contents. One bus ticket, one paper clip and twenty euro. Mark had given her the note that morning for the salmon. 'You get what you pay for,' he'd often say if they went out to eat. That was why they didn't go to her favourite Italian in Terenure any more, where Nonno would plant big kisses on her cheek and tell her she was half-starved before serving her enormous portions of pasta and vitello tonnato, creamy slices of veal that made her heart sing. Mark didn't believe that good food could be that cheap.

She missed Nonno, she thought, but that was the thing when your life changed in a big way, as hers had done in the past couple of years — certain things just fell by the wayside and other things took their place. What was it Phyllis at St Dympna's used to say? 'Every loss comes with a gain and every gain comes with a loss.' Jane wondered where she was on the spectrum right now, as she took her seat opposite her son's pram and played clap-hands as the bus hurried through the suburban streets towards town.

At first, she'd thought she'd gained in the most spectacular way. Avril, one of the other teachers at St Attracta's, where Jane taught French and Religion — an irony because she no longer believed in God had persuaded her to try internet dating, and she'd agreed, if only for appearance's sake. After all, what nearly thirty-year-old professional woman with her own car and a moderately successful social life didn't date or have a significant other? Women who were afraid of themselves; that's who, Jane had thought, as she'd sat in a coffee shop, waiting to meet her third date, knee jigging furiously under the table. She hadn't been optimistic, having endured the BO of a tech nerd and the monologue of a self-made bore, and then Mark had appeared, confident, urbane and, most importantly, in control, unlike any of her previous boyfriends, such as they were, who might as well have got 'not a keeper' tattooed across their foreheads. Except Tom, who wasn't a keeper for a whole lot of other reasons, reasons that Jane didn't ever want to revisit.

Even in the clatter of a gloomy coffee shop in a suburban shopping centre, Mark had had a certain presence. As he'd walked in, scanning the tables for Jane, the little old ladies with their shoppers had looked at him admiringly, watching him as he'd strode over to her table and offered her a firm handshake, making eye contact, removing his navy padded jacket and hanging it carefully over the back of the chair, then sitting down opposite her in his neat jeans and expensive-looking sweater. His hair had been tidy, a nondescript brown, and his eyes were standard-issue blue, his nose was straight and he was clean-shaven. As she'd furtively examined him, Jane had wondered if she'd be able to remember who he was if she met him again. But that was the appeal, she'd decided, as he'd asked her where she worked and had laughed at her jokes about her students, listening intently to her answers. Mark was tidy, in appearance and in personality. The fact that he'd treated the date as a job interview that he was determined to nail hadn't struck Jane as odd at the time: actually, she'd thought his single-mindedness was impressive.

Later, Avril had met him at a pub quiz night to raise funds for a new school gym and joked that he was Mr Square. That had sealed the deal for Jane. Mr Square fitted the bill perfectly, even though Mark hadn't exactly set her heart aflutter; she'd tried passion before and look where that had got her.

Mark's parents, Jim and Maureen, had been so thrilled to meet her that she should have sensed that all wasn't as it should be. Two months after they'd met, she and Mark had gone for Sunday lunch, Jane clutching a bouquet of lilies, Mark a bottle of Chablis. Maureen had fallen on Jane, fussing over her, offering her tea, coffee, olives and almonds in quick succession, then ushering her into the kitchen, 'Where we can have a girly chat. You sit down and tell me everything,' Maureen had demanded.

Jane had felt her cheeks redden. She wasn't used to girly gossip — it wasn't how she'd been brought up — but as Maureen poured her a glass of white wine, she'd given it a shot, filling Maureen in about their dates, their spins in the car to nice restaurants, their shopping trips, on which Mark had flashed his credit card and told her she could have anything.

'Oh, that's Mark all right,' Maureen had said. 'So generous, just like his dad. Bet you feel like a princess.'

Jane had giggled. 'I do,' she'd agreed.

'Oh, that's good,' Maureen had said. 'He's always treated his girlfriends like that. I keep telling him he puts them on a pedestal, but I suppose he's just a romantic.'

It was true: he liked big gestures, huge bouquets of roses, weekends in Paris and London, and even if Jane sometimes longed for a takeaway and a rom-com on a Friday night, she let him take charge because it seemed that she had no choice: it was like being hit by a tidal wave. 'He's swept me off my feet,' she'd told Maureen, who had clapped her hands with glee.

Just three months after they'd met, she'd taken Mark down home to introduce him to Mam and Dad, speeding along the motorway in his sleek dark-navy BMW before pulling up in front of the two-storey farmhouse, with its mean windows and grubby white-painted front. Jane had felt so ashamed, looking at the moss-covered roof that slightly sagged in the middle, at the muddy dog sitting outside the front door – a liver-and-white springer spaniel that obviously couldn't be Mister Magoo, her much-loved childhood friend.

She hadn't told Mark, but she hadn't set eyes on her parents for many years, not since that last summer at home – after they'd told her that Tom was gone. The time she never wanted to think about again for as long as she lived. She had been shocked to see her father's pale-blue eyes watery and red-rimmed, as he'd stooped to put turf onto the fire, needing help to get back up again. Only her mother was more or less unchanged, her compact body springy with energy in her nylon housecoat, her hair iron-grey under the brown hairnet which she'd always worn everywhere apart from to church. It was good to see that forty years with Dad hadn't totally eroded her spirit.

Mark had been charm itself, sitting on their worn sofa in the kitchen, stroking the dog's head and accepting the tea and stale cake that Mam had provided, a smile on her face, clearly determined to put on a good front for the visitors. Conversation had been stilted, the weight of all that was unsaid hanging in the air, Dad asking, with his usual directness, where Mark's people were from and establishing his bona fides with a speed Jane had found quite impressive. The fact that he was a lawyer had surprised and impressed Dad, and Jane hadn't been able to resist flashing her father a smile of triumph. See? the smile had said. I didn't buckle under the weight of it. I came back, stronger than ever. She'd been surprised though, to feel her mother's soft hand on her shoulder when she'd got up to make more tea, the firm, warm squeeze that had made Jane blink back tears.

I suppose Dad would be pleased, Jane thought as the bus rounded the corner of the main street in Rathmines and she got up to push Owen to the door, giving the bus driver a wave and stepping off onto the hot pavement. 'I told you so,' he'd say. 'It's God's judgement, his revenge on the sinner.' At that moment, Jane looked up at a billboard which had been displaying an ad for Jameson whiskey, but it had now rotated and the words seemed to be spoken to her directly by God. '"Vengeance is mine. I will repay," says the Lord.' She stopped dead, staring at the words, stark black against the white, until the billboard rotated again and they were replaced by a block of cheddar and a smiling cow.

Dazed, Jane wandered along the pavement, the hot sun beating down on the back of her neck, which was exposed as she'd pulled her hair into a bun that morning. She put her hand to her skin, which felt hot and clammy, then took it away. She closed her eyes for a second and the world floated away as she found herself in the school hall again, sunlight streaming through the window as she sang God's words as loudly as she could, under the beady eye of the Catholic nun, Sister Joan — or 'the idolater' as Dad had called her, as he called anyone who wasn't his own Baptist religion. She'd tried not to look at the teachers' bench at the front of the hall, in case she'd see Tom grinning back at her, his blue-black hair gleaming. Sometimes, he'd even risk a little wave, stopping if one of her friends noticed, then turning and pretending to pay attention to Sister Joan, his shoulders square in his maroon jumper.

'No.' She opened her eyes then, wondering if she'd spoken aloud, and found herself back on the busy street. An elderly woman passed by, pulling a tartan shopping trolley, talking to the woman walking beside her about her piles. 'You see, I find that Anusol ointment very expensive ...'

'Kate Moss uses it for her wrinkles,' her friend said, and they both collapsed in laughter.

It was funny, Jane knew, but the two women looked sinister to her, leaning close together, so close that their iron-grey heads almost touched. She blinked again. Stop,

she told herself. Nothing good will come of remembering:
it'll only make things worse.

Outside the café, Jane arranged herself, putting a hand to
her bun, stretching her lips wide in what she hoped looked
like a smile. She pushed the door open and manoeuvred the
buggy in, scanning the busy tables for any sign of Gracie.
She found her sitting by the window, sunglasses on, Jasper
on her knee, immaculate in a pair of denim dungarees.

'Sorry I'm late,' she gushed as she arrived at the table.
'Owen threw up on his T-shirt just as we were leaving.' She
didn't want to tell Gracie the truth — that she'd been lost in
a daydream and that she couldn't really say how she'd got to
the café — because she knew it would make her sound like
a sap.

Gracie's face was expressionless, which Jane knew
meant that she was put out. 'I ordered for us,' she said
as Jane clattered and banged the buggy into place by the
window, lifting Owen out onto her knee and sitting down,
mirroring her friend and half the occupants of the pretty
café, a jumble of buggies and stripy T-shirts, of little
hands bashing tables and licking the cocoa-covered spoons
handed to them by their mothers. 'Earl Grey tea and two
berry scones. They're lovely here.'

'Thanks,' Jane said, feeling a sudden stab of resentment.
What was it about her that made people think she didn't
know her own mind? She was a grown woman, after all.

'Sorry,' she repeated nonetheless, then cursed herself for her cravenness.

Gracie shrugged and made a big deal of looking at her phone. 'I have forty-five minutes before the gardener comes.'

Somehow knowing how little time Gracie had to spare made Jane feel panicky, afraid of being left alone. She found herself suddenly wanting to cry. I mustn't, she thought to herself, eyes scanning the menu as if it were fascinating, even though Gracie had already ordered. I really mustn't let anyone else see.

But Gracie was nothing if not observant. 'Jane? You OK?'

'I'm fine,' Jane said firmly, refusing to lift her gaze from the menu until she'd pulled herself together.

'What is it?' Gracie's voice was gentle now. 'Hmm?'

'Oh, it's nothing,' Jane said, finally looking up at Gracie, whose blue eyes were soft with concern. 'It's just that Mark's at a conference in Cork at the moment and I haven't had much sleep and Owen just kept being sick this morning. I thought I was losing my mind.' It was partly true anyway.

Gracie's hand was warm and firm on hers. 'Poor you. I know what it's like not to have enough sleep — it makes the world seem a totally different place,' she said. 'Tell you what. Let's go home to mine and you can have a nice lie down on the sofa and I'll look after Owen.'

'Oh, no, I couldn't ...' Jane said, the very suggestion of

a sofa making her feel suddenly desperate to be horizontal, to feel the warmth of a pillow beneath her cheek. Especially on Gracie's lovely big expensive sofa, which she'd sunk into that time she'd gone to her house for Jasper's baby shower, to nibble on expensive canapes and to admire Gracie's confident, grown-up friends. But no, she told herself. She'd never be ready for Mark if she did that. She had the salmon to buy and the tenderstem broccoli, and even if she cheated and bought a gratin dauphinois, instead of roasting her own potatoes, she had at least an hour and a half of prep. She needed to be home by five-thirty at the latest. And besides, Dad had always taught her, you didn't 'doss' on the sofa in the middle of the afternoon — idleness was for sinners, not for God-fearing Baptists like themselves.

'You absolutely could, and you will,' Gracie said firmly. 'We are going to eat our scones and drink our tea and then we are going to bundle our crap into a taxi and go home and you will sleep and wake a normal human being. OK?'

Jane might have resented Gracie's bossiness earlier, but now she felt a sense of relief that her friend was taking charge like this, making Jane's mind up for her, so that Jane didn't have to succumb to the swamp of confusion and guilt that seemed to rise up any time she was required to make a decision these days, but she knew she had to say no now. She thought of the bright, pointed toe of Mark's brogue, the hardness of the clay beneath her cheek. 'But I need to get Mark's dinner ...'

'I'll take care of that,' Gracie said in her queenly

manner. Jane hesitated, unsure whether to say anything further. The subject of Mark's requirements had only ever been approached in a sideways manner, before the two of them would scuttle away from it, like crabs. Eventually, she settled on a weak, 'It's organic salmon.'

'Is it indeed?' Gracie laughed. 'Well, organic salmon it will be. We're coming down with the stuff in Sandymount.' And with that, she swept Jane out of the café, ignoring her protests, and into the hot and busy street, where she hailed one of those big ugly taxis that could fit an entire football team in it, and the two of them shoved their buggies and bags and babies in and took off towards Gracie's in Sandymount. Jane felt a sudden sense of elation then, and she wasn't sure if it was joy or alarm. Her logical brain told her that this wasn't a good idea, but as they drove through the streets towards the sea, she began to feel as if she were going on holiday or on a school trip, sitting on the top deck of the bus with Donal, her best friend from secondary school, the two of them sticking their heads out the window to feel the breeze and the sun on their faces.

She had a sense that, for a short while, all of the normal rules of life were suspended, and she and Gracie giggled and chatted as the taxi drove through the sun-washed streets until Jane saw the red-and-white-striped chimneys of Poolbeg and the long, brown-blue line of the beach. She could smell the tang of salt on the air, mixed with something less pleasant, like dog poo and frying. They drove up the sea road, Jane looking at the line of tankers making their way across the bay to Dublin Port, passing the blue-green hump of Howth, before the taxi turned right and down a tree-filled road of lovely mid-century houses. Many of them had been done up, and shiny, expensive cars were parked outside huge extensions with massive grey-framed windows. 'Just here, please,' Gracie said to the driver, shoving a twenty into his hand.

'Let me,' Jane said, hoping that Gracie would say no.

'Absolutely not,' Gracie replied. 'This is on me. You are not to do another thing, Jane, just let yourself be looked after for a bit.' And with this she swept Jane up the gravel drive to her immaculate, cream-painted house and in through the front door, painted a subtle shade of grey.

'Oh, wow,' Jane said as they walked into a huge, bright-white room, with its two big, soft grey sofas on which an array of cushions had been tastefully scattered and large French doors onto an immaculate garden. 'The place looks wonderful,' she said, immediately regretting her gaucheness, but Gracie just laughed. 'That's interior design for you. Nice girl from County Meath. I can give you her number if you like,' she said, going to the huge marble-topped island in the middle of the kitchen and running a stream of water into the kettle.

'Great,' Jane said faintly. Wonder what Mark would have to say about that. The thought made her smile, in spite of herself.

'Sit, sit,' Gracie said then, coming over to her and taking her by the shoulders, steering her towards one of the sofas and lifting a couple of the cushions up. 'Now, lie down there, and rest your head on this,' she said, putting one of the cushions under Jane's head. It smelled of lavender and was so soft that she felt herself melting into it until a sudden cry from Owen, still in his buggy, made her sit up.

'I'll see to Owen,' Gracie said firmly, pushing her gently back on the sofa. She went over to the kitchen door and called, 'Sunny?' There was some whispering then and murmuring, but Jane found herself tuning out, concentrating on the soft feel of the sofa under her back, the warm smell of the garden now wafting in through the open French doors. She could hear birdsong and, far away, the long *toot* of a ship's horn out at sea. She felt her body unwind, and as her shoulders slumped, she realised that she'd been holding them tight for goodness knows how long. Now, she felt light, floating upwards, and when a soft throw was placed over her, she let her eyes close and she drifted off.

When she woke, the light was different in the room, a warm golden colour, and Gracie was sitting at the kitchen table with Jake, two glasses of white wine in front of them. They were talking in low murmurs, and when Jake said something, Gracie threw back her head and laughed.

When Jane lifted herself up on the sofa, Gracie turned and said, 'There she is. You were out for the count.'

'What time is it?' Jane said groggily. 'Where's Owen?'

'He's playing with Jasper in the nursery,' Gracie said. 'It's OK. I have someone who comes in every now and then to help out. She's excellent with babies, so just relax.'

Jane shifted on the sofa, knowing that she should get up and check on Owen but unwilling to give up her paradise. She reached into her handbag for her phone, pressing it to see the time, but the screen was blank. The battery must be dead, she thought, sitting up. I'd really better get a move on, or Mark will be wondering where I am.

But the light in the room was so balmy and the soft music from the giant speaker on the wall lulled her further so that when Jake put a glass of ice-cold white wine into her hand, she didn't protest, just took a long sip, savouring the slight fizz, the taste of apples in her mouth. 'It's heaven,' she said.

'It's actually Aldi's finest, but hey.' Jake laughed. 'How've you been, Jane? You look great anyway.'

'You eejit, the poor woman's exhausted out of her mind, will you leave her alone,' Gracie said, laughing. 'Go and check on the babies, will you?'

'Fine, fine,' he said, shaking his head, shuffling through the kitchen door, throwing a jokey comment behind him as he went — something about Gracie being a slave driver — at which she just laughed.

Jane sat there, watching this scene unfold, marvelling that two people could be like this with each other. Could be so relaxed. Could share wine and a laugh like that. Mam and Dad had always bustled around each other, muttering under their breaths as they did various jobs around the house, Mam asking Dad if he'd ever empty the range and Dad replying that he'd already done it, if she'd only look. Their exchanges had been strictly practical, task-oriented, dominated by Dad's taciturn commands, with which Mam went along, in spite of her softer nature. The man was in charge, as far as Mam was concerned, even if it meant she couldn't be herself. Even if it meant she had to choose between him and her daughter. And she and Mark? Jane took a long sip of her lovely white wine. She didn't want to think about that right now — she didn't want the bubble to burst. But the picture of Gracie and Jake sitting at the table, elbows out, laughing with each other, kept nudging into her mind. She could only manage if she thought that she and Mark were like any other couple, but seeing Gracie and Jake brought it home to her that they weren't. The thought made her close her eyes and take another long, welcome sip of white wine.

'So ...' Gracie said, coming over to her and sitting down beside her, placing a warm hand on her shoulder. 'Feeling better?'

'You have no idea,' Jane said. 'I feel like a different person. This place must be magic.' She gave a soft laugh.

'Hah, you should see it on a wet Monday with Jake's footy gear strewn around the place and the dog shedding all over the sofa.'

The dog? Jane looked over to the basket where a soft, black-coated dog with long ears was snoozing. Even the animals were chilled in this place.

'His name is Topsy and Jake adopted him without telling me,' Gracie said, giving a little mock shudder. 'He's manky but not too badly behaved, so I put up with it. Anything for an easy life.'

You have an easy life, Jane thought, a little meanly. You have comfort and warmth and a lovely partner and a means of 'disappearing' your baby so that you can drink wine. That's what I'd call lovely.

'I know what you're thinking.' Gracie smiled.

'What? That this house is perfect and that you have a fabulous life?'

'Nobody's life is perfect, you know,' Gracie said, picking up the throw and fiddling with the soft fringe. 'Everyone has something.'

'That's true,' Jane said, wondering what Gracie's something could possibly be. She wondered if she might ask, but then Gracie sat up straight, that all-business look on her face.

'So ...' Gracie said.

'So ...' Jane echoed.

'What do you think about the new girl?'

What new girl? Jane thought. Then, as if from a long distance, she remembered Gracie's text, the invitation to the café. So, it wasn't just a social call then, a desire to spend time with Jane. She felt suddenly as if the atmosphere in the room had changed. Topsy, who had been silent since Jane had arrived, suddenly got up from his basket and went out to the garden, barking into the dusk. 'Topsy, be quiet!' Gracie yelled with some force.

'Ehm ...' Jane put her glass of wine down on the floor, wondering if she should ask for a coaster. She felt different now, wary, unsure of what answer Gracie wanted from her. An image of Elise came into her mind, the shorts with the discreet but expensive logo, that huge pink pram that looked a bit tacky. She said carefully, 'Well, she seems friendly.'

'Oh, she's friendly all right,' Gracie said with a short laugh. 'Don't you think she's a bit forward?'

'Forward,' Jane repeated, playing for time. 'She's outgoing, certainly, and chatty, if that's what you mean.' She looked carefully at Gracie. A line had appeared between her eyebrows. So, Jane thought, not what you mean. 'Maybe a little ... overfriendly?' she ventured.

'That's it!' Gracie said. 'I found her a bit "in your face", with all of her "me too"s and asking us all questions about ourselves, didn't you? It was all a bit much.'

'Perhaps.' Jane recognised a defence mechanism when she saw one — and Elise used it well — attack before others get their chance. Make sure you're always on the front foot, armed with a battery of questions that some might consider a bit rude, but others would find flattering. After all, Jane thought, isn't that what most people want — to talk about themselves? 'I think she was probably just trying a bit hard,' she said finally. 'You know the way it is when you're new.' She looked at Gracie, whose face fell, just a little. Wrong answer.

Jane opened her mouth to add something, but Gracie stood up then, putting her hands in her pockets and looking out into the garden. The shadows were lengthening now, and Jane had a vague thought in the back of her head about Mark lying in wait at home. Her heart lurched. She'd really better go, she thought.

'So,' Gracie said.

Jane took the hint. 'So, better make tracks. Mark will be wanting his dinner.'

Gracie gave a small smile, then walked to the kitchen door. There was more murmuring and whispering and then Owen appeared in Gracie's arms, as if by magic. 'Here you go, little man,' Gracie said softly. 'Back to Mummy.'

Owen's face was soft in the evening light and the little blond tuft of hair on his head stuck up, like Tintin's. He was wearing a new T-shirt and shorts and Jane assumed he'd dirtied the last set. She held out her hands to take him and he nestled into her, putting his head on her shoulder.

'Aww, somebody's sleepy,' Gracie said.

'Time for bed,' Jane agreed.

'I've called you a cab,' Gracie said softly, putting a small paper bag into Jane's hand. 'Just a few leftovers — so you don't have to make supper for Mark when you get back.'

'Thanks, Gracie, but you shouldn't have—' Jane began, but Gracie shushed her.

'For God's sake, I only did what any good friend would do. You need to accept help sometimes, Jane,' she said, with a touch of acid in her tone.

'Right,' Jane said uncertainly. She opened her mouth to say something else, but a honk from outside told them that the taxi had arrived.

'So, there we go,' Gracie said, ushering Jane out the front door and onto the gravel driveway. Outside, with the whiff of salt in the air and the low rumble of traffic from the main road, Jane felt as if she were waking up from a spell. She turned to say goodbye and thanks to Gracie but the front door had been shut, and Jane couldn't help feeling that she'd been dismissed.

'What time is it?' she asked the taxi driver now, as he turned left onto the strand road, the sea beside their window now a line of inky blue.

'Nine-fifteen, Madam,' the taxi driver said.

'*Nine-fifteen?*' Jane's heart began to race. How on earth had that happened, that she'd let herself be lulled by Gracie's golden home, let herself relax and settle into the lovely bubble. Mark would have been home for three hours. He'd have had his G&T and would be waiting for his dinner, wondering where she was. She dreaded to think how many frantic texts were on her phone. She'd been home late from the park once, and Mark had called her six times and left as many texts. She looked inside the paper bag and saw two little plates with sushi rolls on them, and her heart sank. They'd never fill Mark. He hated that kind of food anyway. 'Could you go a bit faster?' she said to the taxi driver.

He didn't respond, but the engine's drone got a bit

louder and they whizzed through the streets, up along the canal, where the banks were full of people sitting in groups, packs of beer between them. There was a hum of chatter and laughter through the window and Jane wondered what it might be like to join them, herself and Mark sitting on a blanket, a tub of hummus and a bottle of wine between them. The idea was laughable, she thought, wondering why exactly that was. She was thirty-two years of age, and a summer's evening sitting by the canal was out of the question. The thought made her feel suddenly old and tired and sad.

The house was in darkness when the taxi pulled up, and for a second, Jane debated not getting out but just asking the driver to keep going. She felt a sudden longing for her mum, to feel the powdery softness of her bosom the way she'd used to on the very rare occasion she'd stayed home sick from school. Mam would come up to her in bed and sit beside her and let Jane lean into her while she read stories from the big book of Irish fairy tales she kept on the bookshelf in the kitchen. It was one of the few times that her mother would let herself soften, Jane remembered, when she or Helen was sick. The minute they were better, Mam wouldn't allow herself to show more than folded arms, her mouth a thin line on her face.

Jane tried to pay the driver, to be told that the taxi was on account, so she got wearily out the door, letting him lift her buggy and change bag out of the boot. 'OK, Madam?' he said.

He was a little grey man with receding hair and skin so pale he might have been a vampire. Jane felt a sudden urge to say, 'No, actually, I'm not. I'm not OK at all. Please take me somewhere far away from here.' Instead, of course, she just said that she was 'Fine, thanks' and that she appreciated the help with the buggy. The taxi drove off and Jane looked after it, wondering if she could run after it and hop back inside.

The silence inside the house was thick, like treacle, when she opened the front door. Her stomach tightened as she walked into the hall, putting the buggy down, with Owen, who had nodded off in the taxi, now heavy on her hip. 'Hello?' she said softly. Part of her hoped that if she didn't call out too loudly, he might not realise she was there and she could creep back out again. 'Wonder where Daddy is,' she whispered to Owen, who was still leaning on her shoulder, mouth emitting a soft snore. 'Hmm?' The hall was always gloomy and she debated whether to turn the light on, her feet slapping on the wooden floor as she made her way into the kitchen.

'Mark?'

He must have been waiting for her, behind the kitchen door. The punch to her kidneys was so sudden, so fierce, Jane reeled back, her neck snapping, Owen flailing in her arms. She gave a sharp wail as she buckled, knees hitting the floor with a crunch, arms flung outwards, so that he landed on the floor with a soft thud. The pain radiated out from her stomach down to her pelvis and she felt the tang of bile in her mouth. Owen gave a scream of alarm and she reached out, wanting to lift him off the floor, but when she went to push herself upwards, her legs wouldn't support her. Her mouth opened and a thin stream of vomit and mucous came out as she coughed.

'I'm going to bed. Stay down here and don't come near me.' Mark's voice was a low hiss in her ear. His breath was sour and Jane felt the bile rise in her throat again. She could hear him breathing rapidly, panting like a dog – then he was gone, the kitchen door banging shut behind him, his feet heavy on the stairs. The bedroom door slammed so loudly the house seemed to shake, then there was silence.

'Owen?' Jane said softly into the darkness. 'Owen, pet, are you there?'

His answer was a little sob, as if he didn't want to make any noise and, bent double, Jane shuffled across the floor to him, picking him up and cradling him in her arms as he wailed. 'It's OK, pet, it's OK. Daddy's just tired, that's all. Just tired.'

8

Gracie

She'd hoped she could rely on Jane, Gracie thought as she checked the oven temperature, but she'd been disappointed. When they'd met the previous week, she'd expected Jane to go along with her, to say that she didn't like Elise either, but Jane had been a bit ... unforthcoming. Gracie didn't know whether this was because, eager to please as she was, Jane didn't want to take sides or whether she actually liked the woman, Gracie thought, spooning the mixture that Sunny had made earlier, before going out to meet a friend, into the little bun cases in the muffin tray.

But it wasn't about liking or disliking, Gracie mused

as she pushed the orange mixture off the spoon and into one of the cases, with a satisfying little splat: it was about protecting what was *theirs*. What belonged to the three of them and to nobody else. Everything they'd shared over the past few months, from the terror of those awful antenatal classes, the rabbit-in-the-headlights looks in their eyes as Oona had explained the rigours of childbirth, to their labours, which they'd whisper about as you would a car crash, the trauma still fresh in their minds. Gracie knew that she'd never have got over her own experiences of that time if it hadn't been for the girls' listening to her and nodding in unspoken agreement, as she'd told them about the long, lonely hours she'd spent wandering the corridors, waiting for Jasper to hurry on, that awful TENS machine buzzing away like an angry bee on her hip, the exhaustion as she'd slid into the lukewarm bath poured for her by an assistant midwife and fallen into a semi-coma, fragments of dreams splitting her sleep, waves of pain making her bellow like a cow. Giving birth was a totally animal experience, she thought as she pushed the trays into the oven and set the timer — and Gracie didn't like to think of herself as an animal. She also knew that, even though she wouldn't have picked Lina or Jane as friends in normal life, they understood everything now without her even having to say it.

Which is why Gracie didn't want Elise ruining that, spoiling that connection. It wasn't about her silly doughnuts or her fake tan, Gracie thought — it was about something much deeper than that. Something Elise could never hope to understand.

It was all the more important now because the early months of motherhood were much, much harder than she'd expected, Gracie thought, looking through the oven door at the little orange patties, marvelling at their ability to just rise like that, as if by magic. Sunny's bright, fresh mixture seemed to reproach her as she gazed through the glass, the muffins springing to life like so many orange fairy-tale toadstools. Gracie had tried to make them herself the previous week and had ended up with a livid mess, like Play-Doh, that had stuck to the muffin tin. She'd become so enraged that she'd thrown it across the kitchen, bits of orange splattering all over the floor and up the side of the wall. She'd made such a noise that Jake had come in from the games room to see what was going on, finding Gracie, sobbing, in the middle of the kitchen floor. 'I can't, I just can't,' she'd wailed as he'd put his arms around her.

'Can't what?' he'd said softly, rubbing her back. She liked him rubbing her back – he was very good at it, and he was also very good at stroking her hair and massaging her feet. Jake was very attentive to her and it was one of the things she'd loved about him when they'd first met. She'd dated rugby guys and executives before, and even though their confidence had impressed her – the way they moved through the world as if they were in charge of it somehow – she'd found them boring beyond belief. Mum and Dad loved them, of course, with their excessive good manners, their innate good breeding, the sleek cars they parked in the drive when they'd come for Sunday lunch.

But Jake was different, and when she'd met him at some awful gig in O'Brien's pub in the city centre — a place that she found both smelly and depressing — it had been a complete revelation to her: that men could be different from those she'd grown up with; that they could be warm and funny, able to cook and, most importantly, could ask her questions about herself. After five years of simpering beside the latest bore in her life, looking up at him in mock adoration, she found herself relaxing with Jake. True, he wore battered Converse, T-shirts with Japanese slogans on them and jeans that hung off his backside, and it was also true that he didn't seem to have much of a life plan — unlike her previous boyfriends, who had had their whole futures mapped out — but he treated her as an equal, and she'd fallen for him instantly.

For a moment, she'd enjoyed the feeling of him rubbing her back, trying not to notice that he was wearing nothing but a pair of underpants and a T-shirt with *Jaws* on it. This was his usual uniform these days, ever since he'd been made redundant. She knew it wasn't his fault, and she also knew that he was trying to get his bits-of-scary-movies concept off the ground, but she wished he'd get fully dressed and come out of that dark cave of a games room every once in a while.

'What is it you can't do?' he'd said soothingly, hands gripping her shoulders, giving her a good massage, nice and firm, the way she liked.

'I can't do any of this domestic shit!' she'd said sadly. 'Everything I do at home just turns into a huge mess. I hate housework, I'm a terrible cook and I can't even bake bloody muffins. Who the hell can't bake muffins? The cookbook says they're the simplest thing to "whip up", only I can't seem to even do that.'

'They're not that hard,' Jake had said. 'Just eggs, flour and oil and whatever flavour you decide to put in them.'

'You make it sound so easy.' Gracie had groaned. Jake was a bit of a whizz in the kitchen and often complained about Sunny getting in his way. But then, that's what they were paying her for.

'It *is* fairly easy,' Jake had said, 'but I can't say I've ever felt any pressure to whip up a batch to impress my mates if I have anything better to do.'

'That's because you're a man.'

He'd held her at arm's length, giving a short laugh. 'What the hell does that matter, Gracie? It's the twenty-first century, not the middle ages, and women don't have to be good at that kind of thing any more than men. It's not something women are "born to do" these days, thank God. If I were you, I'd enjoy that freedom.'

Gracie's shoulders had dropped. 'I know. It's just that Mum was fantastic at homemaking. She loved flower arranging and hoovering and pledging and she always made amazing dinners for when Dad got home from work. I remember she used to make these lamb chops with little chef's hats on them — can you imagine? While I can barely pour milk on cornflakes,' she'd said with a sniff.

'"Pledging"?'

'Yeah, she used to have this special can of Pledge with lavender in it and she'd spend Tuesdays polishing every bit of furniture in the house.'

'And that's what you think you should be doing, while you have a full-time job — that you're really good at, by the way — and a baby?' Jake had said. 'Look, that's how your mum found meaning in life, when she probably didn't have much else. Some might even say she was kinda lucky,' he'd said dryly. 'Look at my mum — she worked six days a week and we grew up on TV dinners, but we somehow survived. You don't need to prove anything.'

Oh, but I do, Gracie thought now. I do because I want it all to be perfect. I want to be a wife and a mum and a really good account manager and I want my home to be clean and comfy and to look really nice, and I can do it. I know I can. All it takes is a bit of organisation. Thank God for my secret weapon, Sunny. She might be terrifying, but she's good at her job. And if I feel guilty that my mother managed to rear a family and run a home without any outside help, I can just remind myself that life was different then, less complicated.

The oven timer started to beep and she was jolted back to reality, going over and opening the door carefully, as Sunny had instructed, to avoid a wash of cold air making the little muffins sink. She pulled the trays out and put them on the counter with a sigh of satisfaction. Getting this right made her feel pretty pleased with herself, even if she was faking it, just a bit.

'Right, time to get moving,' she said. It was ten-thirty already, and now that that job was ticked off the list, she realised that she had plenty more to do. She needed to organise a valuation of the house, now that they'd done the renovations, then she had to sort a few things for the charity shop and order a load of logs for the burner: they were cheaper if you bulk-bought in summer. But first, Jasper badly needed a bath and a change, and as Sunny wasn't around, she'd have to fit that in, too.

She walked over to where Jasper lay happily under his baby gym, cooing away as he swatted crinkly bits of plastic and shiny mirrors. Gracie lifted him up and he gave a wail of distress. 'I know – we'll play later, promise. Don't you want to meet your friends in the park?' He drummed his little feet off her tummy and twisted his head to give his toys one last look as she walked out of the kitchen. She passed the games room and hesitated, wondering if she could ask Jake to bathe and dress Jasper, but then he'd been up late working on his scary-movie concept, so she thought it best to leave him. He hadn't even come to bed, as far as she could tell. To think, once he'd been into tantric sex and now – well, now nothing, Gracie thought sadly to herself as she went upstairs. She wondered if he wasn't a bit depressed, but then told herself that she didn't have time for that on top of everything else.

Jasper wailed all the way up the stairs and as she put him on the bed, and no amount of singing and blowing bubbles on his tummy and playing his favourite songs on the little CD player and doing the actions could soothe him. Not even 'Incy-Wincy Spider' and he loved that one. 'Oh, Jasper, what is it?' Gracie said as he wriggled and turned his head away while she tried to put his arms into the little blue gingham button-down shirt that she loved because he looked so cute in it. 'Is it that you don't want to go to the park, is that it? Do you want to stay at home and play? Hmm?'

At the sound of her soothing tone, Jasper quietened and listened, his eyes now fixed on her. 'Don't you like the girls and the babies? To be honest, I'm not sure I like them myself. Jane is such a doormat, and she jumps at the slightest little thing, even though I feel sorry for her because she always looks exhausted — because of that fussy husband of hers. And as for Lina — I mean, you'd think she'd wash every now and then, wouldn't you? Not to mention her attitude. Sometimes, Jasper, I think she's laughing at me. And that's not very nice, is it?'

Jasper gurgled in reply. 'I know,' Gracie said softly. 'And Elise, with those highlights and her too-fancy clothes. Who does she think she is, a WAG?' At this, Jasper gave a soft laugh and Gracie laughed too. I'm a bitch, she thought, but at least Jasper is the only one who hears it — well, the uncensored version, anyway.

As she lifted her baby son, now quiet, up to her and

kissed the top of his head, Gracie found her thoughts straying, once more, to Elise. Honestly, she wondered if she had a tiny bit of an obsession. She tried to locate that feeling she had about Elise, that impulse she'd had to recoil when she'd walked across the grass to them with that hideous pink pram. Was it just snobbery? Or was it something that unsettled her more even than the thought of sharing the girls with someone else. She couldn't put her finger on it, but she had a sense that, with Elise there, someone else would be pushed out. And that someone would be her.

'Silly,' she said aloud. 'I founded the group and I keep it together. Elise isn't going to stop that, is she, poppet?' She planted another kiss on Jasper's head, on the soft, velvety down of it, and she inhaled his lovely baby smell, feeling a little bit better, and when, an hour later, with Jasper washed and beautifully dressed, she went back downstairs and caught sight of the muffins on the counter, their beautiful soft domes of orange, she felt better still. Everything was under control.

She was just putting the muffins into a Tupperware box — a wedding gift from Mum, and one of a whole collection — when her phone rang. She looked at the caller display and tutted. It was Toni — she'd been ringing quite a lot recently, to keep Gracie 'in the loop' about developments at Cutlery. Gracie wasn't all that sure that she wanted to be kept in the loop, not now anyway, but she could hardly say no, and part of her was pleased that her boss valued her enough to keep her posted. Besides, Toni was paying the bills right now, so she'd better suck it up, she thought, pressing the answer button.

'Toni, how are you?' She put on her brightest voice.

'Never mind me,' Toni's soft voice responded. 'How's my warrior queen?'

Gracie giggled. 'I'm grand, thanks for asking.' She wondered if she could tell Toni that she was in a hurry, but as if she'd guessed, Toni said, 'I know your time is valuable, Gracie, as a mum. I really do respect that ...'

But, thought Gracie.

'But here's the thing. We're pitching for new business and we'd really like your input from the get-go. You'll be taking up the reins anyway when you come back and, you know me, I'm a stickler for continuity.' She paused, then spoke in a lower voice. 'TBH, Gracie, I'm not sure that Atiyah has the experience I need to reel this one in, so all hands on deck!'

'All hands on deck,' Gracie echoed, wondering just how much of her precious maternity leave would be eaten into by this. But she couldn't help feeling a little bit pleased that Atiyah wasn't up to the job. 'I can pop in later this week, if you like?'

'Oh, you're such an angel — thanks, Gracie. I knew I could rely on you. There's the first pitch meeting on Friday at ten, but there's a planning meeting today that we need some eyes on from our side. You know what the planners are like — they'll try to get away with anything if you let them,' and she gave a small laugh.

'Today?' Gracie's voice came out a high-pitched squeak. 'Oh, I don't think I'll be free. I have a ... meeting at two-thirty.'

'Oh God, Gracie, I didn't meant you'd have to attend the whole thing.' Toni gave a soft laugh. 'Just the first half an hour — in and out, I promise. And there'll be tea and buns to celebrate little Jonathan.'

'Jasper.'

'Yes, of course. Listen, Gracie, I know it's an imposition, but you'd be saving my life if you came in at twelve. I rely on you utterly, as you know, and I really need your practical eye on things. I promise, I'll have you out of the place before you know it, and I'll owe you one for ever,' and she gave a merry laugh.

'Well—'

'I'll have a taxi at yours at eleven-thirty.' And the phone went dead.

'Bye,' Gracie said softly.

It was only then that she realised that someone would have to mind Jasper, because Sunny was still out. She stuck her head into the games room to ask Jake, but found it empty. She swore under her breath then and ran upstairs to see him rifling through the bedroom closet. 'Did you see my Nudie jeans?'

'What do you want them for?' She'd been unable to disguise her surprise that Jake might like to actually get dressed for once.

'Well, I can't wear this to a business meeting,' he said, indicating his *Jaws*–underpants combo.

'Oh, I don't know, why change the habits of a lifetime?' It was meant to be a joke, but it didn't come out that way. It came out bitter and a bit nasty and she was devastated to see the look of hurt on his face. She'd never commented on his awful clothes, even though, many times, she'd wanted to because it looked as if he wasn't taking care of himself, but now, he just muttered something about how he was trying, if she'd only see it. She wanted to say sorry, but there was no time. She looked at her watch and it was eleven-twenty already. Ten bloody minutes to get ready. 'So, can you mind Jasper for me? Toni's dragged me into this planning thing and there's a taxi coming in ten minutes and I have the mums' meeting later ...' Her voice trailed off as he gave her a look of incredulity.

'Gracie, the investor pitch for Deadkill has been moved forward to today instead of next bloody Thursday, so I'm completely unprepared — and I can't find my best jeans. I can't babysit.'

'You don't babysit your own child,' she snapped, opening the bottom drawer on her side of the wardrobe and pulling out his jeans — he always put them in her side, even though she'd explained to him a million times that they had separate halves of the wardrobe for a reason — then she opened his side of the wardrobe and selected a nice white button-down shirt that she handed to him.

'Well, whatever you call it, it amounts to the same thing. I've been prepping for this meeting for weeks — it's make or break, and I can't, Gracie, I'm sorry. It doesn't look cute if you bring a baby into a pitch. It just looks unprofessional.' His voice was softer now, as he took the shirt from her and removed his horrible ratty boxers, replacing them with his best Superman pair that she'd bought him as a joke, and pulling on the jeans and the shirt.

'And yet it's OK for me to be unprofessional, is it?' she snapped. 'It's so sexist: babies make men look weak and yet it's fine for women to cart them everywhere — it looks cute and maternal and nobody says boo because they don't want to be seen as anti-mum, even though they're secretly thinking, Why doesn't she get her shit together and find a babysitter like any normal person?' Her voice was wobbling now and she could feel that shrill tone beginning to take over, the one that she hated because it spelt 'hysterical woman' and that was *not* the persona Gracie wanted to convey.

'Ah, Gracie, please, no breaking my balls,' Jake said, tucking the shirt into the jeans, then taking it out again. 'It's true — we live in an unequal world, and I'm sorry about that on behalf of all men, but can we have the discussion after I get back? I'm really up against it here.'

So bloody well am I, Gracie thought, and you don't see me going on about it. But she could tell how nervous he was, shifting from foot to foot, turning to look at himself in the mirror, when he never normally did, trying out a range of facial expressions that would have been comical were it not so bloody stressful. She sighed and went over to him and began to smooth the blond frizz from over his eyebrows. 'Here, you don't want to go in looking like Boris Johnson – you'll never get a deal then.'

In reply, he gave her a tight grin and allowed her to tuck in the front of his shirt, letting the back loose. 'It's a French tuck,' she explained. 'It looks professional, but cool at the same time.'

'What would I do without you,' he said, bending down to kiss her.

She kissed him back, for the first time in weeks, and decided not to tell him the reply that had been on the tip of her tongue – that he'd be in a terrible bedsit in Rathmines with an outside loo, spending all day in internet cafés playing violent computer games. It wasn't nice, even if it were true.

The taxi driver had no idea where Cutlery's office was, and Gracie wondered if it was an omen, a sign that the day could fall apart at any minute. He was foreign and told her in broken English that he'd only been in Ireland six months, 'So, just get to know the city.' And you decide to be a taxi driver? Gracie thought, as she directed him through the maze of streets that led from Sandymount to the city centre and Cutlery's offices, fuming as they sat at the traffic lights on Baggot Street for what seemed like hours. Honestly, she thought, whatever happened to the moany old Irish fellows with their whining about the state of the country? At least they knew where they were going.

Cutlery didn't have a lift, so Gracie had to haul Jasper, his change bag, complete with two extra bottles of formula, and the cooler box all the way up the rickety wooden staircase to the second floor, where she broke into the meeting room with a clatter to find fifteen heads suddenly swivelling in her direction.

'It's the cavalry!' Toni stood up and came towards her, arms outstretched. 'You look amazing and you are an absolute angel to lean in like this. I don't know what to say ...' And she gave a sad little shake of her head. 'But listen to me. Time to make room for the two most important people in Cutlery,' she said, guiding Gracie and Jasper to the top of the table and to the huge chairman's chair, a big phallic leather thing with huge man-size armrests on it. Gracie and Jasper were both able to fit in it, side by side, Jasper slumped against her, legs thumping the seat with excitement.

'Gotta take a picture of this, girl!' Gar jumped up from his seat and came towards them, brandishing an iPhone. 'Say "Cork"!' he commanded and Gracie gave a nervous smile, while Jasper started in surprise as the flash blinded him. He looked at Gracie and his chin began to wobble, so she swept him up onto her knee and stroked his head, murmuring into his ear.

'If we could get on with the bloody meeting,' Dom muttered under his breath.

To Gracie's alarm, Toni came towards her and perched on the armrest of the giant seat, her tiny bottom next to Gracie's elbow. Gracie blushed and made to get up, but Toni stilled her with a hand. 'Stay right where you are. Now, to fill Gracie in, we were discussing strategy for the launch of a new cat food. Obviously, this is very exciting news because entries into the feline market are few and far between, and the competition is cut-throat, as we know ...'

As Toni talked, Gracie's heart sank. Bloody cat food. A whole lot of problems and the only reward would be hate mail from cat nuts, outraged that their little moggy had the runs or a less shiny coat after using the brand. Gracie's answer was simple — buy another bloody brand of cat food! She loved curry but it always gave her the runs and the answer was not to eat the stuff — she didn't phone the takeaway and threaten to sue them, issuing dire threats while she was at it.

When they'd been promoting Tibbles organic free-range turkey kibble last year, some woman had sent in an envelope of what looked like ricin, and Tracey in reception had had to be taken to the emergency department, only to discover that it was talc. The accompanying note had said, 'Now you'll know what it's like to be poisoned, like your cat food poisoned my Barry. Beware — this is only the beginning.' Thankfully, the writer hadn't escalated to other bath products, even though Tracey had claimed PTSD as a result of the whole incident — but then, she was an awful drama queen.

'OK, this cat food is a budget brand, aimed at C1/D1 groups, so the message is quality and value for money,' Barnaby, the media strategist, was saying, wiping crumbs from his huge ginger beard. Really, Gracie thought, could he not have eaten before the meeting instead of helping himself to the Danish pastries and spluttering crumbs all over them?

'In other words, shit,' Dom said, to a chorus of laughter.

'Yes, but we'll keep that to ourselves,' Toni said. 'The idea here is that you can treat your pet to the best, without compromising on value, and it contains real free-range poultry ...'

'Ah, "poultry" — in other words, there could be anything in it,' Dom said again, clearly enjoying the sound of his own voice.

Toni's smile was a little less bright this time. 'Look, I have two Russian blues, so I know how expensive premium-brand food can be. Romulus and Remus cost me forty euro a month, and all because my vet told me only to give them the best. But less well-off cat owners want to treat their cats well, too, they just can't afford to do so, and they don't need to be patronised in the promotion. They need to be supported to pick a new brand that will give them what they need but that's also good value, so no cynicism here, folks, all-righty?'

Ouch. Dom was silenced then, looking down at his laptop, face puce, but Gracie didn't even have the energy to cheer inside, the way she usually did when Dom was reprimanded. She felt a sweat break out on her forehead, and as she watched her colleagues' lips move, she felt as if they were talking in a language she didn't understand. Words like 'traction', 'leverage' and 'media focus', which were normally second nature to her, suddenly felt threatening, alien. She gripped Jasper a little more tightly, pressing her cheek against his soft hair, wishing that she were anywhere but here, in a sweaty T-shirt and her absolutely-not-best jeans. She wanted to be in the park, lying under the trees, hearing the sounds of the playground nearby, the chat of the other two girls, the soothing of baby cries and the comforting questions about routine. It was another world, soft and warmly embracing, sleepy and reassuring, not jarring and clattery like this one, with people tapping pens and tutting and jostling for position. She wanted to cover her ears so she wouldn't have to listen to another hard-won position, another pitch to Toni from an over-eager team member — the things that had seemed so important to her just four months ago no longer seemed to matter.

'So, guys, I'm conscious that we've completely landed Gracie in it and that we are forever grateful to her for coming to our aid this morning,' Toni's voice broke into Gracie's thoughts. 'Gracie, we need you and your eagle eye.' She laughed softly. 'Where on earth would we be without you? Thoughts?'

Oh, God. Gracie sat forward so suddenly that Toni wobbled on the armrest of the chair. 'Sorry.' There was a brief burst of laughter around the table and jokes about Gracie literally trying to unseat the boss, which gave Gracie time to think, or at least to try to marshal the jumble of thoughts in her head into something coherent. She couldn't say what she really wanted to say, which was that she didn't give a toss about cats and their food – in fact, she hated the filthy, disease-carrying creatures. Instead, she scrunched her face into a hopefully convincing look of concentration and said, 'Well, cat food is tricky because owners feel so passionately about their pets and they can be very wary about any kind of misleading message, in my experience.' That sounded good, she thought as she spoke. The words sounded vaguely right anyway. She looked around the table then and realised that people were waiting for her to continue, to tell them what kind of message might be required, and she hadn't a clue. What did pet owners want to hear? Buggered if she knew. She felt her throat close and her eyes fill. Don't cry, for God's sake, she thought. She remembered what Dad used to call 'soft' people who cried – 'big girl's blouses'. That's what I am, she thought sadly. I'm a big girl's blouse. 'I'm sorry, I think I have –' she accepted the tissue that appeared in front of her, proffered by Toni '– a touch of hay fever.' She blew her nose, playing for time, wishing that the ground would open up and swallow her. 'Anyway, as I was saying ... yes ...' What the hell was I saying? What are the words you use in this situation? Think, Gracie. Think.

'That cat owners are really passionate about their pets, so we need to give them what they want – passion.' A voice broke the interminable silence. 'Gracie's right. Passion should be the core message here – you care about your precious moggie, and so do we. "Kitty-Kat – your pet, our passion."' It was Atiyah, her hair in elaborate braids which Gracie had to admit looked amazing, a look of intense concentration on her face.

'"Your pet – our passion". I like it,' Toni said softly. 'Nice work, women.' Gracie felt Toni's arm sneak around her and squeeze her shoulder. She wondered if she could just lean against her and have a nice cry but thought better of it, and then Jasper gave a loud wail and the tempo of the meeting changed. 'I think Jasper has called the meeting to a close,' Toni said and everyone laughed. There was a general hubbub then, with chairs scraping and chatter, and Gar came up and attempted to take Jasper off Gracie and there was a bit of a tussle because Gracie did not want to let him go. She wanted to cling onto him, to feel the weight of him in her arms, his reassuring solidity a kind of shield against this suddenly hostile world.

'Gracie, are you OK?' Toni's voice was soft in her ear. The room had emptied out now and there was just the two of them, standing either side of the giant leather chair. Gracie hesitated, wondering if she could confide in her boss. Toni was so cool, so 'down with the kids', so lovely — she'd understand, even if she wasn't a mum herself. She'd know how Gracie felt.

'I shouldn't have pulled you in like that, at short notice. *Mea culpa*,' Toni said, holding her hands up. 'It wasn't fair of me to do that when you'd had no time to prepare. I apologise, Gracie.' And she looked at Gracie earnestly, her eyes soft in her tiny face.

'Oh, no, Toni, it was fine. I was happy to help. I just needed a moment to switch gears, that's all. I haven't been in office mode for a little while ...' She knew that she sounded weak, pathetic, needy. Just the kind of nappy-brained mum that she'd sworn she'd never be, with her silly evasions, her sappiness.

'Of course.' Toni looked at Gracie as if she were seeing into her soul, then she gave her a soft pat on the arm. 'Gracie, you are amazing. You really are. I have no idea what we'd do without you here, but if you want to take more time to be with little Jensen, all you need to do is say — hmm?' There was that soft pat again, and Gracie began to feel like a little dog.

It's Jasper, Gracie thought with a flash of irritation. 'You can rely on me, Toni, you really can,' she said in her most definite tone. 'I'll have a think over the weekend and come up with some ideas.'

'I know you will, you absolute sweetheart. Brainstorm them with Atiyah, will you? The two of you are great together!'

'Yay!' Gracie said and gave Toni a thumbs-up, feeling a wave of shame sweep over her. She had never used the word 'yay' in her entire life, and she did not do thumbs-ups, but she had to at least appear to be positive. Atiyah had saved her bacon in that meeting, yet she'd have to be careful. She didn't want the other woman taking ownership of this project — not if she wanted to prove herself to Toni. If she was to do that, she'd need to be a whole lot sharper, she thought, as she accepted another hug from Toni and went to look for Atiyah, clumping down the two flights of stairs with Jasper and her array of bags and boxes.

She found Atiyah in the sandwich shop next to the office, in a queue for the organic salad boxes that came at a considerable cost in this part of town. Gracie examined her from behind, admiring the way she stood tall, unafraid of her height. Atiyah was that kind of person, Gracie thought — upright, direct, a tiny bit intimidating. Gracie tapped her on the shoulder. 'I just wanted to say thanks for bailing me out there. I really appreciate it.'

She thought that Atiyah would be pleased to be thanked, but instead, she grimaced, her brown eyes flashing at Gracie in disdain. Gracie couldn't understand why she might be annoyed, so she ploughed on. 'I was dying in there, in case you hadn't noticed,' and she gave a small smile. 'Or at least I would have died had you not said something. Anyway, I just wanted to say thanks. Oh, and Toni wants us to brainstorm fresh ideas for the campaign. Maybe some day next week?'

Atiyah shrugged, as if she really couldn't care less.

'You're on maternity leave,' she said in her usual direct fashion.

'Yes, but I can spare an hour for this — it's important that we get this gig. In fact, after today, I'd say my job depends on it.'

Atiyah shrugged and looked deeply unimpressed.

'Atiyah, what is it?' Gracie said. 'Have I said something wrong?'

'What it is, Gracie, is that I'm working my arse off here to prove myself, to see if there's the slightest chance that I can get a foot in the door, because the most I can get is contract work and maternity cover. I have to do twice as much as you to be even seen by people in this business. Twice as much work in half the time to be even noticed. I know what the score is. I've known what the score is for my entire life. But in four months' time, I'll be out on my rear end, and you'll be sitting pretty back in your full-time, well-paid job, so you'll forgive me if I don't jump up and down with excitement.'

Gracie's mouth opened and shut like a goldfish. Who did Atiyah think she was and what did she mean, that she had to work twice as hard as Gracie to even get a contract gig? She didn't understand, and then suddenly she did, and her face flushed. 'I wouldn't be so sure of that, Atiyah. I really wouldn't. I'm a mum now, which means that I have to prove myself too, just like you.'

'Hardly,' Atiyah said briskly, taking the box of miso salmon salad that was being handed over the counter to

her. 'The two things do not equate, Gracie. Not in my
world. If you'll excuse me, I've got work to do.'

'Sure,' Gracie said sadly, thinking, that makes two of us.

Later as Gracie climbed the hill to the park, she thought
more about what Atiyah had implied, about having to work
twice as hard because she was black. Surely it wasn't true?
Nowadays, the world was much more egalitarian, wasn't
it? Atiyah didn't seem to think so, though, and she'd
also got quite affronted when Gracie had suggested that
her difficulties were on a par with Atiyah's. Yet, she was
beginning to get a sense that now that she was a mum she'd
suddenly have a lot to prove: that she was more than just
an account manager and more than just a mum, but was
instead a razor-sharp uber-being, capable of rising early
to fit in a session at the gym, then working a ten-hour day,
then coming home to devote all of her energy to Jasper,
before fielding a few emails before bedtime, only to do it all
again the next day. But what would be left, she wondered,
for Jake or for her?

I need to snap out of this gloomy mood, she thought
as she reached the park gates. The others have never seen
me even remotely frazzled, and I don't plan to start letting
them see me like that now. I need to keep this up or else I'll
crumble. She paused for a minute to strap the cooler box
onto the handle of Jasper's buggy and to assemble her face
into its normal cheery expression, and when she looked

up, she saw them there, under the trees, the little huddle of buggies, and right in the middle of them, an enormous, pink pram. Oh, fuck, Gracie thought. That really is just what I need right now. For a second, she debated whether to turn around and leave, but then she told herself to cop on, walking confidently over to them.

'Hi, everyone! Sorry I'm late — big business pow-wow that I got dragged into.' Jesus, what was she like, with her 'pow-wow' — she'd never used that word in her life — but she suddenly felt anxious and out of place, eager to impress.

Lina had been sprawled out on the grass, Tommy beside her, but now she sat up, her top, which she'd draped over her breasts, falling off them before she said, 'Whoops,' and pulled it back up. God, she was such a slob, Gracie thought. 'We thought you'd never get here. We're starving.' It was a joke, and Lina smiled as she got up to give Gracie a kiss on the cheek.

'Hi, Gracie.' Jane remained seated on the picnic blanket and gave her a little wave. She had huge sunglasses on, but Gracie could see that she was even paler than usual. 'I won't get up to greet you — I've a tummy ache.'

'Oh, poor you. Did you get a bug?'

'Yeah, that's it — I think Owen passed it on to me.' Her voice was even lower than usual, so Gracie had to strain to hear.

'Well, I have some of that fermented stuff from the health food shop that's great for the gut — I'll pour you a big glass of it,' she said, going to sit down on the only bit of the picnic blanket that wasn't occupied, steeling herself to say hello to the new member of their group. She turned to acknowledge Elise, mustering all of her energy to be bright and polite, when she noticed the champagne bottle stuck into a cooler bag in the middle of the blanket. She froze. First doughnuts, now champagne – whatever next: cocaine? Jesus.

'Oh, are we celebrating?'

'Yes – you won't believe it, Elise has only gone and swung me a meeting with the biggest talent agent in town,' Lina said. 'I'm shitting myself, quite naturally, but definitely cause for a celebration – and I wanted to say a little thank you to Elise, hence the fizz. It's only Prosecco, but it's the thought that counts.'

'Ah, don't be daft,' Elise said, waving her hand across her face, as if pushing the thanks away. 'Sure, Mack's a client of Gray's, so it wasn't much of a stretch. Besides, every artist needs an opportunity, I always think. You deserve a lucky break, Lina, so you go for it, girl!' and she raised her hand to high-five Lina.

'Mack McCarthy?' Gracie said. '*The* Mack McCarthy?'

'None other than,' Lina said proudly.

'Wow. That's great, but ... he has a bit of a reputation.'

'What do you mean "a bit of a reputation"?' Elise leaned forward in what Gracie thought was a slightly threatening manner, like that horrible yappy little dog she had. Instinctively, Gracie leaned back as her mind whirred.

'Oh, I believe he can be really tough. You'd want to have

your routine down to a tee before bringing it to him, I'd say.' That was true of what she knew about Mack McCarthy: that he was a real Rottweiler — chewed performers up and spat them out, tweeting ruthlessly about them if he thought they were 'shite', in his words. But there were also the other rumours, of a gang of male power brokers, who expected 'performances' that didn't involve too many jokes — not that she was about to tell Lina that here. She'd have to pick her moment, so that it didn't seem as if she were just jealous of Elise.

'Lina is brilliant,' Elise interrupted. 'She's just been performing some of her material for us and I think it's hilarious. Tell Gracie the one about the orange, go on. Honestly, Gracie, you'll be cracking up.'

'No,' Lina said shortly. 'Gracie's right — I'll hone it all a bit more before letting it into the world.'

Her words sounded placatory, but her sulky tone didn't, so Gracie tried to make up for it, reaching over to the bottle and pouring a dribble into one of the tower of plastic wine glasses beside it — Christ, the bottle was nearly empty. 'I propose a toast. To Lina's audition, which I know will be a triumph. Break a leg, Lina!'

Lina reluctantly clinked her glass against Gracie's and Jane wanly joined in. Then Elise lifted her nearly empty glass. 'Hear, hear, Gracie. Break a leg, Lina, love — you'll be a star!'

Lina, love? Who the hell do you think you are? Gracie thought. She only half-listened to the rest of the chatter, which revolved around the sudden appearance of Lina's mother at her front door, the others nodding in sympathy as Lina explained to them just how awful she was. Gracie's mind was racing. Christ, what a day — first the meeting and now this. She felt as if her world had slightly tilted on its axis and nothing was quite as it had seemed. She needed to regain her balance, to feel that she was on an even keel again.

And then it came to her. Brittas.

Gracie waited until there was a lull in the conversation, when Elise had got to the end of a funny story about her public health nurse, and she said, 'I've just had an idea. How about we go on a little weekend break — the four of us?' Of course, she didn't really mean 'the four of us', but it would have been a bit obvious to tell Elise to piss off, that she wasn't welcome, even if Gracie desperately wanted to.

There was a moment's silence while the others looked at each other warily. Gracie felt her heart sink — what on earth was wrong with them all? A couple of weeks ago, they'd have jumped up and down at the chance of a weekend break, she knew they would. Now, it was as if Elise had cast some kind of a spell on them.

'I'm not suggesting Paris —' she gave a small giggle '— just my mum and dad's van in Brittas Bay for the weekend. Wouldn't it be great to get out of town for a change? It's right by the beach, too. Lina, you could work on your material and we could just hang out and swim and drink Prosecco and have a barbecue on the beach. I think it would be heaven,' she said dreamily, 'and I'm sure we'd all fit in the Volvo — it's very roomy, so you wouldn't even have to drive.' She wanted to make it easy for them, so that they couldn't say no. She eyed Elise out of the corner of her eye, hoping that she'd be put out, but instead, she jumped up and gave an ear-splitting shriek. 'Gracie, are you serious? That'd be fan-bloody-tastic! I'd like nothing better than to lie around on the beach and drink Prosecco — you're an absolute star!' And, to Gracie's horror, she bent over and planted a big kiss on her cheek. She smelled of cheap perfume and, if Gracie wasn't mistaken, cigarette smoke. She wanted to retch, but instead, she just smiled broadly.

'Great!' Lina said. 'I'll bring my laptop and sulk on the beach while you all have a brilliant time. It'll be fun to work my arse off while you all hang out, getting drunk — poor me.' As usual, Gracie wasn't sure whether Lina was joking or not, until she said, 'So, I accept your gracious offer, thanks, Gracie!'

Jane was the only one who was quiet, and this wasn't unusual, but Gracie's heart sank when she saw her pensively tugging at a bit of grass. 'Jane?' she said softly.

'I'll need to get back to you, if that's OK,' Jane said quietly. 'I'll just check my diary at home.'

'Of course,' Gracie said, deflated. Honestly, she liked Jane, but she could be a bit of a damp squib sometimes. She was being offered a free weekend in Brittas — she wasn't being led to the gallows. 'Just let me know — fingers crossed you can come.'

Jane nodded silently, and there was an awkward pause, before Elise wondered if she'd need a wetsuit for swimming and Lina said not unless she was crossing the Channel and they all laughed. Then Lina said she had to get back before her mother burned the house down or did something else really stupid and Elise said that Gray was cooking so she'd better get in a takeaway, and Gracie took that as her cue to pack away the food she'd put out on the picnic blanket, uneaten. She could kill Jane, she thought, as she put the orange muffins back in their Tupperware, but still — mission accomplished. At the thought of her triumph, she gave a little inward shriek of delight.

9

Elise

The surprises begin as soon as I set foot in Gracie's Volvo SUV, when she pulls up in my front drive to collect me. It's not the car that's surprising: I'd expect Gracie to drive a nice car like this, but I can't help thinking that Gray's Audi Q8 is a bit smarter, a bit roomier inside, even though it's the size of a lorry! I'm no car expert, but you need space with a baby because their stuff takes up so much room. When I think of my brothers and sisters and myself, all of us squashed into a Nissan Micra booting up the road on our holidays, it's no wonder we fought like cats and dogs all the way there. Anyway, what's surprising is the fact that there's a track of eighties music blasting from the rolled-down windows, and Lina — who else? — is singing along to 'Eye of the Tiger'. She might be funny and gorgeous, but she can't sing. Good job comedy is her thing.

'Turn it down!' Gracie snaps.

'Fine,' Lina says. 'Keep your hair on.'

'And can we please roll up the windows,' Gracie says, 'so I can put on the air conditioning? It's boiling in here.'

'Do you think we might let Elise in first?' Jane says. 'There's no point in rolling up the windows if you're going to open the door and the boot.'

By this stage I'm standing beside the car, my Louis Vuitton travel bag on the ground beside me: it was a present from Gray when the company began to do well, and I'm always a bit embarrassed by it — as if I'm some kind of footballer's wife! But there's another part of me that quite likes it, to be honest. If you work hard, you should be able to reap the rewards without feeling guilty about it.

When Jane speaks, Gracie looks at me as if I have six heads. Honestly, I don't know what her problem is, but Lina jumps down and pulls me into a hug, then she bends down to pick up my bag. 'God almighty, Elise, what have you got in here? We're going to Brittas for the weekend, not on a polar expedition!' She laughs.

'Oh, is it too much?' I say. 'I wasn't sure what the weather was going to be like and there's all of Chloe's stuff ...'

She pats me on the arm. 'Will you relax? I'm only having you on.'

I laugh. 'Of course!' The place where her fingers were feels warm, and my skin tingles.

She slides the suitcase into the roomy boot, on top of all the travel cots, bouncy chairs and a bottle steriliser that must belong to Gracie. Lina's legs are long and biscuit brown and her hair is an even whiter blonde than before. It must be all the sun, I think. Then I hear a cough and I look over: Gray is standing on the porch in nothing but his shorts and a baseball hat with an extra-long peak, to keep the sun off his face. When I see him I jump with fright. I can't see the expression on his face.

'Well, hello, sailor,' Lina mutters to herself.

I walk around to the passenger side of the car and he shuffles over in his flip-flops, chest gleaming in the sun. He looks amazing, even if I say so myself! I'm about to climb into my seat, when he grabs me around the waist and gives me a long, slow kiss. I feel my cheeks redden and my heart thumps loudly in my chest. I'm flustered, to be honest, because Gray doesn't normally go in for these PDAs, but then Lina gives a long wolf-whistle, breaking the tension, and we all laugh.

'So these are the new friends,' Gray says, leaning on the passenger window, six inches away from Lina. 'Gray Sugrue,' he says, holding out a hand, which Lina takes and shakes firmly, giving a little giggle as she does. Gracie pretends not to see his extended hand, eyes firmly trained on her rear-view mirror behind her giant shades, but Jane gives a shy 'hello', reaching around Lina to shake his hand.

'Well, girls, have a good time. Don't do anything I wouldn't do,' he says, and of course, cheeky Lina says, 'Why, what kinds of things *do* you do?'

There's another blast of laughter before Gracie says, 'Listen, if we don't get moving, the traffic will be awful,' and then there's a flurry of goodbyes and Gray winks at me before turning to go back inside. I don't know what to think. He's not normally like that at all: he could be in a crowd of bikini-clad models and not bat an eyelid. If I didn't know him better, I'd think he was jealous.

The next surprise is the 'van', as Gracie called it. I thought that's what she meant — a caravan, like the one we used to go to for a week in Bettystown, the ten of us cramming into two tiny bedrooms and a kitchen that smelled of mould. We'd look out at the rain, playing endless games of cards and making forts out of the sofa cushions, winding each other up until, eventually, Ma would just throw us all outside into the rain, telling us to go and play, which we would, on the grey, windswept beach, until we got hungry and trailed home again to reheated frankfurters in a bun or, my favourite, Fray Bentos steak and kidney pies. Ma always refused to cook on holidays. 'It's my holiday, too,' she'd say, putting her feet up and reading a magazine. Of course, Da couldn't cook, so it was reheated things out of tins, which none of us minded, even if we nearly killed each other to be allowed to scrape the pastry out of the bottom.

As soon as we pull up outside Gracie's, I can see that
this is no caravan and Brittas Bay is no Bettystown – there
isn't a whiff of Fray Bentos about the place, I can tell you!
It's a mobile home, I suppose, but it's magnificent – a huge
big palace of a place surrounded by a large sundeck, which
has obviously been landscaped, judging by the exotic plants
and the lovely outdoor furniture. And inside ... oh, my
goodness, it's out of this world! There are lovely cream
sofas and really nice black-and-white photos of Gracie and
a chubby-looking guy who must be her husband, the two of
them looking adoringly at Jasper. I have to say, they make
an odd-looking couple. Gracie is so pretty and slim and
clean, with her immaculate blonde hair and her hubby – or
is it her partner? – looks like the kind of guy who takes a
scooter to work in Google, with his scraggy beard and untidy
hair. Then Gracie shows us the four huge bedrooms, two
with en suites, and the fully fitted kitchen, with its huge
American fridge and gorgeous white cupboards. Honestly,
it looks like one of those houses in the Hamptons I look up
on Google when I'm bored, imagining that one day I'll live
in one. Gray says he can't see why not, if things keep going
the way they are with his business, but there's no way he'd
go to the Hamptons. The Algarve is as far as he'll travel,
and even then, he moans about the food. Imagine being
born to this, I think, as Gracie takes us on a tour of the site.
Every 'van' here is more like a mansion, not to mention the
tennis courts, swimming pool and gorgeous horseshoe-
shaped beach – it's like Malibu, only in Ireland. 'You are

so lucky,' I blurt as we stand out on the deck, watching the tanned children running about on the white sand. 'It's like something out of a magazine or a movie.'

As soon as the words are out of my mouth, I want to just shrivel up and die. Imagine showing them how uncultured I am. Ma and Da said that I should never apologise for where I came from, but quite honestly, I feel so inadequate. No amount of Louis Vuitton luggage can make up for the way I feel inside. Gracie pretends to laugh and I want to turn and run, but then Jane is standing beside me. 'I couldn't agree more, Elise, and we are lucky to be here, so, thank you, Gracie,' and she leans over to give frosty Gracie a kiss on the cheek. Gracie softens and says, 'You're welcome, pet,' and I wonder why I couldn't just say something nice and simple, like Jane.

Gracie shows us to our rooms then. Mine isn't the nicest of the four, to be honest: Lina and Jane both have lovely sea views, the little red-and-white sails of the boats out in the bay visible through their large windows, but my 'view' is of patio furniture and a half-wilted palm tree. Oh, well, I think, putting Chloe down on the bed while Gracie shows me around. I suppose the others do know her better and it's natural they'd get first choice.

'There are towels in the hot press and extra blankets in the wardrobe,' Gracie is saying, when I decide to come straight out with it.

'Thanks, Gracie. Ehm, can I just say something?'

Her shoulders visibly tense, but I plunge on anyway. 'I

just want to say thanks for inviting me. I know I'm new to the group and everything, but you've made me feel really welcome.' That's not true, but I'm hoping that if I pretend, she might warm to me just a little bit. 'You see,' I add, my eyes filling with tears, 'I was completely lost before I met you all — I'd just moved to Rathgar and I didn't know a soul, and everyone there is kind of unfriendly. And I wouldn't change Chloe for the world, but you know how lonely it can be. Some days, I think I'm going out of my mind with it.' And then I'm off, blubbing away like Chloe herself, big tears rolling down my cheeks, feeling such a fool. I'm an awful crier. Ma always said that I was too sensitive for my own good, that I was missing an extra layer of skin.

She looks at me for a long time, and you couldn't describe it as a friendly look, but neither is it unfriendly. I find it really hard to read, to be honest. It's as if she's making her mind up about something. I continue to blub away, until she reaches into her shorts pocket and produces a tissue. 'Thanks,' I say, taking it and drying my tears.

'You're welcome, Elise. Help yourself to whatever you need. Cocktails on the deck at seven.'

And then she's gone. I really don't know what to make of it. I'm not doing it on purpose. I really do feel overwhelmed with emotion right now. I don't understand how it is Jane can just say 'thank you' and Gracie's all nice, but when I try, she just gives me that icy Gracie look. I can tell I'm going to have to work really hard to win her over.

I'm determined not to feel down, so I make sure Chloe's

installed in her travel cot, nice and safe, then I have a shower, washing myself with my special cleansing bar and repeating my affirmations as I do. 'I am not what happened to me. I am what I choose to become.' I say this over and over again, emphasising the last bit, and every time I do, I think of all the times I was rejected when all I'd done was try to be friends, just like I'm trying to be Gracie's friend − if only she could see it. Still, by the time I'm finished piling on the conditioner, I'm beginning to feel a little bit better. Those affirmations really do work!

We've agreed to put the babies down before dinner − everyone except Lina, that is, because Tommy goes to bed when she does, apparently. Honestly, I like Lina, but she'd make her life a lot easier if she put the child down at a reasonable time. She's been reading one of those baby-wearing books that says you have to have your child with you constantly, no matter who else is in the picture, which sounds like an awful lot of hard work to me. I try to keep Chloe on a nice sleep schedule so that Gray and I have some quality time together in the evenings − Chloe often has something to say about it, sitting between us on the sofa, propped up on a cushion while we watch the telly, but I try!

Now, I give Chloe an extra-long feed before winding her and changing her nappy. I sit on the bed to feed her and look out at the patio and the blue sky beyond. It's been such a lovely summer: all of June and now July with that hot, bright sun and there's still August to go. I'm such a sun worshipper, so I'm loving every minute of it. I sigh happily as Chloe glugs away, her little hand patting my chest, her eyelids beginning to droop as her little tummy fills with milk. My world, I think, placing a kiss on her soft forehead.

It's very quiet and I can hear voices on the patio, neither of them loud, so it couldn't be Lina. I strain to hear what they're saying, even though Ma used to clatter us if she caught us earwigging, but I can't help it. 'There she was, tears falling onto Mum's nice duvet cover – and it's from The White Company. I didn't know where to look.' Gracie. My heart sinks.

There's a long silence, while the person I think is Jane responds, then Gracie says, 'Well, I only asked her to be polite. I could hardly invite the two of you and not her. It's rude.' Then there's another gap, followed by a heavy sigh. 'Look, we'll just have to make the best of it, but does she have to say the first thing that comes into her head *all* of the time?'

I find my hand gripping the duvet really hard, so I can feel the waffle print on the underside of my hand, and then Chloe gives a wail, as she feels the tension in my body – she's such a mind-reader, that child – and I have to take deep breaths to calm myself down. Maybe they weren't talking about me. It could have been anyone, I think, as Chloe's little body goes limp with sleep in my arms.

I'll just have to prove them all wrong.

*

'Wow!' Lina says when I appear on the deck, twenty minutes later, in my best beach-wear, a nice halter-neck maxi with a tropical print that I bought for the Maldives. I have my bag of party tricks in my hand: Bacardi dark-spiced rum, Coke, a big pack of mint and a couple of lemons. 'No wonder your hunky husband fancies you.'

I giggle, a picture of Gray kissing me in front of all the girls flashing into my mind, and I blush. The other two are sitting on the lovely outdoor sofas, lounging on the hot-pink cushions without their babies, except for Tommy, who is hanging out of Lina, as usual. Lina is wearing a lemon-yellow T-shirt and a pair of denim cut-offs, and it looks cute, even if I thought she might dress up a bit for the occasion. Jane is wearing something boring, as usual, and I wonder if she'd appreciate a bit of fashion advice, making a mental note to suggest that. And Gracie is immaculate in a white summer sweater and expensive-looking linen wide-leg trousers that look amazing on her. Honestly, part of me wants to give her an earful and the other part of me wants to be her!

'Thanks,' I say, giving a little twirl. I hold the bag up to the four of them. 'I've brought my party special, rum and Coke. It's not subtle, but it sure tastes good.'

'Oh, I thought I'd make bellinis,' Gracie says as she spies my giant bottle of booze. 'They're very summery.'

'Ah, Gracie, will you give us a break.' Lina laughs. 'Do I want Prosecco and peach juice or a great big dirty double rum and Coke – let's get the party started! C'mon, Elise,

I'll help you.' We go over to the little bar on a trolley that Gracie has set up on the deck, full of bottles of booze with names I've never heard of: Lillet Blanc, Fernet-Branca, white port, even sherry, which reminds me of my Auntie Linda and how she used to get drunk on it every Christmas.

Lina takes a chopping board and slices the lemon, then chops the mint really quickly, with a skill that I can tell is professional. 'I used to work in a kitchen,' she says, when she sees me looking.

'You must have done a lot of things,' I say, dropping cubes of ice into the four glasses Lina has laid out on the tray.

'Absolutely everything, from sorting potatoes to picking blackcurrants to working in a meat-packing factory — I kid you not,' she says, when she sees my face. 'My mother didn't have much money, so I had to get earning pretty quickly to get myself through college. What about you?'

'Oh, I've never been to college,' I say. 'I wish I had gone,' I lie, 'but I didn't have the patience for it. I like to think I'm self-educated,' I add, in case she thinks I'm a complete thicko. Besides, I read some of that Winnicott, and I've been using a little app on my iPhone to learn French, which Gray loves. He likes me to talk to him in French when we're in bed, even though, quite honestly, it's a bit embarrassing. I'm kind of shy like that. At least, when things don't come naturally to me.

'Well, good for you,' she says. 'The University of Life. Sometimes I think I'd have been better off there than in college, learning to do things I've never needed before or since.' She shrugs. 'A degree in philosophy is sod-all use, as it turns out.'

I feel a bit inadequate, a bit out of my depth, so I try to think of something clever to say while I pour the carefully measured rum over the ice. Then she grabs the measure from me and adds another shot into all of our drinks.

'You're mad!' I say.

Her answer is to take a swig before adding another tot, taking a sip and closing her eyes in joy. 'Ah, that's more like it.' Then she opens them and gives me a wink, and my stomach lurches. That's who you remind me of, I think. Fiona. She was clever, zany and funny too — but look how that ended. This time would be different.

We're tiddled before Gracie has even got the barbecue on, and we all joke about how we'll knock the babies out when they wake for their night feeds later, with the injection of alcohol in the milk. Only Gracie doesn't see the funny side of it, but then she wouldn't because she bottle feeds Jasper — each to their own, even if there really is no substitute for breast milk. What would Ma think of me, sitting, 'like a cow', feeding every four hours? We were all given a bottle, as far as I know, and we turned out OK — but then maybe the old grey matter would have worked a bit better if I had been given the breast!

'Did you try to feed Jasper?' I find myself blurting out

as we sit around, waiting for organic lamb burgers with portobello mushrooms and feta, no less. As I say it, I wonder if it sounds a tiny bit like an accusation and, honestly, I could kick myself. Of all the people to antagonise, I think. 'I mean, I don't want to judge …'

But it must be the triple rum and Cokes, because Gracie replies, 'I did and it was awful. Pure agony. I have never felt such pain in my life.'

'I hear you,' Jane chips in. 'I thought I'd pass out the first time Owen latched on. Why does no one ever tell you this stuff? All the pictures show mums looking fondly down at their babies – I couldn't even look at Owen because I thought the pain was all his fault.'

Lina flashes Gracie a look, and I wonder what it's about, but then Lina chips in, 'I had this awful midwife in hospital who appeared beside my bed in the middle of the night because Tommy was crying, and I can still remember her lifting one of my breasts up and dropping it, as if it was something she'd found stuck to the bottom of her shoe, and then she said, 'You'll never feed a baby with breasts like that.'

'Breasts like what?' Jane gives a little giggle and takes another sip of her cocktail. She's drinking it very fast, I think: hoovering it up. It's as if she's determined to get blotto.

'Defective breasts, substandard breasts – I don't know – they weren't right anyway, and I thought it meant that I wasn't right either. I was substandard and defective too.'

'I know what you mean,' I said. 'I wanted to have Chloe at home, but we had a home visit from a private midwife and she took one look at me and told me that my hips weren't wide enough to deliver normally. I ask you. I was surprised she didn't come at me with a tape measure.'

Lina guffawed. 'What a total bitch. I sometimes wonder about these women, what it is that makes them hate other women so much that they have to put them down like that: make them feel that they're not good enough, when they should be supporting them.'

'Ah, well, that's women for you,' Gracie said, getting up to turn the burgers over. 'We seem to do our level best to pull each other down – we give out about men doing it, but I think we're the real culprits.'

I had tuned out of the conversation to look at a bunch of shiny, healthy kids mucking about on the beach, but now I'm all ears.

'That's not very sisterly, Gracie,' Lina says. She's smiling, but I don't think she finds what Gracie has said funny.

Gracie places an extra portobello mushroom for Lina, a vegetarian, on the grill. 'Well, I'm sorry you feel like that, Lina, but maybe you've just been lucky and never experienced it for yourself. How women are the worst when it comes to supporting other women.'

'OK, give me one example then,' Lina says, sitting bolt upright in her chair, like Poppy when she's about to pounce.

'Well, take my maternity cover, the lovely Atiyah. For a start, she's the "diversity hire"' — as she says this, she makes inverted comma signs with her fingers, the burger tongs in one hand — 'and all she's supposed to do is cover my maternity leave, so when I come back, I can hit the ground running. Instead, she's trying to get my job. She doesn't miss a chance to stick her oar in at meetings and she's always trailing around after the boss with fresh ideas, never missing a chance to pitch something, even if the discussion is about paper clips or replacement loo roll for the bathrooms.'

'The "diversity hire"?' Lina says, incredulous. 'Can you hear yourself, Gracie? Do you know just how racist that sounds?'

Oh, dear. I open my mouth but sensible words just will not come out. I look at Lina, who might as well be growling, ears flattened. Gracie says nothing, turning the burgers over, but a muscle is working in her jaw.

'Maybe you just feel insecure.' It's Jane, a glazed look in her eye. 'Maybe you only think she's trying to take your job because you're not sure how you feel about it yourself. You're not sure if that's what you want to do any more, so you make it about the maternity cover or about her race or whatever.' She takes a big swig from her drink then, as we all look at her. Lina catches my eye and makes a face, grimacing at Jane's glass. I nod — no refill for her, I think.

I'm about to change the subject, to get up and freshen people's drinks — everyone's except Jane's, that is — when

Lina says, 'I don't think that's the issue. I think it's that centuries of oppression have made us turn on each other, scrambling over each other for the few small places that the men will let us have. We're like rabid dogs fighting over a scrap of meat.'

'Oh, for God's sake,' Gracie snaps. 'Will you drop the feminist diatribes, please, Lina? It's supposed to be a relaxing weekend, not an encounter group.'

'Fine,' Lina says, getting up from her seat so quickly that Tommy, who'd been snoozing away, gives a wail of surprise.

'Where are you going?' Jane slurs.

'To get a cardigan. It's cold out here,' Lina snaps, shuffling off in her flip-flops, Tommy on her hip.

It's not cold. It's a lovely, balmy evening, a warm breeze ruffling my hair, my ice cubes rattling softly in my glass. It would all be just perfect if it weren't for these two going at each other. And Jane's no help because she's too far gone. Honestly, the atmosphere is poisonous, and I wonder what Gray's doing right now. Probably sitting on the sofa with Poppy, doing one of his business forecasts. He knows I don't let her up on the sofa, so he makes a big deal out of inviting her up onto my nice, clean cushions when I'm not there. I want to be at home, I think, sipping a glass of chilled pinot grigio and watching some nonsense on the TV. I feel completely out of my depth.

Then Jane pipes up. 'You know what?'

'What?' Gracie says, lifting the burgers off the grill and

putting them into the golden brioche buns she'd brought out from the kitchen earlier.

'I think we're just absolute bitches.'

We're suddenly laughing then, Jane and I, bent over our drinks, guffawing away. Gracie sulks for a bit, then joins in, until the three of us are howling. I have tears in my eyes. 'Bitches.' You said it, Jane, I think, thanking God for the change in tone. And besides, now that Jane has broken the ice, I know that I won't have to say what is on my mind. That, really, I don't believe in feminism. Men are men and women are women, and that's the way it is — we are each born to do different things, and there's no point thinking otherwise. That's why we have a womb: because we will be raising the next generation and passing what we know on to them; and that's why men don't: because they have to go out and provide. You can imagine how well that would go down here!

When Lina comes out, Tommy, now wide awake, on her hip, she's still in a sulk, but then she sees us all laughing and she smiles and I like her all over again. The atmosphere lightens then, as Jane makes a silly joke and Lina says that we should get her drunk more often. Even Gracie softens, insisting that we move from cocktails to champagne, even though we are all really tiddly. Who am I to say no? I love champagne — those lovely, buttery bubbles.

We all fill our glasses and munch on our dinners, which Gracie has served on picnic plates. I think guests deserve the best, so I'm a bit surprised, to be honest, but I suppose that's the tone of this weekend. Super-casual.

'Isn't this perfect?' Lina says then.

'Perfect,' Jane agrees, putting down her plate and leaning back on the cushions, closing her eyes.

Gracie doesn't say much, pushing her burger around on her plate, but then Lina says, 'Gracie, thanks for all of this. This place is fabulous, the food was delicious and the drink copious. A toast to Gracie!' It's an olive branch, and as Jane and I raise our glasses, I can feel us all holding our breaths, waiting for Gracie to respond. Eventually, she lifts her glass, like a queen, and says, 'You're welcome,' and we all breathe a sigh of relief.

Even so, the frost hasn't thawed completely, and we continue to eat in silence. If I don't do something, I think, the party will just peter out. The last thing I want is for someone to get up and announce that they're off to bed, so I say, 'How about a game? Like charades.'

'I'm not eighty yet, thanks, Elise.' Lina giggles.

'Oh,' I say sadly, feeling a bit deflated. 'Well, how about truth or dare?'

'Do you think that's wise?' Lina laughs.

'I think it'll be fun,' I say. 'We don't have to get too serious. We'll keep it light. Or we can just do dares – that's always good for a laugh.' It *is* fun: I can still remember daring my older brother, Joe, to streak through the caravan park in Bettystown, which he did – but then he would because he's nuts. I haven't spoken to Joe in years, thanks to the lot of us falling out over Ma and Da's will and the ownership of a grotty council house in Dundalk. It seems ridiculous, but that's families, I suppose. But I still love truth or dare, because that way you find out what makes people tick. 'I'll start,' I volunteer.

Gracie gives a sigh and mock-rolls her eyes to heaven. 'Oh, go on. It can't do any harm, I suppose.'

'Great,' I say, putting down my drink. 'OK, a question for Gracie. What's the most embarrassing thing your parents have caught you doing?'

'Are you serious?' Gracie looks at me sternly, but then shrugs and smiles and I'm glad about that. I want to catch her off guard, for once. 'OK, well, let me think. Smoking out the bedroom window? No, that's lame. Smuggling booze in my school bag to the disco and dropping it on the front drive so it smashed and went everywhere?' She looked around at us all. 'Nope. Oh, I know — Mum and Dad caught me in their bed with this total jock when I was in sixth year. They'd gone to Rosslare to a friend's house, but they came back early because Mum had an upset tummy — and there we were.'

'Oh, Gracie, I thought you were too good for that,' Lina said. I'm not sure, but I think I can detect a bit of sarcasm in her tone and I think, Don't start, Lina, for God's sake.

'Well, people can surprise you, Lina. He was awful, I remember,' and she giggles. 'So full of himself and so absolutely terrible in bed.' We all laugh along with her, including Jane, who seems to be completely out of it. I feel a bit of admiration for Gracie all of a sudden and I'm glad I got her to open up a bit.

'And now, I have a question for you, Lina,' Gracie says.

Oh no, I think, as Lina sits up on the sofa, mock-tidying her hair and straightening herself. 'I'm ready.'

'Why did you decide to go it alone with Tommy? I mean, if you don't mind me asking.'

Oh. The questions are meant to be jokes, for goodness sake, I think, but Lina shakes her head and says, 'No, I don't mind. I've never found it necessary to have a man to complete my life. I mean, they're fine, don't get me wrong—'

'Oh, I don't know about that,' Gracie interrupts. It's meant to be funny, but I notice that Jane winces before Lina continues. 'When I decided that I wanted to have a baby, I thought it meant that I had to be in a relationship – the two go together, right? That's what we've always been taught, even if I wasn't raised that way. That's what all the movies are about – boy meets girl and they live happily ever after. But women don't even need men to have babies any more, do they? I think it's great, even if I didn't want that for myself.'

'Why not?' Jane asks.

'Oh, I wanted Tommy to know their dad – at least, to know *of* him, if they ever needed him. I don't have a dad, and I didn't want that for them. It's too lonely. I know, it's probably a bit contradictory, but that's how I felt anyway.'

I'm not sure what to make of this. I think Lina's trying to have her cake and eat it. Besides, I'm not really a fan of fuzzy lines – I'm more of a black-and-white girl, which is why I could never raise Chloe to be gender neutral, like Tommy. How would she know herself if she wasn't a girl? It'd be like pretending she was a giraffe or a piranha and expecting the world to go along with it. It just didn't make sense. I suddenly feel a bit tired and fed up. It seems that my plan to lighten the tone has totally backfired.

Then Jane blurts, 'Do you know what? I can't think why I didn't cop on to that sooner. That we don't need a man to have a baby these days. God, I wish I had gone down that road. I'd do things differently, that's for sure.'

'What do you mean?' I say, ignoring the dagger stare that Gracie gives me.

Jane sighs and looks mistily into her glass, which is empty – again. 'You know, we think we can hide things, but they always come back to get us in the end. Remember that.' She's slurring her words, eyes glazed, but she seems to mean every word. I open my mouth to ask her more, because I'm dying to know, but then Lina pipes up, 'Right, Elise's turn.'

Oh, God. I lick my lips and swallow nervously while the other three turn their attention on me. 'Now, let me think,' Lina says thoughtfully, before brightening. 'Oh, I know! That hunky guy of yours. Have you ever felt tempted to cheat on him? I wouldn't kick him out of bed for eating crisps, I can tell you.'

'Lina!' Gracie says in mock horror. 'Surely that's a bit personal,' but she turns her gaze on me and I see that I'm supposed to come up with an answer. The obvious one, like, 'Of course not. Gray's the love of my life.' Which he is. No one understands me better than Gray, and the day I met him was the happiest of my life. At long last, I knew who I was and I didn't have to worry any more about being a freak.

I take a deep breath. 'Well, normally, if you were to ask me, I'd say no ...' I begin.

'Oooh.' Lina's eyes are round.

'But as we're telling the truth ... maybe,' I say, 'if the right person came along.' I can't believe I'm saying this, I think. I really must have had too much to drink tonight, or maybe it's the air, or the girls and the fact that we're together in this place and we're sharing secrets.

There's a sharp intake of breath, then Gracie says, 'I'd never cheat on Jake. Never. Maybe you just don't know when you're onto a good thing, Elise,' she says calmly, fixing me with that stare.

I stare back at her and the two of us lock eyes, each of us daring the other to look away first, but then Lina bursts out laughing. 'Oh, Elise, you really had me going there. For a minute, I thought you were serious!'

The spell is broken and I lean back gratefully on the cushions beside Jane, and I say, 'Gotcha!' And we all laugh.

'Well, I think that's quite enough for one night,' Gracie begins, but then Lina interrupts. 'Ah, for God's sake, Gracie. It's eleven o'clock and it's not even dark yet.' It's true – even though we are a month past midsummer, as we look out there's still a faint line of pinky-blue on the horizon.

'Time for a dare.' Lina's voice is loud — very loud — and Gracie hisses, 'For God's sake, don't wake the babies.'

'Right,' she says in a mock whisper. 'Sorry.' She thinks for a moment, then she brightens. 'I know,' she says, 'let's go skinny dipping.'

Oh, no, I think.

'Oh, no,' Gracie says firmly, echoing my thoughts exactly. 'No one has seen my tummy since Jasper was born, and I plan to keep it that way.'

'I'm with Gracie.' I laugh.

'Oh, come on, it'll be fun,' Lina says, growing bolder now. 'Nobody will look — we'll just whip off the towels and throw ourselves in.'

Gracie gives me one of those looks, the ones that I can't quite make sense of. I wonder if she wants me to say no. Lord knows, I'm only dying to, but I want the girls to see that I'm fun — happy to go along with anything, easy-going — so I have to pretend that I'm really enthusiastic about Lina's plan, while I wish to goodness I'd never opened my mouth about playing this stupid game. 'Let me go and get the baby monitor, so we can hear them if they wake up,' I say, playing for time. I get up off the sofa, making my way into the house where no one can see me panic. 'I'll just get some towels while I'm there,' I throw over my shoulder.

What on earth have I done? I think, as I go to my bedroom and rummage in the press, finding the only towels that don't look like they cost an arm and a leg and tucking them under my arm. My stomach is churning and

I can feel a sweat breaking out on my forehead. I can't do this, I think, as I walk back through the van to the deck.

I stand there for a few moments, watching as Gracie sits beside Jane, who looks like a cornered animal, hand gripping her glass. She's stroking Jane's arm gently and murmuring to her and Lina is leaning over them both, saying something soothing that I can't quite hear.

Gracie looks up at me, then right through me, as if I don't exist. Then she turns to Lina, 'Listen, you go on down, I'll catch up with you.'

Lina hesitates, but then shrugs and says, 'Fair enough — last one in's a hairy elephant! C'mon, Elise.' She stands up and offers me her hand, taking mine in hers and leading me down through the narrow, sandy path to the beach. When we get there, I look at the water, which is a dark, slate grey, a vast, churning mass, and my stomach flips. 'Lina ...' I begin, wondering how I can tell her, but then Gracie comes down the steps to the little path, a pile of towels in her hand. 'You forgot these.' She waves them at us. 'Jane's not going to join us,' she adds quietly. 'She's nodded off. I'll put her to bed when we get back.'

'Is she OK now?' Lina asks.

'She's fine. Just a bit the worse for wear.'

I wonder if I can ask Gracie what the matter is. I really want to know, and to be honest, I feel a bit left out, even if there is some history here that doesn't include me. I told my truth earlier, so why can't they tell me theirs?

'That makes two of us,' Lina says. 'I feel quite woozy – it must be the night air.'

'Me too,' I say hopefully. 'I'm beginning to think this wasn't such a good idea.' I try a little laugh then, to imply that I don't mean it, but Lina says, 'It'll be fun. No chickening out now. Besides, a swim will clear our heads.'

We strip quickly and, for a moment, we all stand there on the damp sand, naked and self-conscious. I wonder if the others were looking at my flat boobs or the little mound of fat on my belly. There is a long silence, until Lina, typically, breaks it: 'Jesus, we look as if we've been through the wars. I mean, look at my stretchmarks,' and she points to a row of silvery marks on the outside of her thighs, the only visible sign that she'd actually had a baby – lucky her. Gracie, too, looks as if she's come away without too much damage, her boobs firm and her tummy still taut.

'I know,' she says to Lina. 'I feel like a total blob – just look at me.'

Only people who don't resemble total blobs in any way talk about being total blobs, in my experience, but I know that we're here to support each other, so we all nod in sympathy. Honestly, though, if I'd known how much it would wreck my body, I'd have thought twice about it, I can tell you. I hear about all of those women having a vajazzle or whatever you call it and I think, where can I get one of those?!

We all slink into the water, and Lina dives in first, with a brief scream, then a loud laugh. 'Nobody told me it was the Arctic!'

'Will you be quiet!' Gracie hisses, but Lina is seized with a fit of the giggles, coming towards me, then grabbing hold of me and pulling me into the water, which is dense and dark and a bit scary. Oh no, I think, but I'm in now, so I make the most of it, kicking through the velvety water in that little doggy paddle I do that Gray says makes me look like a turkey having a swim. It's OK, it's OK, I keep repeating in my head, but when I put a foot down to rest on the bottom, I can't feel it. Oh, crap, I think, pulling at the water to turn myself around.

The others are further away from me than I'd thought, Lina swimming in long, confident strokes parallel to the beach and Gracie bobbing along, head high, hair safely out of the water in a bun on top of her head. I kick a bit to pull myself in, but then my head dips below the surface and I take in a big gulp of seawater, coughing it up again. I'm going to drown, I think, and nobody will rescue me. I cough again, louder this time, to get rid of the taste of salt in my mouth and throat, and then Lina hears me, swimming towards me and grabbing hold of my arm.

'C'mon, I'll give you a hand in,' she says and pulls me gently along with her until we're almost at the edge of the water, where little waves lap on the sand. We stand upright then, and I find myself clinging on to her, feeling her cold skin against mine. I take in great big lungfuls of air and feel my heartbeat gradually slow.

'Thanks, Lina, I got a bit spooked,' I manage after a while, wondering how I can pull myself away from her without making it look really obvious. I like the feeling of another woman's body next to mine — it's surprising: soft and full of hidden places. Gray is hard and tough, like a board. Any woman with half a brain could see that he's gorgeous, but sometimes softness is what I want, even if I know it's not natural. Even if I put all thoughts like that out of my mind years ago.

'You're OK — I was the 1997 Wexford Lifeguard of the Year, I'll have you know.'

'I was in good hands, then,' I say, grateful for the joke. I pull away and give her a friendly pat on the shoulder — kind of matey — and walk over to the little pile of towels, picking one up and pulling it around myself, grateful for the warmth and to feel covered again, to feel like myself, not this silly teenager.

'I'm off to the house,' I say, giving the others a little wave. I turn then to where the two of them are standing, just by the water. Gracie says something in a low voice to Lina, who laughs and puts an arm around the other woman, two naked bottoms facing me, a human wall, keeping me out.

'That's silly, Elise,' I say out loud to myself. 'Off to bed,' I say sternly, 'before you make a tit out of yourself altogether.'

It must be the sea air, because Chloe and I slept like babies last night, even if I had funny dreams about swimming in a weed-filled river, my arms and legs catching in the green fronds. I can hear movement in the kitchen, so I get up and take Chloe out to see who is up. To my surprise, I find Jane putting coffee into the French press and pouring in a stream of boiling water from the kettle. When she sees me, she smiles. 'Hi. How did you sleep?'

'Great,' I say. 'I conked out completely. Must be the sea air. And the booze,' I add, smiling.

'God, yes. I lost count of how many of those rum cocktails of yours I drank – never mind the champagne. Not that I regret a bit of it – it was lovely to overindulge for one night.'

'I know what you mean. When the cat's away, eh?'

She gives a small shrug of her shoulders, and her smile disappears.

I wonder what she means by that, but then she says, 'Toast? Gracie and I went down to the village for bread – they have this fantastic artisanal bakery, so we got carried away, buying a ton of bread and croissants and pains au chocolat. She's gone back to bed for a bit,' she adds.

'As my da would say, "'Twas far from artisanal bakeries you were reared,"' I say, sitting down and helping myself to a lovely hunk of sourdough, smothering it with butter and cherry jam. Sod the diet!

'Hah, you're right,' Jane says. 'They didn't have them in the arse end of Roscommon.'

'Nope – not in Dundalk either, funnily enough.' We exchange a smile and I think that maybe this might be a way in, to find out what's going on with her. 'So, we're both country bumpkins then.'

'Guess we are.' Jane helps herself to a slice of the sourdough, buttering it and smothering it with a veil of the wine-coloured jam. She bites into it and her eyes close. 'Mmm, that's delicious.'

'Whereabouts in Roscommon did you grow up?'

Her eyes open wide. 'Oh, you wouldn't know it,' she says quietly, taking another bite of her toast.

'Try me.' Maybe I'm being pushy, I think, but I need her to know that she can confide in me, that I'm there for her.

She sighs and puts her toast down on her plate. 'Castlemonkstown.' It comes out in a half-whisper.

'Never heard of it.'

'Hah!' She smiles. 'That's because it's a tiny dot on the map, and because it has nothing in it apart from a post office and a church. Oh, and a GAA club,' Jane says, getting up and pouring herself a coffee, holding the jug up and looking at me.

'Thanks,' I say. I don't like coffee — unless it's a nice frothy cappuccino — the strong stuff makes me feel sick — but I let her pour me a cup. 'I know exactly what it's like. Everyone knows everyone else's business and you feel that all eyes are on you every minute of the day.' This isn't really true — where I grew up, no one could give a shit whether you lived or died — they were too busy looking out for themselves, hoping to get through another day. Sharon managed to escape because of the books and I got away thanks to Gray turning up just when he was needed. I'd moved to another travel agent's by then and had put the thing with Fiona long behind me and one day, I'd looked up from my computer to find him standing there, asking about direct flights to Salou. By the time I'd booked his flights and done his travel insurance, he'd asked me out. I can still remember all the other girls giggling behind me. Lucy Lenehan even said 'phwoar' under her breath. I am a lucky girl, I know that, which is why I can think what I like, but I know that it'll be Gray for ever.

She looks up at me, surprised, and I'm pleased.

'Am I right? And you feel that the only thing you want to do is get the hell out of the place as soon as you possibly can. That's your only aim in life. Sad, but you'd go mad if you didn't get out.' I shrug. 'It's like you can't breathe or something.' This bit is most definitely true.

'That's right,' Jane says sadly. 'That's exactly it.'

'And then you discover that there's a big, wide world out there, far from Castlemonkstown, and you never look back.'

She nods her head, then looks at me. 'How did you know?'

'Because that's exactly how it was for me,' I say. This time, I'm not lying. 'When did you leave?'

'Fifteen years ago,' Jane says.

'Wow, you must have been young.'

She gives a small smile. 'Yes, well, there were extenuating circumstances.'

Oh. I wonder if I should say anything, but I decide not

to. Jane butters another slice of toast and helps herself to some more jam, spreading the layer ever so carefully over the bread. She's about to lift the toast to her mouth, but then changes her mind, putting it down on the plate before looking at me with those big grey eyes of hers. 'I had a breakdown.'

'Oh,' I say. 'Oh.' I have no clue how to respond and I'm silent for once, wondering what the best thing to do is. Eventually, I decide. I reach out and pat her hand gently, covering it with my own. 'That's tough.'

Jane nods and slides her hand away from under mine. Fair enough, I think, I've pushed it too far. I'm about to change the subject when I remember something Gray said about 'reverse psychology'. If you want someone to tell you something, you have to say the opposite, so I try it. 'Jane. You don't have to say anything. It's fine. I understand completely.' And I busy myself with the sourdough, smothering another slice in butter and that yummy jam.

It works. Jane is silent for a moment, then says, 'There were a few things. My parents were very strict and we didn't really fit in in town because we were Baptists.' She gives a small smile. 'The only Baptists in the place, as it happens. They were big believers in sin and that we are all doomed forever – it was all fairly gloomy. Then there was the usual stuff with school at that age – you know how it can be.'

I nod carefully. I have a feeling that Jane isn't telling me everything, so I say, 'Girls can be absolute bitches at that age.'

At this, she gives a soft laugh. 'If only it had been the girls. That would have been easy. Give me a bit of bullying any day.'

I don't know what she means because I had plenty of it, and honestly, I'd have done anything to get away from it. What could possibly be worse?

'I had an affair with a teacher.' She blurts it out while I have a piece of toast on its way to my lips and I stop dead, putting it back down on the plate. I can't believe it. Jane? Miss Mouse had an affair with some old guy in a V-neck sweater? No, I think.

'I know what you're thinking,' Jane says. 'There's no way.'

'Ah, no, no, I wasn't,' I begin.

'It's OK.' She smiles. 'Nobody believed me then either. I wasn't one of those girls who wore her skirt rolled up to her waist or who came into school in full make-up. I was a nice girl, a good girl, which is why no one could credit it. Little old me.' She gives an ironic smile.

'Did you love him?'

She shakes her head. 'What do you know about love at that age? It was just a silly crush.'

I don't know, I think. I sometimes wonder if that's the only time we *do* know about love. When our brains aren't working to tell us what a bad idea it is. I think of Fiona and me, sitting up in Ma and Da's bed, the two of us reading *Smash Hits* and sharing a bag of stale popcorn she'd found in her bag, crumbs sticking to our bare limbs. I close my eyes.

'What was his name?'

'Tom,' she says. 'His name was Tom.'

'And you liked him,' I add.

She nods. 'Mam and Dad found out, of course, and all hell broke loose. And you know what small towns are like. Word travels fast.'

'What happened next?'

'Next?' Jane gives a grimace. 'Next, Tom was sent off to Donegal to a boys' school, and I ended up in a mental hospital.'

'Because you'd had a fling with a teacher? Is that not a bit much?'

'You don't know my parents,' she says. 'They didn't like any threats to their authority. Besides, I wasn't well – everyone could see that. It was the best thing for me, really,' she adds sadly.

Oh my God. I don't know what to say, quite honestly. No one's really confided in me like this, unless you count Gray, and we tell each other everything. Well, almost everything. I try giving her hand another squeeze and this time she doesn't pull it away. 'I survived anyway, as you can see,' she says. 'You know how it is. One part of you recovers and you go on living your life. You get a job, you go to college, you buy a flat, you live just as everyone else does. Anyone looking at you would think you were completely normal, and yet, there's another part of you that never gets over it. Ever.' Tears fill her eyes.

'Ah, Jane, I'm sorry. I shouldn't have asked,' I begin.

'That's what I get for prying.' I'm not really that sorry because I can see that Jane and I could grow really close after this. We're bonding, and it feels good — to me, at least. I'm sure Jane feels the same way, now that she's got it off her chest.

She shakes her head and gets up to pull a sheet of kitchen roll off the dispenser beside the sink. She stretches an arm out to reach it, and her jumper lifts up, revealing a patch of livid blue bruises just above the waistband of her leggings. I suck in a deep breath. How on earth did she get those? Then I think of what she was saying last night — the cryptic comments, Gracie and she deep in conversation. She blows her nose, then dabs at her eyes, turning back to me quickly so that I have to take the look of shock off my face.

'I never told any of the others about it, so would you mind not saying anything?'

'Of course I won't say anything, Jane. I'm good at keeping secrets.'

'Thanks.' She sniffs.

'Jane,' I try then. 'Can I ask you something?'

She looks like a deer caught in the headlights, opening her mouth to respond, but then there is a loud rustling and banging at the kitchen door and Lina appears, Tommy in her arms as ever, a towelling bag slung over her shoulder. 'Oh, I was going to go down to the village before everyone got up. Gracie's still fast asleep with Jasper, but you got there before me, thank God.' She plonks herself down, balancing Tommy on her knee, and begins sawing at the loaf of sourdough, cutting off a big hunk and looking around for a plate, which Jane finds and shoves underneath the slice of bread.

'Thanks,' Lina says happily, wrapping an arm around Tommy so that she can butter it, only then noticing our silence. 'What's the matter? Did somebody die?'

Jane gets up then, pushing her chair out from the table. 'Nothing. It's ... nothing,' she says. 'I'm just going to check on Owen. He should be awake by now.' And she closes the door quietly behind her.

'Was it something I said?' Lina looks at me, wide-eyed.

'I think she's just hungover.'

'That'd be it,' Lina says. 'That and whatever caused those bruises.' She puts it out there with her usual frankness, looking me in the eye, waiting for my response.

'I know,' I say. 'I was trying to work out how to ask her, before—'

'Before I came in and ruined the moment,' Lina says. 'Sorry.'

'It's not your fault.' A pause. 'Maybe we should talk to her? I don't know, what do they call it, an intervention?'

'Jeez, Elise, she's not an addict or anything,' Lina says doubtfully. 'Besides, there could be an entirely innocent explanation.'

I'm not really sure there is, but I can take Jane aside later and get her to confide in me a bit. 'I'll have a word with her,' I say firmly.

'OK.' Lina nods, helping herself to another slice of bread, breaking off a little and feeding it to Tommy.

Of course, like a fool, I have to say something. 'Isn't it a bit early for weaning?' I say, nodding at Tommy as she gums the bread. 'The health nurse told me that six months was the right time to introduce solids.'

'They're fine,' Lina snaps.

'Of course, I'm sorry,' I say. 'I didn't mean to interfere.'

Lina nods briefly, biting into the bread, and I breathe a sigh of relief. The last thing I want is for her to think badly of me.

Lina retreats to her bedroom afterwards, leaving me by myself in the kitchen. I tidy up, because I don't want Gracie to have to face it — hosts shouldn't have to do their own washing up! — then I decide to take Chloe for a little walk down to the beach and a swim, holding her over the water, then dipping her little toes into it, being rewarded by a swift little gasp. 'Cold, isn't it?' Her arms and legs kick with excitement, so I swish her through the water again, enjoying her gurgles of delight. I don't want her to be afraid of the water like I am. I wonder what it must be like when everything is new, like this water is new to Chloe. To her, everything is a first, a fresh discovery. She isn't jaded and cynical, like the rest of the human race. Sometimes, I wish I could start all over again, like her.

When I get back, everyone is still in bed, and I sit on the

deck for a while with Chloe, looking out at the blue sea, at the tanned and happy kids playing beachball on the sand. Just then, Gracie emerges and says we're spending the afternoon on the beach with the babies, and even though I wonder why she doesn't ask what we'd like to do, I agree and when Lina appears with Tommy, we help her to lug a parasol down to the sand and to put it up, pushing the pole into the sand and draping a large sheet over it for extra shade. We pop the babies down on the thick beach towels that Gracie's provided, and Chloe reaches over then and pats Jasper on the shoulder, which makes us laugh. Maybe Gracie might begin to thaw out a bit, I think, opening my mouth to say something, but Jane arrives at the beach with Owen, then, covered in a loose linen top which she doesn't remove, her eyes hidden behind sunglasses. She sits apart from the rest of us for a little while, reading, but Gracie goes over to her and whispers something into her ear, and she gives a small smile, getting up and asking Lina and myself if we'll mind Owen and Jasper while she goes to the beach café with Gracie. The two of them walk off, thick as thieves, heads together as they stroll through the sand.

'They're very close,' I say to Lina. I feel a tiny bit jealous, to be honest. I thought that after this morning in the kitchen I might be closer to Jane but maybe I misread things.

'They are — if Jane would confide in anyone, it'd be Gracie.'

'Well, that's great,' I say, seeing the smile that flickers

across Lina's face. I don't know what could be so funny. 'So, how's the routine going?'

She blushes. 'Oh, God, it's a bit rough – I've put together a few ideas, but I'm not sure they're any good.'

'Do you want to test them out on me?' I say, and when Lina hesitates, 'C'mon, there's nobody in earshot.' And I look around as if Lina and I are secret agents, whispering, 'The coast is clear,' and being rewarded with a laugh.

'Oh, well, OK,' Lina says, telling me a very funny joke about her mother and then another one about Seamus, the father of her baby, and the first time he met his daughter. It's hilarious, but it's also touching and real, and I find myself sympathising with Lina, even though my life isn't like hers in any way, with my lovely hubby and my big house. I suppose hers is better material, what with the single parenting and the mad mother descending on her! I find myself laughing out loud, giving her a round of applause for the punchline at the end. 'You're so talented,' I say enviously. 'I have not one single talent.'

'Oh, I'm sure you do,' Lina says. I can tell that she's happy with the applause, and that makes me feel good.

'No,' I say, 'I can't sing, I can't dance. I can't type. I can't drive – I can't even swim!'

'I can see that,' Lina laughs, 'if last night is anything to go by! I learned with Sister Margarita, I remember. She used to stand at the top of the pool in Enniscorthy, dressed head to toe in black and with a big cane in her hand, and if you stuck your hand up out of the water to grab hold of the railing, she'd give it a good, hard tap. How come you never learned?'

I'm too embarrassed to say that they didn't have that many swimming pools where I grew up, and my parents didn't have a moment to be teaching me how to swim, or the money to get someone else to do it. Not like all of those mummies and daddies I see at the swimming pool nowadays when I take Chloe to Waterbabies on a Thursday morning. 'I suppose I never got round to it, and now it's too late,' I say sadly. 'I can only do this stupid doggy paddle and that's it.'

'No, it's not,' Lina says. 'I'll give you a lesson when Jane and Gracie come back.'

'Oh, no,' I say, holding my hands up. 'It's too late to teach this old dog new tricks.'

'It's never too late,' she says firmly. 'Besides, I owe you for listening to my drivel.'

'It isn't drivel — it's great. I think you're brilliant, Lina.' The words are out of my mouth before I can stop them — stupid, gushy words that are all a bit much. Why can't I just be cool? I wonder. Why do I have to behave like that?

But instead of laughing at me, she just says, 'Music to my ears, Elise. Who doesn't want to be called brilliant, even if it's not strictly true. Thanks,' and she pops a kiss on my cheek. I want to put my hand to my cheek and hold it there. 'And now, I see Gracie and Jane coming back, so into your swimming togs — it's an order.'

When the others come back, Jane looking a little bit lighter and Gracie as calm and in control as ever, Lina asks them to mind Chloe and Tommy and she leads me down to the water, holding my hand like a small child. Then she strides in ahead of me confidently and holds her hands out to me. 'Lean forward into the water and I'll catch you,' she says.

I shake my head. 'I need to feel the sand under my feet.'

'I promise. You'll be OK.' She holds her hands out to me again and I dive forward, reaching out until I make contact with them, inhaling a big gobful of water while I'm at it. I cough and splutter but somehow manage to hang on as Lina walks slowly backwards into the water. It is flat calm, but it still feels huge and dangerous. 'We're going out too far,' I say, pulling at Lina's hands.

'We're at my hip height, which is perfect for a little swim. Trust me?' Lina says.

The sun has come out now and it's behind her, hot and yellow, so she has a kind of halo around her, and her skin is golden, a rash of goosepimples covering her belly and arms.

'OK,' I say shakily.

'Now, I'm going to hold you while you lie on your tummy with your arms in front of you and kick your legs, OK?'

'OK.'

'Ready?'

'No,' I say.

She laughs. 'Ah, you are, Elise. You're readier than you think – OK?'

'OK.'

'So ... ready?'

'Ready.' Her hand is solid under my stomach, holding me up as I kick, and I have a sudden memory of Da in Bettystown doing the same thing when I was six, and whipping his hand away so that I sank to the bottom. 'You're not to let go,' I say sternly, kicking hard.

'I won't. I promise. All I'm going to do is give a little push and launch you forward and you just have to kick like a mad thing — all right?'

'If you bloody insist.' Then she gives a little push and suddenly her hand isn't there and I think I'm going to sink, but instead, I begin to move forward, legs going like pistons, arms straight out ahead of me. 'I'm swimming!' I yell over my shoulder.

'Keep going,' Lina urges me from behind, and I do, until I can swim no more and then, instead of sinking and spluttering, the way I would have done before, I put my feet gently down and right myself, feeling the sand firm under my feet. Lina had told the truth — it's only waist-deep here. I was right to trust her, I think. I turn to look at her, in her scarlet bikini, hands on her hips, looking like a proud mother. 'I did it!'

'Well done. You're a natural.'

I get so carried away that I launch myself back towards her, arms out in front, legs pumping, until I reach her and it gets a bit awkward then, me reaching out and accidentally grabbing her bikini bottoms, when I'd meant to hold onto her hips. 'Easy, you'll undress me!' She laughs, taking my hands in hers and setting me gently upright. A thought suddenly enters my head about what it might be like to undress Lina, then I push it firmly away. Get over yourself, Elise, I think. Nothing good ever comes of these things — you should know that by now.

I remember what Jane said this morning, about having a 'crush' on Tom, the teacher, and I wonder if that's what I have, just a bit of a crush on Lina. What's the harm in that? I think. She's amazing. She's funny and good-looking and charming and so confident, all on her own like that. I try to imagine if I could manage to live life on her terms, but of course I couldn't. My life is mapped out ahead of me and that's what I've chosen. I can tell you exactly what's going to happen over the next ten years — or longer. I'll have another baby — a boy this time — who we'll call Leo after Gray's dad, and then Gray's fitness business will expand and I'll help him out at reception, once the kids are in school, then a bit of bookkeeping — helping him to march forward, the way Lina said, while all the time I'll be standing still. I admire Lina because she has the guts to do her own thing, to live her own life. I sure don't! But another part of me, one that I'd thought long buried, knows that it's more than that.

All through the rest of that weekend, the silly formal dinner that Gracie insists we all dress up for — I blow them away with an Alexander McQueen jumpsuit that I haven't worn in ages — when we play charades and I get the title of *All the President's Men* wrong because I've never seen it, which is so embarrassing, and the game of rounders on the beach on Sunday morning, with brunch afterwards, before we all pile into the car, damp and sandy and happy — all that time, I can't take my eyes off Lina.

10

Lina

Elise was very keen, Lina thought as they both sat on her bed, the meagre pile of Lina's clothes between them, Tommy and Chloe kicking their legs on a playmat on the floor. It was kind of sweet, really, how badly she wanted to be friends, like an over-eager puppy. Gracie felt threatened by it, as she would, of course, but Lina thought that Elise was just trying a bit too hard, and where was the harm in that? They all had a friendship and she was new to things, so she was clearly just trying to find a place for herself in the group. Besides, she'd been great in Brittas, a foil for gloomy Jane and uptight Gracie — if it hadn't been for Elise, Lina thought that she wouldn't have had half as much fun. She'd livened the place up, that was for sure. And she'd laughed at Lina's jokes. What's not to like? Lina thought to herself.

Elise's questions could be a bit pointed at times, though. On the way home from Brittas, two weeks ago now, she'd punctured the silence in the car by suddenly asking Lina if she'd ever tried to trace her father. Gracie had got on her high horse, of course, telling Elise that they weren't playing truth or dare any more, but really, Lina hadn't minded that much. At least Elise didn't dance around things, saying nothing and making things bigger in the process, like most people.

'It has never even occurred to me,' she'd told Elise. 'I can't miss what I've never had.' Which was true. Or at least, it had been until recently anyway — until she'd picked Seamus to be Tommy's father. Why on earth couldn't she have picked someone who couldn't give a shit, so obviously like her own father? Why did she have to pick someone who really cared, who made her feel guilty every time she refused his call, his offers to take Tommy for a walk along the canal in the late-summer evenings. But maybe, she'd thought once, lying in bed in the middle of the night, her real father had thought like that, too. Maybe he'd cared, but Inge had pushed him away, just like she was pushing Seamus away. The thought had made Lina feel itchy, uncomfortable; for the first time in her life, she'd begun to wonder if it was good enough to keep things the way they were, just because that was the way they always had been.

'Minxy but not over the top is what we want,' Elise was saying now, breaking into Lina's thoughts. 'You know, attractive and lively, but not desperate. Make it look as if you have something to offer him — not that you're begging him for a gig.'

'Attractive, not desperate,' Lina repeated, shocked at herself even as she said the words. It didn't exactly sound like a feminist statement, but Elise had a certain way of doing things, she'd quickly understood, that kind of sucked people in.

'That's it.' Elise laughed, lifting clothes out of the pile, tossing them behind her onto the floor, proclaiming, 'No, no, definitely not,' as she sorted through them. 'God, you really are a bit of a hippy,' she said, as she pulled a flouncy yellow cheesecloth dress out and tossed it on the bed.

'I like that dress,' Lina protested. 'Besides, hippy is a look right now.'

Elise gave her a stern stare as she held the dress aloft, like an unpleasant specimen, wrinkling her little nose. 'The 1970s is a look — camel coats, chunky heels, polo necks — but this,' she looked at the dress with disdain, 'this was never a look.'

'Oh,' Lina said, stung. She wasn't entirely sure that Elise, with her wardrobe that made her look overdressed for everything, was in the best position to be giving her fashion advice, and besides, Lina had never taken advice from anyone, as far as she could remember. It made her feel a bit vulnerable — but she thought she'd indulge Elise if she wanted to help. After all, Elise had got her this precious meeting. It was a drinks party to celebrate the announcement of Conor Creighton's residency at the Atrium — eighteen whole nights. Maybe one day she'd have a residency, Lina thought, imagining the queue of eager punters snaking along the pavement outside the theatre, all there to see her, to hear her take on life.

'This one's nice.' Elise's voice broke into her thoughts once again. She was holding up an emerald green dress with a soft sheen and boat neckline that Lina didn't even realise she still had. 'Very Meghan Markle. You'll look elegant and sexy at the same time — just the impression you want to make.'

'I thought that I was trying to make him laugh,' Lina said wryly.

'You are,' Elise replied, holding the dress out to her. 'But face it, Lina. You're not one of those girls he sees day after day — you know, the ones who have no choice but to be funny because they're fat or ugly. You're funny and gorgeous, so you have to make the most of it. It's your USP.'

'My USP?' Lina guffawed. 'And by the way, that's a terrible thing to say.' She thanked God that Mama had gone out for the afternoon, so that she didn't have to be offended by this statement. She had a feeling that Inge and Elise wouldn't be natural friends, and the thought made her smile.

'So what?' Elise shrugged. 'It's the truth. Now, off you go to change and then we can work on the make-up.'

Lina took the dress out onto the landing to the grotty bathroom, which even in the muggy heat of mid-August managed to feel dank and chilly. She slid out of her T-shirt and denim cut-offs and pulled the dress on. It was tight on her hips and for a second she thought she wouldn't be able to pull it over them, but eventually, she dragged it upwards, putting her arms into the cap sleeves and extending one arm to pull the zip up. She wriggled a bit and stretched her arm further but couldn't get hold of the zip, so she swore under her breath. This was wrong, she told herself. All wrong.

'I know why I hid this dress away,' Lina said as she came out of the bathroom and went back into the flat, pushing open the bedroom door. 'It's too tight.' She looked down at her breasts, which were straining against the material of the dress, and her tummy bulged against the light fabric, even unzipped. 'I can't wear this, Elise.'

Elise, sitting on the bed, tilted her head to one side, then another. 'I think it looks perfect,' she said.

'Are you mad? I'll burst out of it if I move,' Lina said. 'And I don't feel comfortable, Elise. I feel a bit tacky, to be honest.'

Elise laughed. 'You look like a vamp, Lina, and that's just the look you need. Mack McCarthy will be blown away. Now, just let me zip you up, then show you how to do a sophisticated make-up look for the evening that's in it and you're good to go.'

Lina found herself letting Elise take over. She wasn't

normally compliant like that, but she was too tired to argue. Ever since Mama had arrived, with her peculiar routines and her endless night-time perambulations of the flat, complaining that she was unable to sleep, Lina had found herself growing wearier and wearier. Of course, Mama couldn't stay on the sofa, so she'd had to move into the bedroom with Lina and Tommy, bringing her night-time salves and her tablets and her glass with her false teeth along with her. Every time Lina woke to feed Tommy, she'd see them, glinting in the glass, a bizarre smile detached from a mouth. She had to cover it while she lay in bed, Tommy nuzzling against her, remembering all of the other times she'd shared a bed with her mother in the many places they'd lived. Her favourite bed had been one that floated, hanging from the ceiling on four taut wires – Lina had loved to swing gently back and forth on it, enjoying the sheer expanse of it and the feeling that she could stretch out as far as she liked without encountering her mother's bony form.

They had to share, Mama had told her once, because it was cheaper that way – she could rent a one-bed instead of a two-bed flat – but Lina had never believed that because of the way her mother would burrow down beside her, asking her to stroke her hair or hum a tune to help her to go to sleep. You're scared, she'd thought – that's what it is. She'd put her foot down when she was fourteen and wanted to have a friend over for the night, refusing to share a bed with her mother ever again. And yet, here she was, history repeating itself. Lina had the sense of her life closing in on her again: she'd fought so hard to get out, to leave Mama — there was no way she'd get sucked back in. No way.

Still, dealing with her mother took more strength than Lina had right now, so she was glad for Elise, even if she secretly wondered if they'd be friends by choice. That was the thing about being a new mum — you'd have a cup of tea with a serial killer if you thought it'd pass the time. Not that Elise was like that, she thought, as she let the other woman smooth eye shadow over her eyelids, coat her fair eyelashes with a thick slick of mascara. She was maybe a bit overenthusiastic, but she was harmless. She just wanted to banish the loneliness for a bit, just like the rest of them. Or at least Lina thought she did — she'd catch Elise looking at her a bit too hard sometimes, an expression on her face that looked uncomfortably like adoration.

'Now,' Elise said, taking a little black purse out of her bag, extracting what looked like a stencil and placing it on Lina's left eyebrow. She then took a brown pencil out and proceeded to fill in the eyebrow-shaped gap, humming to herself.

'Are you giving me eyebrows?' Lina said warily. She liked her eyebrows as they were — pale and barely visible. They suited her face.

'Eyebrows give shape to your eyes and your face — they're very important,' Elise said. 'You want to look fierce, but intriguing.'

Oh, Jesus, Lina thought.

Elise hummed away as she worked, before saying, 'Lina, what do you know about Jane, about her past?'

'What do you mean, what do I know?'

Elise continued to fill in the stencil, her tongue sticking out as she concentrated. Then she said, 'The time in the mental hospital.'

'What mental hospital? I'm not sure what you mean.'

'Oh.' Elise stopped working for a moment and put a hand to her mouth. 'I'm sorry, I thought you knew. I shouldn't have spoken. Forget I said anything.'

'She was in a mental hospital?' Lina said.

Elise sat back on the bed, a guilty look on her face. 'I feel terrible, Lina, I thought you knew. And I promised I wouldn't say anything.'

'It wouldn't surprise me,' Lina said. 'She has that look about her. Too quiet. You kind of wonder what she's hiding.' Elise locked eyes with her in that intense way she had, and Lina knew what she was thinking. The bruises. She felt suddenly uncomfortable, faced with a problem for which she had no solution and which she'd put away in the dark cave in her mind where she stored things she didn't like and which she hoped would magically disappear.

'Promise you won't say anything, though, will you?' Elise said, as she put the stencil back on Lina's eyebrow and continued her work. 'I'd hate her to think that I was the kind of person who couldn't keep a secret.'

'Promise,' Lina said, feeling that if she were Jane, that's exactly what she'd think. 'Scout's honour.'

She let Elise continue then, wondering why exactly Elise had told her. Was it out of concern for Jane or did she simply want to impress, knowing a secret that Lina didn't, even though she knew Jane better? Lina felt guilty and wrong-footed at the same time. She'd talk to Gracie, she decided. She'd know what to do.

'Ta-dah,' Elise said eventually, and Lina blinked, opening her eyes. She gave a little start at the woman staring back at her in the mirror. Lina had never worn much make-up, but this person was wearing a thick coating of it, like varnish. Lina's pale skin was now a kind of bronzy colour and her eyelashes were so long, she could feel them batting off her cheekbones. And, sweet Jesus, her eyebrows – great big black slashes over her eyes. Kim Kardashian would have been proud of them. 'Oh,' she said, unable to think of anything else to say – 'I look like a tramp' wouldn't do it, she thought.

'Amazing, isn't it? A few touches here and there and you're a whole new woman.' Elise popped a kiss on the top of Lina's forehead. Lina felt herself blanch – she didn't really like the touchy-feely stuff, and she wondered just how quickly she could get this gunge off without seeming rude. And as for the heels that Elise was lending her – a horrible nude pair that didn't match the dress – she'd be surprised if she could get to the bus stop in one piece in them.

'It is amazing,' she said faintly, getting up from her seat. 'I really am a whole new person,' and she gave a shaky laugh.

'Off you go then – break a leg!'

Lina looked at herself in the mirror again. I look like a tart, she thought miserably. 'Elise, I'm not sure. It's just a drinks thing ...'

'And you need to make an impact — you're not just another Mary or Anne from the arse end of nowhere — you're special. You're different.'

'I am?'

'Of course you are — you're exceptional, Lina, and you need to show it.'

'I'm exceptional,' Lina told herself.

'That's right. Keep telling yourself that and you'll begin to believe it,' Elise said, coming to stand behind her, placing a hand on Lina's shoulders. She tilted her head to one side. 'Hmm? You just need to believe in yourself.'

'I just need to believe in myself,' Lina said faintly.

'That's the spirit,' Elise said. 'Have you tried affirmations?'

'I'm not sure they're my thing,' Lina said.

'Oh, they are amazing. Gray told me about them and I can't stop myself now. Every morning, I wake up and I say something like, "I am glad to be awake for another wonderful day." It might seem a bit simplistic, but it's totally changed my perspective on life. I'm much better at gratitude now, for everything I have. I don't spend all my time moaning about what I *don't* have.'

Crikey, Lina thought. She'd never believed a word of that stuff, but faced with Elise's intense, hopeful stare, she tried, 'I am looking forward to this evening.' It wasn't true, but maybe if she said it often enough, she might begin to believe it.

Elise guffawed. 'Oh, for God's sake, you can do better than that. Try ... "I deserve success and I'm going to make it happen."'

'I deserve ... ah, no, Elise, I can't say that. It sounds silly.'

'Try it,' Elise said, fixing Lina with the kind of stare that told her she wouldn't give up in a hurry.

'I deserve success and I'm going to make it happen,' Lina repeated obediently. 'I deserve success and I'm going to make it happen,' she said again and again, as Elise looked on. After ten repetitions, Lina began to feel a tiny bit different – more together, more hopeful. 'I think it's working,' she said.

Elise clapped her hands with glee. 'See – told you!'

'Thanks, Elise,' Lina said.

'You are so welcome!' Elise gave a little squeal, and before Lina knew it, the other woman's arms were around her, squeezing her uncomfortably tightly. She smelled of something sugary, her hair brushing against Lina's lips. Yuck, Lina thought, extracting herself gently. There was a second's embarrassing silence, which was mercifully broken by the ringing of Lina's mobile, the alarm that she'd set to tell her she had five minutes to leave the house, and she thought, it's too late now. I haven't got time to change. 'Oh, Jesus – Mama! She's supposed to be here to mind Tommy. Where the hell is she?'

'Don't worry. I'll stay with the babies until she comes home. I'm sure she hasn't gone far,' and when Lina went to protest, Elise shook her head. 'Go. And when you seal the deal, we'll celebrate.'

'If there is anything to celebrate,' Lina said, picking up her bag and her notes, remembering her keys at the last minute, popping a kiss on Tommy's head. She'd never left them with anyone else for any length of time because, until now, she'd breastfed them exclusively, but she'd spent the best part of the last week expressing with the help of one of those milking machines, sitting while it buzzed and pumped her milk into the little bottles. She couldn't afford to buy her own, so instead Oona had come to the rescue and lent her one. Lina had let Mama take care of giving Tommy the bottle and she had to admit, her mother hadn't done a bad job of persuading her granddaughter to drink from it, even if it had felt strange leaving the feeding job to someone else: that she, alone, couldn't nurture her own child. She wasn't sure she liked it that much.

'Of course there'll be something to celebrate,' Elise said. 'Just remember your affirmation.'

'I deserve success and I'm going to make it happen,' Lina said.

'That's the spirit!'

'I deserve success ...' Lina repeated to herself as she ran out the door and onto the road, trotting along in Elise's silly heels down to the traffic lights. Someone wolf-whistled as she stood there and she felt as if the eyes of the whole world were on her. But it was too late now — she didn't have time to go home and change, to tell Elise that she didn't feel comfortable like this.

When she got on the bus, she sat behind the driver and caught her reflection in the window, and closed her eyes. She may have been a comedian, but she wasn't bothered about her physical appearance — she preferred to let the jokes do the talking. She didn't mind standing up in a room full of people all waiting for her to say something funny, but it had never depended on how she looked. Her usual gig uniform was a T-shirt and jeans. Women didn't need to dress like tarts to be funny — how she wished she'd had the time to explain this to Elise — nicely, of course. But then, Elise was only trying to help.

She took a tissue out of her bag and rubbed it over her lips, a smear of pinky-red coming away on the white. She wondered if she could just wipe it all off, but then, she'd need proper make-up remover and she didn't have the time. Suddenly, tears sprang to her eyes. Shit. This was her big break, and she was going to mess it up because she looked like a Barbie doll. 'Focus,' she ordered herself, taking her notes out of her bag, scanning the witticisms she'd written down, the list of topics she'd try to cover so that she'd really engage his attention. If she only had five minutes, she'd make them count.

She was concentrating so hard that she nearly missed her stop and had to trot over to the driver and call out, 'Here, please,' as he muttered something about giving a man a bit of notice. She hopped down off the bus and after a short hobble, wondering how on earth Elise managed to walk in these things, found herself standing at the top of a set of granite steps that led to the basement bar of a city-centre townhouse. A discreet brass plaque announced that it was Number 28. So posh it didn't even have a name, Lina thought as she hovered, standing back to let a couple pass. They were dressed in baggy jeans and T-shirts and one of them was wearing a grey beanie hat. Lina felt as if she were going to a hen do. 'Get on with it,' she ordered herself, followed by, 'I deserve success ...'

The steps led downstairs into darkness and she gripped the handrail, praying the stupid shoes wouldn't trip her up. When she got to the bottom, the darkness opened out into a white-painted brick corridor, completely deserted, that she walked nervously along, calling out, 'Hello?'

Eventually, a door opened and Lina could hear a blast of chatter, the hum of a party in full swing, before it closed again and there was silence. OK, Lina thought. If the door opens again, I'll walk through it. If it doesn't, I'll go home. She counted to ten, then twenty, then thirty. The silence in the corridor lengthened, and as she got to sixty, Lina's heart lifted. Right, time to go, she thought.

She was about to scuttle off when the door opened, letting out another blast of chat. Lina swore under her breath. There was nothing for it now. She trotted to the door, which was being held open by a man wearing an anorak. He must be cooking in that, Lina thought absently as he held the door open for her, shooting her a lascivious smile. 'In your dreams, bud,' she muttered as she scooted into the room. She felt like a cowboy who had entered a saloon in the Wild West, standing there, scanning the room, looking for a single person she recognised. Eventually, her eyes fell on a petite woman with dark hair and she swore under her breath. Of course Darcy would be here: her former sparring partner from the comedy world, with whom Lina had dreamt a thousand dreams of fame, before betraying her by having a baby, would never miss a party. Lina dipped her head, hoping not to make eye contact, but it was too late. Darcy was coming over.

'Well, will you look at what the cat dragged in,' she drawled, reaching out to pull Lina into a hug. It was kind of awkward because they hadn't seen each other in a while, so Lina wasn't sure whether to squeeze or to settle for an air kiss. She couldn't hug Darcy anyway, she realised, because she couldn't lift her arms up high enough. Darcy stood back then to look at her, and Lina wished that the ground would open up and swallow her. 'What's with the gangster's moll look?'

'Oh, Jesus, I know. A friend called over to help me get ready and she picked this out. I didn't have the heart to tell her that I don't dress like this ... normally,' she added.

'Well, it has a certain "in your face" quality.' Darcy laughed, her mouth a ring of bright-red matte lipstick. She was wearing skinny jeans and a vintage Guns N' Roses T-shirt and looked completely cool. She always had, ever since they'd met in The Dungeon, the city's grottiest comedy venue, and Darcy had given her the only piece of advice she'd ever heeded: 'Open with your best joke to reel them in, and save the second best for last.' It had worked and then she'd 'thrown it all away', to quote Darcy.

'Piss off,' Lina retorted. 'Listen, where's the drink? I need to forget myself for a few minutes.'

'Wait there,' Darcy ordered, marching off to a table filled with glasses, returning with two livid-looking drinks, handing Lina one and taking a big swig of the other. 'Ah, the watered-down cocktail,' she said, reaching into the bumbag around her waist and taking out a baby bottle of vodka. She poured half into her glass, then offered the bottle to Lina.

'I don't know ...' Lina said. 'I'm breastfeeding.' She was lying, kind of, because her mother was feeding Tommy, but she wasn't sure it was a good idea anyway. She needed to keep her wits about her.

Darcy rolled her eyes to heaven. 'You used to be fun.'

'I still *am* fun,' Lina protested. Darcy's response was to look at her closely, a grin splitting her face.

'What?'

'Nothing,' Darcy said.

'Oh, all right then,' Lina said, holding out her glass. 'It'll help me to relax.'

'Whatever gets you through, baby,' Darcy said, emptying the contents of the bottle into Lina's drink. Lina took a sip. It was sickly, but the vodka helped. She took another sip.

That's better, she thought, beginning to feel her shoulders loosen.

'So, what brings you out? I thought it'd be way past your bedtime,' Darcy said, taking a sip of her drink.

Lina wasn't sure whether to tell Darcy the truth. She was a bit competitive and if she knew Lina had five minutes with Mack McCarthy, she'd probably insist on tagging along, and then she'd outshine Lina with her slick jokes. Darcy was nothing if not well-practised. Her routine of sarky commentary might sound improvised, but Lina knew that Darcy rehearsed and rehearsed, leaving absolutely nothing to chance. She had to admire her friend's work ethic, even if the very thought of it made Lina feel suddenly weary. Am I up for this, she thought, taking another gulp of her drink, wondering what Tommy was doing right now and if they were missing their mum. She felt that familiar lurch in her stomach whenever she thought of her child, an anxiety to be with them, to smell their little baby smell, to feel their heaviness in her arms, their solid little body. Tommy wasn't just a baby, she realised now: they were a little person, a unique human being, which was kind of amazing.

'Oh, I thought it was time I started networking again,' she said vaguely. 'A friend of mine knows Mack and suggested I come along.'

Darcy raised her eyebrows. 'Does she know what he's like?'

'What do you mean?'

'Well, he can stall the most promising comedy career if you get on the wrong side of him.' Darcy gave a short laugh.

'Really?' Lina licked her lips nervously. The lip gloss Elise had applied tasted of Calpol, and she felt her stomach churn. She hadn't eaten anything either, she remembered now. Her head felt suddenly cloudy and she thought vaguely that she'd better put her glass down and concentrate on the matter in hand. 'I'll have to take my chances, I guess,' she said vaguely.

'Don't say I didn't warn you,' Darcy said.

'Job done,' Lina retorted.

'Might be easier if you're drunk.' Darcy giggled, opening her bumbag and taking out another baby bottle, pouring a generous tot into her own glass and then into Lina's. Lina tried to pull her glass away, but settled for a weak, 'Easy, Darcy, that's enough.' She took a tentative sip: it certainly tasted better now that there was more vodka in it than anything else. She held her glass against Darcy's and clinked it gently. 'Here's to making it big.'

'Hah,' Darcy said, raising her glass and taking a large gulp. 'Remember our two-hander?'

Lina blushed. She and Darcy had started to write a show a year before about two women in their early thirties who refused to grow up — basically, they were writing about themselves. They'd met every morning in a nondescript coffee shop near the train station, one laptop between them. Commuters sat around them sipping on coffees and looking at their phones, being generally busy, while the two of them guffawed at their own cleverness and wit. It seemed like a lifetime ago, Lina thought.

'Maybe we could pick it up again,' she said hopefully. 'I've a bit more free time now that my bloody mother has come to live with me.'

She was waiting for a response, but then she realised that Darcy wasn't listening. She was looking over Lina's shoulder, and when Lina turned to see, a handsome guy with shiny teeth and a bright, white T-shirt, auburn curls framing his face, was smiling at her friend, giving her a little wave. She suddenly understood the chasm that lay between her and her once-best friend, who, quite naturally, wasn't even slightly interested in Lina's bloody mother or the life she now led. She hadn't asked Lina one question about Tommy — not one.

'I'll leave you to it,' she said smartly. 'Thanks for the drink. It was great to catch up,' she lied.

'Hmm ... yeah, see ya,' Darcy said, still not looking at her. 'Coffee sometime, yeah?'

'Sure,' Lina said, knowing that she'd avoid it like the plague. 'See you around,' she said and attempted to shimmy off into the crowd in search of her five-minute meeting, except she realised that she was kind of drunk and the shimmy was more of a stumble. 'Whoops, sorry,' she said to one woman, who tutted and looked at her sternly.

'I am going to nail this,' she told herself firmly, pulling the dress down as far as it would go over her hips, and scanning the crowd for any sign of Mack McCarthy. She knew that he was small, but he always wore a cowboy hat, a big ten-gallon one — it was his trademark — and as she looked around, she caught sight of it in a corner. She made a beeline for it, elbowing people and muttering 'excuse me' as she pushed her way through. She *had* to see Mack McCarthy — she just wasn't leaving without having had her five minutes. Something about the encounter with Darcy had made her even more determined. She wasn't just some mummy has-been, all dreams of a career now out the window. She was a woman with something to say, and she was damn well going to say it. What was it Elise had urged her to repeat? 'I deserve this and I'm going to get it.'

Eventually, she reached the corner of the room where Mack McCarthy was holding court, sitting in a rattan chair under a fake palm tree, like an emperor. He was tiny, Lina realised, a weenchy little man under a huge hat, his feet, in faded red Converse high-tops, not even reaching the ground. She had the sudden urge to laugh and had to put her hand over her mouth to stem the giggles that threatened to overcome her. She coughed loudly to settle herself and went towards him, her hand outstretched.

'Hi, Mack, I'm Lina—' She was mid-sentence when she found that a girl with bright-pink hair, a T-shirt with the slogan 'Girl Power' on it in bright pink and black baggy jeans was standing in front of her, obscuring her view of Mack McCarthy. She looked like someone from an anime cartoon, with her huge blue eyes outlined in thick black eyeliner, her mouth a bright silvery-blue.

'Hi!' she said gaily, tilting her head to one side. 'I'm Abbie. And you are …?'

'Here to see Mack McCarthy,' Lina barked, craning her neck to see around Abbie, who'd placed herself even more firmly in Lina's line of sight. 'I have an appointment,' she added, as if she were at the dentist for a scale and polish, not watching an opportunity slip through her fingers.

'Uh-huh,' Abbie said gaily, still not moving.

'So, if you could just …' Lina made a batting movement with her arm, indicating that Abbie, whoever she was, should move out of her way and let her get on with the matter in hand.

'I'm Mack's PA. I take all pre-meetings for him.'

'Pre-meetings? What's a pre-meeting?' Lina was suddenly aware that she was slightly drunk, her words slurring. She thought that if she formed the words more carefully, this Abbie person would understand. 'I'm sorry,' she said, shaking her head. 'My friend Elise, her husband Gray trains Mack and she said I could have "five minutes". That's all I need, Abbie, so please let me just talk to him. Please?'

Abbie did that head-tilting thing again, looking at Lina like a cat looks at a hapless, wounded bird. Then she said, 'Tell you what. Give me your number and I'll see what I can do. It won't be tonight,' she gave a small smile, as if that was obvious, 'but I'll call you — 'kay?'

''Kay,' Lina agreed miserably, knowing that she'd blown it. Abbie was just being nice, giving her the brush-off without saying as much. She thought of Elise's hopeful face, all the effort she'd put into making Lina look like a Victorian prostitute, and she wondered how she'd tell her that she hadn't even spoken to the great man.

'Look, Abbie,' she said. 'I'm a comedian, a good one – or at least, I was, but now I have a five-and-a-half-month-old baby at home and a mother who is driving me insane, and this is the first time I've been out at night since before she was born – the baby, that is, not my mother, although it kind of feels like that – and I have this new routine in my head and I really, desperately need to feel that I have something else in my life, something to hang onto, to work towards, or else I'll lose my mind.' She felt the tears spring to her eyes and she had the sensation that she was somehow outside herself, looking down at this woman who, last year, would have marched up to Mack McCarthy, Abbie or no Abbie, and asked for what she wanted. Now, she was just some pathetic, washed-up mum, begging for a break from a teenager. She felt utterly humiliated, standing in front of Abbie like this, but she also felt that she couldn't go home empty-handed.

Abbie sighed and shook her head softly, a regretful look in her eye, acknowledging how pathetic Lina was. 'Look, don't tell another living soul, but there's a thing on after.'

'A thing?' Lina said hopefully.

'Yeah, in the Nameless Bar, do you know it?'

'Eh, yeah, of course I do,' Lina said. She had no

intention of admitting that she didn't — cool girls knew all the best places, and she was going to be cool if it killed her.

'Right, so, it's a small gathering, up close and personal, know what I mean?' Abbie gave her the tilted-head look again and Lina found herself nodding obediently, even though she wasn't entirely sure she did. 'You'll get your five minutes,' Abbie added with a patronising smile. 'Kay?'

''Kay!' Lina said, unable to believe her luck. She wondered if she should hug Abbie, but thought better of it. 'See you later!' she said brightly, weaving her way back through the crowd. She really couldn't wait to get to the Nameless Bar — but first of all, she had to be sick.

The night was cooler than it had been all summer and Lina stood outside the club, sucking in deep lungfuls of air. She felt slightly better now that she'd thrown up those dreadful cocktails — a little less woozy, even if her head was a bit woolly and she had a nasty taste in her mouth. Must find a newsagent's and buy chewing gum, she thought. But first, she had to find this mystery bar. She bit her lip, then opened her phone and composed a text: *Where's the Nameless Bar?* She waited, staring at the phone, cursing under her breath. 'Come on, will you?'

Why do you want to know? came the reply.

'For Jesus' sake!' Lina swore out loud. 'Can you not bloody give me a straight answer?' She tapped in a terse *Work*, then waited. She wondered why she had contacted

Seamus when she could have just looked it up on Maps. She felt a bit foolish then, a silly girl who needed a man to lean on, not a grown woman. She typed, *It's OK, I've found it*, just as his reply to her earlier question pinged. *Round the back of Dunnes Stores. Hipster place, no name on the door — you just knock three times to get in. You probably have to do some kind of shamanic ritual as well, but hey, hope it's worth it.*

Thanks for your sarcasm, she thought, typing a smiley face and sending her reply. *It could be my big break. Wish me luck!*

In reply, he sent her a dancing leprechaun, waving and wishing her a top of the mornin'. She found herself laughing out loud. He was quite funny, Seamus, she had to give him that — annoying, but funny. She looked at the exchange again on her phone, fully expecting him to add, *Wonder if you and Tommy would be up for a visit?*, the way he usually did, but when she didn't see anything further, she felt oddly disappointed. She'd thought she was in the driving seat, but maybe she'd been wrong.

She wished she'd brought a coat, she thought, as she walked quickly up Exchequer Street, her sandals clattering on the cobblestone path. She felt half-naked in the stupid dress, and she was cold for the first time in about three months. The summer had been so long and hot, each evening a muggy, heavy mix of noise and chatter from the bars and restaurants near her flat, which she'd listen to as she lay awake in the dense heat. Now, as August wore on, the nights had begun to cool down a bit, but the streets were still filled with people, crowds gathered outside the pubs, pint glasses in hand; people sitting at pavement café tables, looking out on the world going by, like sophisticated Europeans.

I could be in Paris, Lina thought, until a group of men in matching T-shirts with 'Craig's Stag' on them wove towards her and she debated whether to cross the street before they got to her, but in the end, she decided to brave it out. It didn't matter a bit how she was dressed: she deserved respect, she thought firmly, as one of them caught her eye. "Allo, luv!' he roared.

Lina rolled her eyes to heaven and kept walking, even as they formed a line across the pavement as if to bar her way. As she got close to them, one of them dropped on his knee and proclaimed his undying love for her. She stepped around him and kept on walking.

'Frigid bitch,' he shouted after her. She raised her middle finger in response and there was a roar of laughter. Lina felt instantly better, taking the bastards on like that and winning. Emboldened, she strode up the busy street, turning left and spotting a tatty metal doorway, just where Seamus had said it would be. She sucked in a deep breath. 'I deserve this and I'm going to get it,' she said to herself.

'Good for you,' a voice said beside her. Lina turned and found that she was staring at the top of a ten-gallon hat. Oh. My. God, she thought. I'm not ready. But she pinned a smile on her face and extended a hand. 'Hi, Mack, I'm Lina.'

He took her hand and she gripped his firmly, but then

found that he wouldn't let go. They both stood there for a while, holding hands, until he let hers drop. 'You joining us?'

'Sure,' Lina said. It was meant to sound sophisticated, but had come out of her mouth sounding like a bat squeak. He smiled and, when he'd knocked three times, held the door open for her. 'After you.'

'You're a gentleman,' she cooed, stepping into the gloom. Did I really say that, she wondered as she hesitated at the edge of the bar area, an orange-lit expanse of birch ply, that looked chic and homemade at the same time. A man in a huge beard was vigorously shaking a cocktail shaker, pouring a stream of green into a frosted champagne flute. Lina's stomach heaved. She looked to her right, to make some clever remark to Mack, but he'd vanished, and her heart sank when Abbie appeared beside her, like a bad fairy.

'You made it!' she said. She tilted her head to the side again and started furiously scribbling on the clipboard she was holding. 'So ...' she said. 'Mack has to talk to Darryl Dunne, the promoter,' she rolled her eyes to heaven at the mere mention of the country's top live-gig promoter, as if he were some boring parish priest who had to be entertained, 'but let me just bring you over and see if we can catch their attention, 'kay?'

''Kay!' Lina repeated cheerfully. She didn't want to let on to Abbie that she'd already met Mack and let him slip through her fingers — and besides, Abbie seemed to be the gatekeeper, so she'd better do as she was told.

Abbie turned and walked towards a roped-off section at the corner of the bar, which looked like the kind of VIP area Lina remembered from discos in Enniscorthy. It was all a bit dismal, she thought, as Abbie continued to scribble on her clipboard. Lina wondered what on earth she could be writing, but then she found herself standing in front of two middle-aged men: the tiny form of Mack lost on the cowhide banquette and, beside him, the considerable form of Darryl Dunne, a scruffy-looking man with a huge tangle of curly hair, which didn't look very clean, and a death metal T-shirt that strained to cover his big belly.

'Guys, this is Lina,' Abbie announced, as if Lina were the entertainment for the night. Lina cringed but pinned a big smile on her face and stuck out her hand. Mack did that hand-grasping thing again, taking her hand and holding onto her elbow, like a politician, and when she extended her hand to Darryl, he grinned and took hers in a limp, damp handshake. Lina wanted to shiver with repulsion. Still, she thought as she sat down on a little cowhide stool and accepted Abbie's offer of a drink, she supposed she *was* the entertainment in a way, and she'd just have to grin and bear it. This was her big break after all.

'So, a tequila sunrise for Lina,' Abbie said, as she returned to the table with the drinks, 'and two scotch 'n' sodas for the boys. Enjoy!' Lina turned to ask Abbie what was with the tequila sunrise and why she couldn't have a scotch, like the 'boys', but she supposed she'd better do what she was told, so she took a tentative sip. God, another sugary drink, she thought.

The two men ignored her for a while, in a huddle, clearly doing business, and Lina began to feel increasingly foolish. She took a couple more sips of her drink, then noticed, to her surprise, that her glass seemed almost empty. How did that happen? she thought. Still, she felt a bit better, a bit less conspicuous. She closed her eyes for a second and listened to the music, some deep house mix that she found herself moving to all of a sudden, her limbs seeming to follow the beat as she nodded her head in time to the rhythm. When she opened her eyes, she saw that another glass had been put in front of her, full of the same orange-and-red cough-mixture liquid. She lifted the glass to her lips and took another sip. Actually, it wasn't that bad.

When she opened her eyes, Mack was suddenly perched beside her on his own little cowhide stool. 'So ...' he said. 'Another bloody Irish comedian.' His tone was soft, and he was smiling under his hat, but Lina could detect more than a touch of the world-weary about it. Across from them, Darryl Dunne gave a cynical laugh, his belly jiggling up and down.

'Well, yes,' she said, eager to prove him wrong. 'But how many Irish comedians have a great routine about motherhood?'

'Motherhood,' he repeated, as if Lina had said 'rabies' or 'piles'.

'Look, I know it's not hip, but half the population are

parents' — she wasn't sure of this, but it sounded about right — 'yet all of the comedy they see is about thirtysomethings behaving badly, snorting too much and spending whole weekends at parties and it doesn't have any relevance to them. I think there's a lot of comedy in smelly nappies and the sheer grind of it all.'

'Smelly nappies don't fill clubs, Lina,' he said, shaking his head sadly at her naivety. 'Am I right, Darryl, or am I right?' At this, Darryl gave another chuckle, lifting his glass and swigging the whiskey as if it were orange juice.

'I know, but what about comedy podcasts or five-minute shorts on the other side of motherhood? It's not all fluffy bunnies, you know. What about cracked nipples and bad sex and all-night vomiting?'

Mack didn't say a word — instead he folded his arms and bent his head, as if in prayer, before letting out a big, deep sigh, as if he was carrying the weight of the world on his tiny little shoulders. 'How much have you got?'

'How much material? I'd say enough for five five-minute shorts, maybe more. I'm really fast,' she added. She wasn't really fast, not nowadays, with Mama 'babysitting' for half an hour at a time before presenting Tommy to her, announcing that they needed a nappy change or a feed. But she could be fast, she thought now, seeing a glimmer of hope on the horizon.

'Next week, in the International Hotel. Know the place?'

Next week what? Lina thought, taking a big swig of her

cocktail, pretending to be utterly chilled out about the prospect.

'I'm meeting Graham McSween. He's got a new digital-only TV channel. He's always on the lookout for stuff. Bring whatever you have and we'll see if we can get him interested.'

'Really!' Lina squealed. 'Oh, God, Mack, that would be amazing!' She threw her arms around him then, feeling his diminutive frame pressing embarrassingly against her uplifted cleavage, extracting herself rapidly. He was looking at her closely now, giving a small, knowing smile.

'Can't promise anything, but he's the man anyway. So … now that's out of the way, you up for a party?'

'God, yes!' Lina said, finishing her cocktail.

'That's the spirit,' he said, looking a great deal more cheerful. He looked around and, as if by magic, Abbie appeared with her giant clipboard to spirit Lina away. Five minutes later, she found herself in a taxi with Abbie, driving very slowly up a crowded Camden Street, drunken students tottering across the road between the busy bars and nightclubs, a smell of frying onions in the air from the hot-dog stands. Lina's stomach rumbled and she remembered that she hadn't eaten.

Abbie was friendlier now. She'd put away the clipboard, thankfully, and they chatted about college and careers – Abbie had laughed when Lina had described life at Download, the hours spent combing content, how there really was no end to the number of videos with dogs singing or cats re-enacting scenes from *Game of Thrones*. 'God, that's so funny,' she said. 'You could do a routine on that alone, it'd be hilarious!'

'Maybe I will,' Lina said happily, feeling herself blossom under Abbie's appreciative gaze. No one had told her she was funny or talented since the good old days with Darcy — apart from Elise, which didn't count because she was a friend. Sure, people had laughed at her jokes, but nobody had ever taken her aside and said that she had potential, that she could actually make it in this business. And now, just when she'd thought that door had more or less closed for her, it had opened, and a bright-yellow light was streaming through it, beckoning her. She hadn't felt as excited, as energised, in ages.

'So, how did you start working for Mack?' she asked Abbie.

'Oh, my dad has a production company,' Abbie said vaguely, waving her hand as if to bat away the question. 'Ooh, hot dogs,' she said as the taxi passed another stand. 'Driver, can you pull up for a second?'

The two of them clambered out of the car, all giddy giggles, and skipped the queue for the stand, Abbie striding imperiously to the front and informing a boy with acne that she was, 'like, super-busy, so if you don't mind ... you're an angel!'

Lina laughed as she joined her. 'That's so cheeky!'

'Listen, cheek is the first thing you learn in this business,' Abbie said. 'You should know, Lina.' She was smiling, but she had her killer-cat expression on and Lina wasn't entirely sure that Abbie was joking. 'Still, I have to give it to you — you've boldly gone where no man has gone before! Good for you. Mack likes that — he likes guts. You'll go far.'

'I will? I mean, I will,' Lina said firmly, after she'd told the man to hold the onions — she didn't want to breathe fumes all over Mack. And when Abbie high-fived her, she high-fived Abbie back, the two of them collapsing in giggles as they climbed back into the taxi.

'Onwards, my good man,' Abbie said, and the two of them exploded with laughter, the smell of fried sausage now mingling with air freshener in the cab.

'Where exactly are we going?' Lina said, mouth half-full of hot dog. They were driving over the hump of a bridge on the canal now, turning left down a narrow laneway. The street lighting was poor and the rows of tall Georgian houses seemed to loom over them, dark shadows filling the car. They'd left the jollity of Camden Street behind and suddenly Lina felt uneasy. 'It's just, I said I'd be home. My mother's minding the baby, you see ... What time is it anyway?' She made to reach into her bag to lift out her phone, but Abby's hand on her arm was firm.

'Will you relax? It's just an after-party for Conor Creighton — everyone will be there. Of course, if you'd rather head home, that's no problem. I'll just tell the driver to drop you off. It's on account,' and she gave a little shrug, as if she wasn't bothered either way.

'Well, maybe I could just stay for a half an hour ...' Lina found herself saying.

Abbie shrugged. 'Sure, whatever.' She made it sound as if it didn't matter to her, and when Lina looked at her, her face was closed. She took a giant phone out of her pocket and started tapping rapidly on it, giving a little chuckle and shaking her head as she did so. 'You. Are. So. Fucking. Funny,' she told the phone.

Lina found that she wanted to know who Abbie was laughing at or with. She wanted to be part of the gang – to feel that she was one of them, whoever 'they' were; that she was in on the joke. She nudged Abbie and said, 'C'mon, let's party!'

'That's, like, so amazing! Let's do it!' Abbie said. They high-fived again and got out of the car, laughing away.

11

Jane

It was the waiting that was the worst, Jane thought as she lay back in the dentist's chair. Mark hadn't laid a finger on her since that night, over a month ago, when she'd come back late from Gracie's, but that didn't matter. It had happened twice now and Jane knew that it was only a question of time before it happened again. She wished there was some kind of sign that she could look out for. She remembered how Mister Magoo, her childhood dog, would lift his ears and his tail would stand up on end when he was about to attack another dog. He'd circle the other animal more and more rapidly, nose twitching, and then, with a growl, he'd launch himself at it, and Jane would have to grab hold of his collar to extract him from the fight. But no matter how carefully she monitored Mark, how vigilant she was, examining his every expression, watching his body language like a hawk, she realised that she just couldn't tell when he was about to strike.

Waiting and watching, Jane had found herself reliving the punch, a flashback playing in her head whenever she had a quiet moment: she could feel the pain in her gut, the nausea as she'd doubled over and hit the travertine tiles. *It's wrong, it's wrong, it's wrong*: the mantra kept playing over in her head, even though she tried to quieten it by keeping busy, cleaning the house as never before, chopping and stirring and cooking and hoovering under every mat and into every corner, Owen on a playmat beside her, her face setting into a kind of mask, a tightness settling on her forehead and pulling at her lips and jaw. Sometimes she'd wake up at night lying beside Mark, and she'd feel the throbbing in her temples, the hot-poker jab to her upper jaw from the tension of clenching it so tightly. It had got to the point where opening her mouth to eat or brush her teeth caused her excruciating pain, which was why she was in this pink-painted dentist's room now, lying back in a comfy grey-plastic recliner, the dentist looming over her with his orange-tinted specs.

He'd been recommended by Gracie and, to pay for this consultation, she'd had to hide away little bits of housekeeping money so Mark wouldn't notice, which was hard because he checked all the receipts forensically. But somehow she'd managed, 'forgetting' to bring one home after a trip to the organic supermarket, and because it was so hideously expensive, she'd buried forty euro there. And there had been an extra dry-cleaning trip, which he also hadn't picked up on. Jane found that lying was effortless, but then she'd already known that. She'd learned that all those years ago.

'Hi. Graham Byrne,' the dentist had said, when she was ushered in by the dental nurse, extending a hand and giving Jane's a firm shake.

'Jane,' she'd muttered, unable to open her mouth wide enough to say it loudly. In spite of his dark-ginger beard, he looked about fifteen, but his teeth were helpfully shiny, and Jane had felt slightly more reassured as she'd followed his gentle instructions to lie back in the chair. 'Svetlana will just put on some glasses for you,' he said soothingly, and the dark-haired dental nurse slid a pair of plastic goggles onto Jane's face.

'Now,' he said happily, putting on his giant dentist's torch so he looked like a miner going down into a deep cave. 'Open for me now, please, Jane, nice and wide.'

Jane tried, but all she could manage was about an inch. 'Say, ah,' he added helpfully. Jane tried again, but the sound was more of an 'uuh' because of her jaw. 'I'm sorry—' she began, but he just said, 'No problem, Jane, you don't have to worry about anything.' Then he pressed each temple with his fingers and the pain was so bad Jane gave a little scream.

'Sorry, Jane, I'll be just a jiffy. Ah-ha, ahum ... ah, yes,' he muttered, before standing up, switching off his caver's torch and leaning on the counter behind him, which was filled with plaster moulds of wonky teeth. 'You've got very bad TMJ,' he'd said matter-of-factly.

'What's TMJ?' Jane managed eventually.

'It stands for your temporomandibular joint,' he began, and when Jane looked at him blankly, added, 'It's a very nasty disorder that affects the joint at your temple. Lots of teeth-grinders get it, or people who have a lot of stress in their lives,' he said. 'They're inclined to clench their jaws without realising that that's what they're doing, and it causes considerable pain. Would that describe you, Jane?'

Jane felt like laughing in his face but found that she couldn't open her mouth wide enough to do so. 'I suppose I could be a bit stressed ...' she said. 'I've just had a baby and there have been a lot of late nights.' She tried to smile then, as if having a newborn and late nights made her deliriously happy and, at the same time, just the teensiest bit stressed. She wondered what Graham would say if she told him the truth.

He looked at her carefully, and she realised that even though he might look about fifteen, he was astute. He didn't say anything for a few moments, and Jane understood that he was inviting her to talk. She nearly blabbed then, lying with her protective glasses on in the chair of this complete stranger, but she stopped herself in time. She didn't trust people in positions of power like this — they said they only had your best interests at heart, but Jane knew from experience that that wasn't true.

'Well,' Graham said, when Jane remained silent, 'I'd recommend two things. First, help with your TMJ to return movement to your jaw and, second, a mouthguard to stop it happening again.'

'What kind of help?'

Graham bustled towards his computer and started tapping. 'This might sound a bit left-field, but a few of my patients have had great success with cranial osteopathy. Now, let me see ...' His printer whirred into action. 'It's a very gentle therapy that helps you to loosen the muscles in your temple. Give it a try.'

'Thanks,' Jane said, taking the piece of paper from him. She didn't even look at the address because she knew there was no way she could afford it. There was only so much squirrelling away of supermarket money that she could do.

'And then there's the mouthguard. Svetlana will take the impressions,' he said, 'and we'll put that in motion. That really helps with the grinding. Svetlana, can you do a couple of impressions for me?'

At this, Jane sat up, the piece of paper in her hand. 'Sorry,' she murmured. 'How much would a mouthguard be? It's just ... I'm a single mother,' she lied, hoping he hadn't noticed her wedding band.

'Ah. Well, normally they're about three hundred euro,' Graham said cheerfully, 'but you can claim some of the cost on your social insurance. And we can waive the factory fees, which will bring the cost down. Oh, and we have an instalment plan that's very reasonable ...'

He was practically giving the mouthguard away, and both he and Svetlana looked at her hopefully. 'Let me think about it,' Jane said, getting up out of the chair, thinking, I need more than a mouthguard to fix my problems. 'But thank you,' she added, surprising herself by wanting to give him a little hug. Kindness was somehow harder than cruelty, she thought. It made you feel like jelly inside.

'Come back to me any time, Jane,' he said.

Gracie had offered to babysit Owen while Jane went to the dentist's and she returned to find the babies playing in the garden with Gracie's au pair, or whatever she was. Gracie behaved as if Sunny wasn't there, which Jane thought was a bit odd, but she didn't question it. Gracie didn't like being put on the spot.

'So, how did it go?' Gracie said now as Jane took Owen from her, holding him tightly, feeling his lovely soft skin next to her cheek.

'He was very nice,' Jane said. 'He recommended cranial osteopathy for it, but I don't know ...'

'Oh, it's brilliant,' Gracie said. 'I got some done on Jasper when he was born and it really seemed to settle him. Did he give you Jasmine's details?'

Jane really didn't want to entertain this nonsense that she couldn't afford, but she rummaged in her bag and extracted the card, examining the words 'Jasmine Devlin: Cranial Osteopathy', with a mobile number. 'Oh, yes, it is Jasmine,' she said. 'I must give her a ring.'

'She does lots of low-cost work,' Gracie said softly. 'So don't be afraid to call her. I'm sure she'd be happy to work something out.'

How do you know? Jane wondered, as her friend stood in the back garden, in her rainbow-coloured leggings and vest top, looking as if she were about to run a quick marathon, having first whipped up a batch of scones and taught Jasper long division. How do you have this sixth sense? Is that what friends do? She wasn't sure because she'd never really had that experience before. She'd thought she'd had it with her sister, Helen, the two of them allies against their parents on the long, dreary Sundays after church. She could remember them now, doubled over with laughter in the kitchen as they sliced white-bread sandwiches into quarters for the twenty or so from the congregation gathered in the 'good room' at the front of the house. They'd sing all the hymns from that morning's service, this time inserting their own lyrics, rude or funny: it didn't much matter — anything was material. They'd collapse in laughter as they imitated the Reverend Conander, their visiting priest, with his long, mournful drawl, the two of them making so much noise with their stifled giggles that Mam would beetle through the kitchen door: 'Will the two of you just whisht?' she'd hiss, trying to hide the smile on her face. 'The whole of Castlemonkstown can hear you laughing away, like the village fools you are.'

As soon as Mam had left, they'd succumb to the giggles again. 'You and me against the world,' Helen used to say, as the two of them would pile the sandwiches onto plates, filling the big teapot, into which Mam had dumped half a tea caddy of leaves, with hot water. Then, assembling their expressions into the right ones of reverence and politeness, they'd busy themselves serving the county's Baptists, trying to keep a straight face at the sheer dullness of the conversation. After that, to while away the interminable Sunday afternoons, they'd go up to their shared bedroom to listen to *The Chart Show*, singing Avril Lavigne or Christina Aguilera's hits as loud as they could manage without Dad finding out that they were listening to 'the Devil's music', as he called it. 'Honestly,' Helen would pronounce, as she stuck her head out the window to smoke the cigarette she'd filched from someone at school, 'you'd swear we were bloody Amish, we're so backward. It's 2003, for God's sake, not 1953.'

Helen used to be the bold one, the boundary-pusher, in the very limited way allowed her by Mam and Dad, and she, Jane, had been the good girl. They'd assumed their roles without question – until Tom. Jane never could understand why her sister had betrayed her like that, had sat in front of her on the sofa in the good room that Saturday afternoon and said those things: that it was for her own good, that it was a sin and that telling Mam and Dad had been the only choice open to her. 'Don't you understand?' she'd said later, as they'd stood in the porch of St Dympna's. No, Jane thought now. No, I bloody well did not.

Now, here Gracie was, inviting her to say something, to confide in her. Jane found that she'd desperately wanted to tell her friend, but she also understood that she couldn't because she knew what would happen next: that Gracie would tell her she was a complete fool to stay with Mark, that she should leave immediately, that no woman should put up with it and so on. And Jane didn't need to hear that because she was all out of options. All that she had was Mark and Owen – nobody else. The rest, she'd left behind fifteen years ago. Gracie was so kind, taking her under her wing that day, letting her rest in that lovely golden home of hers, minding Owen today, so she could see that kind dentist – but could she trust her? Jane bit her lip. No, she decided. No – she could trust no one.

Now, leaving Gracie's, she put the backpack on the ground, balancing it on the handy little legs that folded out from the main frame and slotting Owen in. He kicked his feet with excitement, babbling away as Jane lifted the backpack up.

'Here, let me help you,' Gracie said, lifting it onto her shoulders. 'There,' she said, when Jane had adjusted the straps. 'You look as if you're off to climb Everest!'

'Not quite,' Jane said. 'Unless you count making chicken Kiev Everest.' Chicken Kiev was one of Mark's favourites and Jane tried to make it once a week for him, even though the greasy garlic butter that oozed out of the rolled and breaded chicken breasts made her stomach heave. He would be happy, though, which was what mattered.

'I do nowadays,' Gracie said. 'In fact, the smallest things feel like Everest these days.' She gave a little shrug. That wasn't like Gracie, Jane thought, as she looked at her friend, noticing the dark shadows under her eyes, the way she stood, shoulders hunched, on the doorstep, as if bowed under a heavy weight. She hesitated, unsure what to say or do; she wasn't used to being in charge — to being a leader rather than a follower. 'Ehm, is it work?' she tried timidly.

Gracie shrugged. 'Work, home ... I'm not sure any more.' She rolled her eyes to heaven. 'Does it sound terrible if I say I sometimes wish I'd never had Jasper?' She whispered the words, as if Jasper, inside with Sunny in the lovely playroom, might hear her.

Jane reached out a hand. 'Gracie ...'

'Oh, I don't mean it like that — that he'd never been born. I mean that sometimes I wish I could go back to my old life, when things were simple, you know? All I had to do was concentrate on one thing — now, I feel that my brain is constantly flitting from one thing to another: from Jasper and wondering if he's OK or happy or if I'm doing a single thing right with him, to Jake and that website of his and wondering when on earth it will make us money or if he'll just have to keep buying new jeans and T-shirts for the next hoop they make him jump through. I've a feeling that development company is going to pump him for secrets, then get someone else to do it, but can I tell him that? Oh, no,' she said bitterly. 'He'll say I'm "wrecking his buzz", ruining the one good thing in his life — as if we don't matter. As if *we're* not good things in his life, do you know?'

Jane nodded. She wanted to feel sorry for Gracie, she really did, but part of her wished she had plausible, normal problems like Gracie's — problems that could be fixed. 'Maybe he has to work the website thing out for himself,' she said. 'That way, he won't blame you if the worst comes to the worst.'

'I know,' Gracie said. 'It's just I want to save him from the hurt. He hasn't been himself since he was made redundant and I couldn't bear it if he was to get shafted again.'

'But you can't help him,' Jane said. 'He's a grown-up and you can't control what happens to him.' In fact, she thought, control is probably your issue — not that I'm about to say that to your face.

'Sometimes I think I have two children, not just one,' Gracie blurted out.

'Oh, Gracie,' Jane said, putting her arms around her friend. 'Have you talked to him about how you're feeling?'

Gracie shook her head sadly. 'I don't know how. You know what it's like: the days pass in this haze of nappies and bottles and your whole being is just focused on this new baby, and so you ... forget each other.'

'Hmm, I know,' Jane said vaguely. She didn't really know and as she listened, and nodded and gently suggested that Gracie talk to Jake, she thought about how lucky

Gracie was that she could just 'forget' Jake like that, as if he was something she'd left under the sofa cushions. How she wished she could forget Mark, just blot him out of her mind, as if he'd never existed.

At the thought of him, Jane automatically checked her watch, trying to do it furtively, so Gracie wouldn't notice, but of course she did, and Jane saw the look of hurt in her eyes. Sorry, she thought, but I have to get home. My life depends on it. 'So ...' she said. 'Listen, Gracie, I'm sorry, but I have to get back.'

Gracie nodded miserably.

'We'll talk again, OK? I'll give you a call,' Jane said, as she turned and walked down Gracie's gravel driveway, feeling like the worst friend in the world.

She didn't know why she'd suddenly begun to think about Tom now. Or rather, she did: because it was the only real relationship she'd had before meeting Mark. Imagine, she thought, as she sat on the bus, looking out at the late-summer suburban streets, that that was the sum total of her experience. No wonder she hadn't seen Mark coming.

Tom had been the new English and Drama teacher, and the first person under the age of forty to grace Sacred Heart secondary school, Castlemonkstown, in a century, as her friend Donal used to joke. With his dark hair, intense blue eyes and his lace-up Doc Martens, Mr Moloney had been the talk of the school when he'd arrived. 'Sure, I'd nearly fancy him myself,' Donal had said the first time he'd walked into their fifth-year classroom, a copy of *Macbeth* under his arm. 'He looks kind of Byronic,' he'd added, doing a little sketch of the teacher in the margins of his textbook.

Ironically, Jane hadn't liked him at all. She'd found his intensity irritating, the way he'd perform the long soliloquies in 'the Scottish play', as he insisted they all call it, taking both Macbeth and Lady Macbeth's parts, giving it both barrels as he strode around the classroom. She'd found him over the top, too emotional. She wasn't used to that because everyone at home went to so much trouble to keep emotions hidden. So, when he'd pointed at her one day and asked her to come to the top of the class, she had no idea what he wanted. Jane had never been asked to come to the top of the class in her life. She'd always hidden safely away at the back, where no one would see her, and as she'd stood there opposite Mr Moloney, she could hear the whispers and titters of the class.

'Right,' he'd said. 'You be Lady Macbeth and I'll be her wimpy husband, who's too scared to kill Banquo. Remember, you're much stronger than me, so you have to urge me along to get me to see things your way.' He'd fixed his blue eyes on hers. 'Right, I'll cue you in.'

Jane had nodded obediently.

He'd tutted then. 'Where's your book,' he said, 'so you can read the lines?'

'Oh, I don't need it,' Jane had said. 'I know them all already.'

'"I know them all already,"' Mia Delaney mimicked from the back of the class, and there had been a guffaw of laughter.

'Mia, do you want to come up here and perform for us all, then?' Mr Moloney had said sharply.

'No,' she had replied quietly.

'No, what?'

'No, Mr Moloney. Sorry.'

'That's more like it,' he'd said. 'Now, Jane, from Act One, scene seven.

'"Prithee, peace:

I dare do all that may become a man;

Who dares do more is none."'

The class had been so silent then, you could hear a pin drop. Jane had felt a buzzing in her ears and she could see Donal out of the corner of her eye, holding up the relevant scene in the book. She had taken a deep breath.

'"What beast was 't, then,

That made you break this enterprise to me?

When you durst do it, then you were a man;

And to be more than what you were, you would

Be so much more the man."'

The deafening silence continued when she'd finished and then Donal had murmured, 'Holy cow.' There had been laughter and a ripple of applause and Tom — Mr Moloney — had told them to pipe down. He'd put a hand on her shoulder then, warm and firm. 'To your seat, Lady Macbeth.'

It had been like an electrical current flowing through her, she'd thought later as she'd put her books in her bag, something that had made her feel truly alive. All she could think of was how she might do it again, might perform with Mr Moloney. She'd found herself half-looking out for him all day, seeing if she could spot his leather-jacket-clad figure disappearing into the staffroom or could hear him admonishing the third years, telling them that they were like a pack of hyenas with their baying and howling when they should have been quietly at work. But there'd been no sign of him and Jane had found herself oddly disappointed.

But as she'd been leaving to get on the school bus, herself and Donal walking across the windswept school car park, a voice had called her. 'Hey, Lady Macbeth.'

'I'll catch you up,' she'd told Donal, making a face when he'd given her a look, and she'd turned to see Tom standing beside a silver Ford Fiesta, his leather satchel slung over his shoulder.

'You were very good in there. Very powerful.'

'Thanks,' Jane had said, all traces of her Lady Macbeth energy having left her now. She'd felt as if she were herself again, small, pale brown, insignificant.

'Don't be afraid of it,' he'd added as she'd shuffled off again. 'It's your gift.'

My gift, Jane thought as the bus neared her stop and she packed Owen back into his little backpack, pressing the bell and waiting for the driver to stop. See where that got me.

*

Jane looked around the hall when she got home, as if Mark might be lurking somewhere, before realising that he wasn't home yet, a lightness filling her as she put her handbag down and took Owen off her back, placing the backpack gently on the ground. 'Right,' she said brightly to her baby boy as she took him out and slipped him into his little bouncing chair. 'Let's get dinner underway.' At the sound of her sing-song tone, Owen let out a little chuckle and reached out to grab one of the plastic teddy bears on the bar in front of him, sending it rattling around and giving a gurgle of satisfaction as he did so. 'Good boy,' Jane said. 'That's new — you're very clever.' His response was to bash the bears again and again, each rattling turn sending him into a gurgling fit.

'Silly boy.' Jane smiled, as she sliced a chicken breast open, flattening it out on the counter. She washed her hands and opened the fridge to get the butter, popping a chunk into the pestle and mortar, and then chopping garlic and parsley, adding them to the butter. When she'd finished, she put the Kievs in cling film and placed them in the fridge. 'Now what?' she said to herself as she wiped her hands on some paper towels. 'I know,' she said to Owen, 'I'll make you some stewed apple for when you start eating solids — would you like that?' Owen's answer was to bash the teddy bears again. 'Well, good,' Jane said, bending down to the vegetable basket in the cupboard and pulling it out, extracting a couple of sweet apples from amongst the neat piles of potatoes and onions.

When Mark walked into the kitchen and said 'hello', Jane shrieked, a hand, with a vegetable peeler in it, to her throat. He put his hands up, as if in surrender.

'Sorry, I thought you'd heard me come in.'

Sorry? Jane looked at Mark warily, wondering what the sorry was about, mind whirring. 'I was just getting the dinner ready—' she began, but he interrupted her.

'I have good news.' His normally stern features broke into a smile, which made him look about ten years younger, and Jane had the tiniest glimpse of who he might have been once, before he became this ... She tried to think of the word and her mind kept fixing on 'monster'.

'Oh.' Jane had trained herself not to react, not to make anything other than the blandest statements, a carefully neutral look on her face. 'That's nice.'

'Nice? It's fantastic!' he said happily, coming towards her, arms outstretched. Jane recoiled, leaning back over the worktop as far as she could. For an awful moment, she thought he was going to hug her, but instead he rested his hands on her shoulders paternally. 'I'm going to make partner! Isn't that great?'

'It is? I mean, it is,' Jane agreed. 'It really is. Well done,' she ventured.

'Well, it's not in the bag yet, but John Fogarty says it's as good as,' he said. He suddenly grabbed Jane by the waist and pulled her to him. Oh God, no, she thought. Please, no.

But it turned out that all he wanted to do was dance,

placing an arm around her waist, lifting her hand in the air with his and beginning a slow waltz around the kitchen. She'd forgotten Mark could dance: he'd taken lessons before their wedding so he 'wouldn't make an ass' of himself when they took to the floor. She'd thought it was charming, and it was at the time — there were lots of fond *awws* from the guests, all of the teachers at St Attracta's forming a circle and clapping along in time with the music. But it was also typical of a man who wouldn't let himself, or anyone else, make a single mistake, in case they'd be 'shown up' in some way. As they waltzed around the kitchen, Owen gurgling in the background, Jane followed her husband's footsteps, a rhythmic one-two-three, and she wondered which Mark was real — this one, or the other, the one who could punch her like a boxer and leave her on the floor.

Later, after dinner, when she'd listened patiently to him explaining how he'd initiate a new invoicing system when he became partner, nodding and smiling away, accepting the glass of champagne from the bottle that he insisted on opening, even though, as far as she could tell, he hadn't actually got the job yet, the phone rang. Mark had insisted on installing a landline, even though not a living soul used them nowadays, and for a second, Jane didn't recognise the ring tone, but when he said, 'Who could that be?' she said, 'I'll get it', desperate to get out of the dining room, to suck in deep breaths in the hall as the phone rang and rang.

'Darling?' he said from the dining room.

'I'm just picking up,' she said, bending down to the

phone in its cradle on the hall table. The shrill ringing
made her ears hum. She picked the phone up, pressed the
green connect button and put it to her ear. 'Hello?'

'Jane?'

At the sound of her sister's voice, Jane collapsed on the
floor, the phone clattering off the white tiles.

12

Gracie

Sunny had done a brilliant job, Gracie thought as she and her mother sat down to lunch in the den: salmon with a mixed-grain and pomegranate salad. She'd made a little tower of the salad, with the lovely jewelly pomegranate seeds and baby carrots, a sprinkling of feta to finish it off, and on top, had lain a perfectly cooked piece of organic wild salmon. Others might say it looked like a beautiful painting, but to Gracie it felt like a reproach, particularly with her mother sitting across from her, a woman who had been able to conjure up a three-course meal out of half a tin of peas and a sliced pan.

The lunch was a thank-you for the loan of the place

in Brittas, but already Gracie was beginning to wonder if she couldn't have just sent a card in the post. She looked longingly at the bright, hot late-August day and wished that she was anywhere but here.

'My goodness, this is delicious,' Mum said. 'What a treasure Sunny is! But then, I suppose you never were much good at anything domestic, were you?'

'Well, I wouldn't say that, Mum,' Gracie said sharply. 'There was that pillowcase I did for my Junior Cert project. That turned out well.'

'Colette finished it off for you – do you not remember?' her mother said, helping herself to another delicious mouthful. 'No. Your sister was the domestic one.'

And I was the failure on all fronts, Gracie thought miserably. Colette, her older sister, was the Golden Child: brilliant at camogie and tennis, a straight-A student who cooked like an angel. Not that it had got her anywhere. Now, she lived with her husband and five children in a lovely semi-rural location and spent her entire time in the car, ferrying the kids to their activities and playing tennis. All that talent for nothing. She wanted to say that to her mother – look at me now, Mum. I may not have any real talent, like Colette, but I can get things done; I'm essential to my company, a good mum to Jasper and ... and ... there, her mind seized, as she felt the first tingling of the headaches that had become so regular recently. She had never had a headache in her life, but now her scalp began to tighten and she had that cotton-wool feeling in her head, which was so crammed with things she thought it might burst. She'd wake in the middle of the night, chest pounding, and go over it, the long list of things that had to be done every day, mentally ticking each item as she went. The problem was, she couldn't remember what she'd ticked by the time she got to the bottom, so she'd have to get out of bed and write everything down. Only when she'd committed the list to paper would she be able to lie back down in bed, mind empty at last.

She had thought her maternity leave would be so different: she'd relax, spend more time with Jake, bond with Jasper, do a little yoga, hang out with the girls in the park, but ever since Brittas, which had only been three weeks ago but felt like a lifetime, things seemed to be sliding out of control. For a start, Jake and she were sort of not talking, ever since she'd forgotten to collect Jasper from Mum's on the one occasion that Mum had reluctantly agreed to babysit while Sunny was on holiday for two long weeks. Mum rarely babysat, and after this latest episode, Gracie could remember why. They'd had to call Jake out of a presentation to the board of the venture capital firm who were to invest in his business. 'And I had to explain,' he'd said, face red with indignation, 'that I would have to reschedule this critical meeting, to which thirty people were dialling in from five different time zones, because I had to collect my child from my mother-in-law so she could play her Thursday round of bridge.'

When he put it like that, it didn't sound good. He had

apologised later. 'I'm sorry, hon, I sounded like a complete Neanderthal there. I'm just under pressure, that's all. There's no reason why my work stuff should come before yours.'

She'd been magnanimous about it, but only because she'd hidden the fact from him that she hadn't been in work at all that day, as she'd said she was. Instead, she'd switched off her phone, so no one from Cutlery could get hold of her, and wandered down to the beach at Sandymount, by herself, and walked the vast expanse of muddy sand all the way to Booterstown, four miles away. Even on a hot, sunny day, the sky a bright blue, this walk was always a bit bleak, with its view of the silver hulk of the city's incinerator and a huge plume of smoke rising into the sky as people's rubbish was burned to a crisp; the little bump of Howth always looked like the shell of a tortoise from this distance, and a huge rusting tanker had slid across the sea. Gracie wasn't much of a walker, but she'd found herself pounding the sand, the rhythmic slap of her feet on the silt a comfort, a release from the thoughts whirring in her brain, which never seemed to stop.

Besides, she thought now, as she picked at her food at the lunch table, she was glad that, after a year of moping around the place, Jake seemed to be happy, even if she did have her doubts about the pace of progress with his new company. He was all smart dress and busyness, tapping away at his laptop, his mop of blond hair now neatly trimmed; there were long phone calls to far-flung places and virtual high-fiving of people on Skype and breakfast meetings in the kitchen, which she would have to vacate to allow men who looked just like Jake to sit around and earnestly discuss the merits of slasher versus supernatural horror 'genres'. When she'd pass through the kitchen, drifting in to get a coffee or something for Jasper, heads would turn and she'd be given polite, pitying glances. The Little Woman.

If only, Gracie thought now, as her mother updated her on everyone in the old neighbourhood who was dead or on their way there. She didn't even fit that role, with her housekeeper and the job which, as she'd suspected, was now inching into her maternity leave, like a supertanker sliding through ice. She had a meeting in work this afternoon, one of three that week, and even though Gracie was pleased that they needed her so much, the meetings were exhausting, big, long epics full of bluster and faffing, which she thought could actually be done in a third of the time and without the verbal jousting, so that she could go home and put her five-month-old child to bed. Worse, Jasper had taken to waking two or three times a night. Gracie knew that it was because she'd eased off on the discipline of the sleep routine, too exhausted to keep it going, but as a result, she was caught in a vicious circle of Jasper waking and needing a bottle to nod off again, with her lying wide awake beside him, her mental to-do list working away inside her head.

Toni insisted that she bring Jasper into work with her because Cutlery was a 'family-friendly' place, even though Gracie would have preferred not to. She couldn't concentrate with Jasper there: the last time, he'd reached out for the coffee pot in the middle of a meeting, burning his little hand in the process, and she'd had to bring him to A&E. And the time before that, he'd choked on a Rich Tea biscuit he'd somehow got his hands on. Sometimes, she'd have to get Gar to look after him, but he wasn't a babysitter, nice though he was – and besides, Jasper would always come back to her trailing some bit of Cork memorabilia. The last time, Gar had had the nerve to paint his little cheeks with two livid stripes of red, because Cork had got into the All-Ireland hurling semi-finals, and it had taken Gracie an age to get it off.

Now that she thought about it, Gracie wondered why Toni insisted on her bringing Jasper into work. It was nice of her, certainly, and very accommodating, but Gracie had the tiniest feeling that Toni was doing it not out of kindness, but out of a desire, somehow, to show her up. But that was silly, she thought now, nodding as her mother gave her the rundown on Mrs O'Brien's cancer diagnosis. Toni was an empowerer; that wasn't her style at all. She was just being paranoid.

Must be the lack of sleep, she thought miserably, that or the fact that the trip to Brittas Bay hadn't really had the intended effect on the Tuesday group. She'd really hoped that the girls might appreciate what she'd done for them a tiny bit more, but all they seemed to want to do was giggle and eat those disgusting doughnuts that Elise insisted on bringing every single week. They made Gracie feel sick with their synthetic ingredients, and the others were like children after a sugar rush then — but if that's what they wanted ... Even Jane didn't seem to have time for her any more. Look how she'd rushed off the other day, and after Gracie organising the dentist for her and everything.

Her mother was in mid-sentence, going on about some rule change in the bridge club, when Gracie interrupted her. 'Mum?'

She stopped, fork hovering over her plate. 'Yes, love?'

Gracie wanted to smile. When she was small and Mum would be cooking or cleaning or humming along to the radio, when Gracie would call her, she'd always answer in the same way: 'Yes, love?'

'Did you find it hard when we were born?'

'Oh.' Her mother seemed wrong-footed by the question. They didn't do personal in Gracie's family, and it seemed to disconcert her. She looked off into the distance for a while, before saying, 'Well, it was different in my day ...'

Oh, Jesus, Gracie thought, bracing herself for a lecture on how, in the Middle Ages, her mother had been able to raise her family on mouldy potatoes and with no shoes.

'It was so much easier,' her mother continued. 'I really don't envy mums nowadays — it's so tough.'

'It is? I mean, yes, it is,' Gracie agreed, unable to believe her ears.

'Yes, you have to hold down a job and raise a family and

there's no clarity at all to things. In my day, your father did one thing and I did another, and we each knew where we stood. I might have been half out of my mind with boredom, but I knew exactly what my job was: to cook and clean, to bring you lot up and, if I had a minute's spare time, to do something like gardening or to join some boring old knitting club.' She gave a small laugh.

'Did you ever feel unhappy?' Gracie asked.

'Oh, yes,' her mother said cheerfully, cutting into another slice of salmon. 'Most of the time. You know how it is when babies are small — they're not very interesting. But the difference was, we had lots of other women around us all in the same boat, so we could spend whole afternoons together at the park or in each other's houses, all having a good moan. There was a comfort in that. Fridays were my favourite because we'd break out the G&Ts at three o'clock. By the time the dads came home, we'd be catatonic.' She laughed. 'I'll tell you, booze helped us to get through a lot in my day.'

Gracie was stunned. 'I thought you loved being at home with us. At least, you gave the impression that you did.'

'Well, I suppose I did because I didn't know any better. Nowadays, you have to do so many jobs — mother, wife, worker — and you have to be brilliant at all of them, which must be exhausting.'

'It is,' Gracie said grimly. She pushed down the lump in her throat, wondering if she could confide in Mum, tell her just how awful she felt — like a car running on fumes, engine spinning over and over but with no fuel in the tank. She was about to open her mouth to say this, when her mother said happily, 'Well, you're doing a great job, love. Now, what's for dessert?'

'Oh. Apple crumble, I think. I'll go and see,' Gracie said wearily. She was about to drag herself up from her chair, when her mother gave a little scream.

'Sacred Heart, who's that?'

Gracie turned to look through the giant plate-glass window to see a pair of hands pressed against the glass in a circle, and inside that circle, a tanned face with two eyes, like marbles, staring in at them.

'Stay here,' she told her mother sternly, as if Elise, standing outside her window, in her back garden, in a pair of pristine denim shorts and a top trimmed with pink feathers, was about to burgle the place.

'Hi!' Gracie opened the back door, all ready to repel the invader, but Elise rushed across the step to her, in a rush of sugary perfume, and treated her to a giant hug. 'Elise,' she said, when she'd managed to disentangle herself. 'This is a surprise.'

'Yes, well, you weren't answering your phone and so I asked Jane where you lived. And no one came to the front door but I could hear that you were here, so I found my way around the back. I really hope you don't mind. I've been meaning to thank you properly for ages.' She bent down to the wire tray under Chloe's pram and pulled out a huge bouquet of flowers and a bottle of pink champagne —

a very expensive bottle. She handed them to Gracie. 'That weekend was one of the best of my life and, well ...' Her eyes welled up with tears.

Jesus, Gracie thought. Could she just turn them on like that?

'Who's that, love?' Her mother's voice came from behind her, followed, not five seconds later, by the woman herself, face curious. 'Who's this — you don't often have visitors, do you?' she said to Gracie.

'I do, Mum, but I have a meeting ...' Her voice trailed off as her mother said, 'Dervla O'Malley, pleased to meet you.' She shoved Gracie slightly out of the way to offer Elise her hand.

'Elise Sugrue.' Elise beamed at Gracie's mother from under her head of caramel curls. Then the two of them waited until Gracie said, 'Would you like to come in?' She shot her mother, the traitor, a dagger look. Her mother returned the glare sternly and Gracie flushed. Mum believed in making callers feel welcome, no matter what hour of the day or night, and Gracie knew she'd be in for a lecture later. 'We were just about to have dessert,' she added with a degree more warmth.

'Oh, that'd be lovely, Gracie, thanks!' Elise beamed as she lugged that awful pram into Gracie's den, leaving streaks of black on the expensive parquet. Gracie tried not to look as she thanked Elise for the lovely flowers and promised to find an occasion soon to open the champagne.

'I should have brought some for your mum as well,'

Elise said. She then made a big production of taking off her shoes — 'So I don't ruin your lovely floors with my heels!'

Too late, Gracie thought grimly, looking at the wheel-patterned streaks and mentally making a note to look up something to remove them.

'Mrs O'Malley, I'm so pleased that I've got this chance to thank you in person for the fantastic weekend. Your place is just amazing and we had the best time!'

Mum smiled easily, as if she were the queen bestowing favour on her subjects. 'So glad you had a nice time, dear. What is it they say: *mi casa es su casa?*' And she gave a little giggle.

Mother of God, Gracie thought, this is going to turn into the longest half-hour of my life. And the client was coming in for the first presentation of Cutlery's ideas this afternoon, so she had to be in top form, not brain half-fried from inanity and lack of sleep. And what the hell was Elise thinking, rocking up like this? She'd kill Jane, Gracie thought.

Her mother and Elise nattered away like old friends, Chloe sitting up on Elise's knee, looking like the Sugar Plum Fairy in some lurid, utterly tasteless little dress, so Gracie made an excuse about checking on the crumble and took temporary refuge in the playroom, where Sunny was sitting with Jasper, building a tower out of giant blocks of Lego, Jasper propped up on a mountain of cushions, eyes following Sunny's every move.

I just need a minute, Gracie thought, to get away from

the din, to clear my head. There's so much bloody noise in this house, she thought as she sat down on the sofa, pinching the bridge of her nose to help the headache she could feel building in a spot between her eyes. Lina said that if she massaged her sinuses it would really help, but all it did was make Gracie's eyes water.

She looked up to see two heads turned to her, surprised. I don't belong here either, with my own child, Gracie thought miserably. 'Sunny,' she said. 'Thanks so much for lunch. It was absolutely delicious.'

Sunny wasn't used to such effusive thanks from Gracie, and she looked as if she didn't know how to respond, but eventually, she said, 'Thank you, Miss Gracie. I get Jasper ready now.'

'Lovely, thank you, Sunny. And listen, take the rest of the day off,' Gracie found herself blurting. She reached into her pocket and took a crumpled fifty-euro note out of it. 'Buy yourself something nice.'

Sunny looked horrified, retreating from the money as if it were poison. 'Oh, no, Miss Gracie. You pay me very well, thank you. I'm very happy here, thank you very much.' With this, she shot up, lifted Jasper into her arms, where he looked entirely comfortable, and vanished out the door.

Gracie burst into tears, great sobs racking her body. She couldn't go on, she thought. She just couldn't. She hadn't got another ounce of strength in her body, and her mind felt wrung out, like an old dishcloth. She would give everything, she thought, to just go upstairs, pull the blinds down, climb into bed and stay there, watching *Martha Bakes*, to which she'd become secretly addicted, the lady's stern edicts about pastry lamination and measuring dough with a ruler keeping Gracie company in the early hours as Jake snored away beside her. But she had to keep going, she thought bleakly as a gust of laughter reached her from the living room — if she didn't keep going, everything would fall apart. So, she gave herself some time to howl silently, before getting up, taking a wet wipe from the box in the corner and blowing her nose into it, a smell of Jasper in her nostrils. She took a deep breath and went into the kitchen, emerging five minutes later with three bowls of apple crumble and a big pot of tea on a tray. 'I'm afraid there's no coffee,' she said.

'Oh, I don't drink coffee anyway,' Elise said, 'just the odd weak cappuccino. I find it makes me very jittery in the afternoon — do you, Dervla?'

'God, yes, Elise, pet, I can't touch the stuff. Gives me terrible indigestion, and I'm high as a kite!'

So, we're on first-name terms here, Gracie thought, as she put the tray down on the coffee table, feeling as if she'd missed some shift in the atmosphere while she'd been gone.

'So, tell me, Elise,' Mum said, digging a spoon into the crumble, after she'd poured a generous amount of cream on top, 'whereabouts are you from? I can't place that accent.'

Good old Mum, Gracie thought. Wondered when

her inner snob would come to the fore. Mum might be scrupulously polite, but she'd make sure everyone knew their place.

'Oh.' Elise was silent for the first time since she'd arrived. 'Ehm. County Louth.'

'I can't believe it.' Her mother slapped her knees. 'I'm a Drogheda girl myself. What school did you go to? Don't tell me you're a St Jude's girl?'

'No.' Elise shook her head vaguely. 'We were home educated.'

'Oh, that'd be very unusual,' Mum said, clearly not ready to let go of her prey just yet. Gracie felt herself growing just a bit more cheerful.

'Yes, it was. Ma— Mother was a firm believer in educating us herself. She was very well educated and she wanted us to be too.'

Gracie couldn't believe it. She'd bet her last fiver that Elise had no more than the Junior Cert and some hairdressing thing, in spite of the clothes. She knew new money when she saw it.

'I see. And would you have been from Drogheda yourself?'

'Just outside,' Elise said, visibly squirming. Gracie sat forward, interested all of a sudden. 'Bettystown actually.'

'Oh, lovely. I used to walk that beach every Sunday with my own mother after mass. We'd look at the fine houses and promise ourselves that, one day, we'd live in one ourselves,' she laughed. Mum had grown up in a fine Victorian house on the Dublin Road, so Gracie had no idea what she was talking about.

Elise smiled politely, taking a bite of the apple crumble. 'This is gorgeous, Gracie. Did you make it yourself?'

'She did not,' Mum interjected. 'She has this Chinese girl who does everything – doesn't she, love?'

'She's Filipina and she drops in every now and again to give me a hand. I've had to go back to work early—'

'Thank God she's a cook, anyway, because otherwise the crumble would be like concrete,' Mum added before Gracie could finish. She could have strangled her mother, Gracie thought. In front of Elise, of all people.

'Oh, I don't know, Dervla – she cooked for us in Brittas, and it was fantastic. She can really barbecue, and she did this delicious pavlova for dessert, didn't you, Gracie? She was the most amazing host, as well. We didn't want for a single thing all weekend. That's why I wanted to come down to say thanks to you, and to you,' and with this, she reached her hands out in Gracie's and her mother's direction, seizing one each of theirs in hers and squeezing it tightly. 'Quite honestly, your daughter has changed my life.'

For once, Mum was silent, shooting Gracie an anxious look. Gracie smiled benignly. Serves you right.

Elise seemed to be in a hurry to go then, getting up from the table and announcing that it was time for Chloe's afternoon nap. 'It's the highlight of my day!' She giggled, packing Chloe into the giant pram. 'I get two whole hours to sit on the sofa watching true-crime documentaries.

They're about terrible miscarriages of justice,' she said, 'but I can't resist them!'

Mum clutched her throat at this display, shaking her head but managing a smile. 'I don't watch television before the six o'clock news,' she said. 'I find it's an excellent exercise in self-discipline.'

'Well, good for you, Dervla,' Elise laughed, as if Mum hadn't just insulted her. 'I just fire Chloe into the cot, pop on the baby monitor and the kettle, then settle down for two episodes. Half a packet of dark-chocolate digestives, and I'm all set.'

'You have the right idea, pet,' Mum said, a trifle more warmly. 'Gracie's dad and I sit down with a nice glass of chilled Chablis and watch the headlines, and it really helps us to relax. I wish Gracie here could take a leaf out of your book.' She gave Elise a conspiratorial look, and Elise looked at Gracie gleefully, clearly delighted with herself.

You have some bloody cheek, Gracie thought. As if you'd lift a single finger to help me, but no, you're far too busy with bridge and coffee mornings and all that crap you fill your life with, instead of spending five minutes with your grandson. She suddenly felt murderous, looking at her mother with her immaculate wash-and-set, her slacks unmarked by baby sick, unlike Gracie's jeans, which, now that she looked at them, had little splashes of regurgitated milk on them.

'I'm too busy at the moment,' Gracie said pointedly, 'but I'll be sure to make time for it when I've nothing on.'

She hoped, by her tone, that she was conveying that she had far too much on her plate to indulge herself in telly-watching — even though the thought of sitting on the sofa, a big packet of biscuits beside her, suddenly filled her with longing.

Elise was all movement then, disappearing in a flurry of pink pram and gushing thanks. Gracie saw her to the front door with an eagerness that she knew bordered on rudeness, but then Elise probably wouldn't notice. She seemed terribly thick-skinned.

'Well, thanks for calling!' Gracie said cheerfully, eyeing her watch and realising that she had ten minutes to get dressed and out the door for this client thing. Ten bloody minutes. That's what her life boiled down to nowadays — the ten minutes that formed the dividing line between keeping the show on the road and complete disaster.

'Thank you for having me,' Elise said. Her smile wasn't quite as bright now that she was faced with just Gracie, and she seemed to hesitate for a second on the doorstep, her eyes scanning Gracie's face warily.

Gracie debated whether or not to ignore the signal. She didn't have time, she thought. She was about to close the door, then realised she couldn't exactly slam it in the woman's face, so she took a deep breath. 'Is everything OK, Elise?'

'Well ...' Elise said.

Oh, Jesus. 'Look, I'm really sorry, but I have a meeting—' Gracie began.

'It's Jane,' Elise blurted.

'What about her?' Gracie said warily.

'I'm just wondering if there's something wrong with her. Really wrong.'

'What do you mean?' Gracie said. She felt like adding, 'Spit it out, for God's sake', but didn't. She just waited, half-knowing what Elise was going to say and feeling suddenly ashamed that she'd done nothing about it, a shame that found itself transformed into a building anger with Elise, this little cuckoo who had invaded their lovely nest and, as far as Gracie was concerned, was now proceeding to destroy everything. And she needn't think that Gracie hadn't noticed the way she looked at Lina: like a lovesick teenager.

'I mean ... surely you've noticed the bruises – you'd want to be blind not to. And she's so quiet these days.'

'What are you suggesting, Elise?' Gracie knew exactly what Elise was suggesting, but she'd make her say it.

'I'm *suggesting* that Jane might be being knocked about by someone. What do you know about her hubby? She says fuck— I mean, nothing about him, but every time the man is mentioned, she quivers like one of those little dogs.'

The rage felt like a wave rising up through Gracie, from the bottom of her stomach, up to her throat, coming out in a great tidal gush. 'What do you know about Jane?' she spat. 'You're hardly here a wet week and you're digging around, poking your nose where you don't belong, interfering with things that are none of your fucking business.'

Elise seemed to shrink back against the lurid pram. 'I was just worried, that's all,' she said, her hands up in a gesture of surrender.

Gracie realised suddenly how it must look, the loss of control. She didn't know what had come over her. She knew that she should apologise. Mum would kill her if she knew Gracie had been so angry, but she'd rather die than admit anything to this little squit, she thought. 'Look, Jane is my friend and I think I'd know if there was something wrong with her,' Gracie said firmly, trying to get her feelings under control. 'But thank you for your concern, Elise.' This time, she went to push the door closed, but it caught on something, and when she looked down, she saw one of Elise's trainers, hot pink with sequins on it, jammed in the gap.

'Look, let's just call a spade a spade here,' Elise hissed. 'I've seen bruises like that before and, let me tell you, they won't go away. They'll get worse; the injuries will become obvious and we'll all just sit there on the bloody blanket under the trees and we'll be too polite to say a single word about the black eye or the cut to the lip. And you know what?' She came up close to Gracie now, so close that Gracie had to recoil. 'We'll only have ourselves to fucking blame. Now, I don't know about you, Gracie, but I sure as hell don't want that on my conscience.'

Then she was gone, her little shadow disappearing down the drive, and Gracie collapsed on the doorstep, chest heaving. She couldn't seem to get a breath, no matter how hard she tried. It felt as if she were having a heart attack and she wondered if she should call an ambulance, but she didn't have the strength. She clutched her chest for a moment and prayed. 'Please, please, let me just breathe.' She didn't know whom she was praying to – she hadn't prayed since making her first Holy Communion – but she wanted desperately for someone to answer.

'Well, that was interesting.' Her mother's voice, when she appeared behind Gracie, seemed to boom and Gracie had to put her hands over her ears, hoping to God that her mother would be quiet.

'What did she say her name was?'

'Elise,' she managed.

'No, her *surname*. Sugrue, was it? That's not a Louth name. I must look it up.'

Her mother's snobbery suddenly felt like the most irritating and pointless thing in the world.

'For God's sake, Mum, what does it matter?' Gracie said, getting wearily up to her feet.

'It matters, Gracie, because we all have to know our station in life,' her mother replied. 'I know that isn't a popular view nowadays, with all this talk about "diversity", but the world runs a lot more smoothly if we accept what we're given.'

What total horseshit, Gracie thought. For a second, she toyed with saying this to her mother, to watch her clutch her throat, as if mortally wounded, but she just didn't have the energy. It was all she could do to focus on breathing in and out, in and out. 'I have to go,' she said miserably.

'Oh. Well, if you're in that much of a hurry,' her mother said, 'that you're going to kick me out, then I suppose I'd better go too.'

Gracie didn't even argue but instead just trudged miserably up the stairs to her bedroom to put on her armour, removing the puke-spattered jeans and T-shirt and replacing them with a crisp white shirt and black palazzo trousers. She sat at her dressing table and looked into the mirror at her tired, pinched face. I look old, she thought suddenly. Old and tired. Maybe I *was* having a heart attack after all.

She put her second and third fingers on her pulse, the way she'd learned in Transition Year first-aid classes. She could still remember how hilarious she'd found the whole thing when she was sixteen, hovering over Delia Hughes, the two of them doubled over with laughter as Delia played dead. If only she'd known, she thought sadly, listening to the flicker of her pulse, that life would be this difficult. Maybe it was Mum and Dad's fault for wrapping her up in cotton wool, encouraging her to think that life would be one happy sequence of lovely things, from marriage to family to home, but it sure hadn't worked out like that. Life was hard, Gracie realised, and with a jolt, she wondered what it must have been like for Elise. That woman didn't look as if things had come easy to her, even if she did have a cheek telling Gracie about Jane — as if Gracie didn't already know. Jane was her friend after all.

Just then, Gracie's phone beeped. *Are you on your way? We're getting set up here.* Oh, fuck. She picked up a pot of foundation and began to dab it on her face, filling in the cracks with her very own ready-mixed concrete. Hurry, hurry, hurry, she thought as she dabbed. Then she heard her mother call up the stairs. 'Well, goodbye then. I'll call you!'

'Piss off,' she muttered under her breath.

13

Elise

I'm sitting, waiting for the others, at the park café rather than in our usual spot under the trees because there's a Zumba class on, and if I wasn't in a bad mood before I arrived at the park, I am now, drinking my one-shot cappuccino, watching forty people gyrating on the grass to the roar of Latin music. That's *our* spot, I feel like telling them. Bugger off and find your own.

The reason I'm so angry is because Gray and I rowed last night. We have never exchanged a cross word, not since the day we met, but we had a full-on shouting match, the two of us roaring at each other over the table. The only good thing was that Chloe wasn't awake to hear it. She'd have been scarred for life. And all because I made *coq au vin*. I thought he'd love it, but he just accused me of getting above myself by cooking pretentious food: he says that I haven't been the same since I came back from Brittas, that I'm full of 'notions', whatever that means. Honestly, talk about the pot calling the kettle black! He was the one who insisted we move to Rathgar, where none of the snobs will so much as give us the time of day.

I wouldn't mind, but I cooked the meal especially for him – though I think the reason I got so annoyed is because I know he has a point. Even though it's nearly a month ago now, I know that I haven't exactly been myself since I came back from Brittas Bay. I've been distracted and a bit snitty with him. It's just, I can't really put it out of my mind. The golden sunshine, the lovely clean sand, the way everyone just seemed so shiny and well fed: they were like Labradors, no scrawny little Jack Russells like where I grew up. And of course, there's Lina. I know it's just a silly crush, but I can't get her out of my mind. I always knew that once I opened that door, I wouldn't be able to close it again. What Ma and Da would make of it, and me a married woman!

I got the *coq au vin* recipe from Jane at last Tuesday's meeting. She said that it was one of Mark's favourites, and Gracie shot me a look that would curdle milk. I felt like telling her that I wasn't going to embarrass Jane like that. I have a bit of cop-on, unlike her, Jane's so-called friend, who is doing sod-all to help her. But then, neither am I, apart from passing the buck by telling Gracie. Maybe that's why these things go on: because everyone's too scared to do anything. It's too awful to think about, so we all look the other way.

I told Jane that the dinner was for Gray and that I wanted to impress him, and she gave that little laugh of hers and said that it would certainly do that, whatever she meant by that. I had high hopes, but still, my eyes were out on stalks when I read the recipe. A whole bottle of wine in one dinner! I couldn't believe it. Anyway, last night, I poured it all into the giant Le Creuset casserole dish that I'd bought in Arnotts — also at Jane's suggestion, because she'd got a nice one from there as a wedding present. Glug, glug it went, a big sea of red over the free-range, organic chicken. As I poured it in, I wondered what Ma would have made of it. She raised us all on mince, as she was often fond of saying, and, 'Sure, you didn't suffer.' I'm not convinced that she's right about that, if you think of the way we've scattered, but she did her best. Sometimes, I really miss my brothers and sisters and I'd love to be close to them — even though we were too bloody close for comfort once upon a time, four of us sharing bunks in the second bedroom, the boys in the dining room downstairs. I can understand why we aren't — we remind each other of that crappy place we worked so hard to escape.

After leaving it in the oven for four hours, I took the casserole out and, I have to say, it looked great and it smelled even better. The wine wasn't too wine-y, but had reduced down to a rich gravy. I couldn't wait to serve it to Gray. I was so excited!

Alison Walsh

I should have known that he was in a bad mood because he went straight into the living room, flicking on the telly, instead of coming in to see me in the kitchen, the way he normally does, snaking an arm around my waist and kissing the back of my neck. He's very affectionate, Gray, very touchy-feely, and I think that's great in a man — that he can show his feelings like that. But recently, he hasn't done it as much and I wonder if he senses something in me. I hope to God not. I can have all the crushes I like, but I know the way the land lies.

I left him to it because I know that he's under a lot of pressure. The bank are being a bit iffy about some new business plan he sent them, and it's been driving him mad. I could hear the sound of a Champions League game in progress as I sprinkled some baby potatoes with rosemary and salt and laid the table with the new crystal tea lights I'd bought in this cute little gift shop in the village. I'd popped Chloe down for the night early, so it'd just be the two of us. I'd made sure that we had a really busy afternoon and that she had a good feed around teatime so that she'd sleep through, and, sure enough, her little eyelids drooped the minute I put her down. Everything was just as it should be, I thought, calling out to Gray that dinner was on the table.

I might have known that it wouldn't go well when he shuffled in, still in his grubby sweats from work. Normally, he's had a shower and changed: he always says that he hates to bring the office home. Still, I ploughed on. 'Ta-dah!'

I said, lifting the lid off the huge orange pot, which I'd placed on a mat on the table between us.

He peered inside, sniffing suspiciously. 'What is it?'

'It's *coq au vin*.'

'Translated into English, what is it?'

'Chicken in red wine. You'll love it.'

He shook his head, looking at it as if it was bloody nuclear. 'Ah, I'm not sure, love. I like things simple.'

'Just try it,' I insisted. 'I'm trying new things, so you can too.'

'What if I don't want to?' he said.

'What do you mean by that?' I snapped. I know that I shouldn't have, but I couldn't help myself. I'd slaved away in the kitchen for the whole afternoon, so he could bloody well like it.

He sighed. 'I mean, you don't have to be like them. Like your posh new friends.'

'But I do!' I wailed. 'What do you think I'm doing it all for? I want to better myself, Gray. How do you think I'm going to fit into this place if I don't learn?'

He got in a bit of a snit then, truth be told. He shoved his hands in the front pockets of his hoodie, even though he knows I don't like him doing that because it pushes the thing out of shape. 'What do you mean "better yourself"? Is what we have not good enough for you?' He waved his hand at our new kitchen and the marble floor tiles I'd insisted on — because marble is very hard-wearing, as well as looking nice. 'I've worked bloody hard for this, love,' he'd said. 'And I don't like you looking down your nose at it. We've got everything we have through honest work. We've nothing to be ashamed of.'

Normally, I'd have agreed with him then, because it's true. We have nice things because of Gray's hard work, and I'm grateful, but after a day fussing in the kitchen, the sweat pouring off me because of the heat, I was not in the humour. And besides, I'm not really sure that I'm all that happy with things being the way they are: I want to shake them up. Suddenly, it doesn't seem enough to just go along as we are, with me playing the little wife and Gray going out there to kill a woolly mammoth every day. I know that's what I signed up to, but being with the girls has made me realise that there's more to life than marble floors and a nice car.

'I didn't say that there was anything wrong with what we have,' I began, 'but I want to try new things. You always said that life wasn't about standing still, but keeping moving forward, to something better. That's what I'm doing — moving forward, just like you, and I'm sorry if it makes you feel uncomfortable.'

Gray got up from his seat so quickly that the chair fell on the floor behind him with a crash. 'Uncomfortable?' he said. 'I'll tell you what makes me feel uncomfortable. You waltzing in and out of here with a big puss on your face, complaining all the time about the food we eat and the TV shows we watch, when a few weeks ago they were just fine. Not to mention trying to persuade me to join the golf club because Gracie's dad will put in a good word for me, and that's before we get to the holiday brochures for the Italian feckin' Riviera.'

'Gracie went there last year and she said it was lovely. Full of old treasures and lovely restaurants. It's romantic,' I said quietly.

'Yeah, well, maybe it's her idea of romantic, but it sure as hell isn't mine. I don't need the "treasures of Italy" tour to feel good about myself, Elise, to feel that I'm a worthwhile human being because I know the difference between Michelangelo and Leonardo da Vinci, like your snobby friends.'

'That's just ignorance,' I shouted back. 'It's fine if you want to spend your whole life like some bloody ape, afraid that knowing stuff will turn you into a snob. It won't, it'll just turn you into a person who knows things and who's able to make interesting conversation. You should try it,' I finish. 'You never know, you might actually enjoy it.'

His answer was to mutter a string of curses and storm off, kicking the chair on the floor for good measure.

I know that I should have gone up to him, to make up, to tell him that he was the man for me and that we shouldn't let my new life come between us, but I didn't. Instead, I served myself another helping of coq au vin, the delicious, rich sauce slipping down my throat — then another and then another, until I thought I'd burst. And then I went and threw it all up.

*

Now, I take another sip of my cappuccino and try to put last night out of my mind. Then I remember that nice youth-club leader we had, Mrs Hennessy, who was forever going on about being yourself. That it was OK, that you were good enough as you were and all that, and honestly, I thought she was mad. Everything I'd learned until then had told me that it wasn't OK to be me at all. That it wasn't all right to be poor, or not very good at school, or never to be able to think of the right thing to say. Being yourself was for other people, I always thought, not me.

And then I met Fiona. I was only sixteen. I'd left school the year before, after the Junior Cert, with three Cs to my name and a computer night course at the tech behind me. I wasn't exactly going to take on the world, but at least I wasn't sitting at the back of the class every day, squinting at the board, words and numbers swimming before my eyes. I got the job in Zen Travel pretty easily because one of Ma's friends worked there, and I enjoyed it. Bit of a natter in the morning and during coffee break, lots of customers ringing in to book exotic holidays. It felt like freedom and not even the complainers wore me down, with their whingeing about scruffy hotel rooms and dodgy food.

Fiona had been working there for three months at that point. She was older than me – nearly eighteen – and sharp as a tack. I'd say she could easily have gone to college – in fact, she did later, I found out, and I was pleased about that – but she'd got kicked out of school for thumping a girl who called her a dyke. She told me this on our first day at work, and my heart fluttered with excitement. I've never met a lesbian before, I thought, before she added that she wasn't one, in case that's what I was thinking. 'I just don't like bullies,' she added, pinging an elastic band at spotty Dave, the IT guy, and giggling when it hit him on the backside.

'The thought never crossed my mind,' I said. Of course, the thought had crossed my mind more than once, but until then, I'd never dwelt on it. I'd always thought that I hated the boys in school because they smelled musty and because they'd stick their tongues down my throat at socials, but when I met Fiona, it was like a lightbulb going off in my head. Oh, I thought. That's what I want.

We spent every lunchtime together after that, telling each other silly jokes and gossiping about the others at the agency: Doreen, with her moustache, or Karl, who had a thing about Kathleen from accounts. Then we were spending Saturday afternoons together, shopping for cheap clothes with our wages, and then she asked me if I'd like to take a day trip to Skerries on the train. I couldn't believe it. Fiona was the first real friend I'd ever had and I hadn't even had to try. It had just come naturally.

We first kissed at the Christmas party in work. She was wearing those reindeer antlers on her head and I had two Christmas puddings on springs sticking out of mine, and they got tangled, I remember, when we kissed. She'd taken me into the photocopying room and asked me if I'd like to kiss her, straight out, no messing around. And because she'd been direct, so was I. 'Yes,' I'd said. 'Yes, I would.'

She'd leaned her head to one side then, her bright-red curls brushing her shoulders, her antlers tilting, and she'd said, 'C'mere.'

I'd shuffled towards her, wondering if I was ready for this and what it might feel like to kiss a girl instead of a boy. Would it feel like Jason Beecham, the first boy I'd ever kissed, who nearly tore the lip off me with his braces? It turned out that it didn't feel like that at all. It felt warm and soft and light, like air. I've never been kissed like that before or since.

From that day on until the day Ma stood at the end of my bed six months later, her face a picture, we were never apart. Nobody remarked on it: we were just two friends having a ball, going out to pubs and clubs and coming to work the next morning, eyes bleary, collapsing in giggles at the slightest thing. No one ever suspected.

We only 'went public' once, at a sales conference in Sligo, holding hands as we walked along the beach at Enniscrone, watching the surfers. The others had all gone on a day trip to Salthill, to the amusements, but Fiona had pretended to have a bug and I pleaded a hangover, so we had the day to ourselves. We walked the beach, and we kissed and we ate ice-cream and we lay in the dunes, the sun on our faces, and I began to imagine what it would be like to do this every day. Just to be together like this, like a normal couple. I talked about the great future we'd have together, like a fool. She just laughed. 'Ah, Elise,' she said. 'You know it can't last.'

I was outraged, of course, demanding to know why not, but obviously Fiona was cleverer than me: she knew that the pull of my life, my family, would be too much for what we had together, and she was right. She even said, after Ma found us, that I'd made it happen to push us both apart because I couldn't bear to do the deed myself. To tell her that I didn't have the courage to live like that. To be open about who I was. I denied it, of course, but deep down I knew that she was right. Wanting to be liked has always mattered more to me than being who I am.

Fifteen years, two boyfriends and a husband later, here I am, staring down the barrel of my life, all of the feelings that I'd squashed down coming back to the surface. Only now, there's so much more at stake: the life I've built with Gray and my lovely Chloe. For a second, I try to imagine life without her, but even the thought of it makes me feel sick.

Where on earth are the girls? I wonder. I begin to fidget in my chair now, and Chloe begins to cry – she's like that, Chloe: she picks up on everything. If I'm in a bad mood, she'll start to grizzle or give a sad little wail, as if in sympathy. She has amazing emotional intelligence, even though she's only a baby. 'It's OK, pet,' I say, lifting her out of her pram and sitting her on my knee. She reaches out then and sticks her little fist into the foam of my cappuccino, putting it into her mouth and sucking vigorously. 'So, you like coffee then?' I laugh, cheering up immediately. She's my little ray of sunshine, Chloe. I know that, no matter what, she'll never reject me. And, until last night, I would have said the same about Gray.

Then I see Gracie walking slowly down the path towards me. I pin a great big smile on my face, pretending that she wasn't an absolute bitch to me that time I went to her house. 'Hi, Gracie!' I say and give a little wave. I can't see her expression behind those huge sunglasses of hers, but she waves back and I feel a tiny bit better. Maybe all is forgiven and she doesn't hate me quite as much as she lets on. I know that I shouldn't have called around like that, but I couldn't think what else to do – and besides, Ma always made us say thank you for everything. Although that mother of hers is something else. What a wagon. She's like a sniffer dog, hunting out the lower classes.

'Well, this is different,' she says when she gets close, pulling out a chair and manoeuvring Jasper's all-terrain buggy into position beside her.

'I know. I felt like telling them all to piss off when I saw them there,' I say.

She gives a small smile. 'Well, I suppose we don't own it.'

'No, but it feels as if we do,' I say. 'It's part of the whole thing, isn't it? I mean, we can't really have a mummies' meeting in a different place. It won't be the same.'

I thought she'd laugh, but instead, she just shakes her head sadly. 'No, you're right, Elise, it won't. It feels like everything's different all of a sudden,' she adds, wrapping her arms around herself, as if it isn't thirty degrees in the shade. 'Haven't you noticed?'

'Yes, I have,' I agree, even though I'm not sure that we're talking about the same thing. 'I suppose everything has to change sooner or later. That's life, isn't it? We think nothing's happening, but it's all going on under the surface.'

'Well, I wish it wasn't,' Gracie says. 'I just want it all to stop for a while, so I can catch my breath.'

'Ah, but no man ever steps in the same river twice,' a voice says behind us. I turn to see Lina, with Tommy in her usual place in a sling around her neck. My heart stops. How can she get away with that bright-blue T-shirt and the kind of hippy Aladdin trousers in green that would have looked stupid on anyone else? 'Heraclitus, in case you're wondering. Miserable git, but he was a believer in nothing remaining the same. First-year philosophy,' and she gives a little bow.

I find myself giggling like an idiot as Gracie says, 'Well, I wish to goodness Heraclitus had kept his mouth shut.'

Lina shoots me a look over her head, a 'what's up with her' expression on her face. I shrug because I really have no idea. Gracie is a complete mystery to me.

Lina gives me a careful look, then says, 'But enough about metaphysics. I think I'm going to get a lemonade — Gracie, do you fancy one? Elise?'

'Lovely,' I gush.

'Three lemonades then.' Lina smiles, reaching into her purse and taking out a five-euro note.

'Let me,' Gracie says immediately. We both know that Lina's broke, but even so, I don't think she needs to be patronised like that.

'It's fine,' Lina says. 'I get a carer's allowance now, thanks to Eileen in the social welfare office, which just about makes Mama's presence bearable. Three lemonades it is.' I watch her walk under the awning into the shade of the café, her limbs long and brown and strong, Tommy's little legs, in the sling, sticking out either side of her. She bends down to reach into her little shoulder bag, and a voice beside me says, 'Be careful, Elise.'

I turn to Gracie, but as usual, I can't read her expression behind those giant shades. I swear she does it on purpose. Honestly, the woman thinks she's Jackie Kennedy. Apart from the one slip, when she'd completely lost it, which made me think that maybe she's not as in control as she'd like us to think.

'What do you mean "be careful"?' I try not to sound too annoyed.

'Lina's a real force of nature, but she's not exactly ... steadfast,' she finishes. 'She's easily distracted, if you know what I mean.'

For God's sake, I think, will you stop talking in riddles! I have no idea what you're on about. Seeing the expression on my face, Gracie smiles. 'Look, I know Lina. She was like that in the antenatal class: when she gave someone her attention, it was like the sun shining on a little plant. I could see people bloom in it, stand taller, because of that beam of sunshine. She pays attention to people and that's what everyone wants, isn't it, to be listened to? And by someone as charismatic as Lina? But then she stops looking and you can just wilt.'

'I'll be sure to remember that,' I say. I'm hoping I sound sarcastic and cool, when, really, I want to shrivel up, like one of those plants Gracie's talking about. How on earth does Gracie know? Is it written all over my face? Or is the woman trying to get her own back after what I said about Jane?

'I hope you do, Elise,' Gracie says. 'I wouldn't want you to misunderstand ...' She gives me that frosty smile of hers, but then her voice trails off as Lina comes back towards us, three plastic cups of lemonade in her hand. 'Let me help you with that,' she says, getting up to take the drinks from Lina. I don't move because I'm in shock, and Gracie puts the cup carefully down in front of me.

We drink our lemonades in silence, looking at the crowd on the green dancing away, bums jiggling. A stray Labrador has got into the middle and is running around the instructor, barking loudly. I try to look at Lina out of the corner of my eye without Gracie noticing and giving me one of her superior smiles. Lina's leaning back in her chair now, Tommy resting against her, her little face pressed to her mother's bosom. That must be nice, I think, to be carried around like that all day, to be able to listen to your mum's heartbeat. Maybe Lina has the right idea, I think, as I stroke Chloe's little foot in the pram beside me. I might give it a try.

'Jeez, I'm wrecked,' Lina suddenly says. 'And all thanks to you, Elise,' and she gives a small smile.

'It went OK then?'

She shrugs. 'You could say that.'

'So what happened?' I say, sitting up and leaning forward on my seat, all ears.

'Well, we went to this after-party thing in the Nameless Bar and then to an after-after-party for Conor Creighton.' She gives a small shrug, as if going to a party for the country's favourite comic is all a bit of a bore.

'And? What the hell happened, Lina? I'm dying to hear.'

'Ah, nothing really. There was dancing, would you believe, in this little flat in Rathmines. God, I felt like a teenager again, waving my arms in the air. I even snogged someone.' She gives a giggle.

'Oh, who?' Gracie says, shooting me a look.

'Ladies, you are speaking to the woman who has locked lips with none other than Conor Creighton,' Lina says gleefully.

'You are joking!' Gracie says.

'No, I'm not,' Lina answers, a cat-that-got-the-cream look on her face.

I don't know what to say or where to look. It kills me to even think it, but maybe Gracie was right. I thought

Lina liked me: she told me all her jokes and gave me that swimming lesson and I felt like the most important person in the world. Now, it really does feel as if the sun has gone behind a cloud and I feel chilly and exposed. Maybe I misread the situation: it wouldn't be the first time.

'Oh, Lina,' Gracie is saying softly. 'You do know he's married — or as good as, anyway.'

'So? He says his partner and he are on a hiatus, so it doesn't count,' Lina says happily. She looks at me then, as if waiting for me to back her up, but I'm silent. I can't say a word.

Gracie rolls her eyes to heaven. 'For goodness sake, Lina, I'd have credited you with a bit more cop-on. I saw a picture of them both at an awards ceremony last week, looking very much a couple.' Gracie whips her phone out of her pocket and scrolls through it for a moment. 'There,' she says triumphantly, as a picture of Conor Creighton and a dowdy-looking woman in an ill-fitting black dress flashes up on screen.

'Can you blame me if the missus looks like that?' Lina says. Then she puts a hand over her mouth to conceal a laugh, and looks at me, waiting for me to join in. I don't know what's come over her, I think. What about all that stuff about women standing up for each other? I suddenly find Chloe's waffle blanket fascinating and I busy myself rearranging it around her, which she doesn't like, kicking it off with a wail.

'Honestly,' Gracie says, putting her phone on the table.

'Lina, I'm a bit surprised at you. All that feminist talk, all that stuff about the sisterhood and about how we have to support each other and look at you – doing another woman down like that.'

'Ah, come on, Gracie,' Lina says, eyes wide. 'It's not like either of us was taking it seriously – we were in it for the laughs, as it were. We didn't sleep together – I went home in a cab and I'm sure Conor went home to his wife and children too. No harm done.'

Gracie shakes her head. 'God, you're naive, Lina. Conor Creighton is a player – everyone knows it – and you're just another silly woman who's fallen for his schtick.'

'Really? I thought we were two grown-ups having a no-strings nice time, but thank you for the lecture,' Lina says. 'I'll be sure to remember it when I nail my first TV show, which I will be doing in about a week, I'll have you both know.'

She's looking directly at me now, her eyes scanning mine for a sign, so I give a little scream then, jumping up and nearly knocking the table over. 'Lina, that's fantastic!' I can't help it – I put my arms around her and give her a squeeze, ignoring the look Gracie shoots me over her glasses.

'Easy, Elise, it's not in the bag yet. I have to pitch it to Graham McSween, the TV producer – and it's digital-only, but it's a start,' Lina says happily.

'Well, that's fantastic – isn't it, Gracie?' I say.

Gracie looks as if she's sucked on a bitter lemon, her lips

puckering with distaste. 'Well done, Lina,' she says quietly.

'Yes, well done. You're going to be a star!' I feel like breathing a sigh of relief that I've pulled it back from the brink.

'Where's Jane?' Gracie suddenly says. 'It's half-past three. She should be here by now.'

Lina and I look at each other guiltily, sharing the thought that we hadn't even noticed.

Gracie tuts. 'I hope she didn't see the Zumba class and think we weren't here.' She picks up her phone. 'I'll text her,' she says, typing rapidly. She puts the phone down on the table and we all look at it, waiting. It buzzes then, rattling the cast-iron table, and Gracie picks it up. 'Oh.'

'What is it?' Lina says.

'Her dad's died. She's gone home.'

'I didn't even know her dad was still alive,' Lina says.

'Neither did I,' Gracie replies. 'Poor Jane. Do you think we should go down for the funeral?'

'Yes, we should,' Lina says. 'I think it'd be a good idea.'

'I haven't a clue where she's from, though, have you?' Gracie says guiltily.

'No,' Lina says. 'That's kind of embarrassing.'

'Castlemonkstown,' I pipe up. 'It's in Galway or Roscommon or somewhere.' I add, 'She told me in Brittas,' in response to the unspoken 'how did you know?'

'Right,' Gracie says, tapping away. 'Castlemonkstown, County Roscommon. It looks really small,' she adds. I can see her little south-Dublin nose wrinkle with distaste.

Alison Walsh

'I can't see what that has to do with us going to the funeral,' Lina says.

'I didn't mean it like that,' Gracie snaps.

Lina sighs. 'I'll text her and see if it's OK to go.'

She rummages in her pocket for her phone, but Gracie puts out a hand to stop her. 'Leave it to me,' she says firmly. 'She'll take it better from me.'

Nobody asks me at all.

Lina nods and sits back, waiting. Neither she nor Gracie look at me and I know that I'm not going to be invited. I thought I belonged, but now it feels as if they are both in their own world, and I'm on the outside, looking in, the way I always have been.

14

Jane

Jane thought it was sweet of the girls to offer to come to the funeral, but she had said no, because she didn't want them to see where she'd come from. She was ashamed, she realised now, as she piled a tower of white sliced pan filled with ham onto a chopping board and sliced through it in a criss-cross fashion, and then again, until she was left with four triangles. Elise had even sent a condolence card: a picture of St Thérèse of Lisieux, decorated in lurid gold, and a promise that a priest would pray for the 'repose of his soul'. Jane wondered what Dad would have made of that, even if it was a nice gesture. Thoughtful, if a bit blingy.

'Have you finished yet?' Helen, her sister, blustered into

the kitchen and grabbed a plateful in each hand, turning and pressing the door handle down with her elbow, prising the door open with her foot and then hooking the same foot around it to close it behind her. She'd been doing that since she was a teenager, coming down to the kitchen for toast while she was studying, hooking a socked foot around the door behind her in response to Dad's bellowed, 'Door!'

Dad. Jane thought about the last time she'd seen him, when she'd visited with Mark, how his hand had shaken as he lifted the teapot to pour the tea. 'I'll be mother,' he'd said, his one and only attempt at a joke. Dad couldn't really be said to have had much of a sense of humour. Was it possible to love, but not like, your parents? Jane wondered, as she put more plates of sandwiches onto the tray Helen had left on the table. To understand that they wanted what was best for you, while having severe reservations about the way they'd gone about things? She'd be different with Owen, she thought, putting a white-bread finger on to the table of his little high chair, watching him pick it up, finger and thumb in a pincer grip, eyes almost crossed in concentration. That's what marks us apart from animals, Jane thought: that movement, and not a lot else, despite what we might believe.

Helen really hadn't aged that much in the fifteen years that had passed, Jane thought and yet, she'd changed completely. Her face, which had once been so bright, so full of life, had dulled, her mouth pulled down at the corners, her jaw set. She had a line on her forehead, a deep vertical gash that bisected her brows, that made her look permanently angry. Maybe she *was* angry, Jane thought as she took the tea brack that Mam had left out, placing it on the chopping board and hunting for a knife in the cutlery drawer. Jane had thought that she was the angry one: enraged at her sister's betrayal, but now, as she sliced into the rich dark cake, she wondered what it must have been like to be Helen. Jane was the black sheep, but Helen was the one left behind.

Jane knew that the idea of her being a black sheep would be hilarious to Gracie and Lina because they thought she was a doormat, and she was, she knew — or at least, she'd become one. For that one sin, she'd spent her whole life atoning, following other people's rules, doing what they wanted and packing her own self away. And now, here she was, with a husband who physically attacked her, who left her with visible marks on her skin, in a lovely, comfortable middle-class prison, no better in its way than St Dympna's, with its distemper yellow walls. And all because she felt it was what she deserved. It was her punishment.

The door swung open again and Jane's head snapped up, her knife, with a chunk of butter on it, poised over a slice of brack. 'I'll be in in just a second, Mam. I wanted to bring a bit of food in with me ...'

Her mother nodded absently, going over to one of the kitchen cupboards, opening it, looking inside and closing it again. She stood there for a few minutes, hands in the pockets of her black cardigan, before she took a tissue out and blew her nose, putting it back and then just standing there again.

'Mam?'

'What?' Her mother turned around, as if seeing Jane for the first time.

'I was saying that I have some brack ready to bring out to the good room.'

Mam made a dismissive gesture with her hand. 'If we give that lot any more food, they'll never leave.' It wasn't true: people in Castlemonkstown had respected Dad, but they hadn't liked him, so the group of people huddled in the good room would be gone before long.

Jane continued buttering, her mother coming over and pulling out a chair, sitting down beside her. 'I'd murder a cup of tea,' she said suddenly. 'You'd think I wouldn't, after the amount I've drunk, but I just can't think of anything else to do,' and she gave a small wail.

'Ah, Mam,' Jane said, reaching an arm around her mother's back, which felt small and bony under her hand.

Mam shook her head then, taking the tissue out of her cardigan pocket again and giving her nose another blow. 'It's not him dying that has me like this – sure he's been up at the hospice for months, and I'd made my peace with him going – it's the not knowing who I am without him, do you know what I mean?'

Jane nodded guiltily. I should have been here to say goodbye, she thought, me and Owen – and Mark, she added reluctantly to herself. The thought of her husband made her feel light-headed, giddy almost, with the freedom of being away from him for two whole days. He'd said to give Mam his 'best regards' but because of the partnership he couldn't afford to leave the office even for a few hours. 'I'm sorry,' he'd said.

You have no idea how happy that makes me, Jane had thought.

She'd dreaded coming back to her childhood home, herself and Owen sitting on the bus, speeding through the countryside that had once seemed so familiar: the little patchy green fields bordered by whitethorn; the clumps of rushes that were Dad's enemy because they made the ground soggy; the standing stones and ancient graves a testament to everyone who'd gone before them. And yet, as she'd left Dublin behind her, the choked streets, the smell of rubbish under the hot sun, the constant whirr of ice-cream vans and the noise of kids playing in the park, her spirits had begun to lift. 'This is where Mummy comes from,' she'd told Owen, sitting him up on her knee, pointing out the window, his little hand pressing against the glass. 'So you kind of come from here too.' Funny that the place she'd been so desperate to run from could change like that, could become a refuge. But maybe that was just her emotions getting the better of her.

'Your sister's been driving me up the wall,' Mam said, a sly grin on her face.

'She has?' Jane said neutrally, continuing to butter, ears pricked.

'She has. Helen can be impatient. Quick to judgement, you know.'

'You don't say.'

'It's a terrible curse, really, to look at the world and always find it wanting,' her mother said, looking at Jane carefully.

'It is,' Jane agreed, thinking that she wouldn't say another word. That subject was closed and she did not want to reopen it.

'Still, you can hardly blame her, having to put up with Dad and me for all these years and Dad wasn't a bit well these past few months,' Mam said.

'No,' Jane said softly. She looked at the brack and had a sudden desire to devour it. She bit into a slice, feeling the rich fruit fill her mouth, the slight saltiness of the butter. She'd forgotten how nice Mam's tea brack was. 'I'm sorry,' she added, through a mouthful of crumbs. 'I should have been there.'

'Well, it's too late now,' her mother said in her matter-of-fact manner. 'Still, it would have been nice if you'd made your peace with him.'

Jane nodded miserably. It would have been 'nice' but it would also have been impossible, not without acknowledging that Dad might actually have been right.

Her mother's hand was soft on Jane's, but firm. 'We thought we were doing the right thing, love. You were led astray, half-mad after that ... that man,' she said, her voice shaking.

'I was upset, Mam, and angry – but I wasn't mad,' Jane said. 'I was just young, that was all. Young and stupid.' All of which was true.

Mam nodded her head sadly. 'You were, but you paid for it.' And she gave Jane's hand a tight squeeze.

And how, Jane thought.

After that day in the class, when Jane had read Lady Macbeth's part, Mr Moloney had focused his intense blue-eyed stare on her more and more. At first, she'd been embarrassed because people kept coming up to her at break time, saying things like, 'Ooh, how does it feel to be Mr Moloney's girlfriend?' and making loud kissing sounds. Jane wasn't used to being singled out. She'd always blended in and it had suited her perfectly. She'd been taught that way by Mam and Dad because to stick out, to draw other people's attention to you, was sinful. As far as they were concerned, life was about keeping your head down and avoiding damnation, until the time came for you to meet your Maker, when you could show Him your clean slate. But Mr Moloney made her see things differently.

They'd started to meet after school to rehearse, because *Macbeth* was to be the school production that year; Mr Moloney had said she was the obvious choice for the part of Lady Macbeth, but he hadn't found the perfect 'foil' for her yet, so he'd have to read the role of Macbeth himself, which Jane had found thrilling. The two of them would sit in the

semi-dark school hall, Mr Moloney turning the chair back
to front, so he could sit on it, and rest his elbows on the
back, chin in his hands, Jane with her notebook and pen,
so she could listen and make notes on their performance.
Jane had been entranced. Mr Moloney didn't even sit like a
normal, boring person. He was too full of energy. They'd
go over and over the lines together, with him playing the
role of the cowed Macbeth and Jane slowly becoming the
real power behind the throne. She found that she enjoyed
it: it was good to be a scheming murderess, washing the
blood off her hands and roaring at her husband. She'd felt
special under his laser-like focus, as if she really mattered.

The trip to Galway had been his suggestion, to take a
'select few enthusiasts from the cast', as he'd put it, to see a
real, live performance of *Macbeth*, and even though there'd
been five of them squashed into his car, Jane had felt that
she was the only one. Sitting in the front passenger seat
beside him, she'd listened as he'd told her about where
he'd grown up, by the sea in Donegal, and she'd found
herself imagining him standing by a clifftop, the wind
blowing his inky-black hair. He'd told her about his first
teaching job, in a rough girls' school in Dublin. 'They
were like animals,' he'd laughed, and she'd found herself
imagining him sitting on the chair, the way he always did,
and trying to engage them with Seamus Heaney poems, the
class falling silent under his spell. Then he'd shown her a
picture of his eight-month-old baby, Victor, handing her
the crumpled photo he'd taken from his back pocket of a

little baby in a high chair, a shock of black hair standing up on his head. She'd looked at it for a long time, at this glimpse into a grown-up world that was far beyond her understanding, and then she'd handed it back to him. 'He's lovely. He looks just like you.'

He'd grinned then, eyes fixed on the road ahead. 'He's lovely because he looks just like me?'

Jane had blushed then. 'No, I mean – yes. He's very cute.'

'Aha,' he'd said, a small smile on his lips. Jane had thanked God for the darkness in the car so he wouldn't be able to see the colour of her face. There'd been silence then as they'd both listened to the crowd in the back, singing silly songs at the tops of their lungs, and then he'd said, 'You're not like all the rest of them in this place, do you know that?'

'What do you mean?' Jane had said, as Donal, who was to play Banquo and Caitriona Dooley, who was a wooden Lady Macduff, fought each other in the back of the car over a stick of chewing gum. She'd wanted to yell at them to shut up because she desperately wanted Mr Moloney to explain and to hear every single word.

'Is it because I'm a Baptist?' she'd blurted eventually over the din.

He'd laughed so much that tears had rolled down his face, and Caitriona Dooley had leaned into the front to ask him what was so funny. He hadn't been able to answer because he was choking with laughter, and Jane had wanted to reach out and cover his hand on the steering wheel. She wasn't even that annoyed at him laughing at her like that: at least she was special, she'd thought. Not like all the others.

Jane had never met anyone like Mr Moloney, certainly not at the dry Sunday-school gatherings that Mam and Dad had dispatched herself and Helen to, to sit colouring in pictures of Jesus, along with other dull, pale-faced children, and to have nice Dorothy tell them all about God. Mr Moloney gave her books by poets like Byron and Shelley, poems by Sylvia Plath, telling her all about her ill-fated marriage to Ted Hughes, Jane's face blushing bright red in the process. Mr Moloney was opening her eyes to a whole new way of looking at the world, and as winter became spring that year, Jane had found herself becoming different — taller, stronger, not afraid to voice an opinion. She'd even started smoking, Helen laughing at her as she cadged cigarettes off her. 'All the best actresses smoke,' had been her snooty explanation. Really, she'd thought as she'd puffed away out of her bedroom window, she felt a bit sorry for Helen, head down in her books and her tiny little dreams of being a teacher. 'The world isn't helped by you remaining small,' Mr Moloney had told Jane once, putting a hand on her shoulder. 'Remember that.'

When Jane had come home to tell her parents that she'd got the part of Lady Macbeth in the school play, Dad had said he'd have to think about whether to let her take part. He'd asked if Danny O'Brien, who was to play Macbeth, was a Catholic, by any chance, which was stupid, Jane had thought. Then he'd asked her for a copy of her textbook, putting on his reading glasses and scanning the lines for anything suspicious, and Jane had thanked God for his primary-school-only education, hoping that he wouldn't read the modern version at the back of the book. Mam, on the other hand, had gone along with it with great enthusiasm, taking out her sewing machine and spending a whole week trimming the green velvet of Lady Macbeth's cloak with fur from Granny McCarthy's old coat. And when Jane had taken her bow, when the play was finished, her mam had got up from her seat to applaud, only sitting down when Dad had tugged at her sleeve, giving her that look that told her she'd stepped out of line.

'Do you remember the school play?' Jane suddenly blurted to her mother now.

Mam was buttering a slice of brack and she put her knife down and smiled. 'I do. You were better than Vanessa Redgrave, so you were.'

'I was not, but thanks,' Jane said.

'I used to want to be an actress, you know,' Mam said wistfully.

'You did?' If Mam had said she'd wanted to be an astronaut, Jane could hardly have been more surprised.

'I did.' Mam laughed. 'Can you believe it — me? Maybe in another time I might have been, but our expectations were so low for ourselves. We'd no more have gone to acting school than fly to the moon. I wonder how many people in this place might have done something completely different if they'd had the chance.'

'I wonder,' Jane said neutrally.

She'd kissed Mr Moloney after the first-night celebrations, the whole of fifth year packing into the staffroom to drink Club Orange and eat crisps. They'd never been allowed past the door of the place, so standing in this grown-up room, with the mugs with teachers' first names on them and the tins of biscuits, it might as well have been a New York nightclub, Roscommon's answer to Studio 54. Mr Moloney had let them play their own music, the sounds of Eminem and his bad language blasting out from the speakers. He'd even let them smoke, telling them to go behind the bike sheds and not to let anyone see them. 'Or my reputation in this place will take a bashing,' he'd laughed. 'Not that I have one,' he'd added, to a chorus of giggles.

Jane had known he'd kiss her. He hadn't been able to take his eyes off her when she was on stage and she'd felt powerful, a vibrant life force full of rage and ambition, not a mousy teenager. She was kind of still in character, she'd thought to herself as she sipped on her drink and listened to some long and boring story that Donal was telling her. She was far away from the muddy ground and the little streams of Castlemonkstown, in a Scottish castle, plotting great things. So, she'd let the others drift off, refusing

Donal's offer to walk her home, telling him that Helen had said she'd come down in the car to pick her up. She'd got her driving licence that summer and availed of any excuse to take the car out for a spin, so it wasn't that much of a fib, really.

'Don't you have to get home?' Mr Moloney had said to her while she'd busied herself putting plastic cups into binbags and sweeping crisps and sweet wrappers off the ground.

'Don't you?' she'd responded, leaning on the sweeping brush.

He'd laughed. 'I'm not in a hurry, believe me.'

'Why not?' She'd known that asking the question was crossing a line. That she could just let it go and then they could both step back from the brink, but she couldn't help herself. She'd felt that her courage that night wasn't fully her own and she had to see it through, just like Lady Macbeth – she had to 'screw her courage to the sticking place', she'd thought, feeling quite pleased with her analogy.

'Ah, it's a bit of a mess, really,' he'd said, running a hand through his hair. He'd shaken his head then. 'It's grown-up stuff.'

'What kind of stuff?' Jane had said, inching towards him, broom in hand.

'It's just ... life kind of gets to you after a while, you know? Victor's teething, Melissa's complaining about the damp and the bills and I'm stuck in the middle, the wimp who can't earn enough to provide for his family. And she hates this dump ...' He'd waved a hand then. 'Sorry. I didn't mean that.'

'It *is* a dump,' Jane had replied. 'And I can't wait to get out of it.' And then she'd rested the broom on a table beside her and she'd come over and stood opposite him. 'You've changed my life,' she'd told him, unembarrassed by her words. 'If it wasn't for you, I'd still be sitting at the back of the class hoping no one would notice me, but now I feel that I want the whole world to see me,' she'd said with a soft giggle. 'I feel that I can do anything.'

He'd looked at her then, fixing her with his intense gaze. 'I'm glad of that, Jane. It's what's good about teaching, that you really can make a difference.'

He'd been reminding her of who he was, but Jane hadn't really been listening. The staffroom was completely silent except for the hiss of the Burco water boiler in the corner, as they'd stood facing each other. He hadn't fixed her with those eyes then – instead they'd looked away from her, over her head, and she'd had to put a hand up to turn his face to hers.

'Jane ...' he'd begun, but she'd kissed him anyway and it was unlike any other kiss she'd ever had, at least the rubbery ones she'd occasionally received from the local boys at the awful GAA discos that her parents let her go to, on condition that she was home by ten. She'd felt like a grown-up then, sophisticated and world-weary, not like a silly teenager with a crush on the drama teacher. And even though he'd said it wasn't supposed to happen and it would never happen again, she didn't care, because she'd known it would.

'You know, Donal's home every weekend now, ever since his mother got dementia, God help her,' Mam's voice broke into her thoughts. 'I don't think it'll be long before she'll be in a home, but, sure, he's doing his best. He has the house plastered with them what-do-you-call-it, Post-its, with the names of things on them, like "Cooker" and "TV". Can you imagine being so far gone that you don't know what a television is?' She shook her head sadly.

Donal — Jane hadn't thought about him in years. She'd blotted him from her mind, just as she'd blotted out everything else about Castlemonkstown.

'I always thought the two of you would have made a nice couple, young though you were. You seemed to care a lot about each other.'

'We did,' Jane said, surprised for a moment because it was true. She remembered that Donal was the only one of her friends who'd call to the door, and because he was so polite, Mam and Dad actually let him in, and Jane would often find him sitting at the kitchen table, tucking into a sandwich, the biscuit tin, which was normally only for the Reverend Conander, on the table in front of him. 'Will we go for a walk?' he'd say when she'd appear, Mister Magoo at her feet, as usual, looking eager. The two of them really would go for a walk, too: it wasn't a euphemism for smoking in front of the petrol station or hanging around outside the chipper — they'd take long rambles across the fields to the standing stone at the top of Tullis Hill, and they'd talk about everything they'd do when they left Castlemonkstown. 'The world is at our feet,' Donal was fond of saying. She wondered what he'd say now.

He'd tried to warn her about Mr Moloney, to tell her that the whole school was talking about it and to stop before it was too late, but she'd ignored him. She'd simply pushed him away, making up excuses when he'd call to the door, telling him that she had a headache or was busy revising until he got the message. Evenings that would have been spent with Donal were now spent with Mr Moloney at the river behind the GAA pitch, which wasn't overlooked, the two of them sitting on mossy stones, him telling her of his latest domestic woe and she listening, rapt, at this glimpse into his world. Never had a broken boiler or a child's sore throat seemed so exotic. At other times, he'd take her for drives in his car: he'd collect her in front of the disused petrol station on the old road to Galway and she'd have to duck every time they passed another car, in case it was someone local who'd recognise them. She used to shake so much with laughter at this that she thought she'd wet herself, his hand pressing on her head as she bent over in the passenger footwell.

'I think he wanted to be a poet,' Mam said.

'Who?' Jane said, tuning back in to the conversation.

'Donal. He had a couple of things published in the

Tribune, but I'm not sure if it came to anything. Talent gone to waste, but then, that's what this place will do to you.'

There was a long silence while they both absorbed this, which Mam broke. 'Tell me, do you have any friends above?'

'I do, Mam. I have good friends.' Jane thought of Gracie and realised that she was a real friend.

Mam picked up her hand and squeezed it tightly. 'I'm glad to hear it. Hang onto them, pet. You don't know when you'll need them.'

I've a feeling I do, Jane thought.

The rest of the evening was spent clearing up after the guests, Jane stationing herself at the sink, washing every cup and saucer in hot, soapy water, looking out the window onto the little garden so that she wouldn't have to make conversation with Helen. Behind her, her sister and mother shuffled back and forth from the good room, bringing in plates and cutlery, then wrapping leftovers in cling film. They worked in silence, punctuated by the odd, 'Throw that out, we'll never eat it,' or, 'Would you not take that home to Peter and the girls? It's got fresh cream in it, so it'll only spoil here.'

'Peter and the girls'. Jane realised that she'd never met Helen's husband or children, who'd been whisked away after the Church service, and until today, Helen had never met Owen. The losses suddenly seemed overwhelming to Jane and now she couldn't really understand why they'd both let it go on for so long. But they had, and there was nothing to be done about it at this stage, she thought, picking up another bowl, with its pattern of roses bordered by a line of gilt, and holding it to the light to check for smudges. It was too late. She didn't want to forgive Helen for betraying her and Helen didn't want to forgive her for having been the one to get away, to leave home, unlike her, still stuck here after all these years. If only her sister knew, Jane thought. Maybe she wouldn't envy Jane's life quite so much.

She went to bed early, pleading a headache and Owen needing an early night, giving Mam a squeeze and Helen a vague wave and climbing the stairs to her childhood bedroom, one that she'd shared with her sister until she'd left home. She'd forgotten how quiet the nights were here, the silence a dense blanket that covered the country, broken only by the shriek of a bird woken from sleep or by the noise of a car passing on the road. Jane kept the curtains open so that she could see the moon outside, bright yellow in the still-pink sky.

She remembered that other summer, the summer Mr Moloney had left Castlemonkstown, his little car crammed to the roof with stuff, his wife sitting bolt upright in the passenger seat beside him, a look that would curdle milk on her face, according to Aisling Farrell, the school gossip, whom Jane had overheard when she was searching for baking powder in the local shop. 'It's the most exciting thing to have happened in this dump in forever,' she'd tittered to Shauna, the girl who worked behind the counter. 'Who'd have thought it, though? That wimp Jane, of all people. I didn't think she had it in her.'

It was a compliment, of sorts, but Jane hadn't seen it that way: Mr Moloney wasn't leaving because of her. He was leaving because of what she'd told her sister.

She'd been so angry, she'd had to confide in someone. She could still remember the white-hot rage she'd felt when he'd told her it was over, that he couldn't go on seeing her like this. 'I'm a teacher, Jane,' he'd said as they'd both stood in the classroom a week before the summer term was to end. 'It's an abuse of trust.'

'Oh, now you remember?' she'd hissed. 'It didn't seem to bother you before, did it?'

He'd shaken his head sadly, guiltily. 'I know and I'm sorry, Jane, sorrier than you'll ever know.'

'So, why?' Jane had said, eyes filling with tears. 'If you're all that sorry, why finish things?' The thought of being without him, of not listening to him talk about his grown-up life, had been so devastating to Jane. She had to tell someone, she thought, or the feelings would just wipe her out. Then it had come to her: Helen.

Telling Helen the truth about her and Mr Moloney had been the most foolish part. She should have known that Helen would tell Mam and Dad, but to Jane the risks were outweighed by her need to unburden herself.

She could still remember where she'd told her sister — in the bathroom, with its horrible puce bathroom furniture, the shell-shaped sink and the cistern that dripped; the icy wind that always blew in the ancient window. Helen had been getting ready to go to a GAA fundraiser – the only entertainment that Mam and Dad considered suitable – and Jane's stomach had heaved as she'd smelled Helen's cheap perfume. She could still remember the look on Helen's face – a mixture of concern and horror.

'Please don't tell Mam and Dad,' Jane had begged, 'Please, Helen. You know what they're like. They'll kill me.' And God knows what they'd do to Mr Moloney, Jane thought, if they ever found out.

Helen had said nothing for the longest time, she sitting on the closed lid of the loo, Jane on the edge of the bath in her furry pyjamas, like a nine-year-old. They had been holding hands and Jane's were cold and clammy, Helen's warm and safe. Jane had wanted to climb onto her sister's knee, put her head on her shoulder and cry her heart out.

Helen had that crease between her eyebrows, indicating that she was thinking, and Jane had hung onto that expression as if it were a life raft. Eventually, Helen had put an arm around her sister. 'It'll be OK – I won't tell. I promise.'

Helen had lied, and in the days and months that followed Jane would wish that the clock had turned back, that she'd kept her secret to herself. She'd imagine that her teacher wasn't being dragged before the school board, then being hustled off to a boys' school in the wilds of Donegal. How she'd longed to be just her old self getting up to the odd bit of mischief or walking around the fields with Donal, talking about books and poetry. How she'd wanted desperately to be bored out of her mind again, as she'd been for almost her entire life. Being bored, it turned out, wasn't the worst thing that could happen to you.

Instead, Helen had stood at the foot of the stairs the following morning and called her down. Her parents had been sitting on either side of the kitchen table, the teapot, in its multicoloured cosy that Jane had knitted in third class, in between them. And Jane had known. Her parents hadn't shouted and screamed, ranted or raved. Her father had simply told her that it was Mr Moloney's fault and he would have to accept the consequences of what he'd done.

'But it was *me*,' Jane had protested. 'I led him on, I—' she'd begun, but her father had lifted his hand and smacked her across the face. 'That's enough! There's a word for men like him, but I won't defile our home by saying it.'

The only thing she'd been able to do for Mr Moloney was to deny everything when Sister Monica grilled her in her office. She'd had to directly contradict what she'd said to her sister, agreeing with Sister Monica that her parents had come down to the school for nothing, concocting a story about having been disappointed that he hadn't picked her for the summer musical. She'd had to deny it even when the garda had come to see her. The only relief to her had been that it wasn't Garda Hannity, who'd known her since childhood, because he was in Galway on a training course. This man was from Dublin, and he'd taken her statement with great seriousness, making scrupulous notes in his notebook, asking her if she fully understood that if a teacher did what her parents said Mr Moloney had done, he'd be breaking the law, 'in the most serious manner'.

'I do understand,' Jane had said. 'I'm sorry. I made it all up.'

She'd stayed at home for the rest of the summer, forbidden from setting foot outside the door. Donal had called once, and Mam had told him she had glandular fever – why, Jane couldn't understand as the whole county knew by that stage. Jane had wanted to run down the stairs, grab him by the hand and tell him to run with her all the way down to the road, where they could hitch a lift and be in Dublin by lunchtime. But she didn't, because it was bad enough to ruin her own life – she didn't want to ruin his too.

Jane had never spoken to her sister again. They'd lived in complete silence for the following year, when Jane had taken the bus to the technical college in town to do her Leaving Cert, getting honours in Art and Home Economics. And then the following summer, Jane had gone berserk one morning, smashing up her bedroom and breaking her sister's collection of china dolls, given to her by Granny McCarthy, gouging great holes in their horrible faces – and she'd ended up in that awful hospital. Helen had visited her then, she remembered, the two of them sitting in the overheated green-painted TV room, *Neighbours* playing behind them while Rebecca, one of the other patients, sang at the top of her voice, and Helen had told her that she'd done the only thing possible in telling Mam and Dad, that there was no other way, and didn't Jane understand that she was trying to protect her. 'Men like him need to go to jail, Jane,' she'd said, tutting and turning on her heel when Jane had just looked beyond her out the window to the fields.

When she was judged to be better, she'd once more followed Mam and Dad's instructions, moving to Dublin and in with Auntie Kathleen, the two of them sitting by the fire in the evenings, eating cheese on toast on trays in front of *The Late Late Show*. She'd dragged herself through secretarial school, again at her parents' insistence, then teacher-training, and all the time, she'd thought of Mr Moloney and how bright he'd made her feel. How capable and talented and as if she could achieve anything in this life.

It wasn't Helen's fault, Jane thought suddenly, the hoot of an owl waking her from her half-sleep. It was mine. Mine and Mr Moloney's. He was an adult and I was still a child. The lines were clear and he blurred them, inviting me into his confidence, into a world for which I wasn't ready. But I hadn't seen it that way then. Then, I was Lady Macbeth, capable of anything and he was my wimpy husband, doing what I wanted.

When Jane went back to sleep, she dreamt that her sister was lying beside her in the bed, and she seemed to be dead, her face blueish-white, cheeks sunken, just like Dad's had been in his coffin, a wisp of white hair on his forehead. She woke with a start in the dim light of early morning, her mouth dry. I'm a very bad person, she thought, lifting Owen quietly up from his place on the bed beside her and walking onto the landing. She stood at Mam's door for a while, but all she could hear were her mother's soft snores. As she put out a foot to walk down the polished mahogany steps in her bare feet, she had a sudden vision of slipping and falling, herself and Owen hurtling through the air to land in a crumpled heap on the hall floor, both of them never to wake again. She had to stop and grip the banisters as tightly as she could to prevent herself from acting on it, repeating Phyllis's mantra, the one she'd taught her to use when her 'disturbing thoughts' filled her mind. 'They're just thoughts, Jane. They're only dangerous if you act on them.'

She crept downstairs and put Owen into his buggy, tucking a blanket around him, even though, in early September, it was still warm. As she walked down the avenue under the sycamore trees, she could see their leaves above her head, heavy with dust, weary after the long, hot summer. They look the way I feel, she thought, as she pushed the buggy over the bumpy ground towards the Protestant churchyard, where all the local kids had done their teenage smoking and drinking. She didn't see the car until it was beside her and the driver slowed, the window rolling down.

Donal's voice was lower now, richer, and when Jane leaned in through the passenger window, she saw the small lines fanning out from his eyes, the tiny sprinkle of grey amongst the brown of his hair, even though he was only thirty-two. Maybe that's what looking after your senile mother did to you. 'Your mam said you were back. I'm sorry to hear about your dad. I couldn't get to the funeral because I had to take Mum to the hospital.'

'How is she? Mam told me that she wasn't well.'

He shrugged. 'Ah, you know. Yesterday she thought I was the postman and she kept asking me if I didn't have any letters to deliver, and why was I kidnapping her instead?'

Jane gave a small laugh, even though it wasn't really funny. Look at the two of us, she thought. We thought we'd take on the world, and yet here we are.

Then Donal peered around her and said, 'Who's that handsome fellow?'

'Oh, this is Owen,' Jane said, accepting Donal's admiring noises.

'I heard you'd got married to some hotshot lawyer,' Donal said. 'Congratulations.'

Jane thought she might cry, focusing steadfastly on Owen so that she could keep her emotions under control. 'Thanks,' she said eventually. 'It's all been a big change.'

'I'd say so — but a good one.'

'Yes, that's right,' Jane said woodenly.

'Life moves on, eh?'

'It sure does,' Jane said. 'What about you? Any sign of Mrs Donal yet?'

It was an old joke, from when they were teenagers and

he swore he would never find Mrs Right, or Mrs Donal, as he'd used to say.

'Ah, no. Strangely, a man in possession of a mother with dementia isn't all the rage on Tinder right now,' he said. He was smiling, but Jane knew that it must have hurt him. Donal was made for relationships: he was funny, sensitive and well-read. Jane used to joke with him that she'd take him herself if no one else came along. Now, it seemed as if it was too late for both of them.

Donal looked in his rear-view mirror then. 'Uh-oh, here comes Pat Hanratty to run me off the road. I'd better be off – will you call in one of the days if you're passing?'

'I will,' Jane said, not wanting him to go, wanting to hold him back and ask him if he'd like a coffee or a chat – 'It'll be like old times,' she wanted to say, but then he was gone, the car disappearing over the hill.

'C'mon, Owen,' Jane said. 'Let's go and say goodbye to Auntie Helen and try to make it civil this time.' She walked back with Owen to the farmhouse and sat down at the breakfast table with her mother and her sister and the three of them chatted about silly things, like telly and what Helen's kids were into and their summer camps. And Mam had let Helen smoke, opening the window so her sister could lean out, puffing away. 'Maybe you'd call in, the next time you're down. You can see the new house. It has four bathrooms, which Peter insisted on, even if it just gives me more cleaning to do,' she laughed, a stream of smoke wafting out of her mouth.

'That makes two of you,' Jane said.

'Two of us what?'

'Oh, I met Donal down the road, and he said the same thing.'

'Well, then you'll have to come down again, won't you?' Mam said, giving a little smile before getting up to busy herself at the range.

15

Lina

Hey, how did you get on? Bet you blew him away! There was a whole row of emojis beside Elise's text, lots of smiley faces. Lina wanted to throw the phone at the wall, feel it smash into a lot of tiny pieces, but instead, she pushed it down to the bottom of her bag and strode out of the hotel lobby, as if she were just another busy businessperson after a meeting. Her legs felt wobbly, though, and she had to lean against the door for a few moments and the doorman asked if she needed a taxi. 'No thanks,' she said. 'I just need some fresh air.'

It was the truth – she needed to suck in deep lungfuls of the cool night air, feel it rinse her clean, but when she got down the steps of the hotel to the street, she found that she needed to sit down again. Her teeth were chattering and her mouth was full of bile. She wobbled over to a bench beside the river and eased herself onto it, perching on the edge of the wooden slats, looking out at the blurred orange and yellow of the street lights reflected in the water. She just wanted to empty her mind of all thought, of all memory of what had just happened.

Abbie had met her at the door of the hotel, her pink hair tied into a ponytail. She had been wearing big round glasses with white frames, her eyes huge behind the goldfish-bowl lenses. 'Hi!' She'd enveloped Lina in a hug. 'How's the head?'

Lina'd giggled, like a fool. 'I haven't felt that drunk since college.'

'I know,' Abbie had said. 'You and me both. Honestly, those boys ... Anyway, Conor's in the bar with Mack.' Abbie had given a conspiratorial wink, her magnified eyelashes like a tarantula behind her glasses. 'He says to drop by as soon as you've finished with Graham.'

'Really?' Lina had squeaked, hating herself for sounding like a starstruck teenager, which she absolutely wasn't. She hadn't really taken Conor that seriously that night two weeks before: she knew that he was just fooling around, or at least, she thought she knew. *She* definitely had been, although when Gracie had waved that picture of him and his missus under her nose, she had been a bit embarrassed — but only because she'd been caught out. She didn't believe that men and women owed each other anything. Nope, she'd thought, as she'd listened to Abbie's excitable chatter as she led her down a long, gloomy corridor, Lina had been quite clear what she wanted from this whole exchange. 'A star in the making' is what Mack had called her. Well, it was time to grab her chance.

'Here we are!' Abbie had said, leading her into a cramped little office filled with piles of paper, a tower of ring-binders piled on top of a chair, which she'd hastily moved. 'Take a seat,' she'd added. 'It's the manager's office, but they've lent it to us for the duration. Now, let's see ...'

'What's this?' Lina had pointed at what looked like a very large lunchbox with a dial at the front, a black flex extending from it to a socket in the wall.

'Oh, it's an egg incubator,' Abbie had said, as if it were perfectly normal to find one in a cramped office in a city-centre hotel. 'Mack's really into hens. I have to carry the bloody thing everywhere.' She had given a small giggle as she checked her laptop.

'Is that in the job description?' Lina had joked.

'Hah,' Abbie had said. 'If only you knew.'

Lina had turned that over in her mind for a few minutes, before deciding to say nothing further. Mack seemed really cool, so was it that much of a disaster if he got Abbie to supervise his egg collection? Still, it seemed a bit ... over the top. Nobody ever asked her to do anything she didn't want to at Download. Once, Tom in accounts receivable had asked her to make him a cup of tea and Magda, the project manager, had practically kneecapped him. 'No one is here to make your tea!' she'd spat at him. 'We have no Irish mammies here,' she'd added, which had made them all splutter into their non-fat flat whites.

'So,' Abbie had said. 'Graham McSween.'

'I know!'

'Just a few tips. Keep it short — he has the attention span of a gnat; put your best material up front because, I guarantee you, he won't be listening after about two minutes; and be confident. He doesn't like wallflowers — but then, you're hardly a wallflower, are you?' She'd beamed, tapping her pen on the table.

'No, no,' Lina had said, with a little laugh. And she wasn't, but she had suddenly been feeling a bit nervous: the other time, at the party, she'd been drunk, so drunk she'd found herself singing some cheesy pop song at the top of her voice with Abbie bellowing along beside her and then snogging Conor Creighton, neither of which had been on her list earlier that night.

'Pity you're not wearing the dress,' Abbie had added casually, getting up from her seat and picking up a lanyard, popping it over her head.

'What?'

'That va-va-voom number. That would have made him sit up and take note.' Abbie had laughed.

Lina had looked down at her neat white T-shirt, jeans

and black jacket. It was her Download uniform, and she hadn't looked at it since getting pregnant, digging it out of the back of the wardrobe and letting Mama iron it for her while she'd washed and dressed. She had been a bit surprised at Mama's offer, but she'd accepted it nonetheless. She'd managed to fend Elise off because she had no desire to look like *that* again, and this look was much, much better. 'I didn't think I needed it,' she'd said, with what she hoped was enough acid for Abbie to understand, but the other girl had just laughed. 'Oh, well, your loss.'

The thought had popped into Lina's head: I can leave. There's still time. But then another thought had followed that: this is your big chance. Are you going to grab it or not? 'I'm ready,' she'd said, with as much confidence as she could muster.

'Great!' Abbie had smiled. 'Let's go!' She had unplugged the incubator and tucked it under her arm, giving it a little pat. 'They come everywhere with me,' she'd said sweetly.

How can a woman who carries an egg incubator be in any way harmful? Lina had told herself, trying to be logical about the creeping unease she felt. Cop on and get on with it. Obediently, Lina had followed Abbie through a maze of gloomy corridors decorated with dated flowery wallpaper and a carpet that seemed to sink damply under her feet. As she'd walked, she couldn't shake the feeling that she was descending into something dark and unpleasant. Don't be silly, she'd chided herself; it's only a cheap hotel, not the seventh circle of hell.

Eventually, Abbie had knocked on a chipped black-painted door. 'Graham — you decent?'

I think I'm going to be sick, Lina had thought as she followed Abbie through the door and into a small, dingy space. Graham McSween had been sitting at a solitary desk in the middle — a balding, overweight man in a grey T-shirt, unbuttoned checked shirt and jeans that were too small for him. His skin had been such a pale white that it looked almost green in the dim light of the little conference room, contrasting with his neatly trimmed dark beard, the only tidy thing about him. He had looked up from his phone and his eyes had flicked over her, like a lizard's.

'Graham, this is Lina — you know, Mack's girl. She's going to perform her new show for you — so pay attention, will you?'

'I'm not actually Mack's girl ...' Lina had said, really quietly.

'Well, whatever,' Abbie had said, raising her eyebrows as if to say 'behave'. 'Be nice, Graham,' and with that, the door had closed behind her and Lina had been alone in the room with Graham McSween, a man she didn't know from Adam.

She'd pulled her jacket close around her.

'Cold?' he'd said, getting up from the desk and going to the air-conditioning unit in the corner. As he'd bent down, Lina had caught a glimpse of the waistband of his boxers, and above that, a fine display of builder's arse.

Yuck. 'We can fix that,' he'd said cheerfully, flicking the switch on the side of the unit. 'Water?'

'Ehm, thanks,' Lina had said, accepting the plastic cup of water he poured from a jug on his desk. As he'd handed it to her, he hadn't released his grip, his hand over hers, so she had to wrench it away slightly. 'Thanks.' She had taken a too-big swig of it and found herself choking, coughing and spluttering and trying to catch her breath.

'Whoopsie,' he'd said, coming over to her and patting her on the back, a look of concern on his chubby face.

'It's fine,' Lina had said, wishing he'd stop. 'It just went down the wrong way.'

'Sure,' he'd said, continuing with his patting.

'Ehm, will I start now?' Lina had said, hoping to distract him.

'Ah, sure, why not,' Graham had said, not moving. He hadn't sounded like a man who'd been waiting for her pitch, for her ideas and her material, but maybe he auditioned everybody like this — kind of casually. Maybe it was a good thing, Lina had thought, as she had tried to find her centre, the place from which she could be herself, but all she could feel were the damp patches of sweat under her arms, the itch of the foundation she'd applied to her face, just to even her out a bit. She never normally wore the stuff, mainly because it made her skin itch, but also because it cost too much, but she'd gone into Boots earlier that afternoon and the nice girl behind the counter had given her a sample.

She'd cleared her throat and begun her opening gag. 'I sometimes think ... I sometimes think that being a mother is like being ... like being ...' She couldn't for the life of her remember what it felt like being. This person standing in front of Graham McSween had seemed to be someone else, someone not in possession of jokes or a routine. 'I'm sorry,' she'd said eventually. 'I'll start again.'

He'd nodded pleasantly enough. 'Deep breath, love. Here, let me help you.' For a big man, he could move very quickly, Lina had thought, as he stood behind her and placed a meaty, clammy hand on each shoulder. 'Now ... let me feel you breathing ... that's it, in through the nose and out through the mouth. It's a yoga technique.'

'Right,' Lina had said, desperate to shake his hands off her shoulders. She'd cleared her throat again and began. 'I sometimes think ...' but it was no good. Her mind had been a complete blank. She'd felt the seconds tick away, the silence in the room grow more deafening until eventually all she could hear was her own heartbeat, thumping away in her ears, the weight of his hands on her shoulders, the hiss of his breath beside her ear. She'd known he was close, but she hadn't wanted to turn her head to see, so she'd just stared straight ahead.

'I sometimes think ...' she'd begun, closing her eyes, then opening them again. 'I'm sorry,' she'd said, 'do you think you could ...?' and she'd gestured towards his hands.

He had looked at them as if they didn't belong to him, but he'd removed them and came to stand in front of her, hands in his pockets, a big grin on his face. 'You seem very tense.'

'Do I?'

'Yeah – just relax, take a breath and we can do it again. 'Kay?'

Did everyone here say ''kay'? Lina had wondered, but she'd felt grateful to him for giving her a second chance, and she'd given him a small, nervous smile. He'd returned it, but the expression on his face had been oily and she'd felt her stomach heave.

'OK then, deep breaths, in and out, until you feel yourself settle.'

'Right,' Lina had said obediently, sucking in a deep breath. She'd been about to start when she noticed how close he was to her, standing barely a foot away. How had he done that? she'd wondered, looking down at his feet, then up at him.

'Are you breathing?' His breath had smelled of garlic and Lina had wanted to be sick.

'Yes,' she'd squeaked.

'Great, well, then, let's go again. You tell me your little jokes, and I'll listen really hard – 'kay?'

Definitely not 'kay, Lina had thought, but I'm stuck here and I have to make this work. I have to. 'I always think …' she'd begun. At this, she had felt him move even closer, so that the edge of his considerable belly was pressing into her. Oh, Jesus. Lina had known she'd have to think of something, so she'd said, in her best feminist voice. 'I'd really rather you didn't do that, Graham.'

'Didn't do what?' Suddenly he'd leaned towards her, his voice hot in her ear. 'I'm doing nothing but offering you an audition for your mummy gags out of the goodness of my heart. Quid pro quo, pet. Quid pro quo.' With this, he had pressed his mouth to her ear and blew. The next thing, she'd felt his tongue flicker in her ear.

She'd had to resist every impulse to deck him as she'd closed her eyes and willed the wave of nausea that rose from her stomach to subside. All rational thought had left her head and her senses had suddenly been on high alert — she had been able to hear an ambulance siren in the street outside, where it all had been normal, where people shopped and ate and went about their sunny, daily business. But in here, she had been able to smell nothing but rancid garlic, the taste of it filling her nostrils.

'So,' he'd said, his breath hot in her ear. 'What's it to be? Do you want to leave here with a deal under your belt, or to go back to your little cave and toil away hopelessly for ever?'

Lina had had to quell the urge to be violently ill all over Graham McSween's blue suede shoes. I would really like to crush your skull with my bare hands right now, she'd thought, but because I really, really want to be a successful comedian, I will have to go along with your sick agenda.

'What'll I get if I do it?'

His head had snapped back and he'd laughed. 'Well, I wasn't expecting that.'

'What were you expecting?' Lina had said. 'Me to run from the room screaming?' She had been trying to keep her voice low and steady, so she wouldn't betray her inner panic at the thought of what she might be permitting this man to do.

'Well, the thought had occurred to me,' he'd said. 'You wouldn't be the first,' and he had given another laugh that sounded like a girlish giggle.

'You'll get five minutes and, this time, I'll listen,' he'd said. 'And if you're good enough, you'll get your series — but that's a big "if".' He'd made little air quotes with his fingers, meaty, flabby sausages of white.

'Deal,' Lina had said.

She'd had to sit on his knee and let him remove her jacket, his breath coming in short, garlicky puffs, then she'd had to let him remove her freshly ironed, clean white T-shirt and place his hands on her breasts, which she'd thanked God were at least shielded by a giant maternity bra. Then she'd had to let him bury his face in her chest, making animal noises. She'd found that if she turned her head away and looked at the terrible painting beside the door, a portrait of Merrion Square with misshapen flowers and neon-bright grass, she could pretend that this man was not wallowing in her cleavage. But when his hand had moved downwards, she'd stood up so abruptly, he'd banged his nose off the belt of her jeans. 'Ow, Jesus!'

'Sorry. So, will I start?' she'd said.

He had managed to nod, cupping his nose, which was

now bleeding, with his hand, producing a hankie and holding it to it.

This time, when she'd opened her mouth the words came out, a fluent stream of jokes about motherhood, even as in her mind she had gone somewhere else, far away from this dungeon. When she'd been finished, she'd said, 'Thank you for the opportunity, Graham', and she'd held out her hand, even though she'd wanted to grab his in hers and fling his flabby body to the ground.

He'd removed the now-bloodstained hankie and looked at it sceptically, before deciding the bleeding had stopped, taking her hand gingerly in his. Recovering, he'd smiled that oily smile of his, pulling her towards him and enveloping her in a smelly, moist hug. 'You're a special talent, do you know that?' He'd said into her hair.

'Yes, Graham,' Lina had managed. 'In spite of everything, I do.'

She'd held her head up as she left the room, walking back through the maze of corridors, hearing the solid thunk of the lift, the rattle of a tea trolley on another floor, and then she was in the lobby. She'd wanted to run outside onto the street, where it was still light, but instead, she had hesitated there for a second, peering into the bar, spotting, to her mortification, Conor Creighton, then Mack's Stetson and, beside it, the pink of Abbie's hair. The two men had been talking and she'd been taking notes, the three heads together as if they were plotting something. Then Abbie had spotted her and beckoned her over. 'So – how'd it go?'

'Marvellous, it was just amazing,' Lina had said blankly.

Abbie's eyelashes had batted behind her glasses. 'Well, I'm glad. Drink?'

'No, thanks. I just wanted to thank you both,' Lina had said, leaning over to Mack as if she was going to kiss him on the cheek, swiping his pint with her hand as she did, so he'd got a glass of chilled Guinness in his lap. 'What the fuck?' he'd said.

Specks of treacly porter had splashed onto Conor Creighton's boxfresh white trainers and he'd looked at Lina as if she'd betrayed him.

'Oh my goodness,' she'd said, 'I'm so sorry.' She'd reached into her pocket and pulled out an ancient, balled-up bit of tissue and handed it to him. 'You'll need this,' she had said, as Abbie had returned with a bar cloth. 'So sorry,' she had said to Abbie. 'I'm really very clumsy, you see.' And with that, she'd given a little wave and left Abbie dabbing her boss's crotch with a probably filthy bar towel.

In a daze, Lina walked towards the river now, taking off her uncomfortable, pointy work shoes and feeling the bare, dirty concrete under her feet. She had a sudden longing for chips, to feel their hot saltiness in her mouth, but when she looked in her purse, she found she had no money. She'd given it to Mama to buy groceries. Oh, fuck, she thought. It was then that the tears of self-pity began to flow — self-pity and self-reproach.

Her thoughts turned to Elise then and to her silly text, to which she replied in her head. No, it didn't exactly go well, Elise, but it might not have gone quite so badly if you hadn't persuaded me to dress like a slut in the first place – to be someone I wasn't. But then, she thought, that wasn't fair – dress had absolutely nothing to do with it and Elise had only been trying to get her to put her best foot forward, albeit in her own tacky way. No, the deal she'd just made with the devil was her own responsibility entirely. She probably wouldn't even get a spot out of it, knowing that prick – but then, she thought miserably, maybe I don't deserve it. Maybe I'm not the world's next comedy star, or even Ireland's – I'm just a comedian with a line in mediocre mummy gags who is doing what so many have done before her: going along with creepy gits like Graham McSween to get ahead. Look at you, she thought – call yourself a feminist now? You think that you're in control, that you can dictate the terms, but you're wrong.

She reached the river and, out of her bag, she pulled her notes, with their bolshie, upfront stories about motherhood that now seemed utterly pathetic, tearing them into tiny pieces, watching them spill like confetti into the water and swish away. She felt as if she were saying goodbye to a part of herself and to her dreams, and at the thought, the tears of self-pity started again, until she couldn't stop. She trudged across the Ha'penny Bridge, the river a pinky-blue beneath her as the sun set. For some reason, Seamus came into her mind for the first time in ages. She thought about him in his smart casuals, holding his child. No, she decided — she didn't need another man to comfort her, to make her feel better. That was weak and silly. She needed ... what exactly? She stopped so abruptly that someone ran into her from behind and she had to apologise. There was no way that the thing missing from her life was a man — no way.

She took her phone out of her bag and rang his number.

Seamus hadn't asked a single question, but had simply tucked her arm into his and said, 'Let's go to some old-man place.' How did he know that an old-man place, with its comforting smell of beer and toasted-cheese sandwiches, was just what she needed? He led her to a seat down the back of the pub, a squishy red banquette with a scattering of cigarette burns in the fabric, said, 'Back in a sec,' then returned with two pints and two packets of cheese and onion crisps, along with a double whiskey in a small glass.

'This is for you,' he said, putting it front of her.

'Thanks,' she said, picking the glass up and knocking it back. 'Jesus,' she wheezed. 'That's strong.'

'You looked like you could do with it.'

Lina thought she wouldn't be able to eat, but with the whiskey inside her, she felt a sudden warmth filling her chest, and her teeth stopped chattering. Suddenly, she'd never felt so hungry in her life, tearing into the packet and scoffing the crisps. She then took a big swig of the pint.

Seamus remained silent throughout, taking small sips

of his drink, waiting. 'So ...' he said eventually. 'What's the matter?'

Lina shook her head, taking another mouthful of her pint, feeling the chill of the beer fill her stomach. 'If I tell you, you'll think it's all my fault. You'll think I'm one of those girls.'

'One of what girls?'

Lina sighed, and then the tears came again, hot and fast, and she needed three red-paper serviettes to mop them up, as she hiccupped and tried to get the words out — about Graham McSween, the feeling of his hot, clammy hands on her shoulders, his nasty tongue in her ear, then the rest. She wondered briefly whether to hold back on the breasts bit, but decided to tell Seamus everything. She knew she could trust him. He was the father of her child, even in board shorts and a Hawaiian shirt, bare feet resting on the bar of the stool, his flip-flops cast off under the table.

'That's what I can't forget,' she finished. 'He smelled like ... an animal, that's what it was,' she said sadly.

She looked at Seamus warily then for any sign that he was judging her, but instead, there was a look of horror on his face. 'Lina, for God's sake, that's assault. You should go to the guards.' He went to get up, putting his feet back in his flip-flops, patting his pockets for his mobile phone. 'C'mon, I'm taking you.'

'No!' Lina shouted, so loudly that the old men at the bar swivelled their heads to look at what was going on. 'No,' she repeated more quietly. 'You see, it was kind of my fault,' she began.

'What do you mean? You were alone in a room with this prick and he attacked you — end of.'

'I told him he could,' Lina said sadly.

'What do you mean, you *told* him? Who in their right mind—?'

Lina put a hand up to silence him. 'A quid pro quo, he called it. That means—'

'I know what it means,' Seamus said shortly. He was sitting back down now, hunched over himself, a muscle working in his temple.

'He said that he'd give me a slot on his digital TV channel if ... if I ... and I know that I could have decked him or something — I should have decked him or even run from the room screaming, but that would have been it. My career would be flushed down the toilet.'

He shook his head, 'No, no, no, it's not right,' he said. 'That can't be the price of a crappy slot on a digital-only show. It can't be.'

'It might be crappy to you, Seamus, but to me, it was my big break,' Lina said, realising that she sounded pathetic. But there was no way she was going to report Graham McSween. She knew that. She'd remain silent and feel guilty about it because she knew the way things worked. Speak up and you'd never get another gig as long as you lived. Suck it up and you'd live to fight another day. She was beginning to understand just why her mother had been so disdainful – not of men, but of the way the rules of the game were so rigged.

'I'll go in tomorrow,' she lied.

'Good,' Seamus said, clearly relieved. 'Would you like me to go with you?'

'God, no ... I mean, no, thanks.'

'OK,' Seamus said, looking a bit miffed.

Lina couldn't be bothered apologising for not letting him do his knight-in-shining-armour routine. She just didn't have the energy for it. She felt sick and sore and sad. 'I think I'd like to go home now, Seamus,' she said quietly, letting him help her up. 'Whoops,' she said, wobbling a bit because of the whiskey and the Guinness, hoovered up with only a packet of crisps for soakage. Seamus put an arm around her shoulder, but she shook it off. 'I'm fine,' she said crossly.

In response, he just shrugged, waiting patiently while she faffed with her jacket and bag, putting her feet back into her horrible pointy shoes and following him out past the old men, eyes glued to the giant TV screen. 'Cheer up, love,' one of them said. 'It's not that bad, is it?'

'It fucking is,' Lina muttered under her breath.

She had to borrow money from Seamus for the taxi, which provided further mortification. 'I'm sorry, my dole money's not due until tomorrow,' she said, as he looked up the taxi app on his phone, wondering what Mama would think of her meekly accepting his help.

He shook his head and said, 'It's not a problem. There's one a minute away.'

They stood in silence then on the busy pavement, people moving around them. There seemed to be nothing more to say. And then the taxi appeared and he opened the door for her, helping her in. She sat back on the warm leather and closed her eyes, then flicked them open again and rolled down the window. 'Thanks,' she said. In response, Seamus gave a little wave and shuffled off up the street, hands in his pockets.

She was praying Mama wouldn't still be up, but sure enough, as Lina wearily opened the hall door and trudged up the stairs, she could hear the siren blast of reality TV, which was all her mother seemed to watch these days. Lina wondered if she was developing dementia, so changed were her viewing habits.

'Hi,' Lina said quietly when she opened the flat door. Her mother was sitting on the sofa, Tommy perched beside her on a bundle of cushions, the two of them watching repeats of *Love Island*.

'Kacey has dumped Kevin for Blair, but I think he's such a creep. Who wants a man with muscles like that? He's like a triangle,' her mother said, not taking her eyes off the screen.

Lina sat wearily down on the sofa, picking Tommy up and kissing her lovely baby forehead. She went to feed her, but her mother said, 'No need. She liked the bottle. Drank it all up.'

'Oh,' Lina said, sitting there for a few moments, watching the parade of gorgeous, tanned people in tiny swimsuits cavort around a lovely blue swimming pool. It was a parallel universe, she thought grimly.

'So — *wie ist es gelaufen?*'

'Oh, it went fine,' Lina said.

'Aha,' her mother replied, as they both sat there for a few moments, digesting the obvious lie.

'I think I got the spot anyway,' Lina said. 'So I suppose that's good news.'

'*Gratuliere,*' her mother said, and when Lina didn't reply, she turned to her and said, 'What happened?'

'Nothing,' Lina said, focusing really hard on a buff couple in matching swimming costumes who were sitting on inflatable pink flamingos in a swimming pool, sipping large bright-yellow drinks, but her mind kept wandering to the feeling of his soggy, fat hands on her shoulders, tracing the lines of her broderie anglaise maternity bra, an avid look on his face.

'Lina?' her mother said, in that tone that said everything. Mama had always been able to winkle things out of her, from missed schooldays to furtive cigarette smoking, to a trip to Dublin to get the pill. That's what came with living with one other person 24/7, Lina thought — there was nothing they didn't know about you, nor you about them.

'Oh, Mama,' she said sadly. 'It was awful, so awful.' Then she cried, for the umpteenth time that night, repeating the story to her mother in German, feeling the language comfort her, reminding her of what they both shared. And her mother took her in her arms and stroked her hair and patted her head and murmured soothing words and, to her credit, did not turn it into a diatribe against the entire male race. And when Lina had let it all out, her humiliation and her rage, Mama said, 'Cocoa'.

'What? I don't think that'll fix anything,' Lina said.

'No,' her mother replied. 'It will fix nothing, but we'll feel better anyway. There is no problem that cannot be made better by food and drink.' She got up from the sofa, going into the kitchen and turning on the light, humming to herself as she clattered and banged.

'Do you need any help?' Lina said wearily.

'*Nein*. I know where everything is.'

There was more humming and singing as Lina patted Tommy, who was back in her nest of cushions, on the head and squeezed her tight. 'I'm sorry, love. I just had a bad day.'

Tommy gurgled in response and lifted a foot to her mouth, sucking on her toes with great concentration, and Lina suddenly wished to be small again, to be beyond conscious thought. Life was so much easier then.

Her mother returned to the living room carrying a wicker tray that Lina had never seen before, with a jug on it, two mugs and a plate of pastries. '*Bitteschön*,' she said softly, handing Lina a mug filled to the brim with rich hot chocolate. I'm going to be sick, Lina thought, after the Guinness and the crisps, but one sip of the drink returned her to her childhood, sitting with Mama in front of whatever fire they had — a little two-bar electric or the giant open fireplace that had been in one house, their nightly ritual keeping them anchored, keeping them safe.

'*Dankeschön*, Mama,' she said, gratefully sipping, nibbling on the edge of a pastry. 'These are nice — where'd you get them?'

'The little Indian man — he says they're native to his country. His wife makes them — she said she'd teach me. I must say, they're very charming, for foreigners. We've become friends.'

'That's nice.' Lina decided not to say anything to ruin the moment. She was all out of conflict tonight, for a start, but Mama was right. The Abdallahs were lovely people, plain and simple. They were family.

'So, what are we going to do about this man?' Mama said, brushing crumbs off her worn jeans.

'What do you mean, what are we going to do about him? We are going to do nothing,' Lina said. 'And the reason why is that if we do, I'll never get a single comedy gig again, never mind my TV slot. I might as well get something out of the transaction, if you can call it that.'

Mama's mouth set in a thin line.

'What? Mama, you are to stay out of it.'

Mama nodded her head, a determined look on her face. Lina knew that look — it spelled trouble; so she was surprised when Mama simply picked up the remote control. 'Oh, they have *Love Island Aftersun* on now. Let's watch it — the gossip is the best bit.'

'Mama, have you lost your mind? You hate this kind of thing — you always called it trash, and you wouldn't let me watch it, what's more.'

'I have changed, Lina. I now realise that I was missing so much. What's wrong with a little fun anyway? It never hurt anybody.'

'I suppose it didn't,' Lina said doubtfully, sitting beside her mother, resting her head on her shoulder, watching a girl in a yellow jumpsuit tell the presenter why she fell in love with Zak on the island. It was just a silly show, she thought, full of people with straightened teeth and shiny smiles — and yet, the girl seemed to be really sweet and the guy, even with his painted-on six pack, seemed relatively normal. It really is love, Lina thought sadly, and when have I ever experienced that? Never. Never once in my whole life.

She was almost asleep when her phone beeped. Groggily, she pulled it out of her pocket and peered at the text. *I'm going out of my mind here, Lina. Let me know how it went!!! Elise XOXO.*

'Who is it?' her mother said.

'No one. Just one of the mums,' Lina said vaguely.

'That girl with the big hair?' Mama said. 'I don't like her.'

'Elise? I'm beginning to think I don't like her much myself,' Lina said, pressing Reply and typing: *Let's talk tomorrow. I'm bushed.* She did not add any silly emojis or kisses, and when she didn't receive a reply, Lina felt a certain grim satisfaction.

16

Gracie

Gracie was late as usual. She always seemed to be late these days, constantly trying to catch up with herself. She felt as if the world was a merry-go-round and she was desperately trying to clamber on, watching the horses speed past as she tried, and failed, to sit in the saddle. Whirring day and night, her mind just wouldn't leave her alone, and the only thing that calmed her was her now-daily early-morning walk on the beach. She'd leave Jake and Jasper, in his new place, right between the two of them in the bed, arms and legs outstretched, taking up the space of a fully grown adult, and she'd go quietly downstairs, slipping out the front door and walking around the corner to the seafront, sucking in a deep breath of sea air before striding along the raised walkway and past the granite hulk of the Martello tower, waving to her fellow travellers, the mix of elderly people with small white dogs and Jack Russell terriers, outdoor gym enthusiasts and the obvious insomniacs, with shoulders hunched, like hers, as they shuffled along. It was the only time in the day when she felt she could just be, without having to wear one of her many masks: mother, daughter, partner, friend, professional, taking each one off and throwing on another, hurtling through the days, feeling herself being stretched more and more thinly until she wondered if she'd simply snap, like a piece of elastic pulled too taut.

Today, she was racing around like a headless chicken, much to Jasper's amusement from his perch in the middle of her bed. Sunny was off, yet again, this time because she was seeing an orthodontist about Invisalign braces, which made Gracie think she was paying the woman far too much, and Jake was downstairs in the games room, no doubt snoring away on the sofa, because they'd had a huge row the night before. He'd known perfectly well that today was Gracie's big day – she'd been telling him for the best part of a fortnight – but had to choose it for a 'top-level' meeting about financing. She'd lost it completely when he'd casually dropped it in over dinner the night before, poking the gnocchi in pesto sauce that Gracie had snatched from the deli, rustling a meal up in fifteen minutes after her long day in pitch rehearsals with Atiyah and Toni and the team.

'I'm not sure I like gnocchi,' he'd said. 'They remind me of snails.'

'Well, they're quick, and I didn't have time to go to the supermarket,' Gracie had said tightly.

'I wasn't criticising you,' Jake had said. 'I was just making a comment about gnocchi.'

'Fine,' she'd replied, taking a big swig of red wine, eyeing the bottle and wondering how she'd managed to get through half of it by herself. 'Would you like some?' She'd lifted the bottle and went to pour some into Jake's glass, but he'd covered it with his hand.

'No, thanks — I need to be fresh for tomorrow.'

'What's on tomorrow?' Gracie had asked.

'I told you — it's the financing meeting. Do or die for Deadkill, if you'll excuse the pun,' he'd added, spearing one of the little balls with his fork and lifting it to his mouth, before making a face and putting it back on his plate.

'*What?* But I have the client presentation tomorrow!' Gracie had shrieked, thumping her glass down on the table.

'Jeez, will you take a chill pill?' Jake had said casually. 'It'll be fine.'

Gracie had found herself grinding the reply out from between clenched teeth. 'How will it be fine? Sunny's off — again — and you know what happened the last time we asked Mum to babysit.'

In reply, Jake had simply shrugged. 'So, take Jasper into work. I thought you said they all liked having him — that it was very empowering.' He'd given a small, patronising smile.

Gracie hadn't been able to believe her ears. 'I cannot take Jasper into a client presentation, Jake. You'd hardly take him to your financing meeting, would you? What was it you said, "it doesn't look cute — it looks unprofessional"? Well, the same applies for me, no matter what Toni says.'

Jake had absentmindedly twiddled the stem of his wine glass in a way that made Gracie want to reach out and slap his hand. Then he'd said, 'It was your choice, you know.'

'What do you mean?'

'Well, you're on maternity leave, aren't you? You could just have said no and gone on with your life and enjoyed the time to which you're entitled, but instead, you high-tailed it off to that place without a second glance: it was as if you couldn't wait to be rid of us,' he'd snapped, throwing the linen napkin that Gracie liked to use for suppers onto the table.

'What on earth are you talking about? In case you don't remember, Jake, I pay the bills around here, so you'll forgive me if I have to work,' Gracie had said acidly.

'A fact that you won't let me forget,' Jake had said, putting his fork down on his plate with a clatter. Jasper, who'd been fast asleep on the sofa, woke up with a startled wail. 'For a start, you get maternity pay, so you don't have to work at all until you go back to the office in January —

that's four months away. And you've never forgiven me for being made redundant, as if that made me even more of a spare wheel than before, and even though I'm trying, I don't think you see it. We live in this giant house that your father paid for, with a nanny we can't afford and a lifestyle that's way beyond our means, and you just disappear every day to work, burying your head in the sand.'

Gracie had been silent for a long time, her mind spinning through smart responses, none of which seemed adequate. He'd been right, of course – that's why she loved him: because he could always be relied on to tell her the truth. But why bloody now, when she was just hanging on by her fingernails? Eventually, she'd said, 'I don't think I've ever heard you make such a long speech, not in all the time I've known you.'

'Well, maybe it's because I've something to say. Look, this isn't working, Gracie   it just isn't,' he'd said quietly, leaving the table and going over to the sofa, picking Jasper up and holding him close, murmuring soft words into his ear. Jasper had settled immediately, resting his head on his dad's shoulder. 'Decide what it is you really want, Gracie, and come back to us.' Then, the two of them had left the room, leaving Gracie sitting in front of her cooling gnocchi until it had finally grown dark.

How can I decide, when I have no bloody choice in the matter? Gracie thought as she picked up her favourite 'presenting shirt', a silk—cotton mix that was lovely and cool but which had acquired a giant stain of what looked like ketchup on the front. She tossed it into a corner and selected a pair of black slacks that were now slightly too small for her and a matching black T-shirt — something professional and yet invisible at the same time, which struck about the right note, Gracie thought grimly.

'I have to keep the show on the road — I just have to,' she said to herself in the mirror. 'I have to nail this presentation, and when I do, I'll tackle the rest.' One more day, she thought. If I can get the Kitty-Kat account, then my future will be secure at Cutlery, at least for the time being, and maybe then Jake and I can talk.

She decided that the quickest way into town was to drive, strapping Jasper into his baby seat and setting off in the baking heat for the city centre. As she drove, she passed a group of mums, dressed in bright summer colours, heading for the beach. They were pushing buggies and holding toddlers by the hand and they looked carefree and happy. How I wish I was there, Gracie thought wistfully, imagining herself sitting on the beach, bucket and spade in hand, watching Jasper grabbing handfuls of sand and letting it trail through his fingers. She longed for the freedom that she'd felt in Brittas, with nothing ahead of her except a bright, sunny day.

But that was silly, she chided herself as she turned left off the seafront and waited in a long line of traffic to cross the train line. Life didn't work like that. There were bills to be paid and, as Jake had so helpfully pointed out, there was a mortgage on that big house that was currently eating into most of her salary. Dad had written them a cheque, lending them the money for the deposit and the refurbishments that were so badly needed — which reminded Gracie: she had to start paying Dad back. He hadn't asked for the money, but she knew he'd be expecting it. 'Neither a borrower nor a lender be,' was one of his favourite sayings. Gracie was both: borrowing and lending to Jake to get his project off the ground, for which he wasn't even grateful. What would Dad make of that? she wondered.

The traffic ground all the way into town, a long line of chugging cars, and Gracie found herself gritting her teeth, feeling the coating of red wine from the night before, which not even vigorous tooth-brushing had removed. I'm going to be late, she thought, but what's new. When she eventually got there, she remembered why she never usually drove — because she'd have to spend a good twenty minutes hanging around outside the office building, waiting for a free parking space. She eyed the lime green Maserati of the tech mogul across the street, proudly parked on double-yellow lines, waiting for the parking ticket, which, of course, he wouldn't pay and wondered how it was that some people got away with things like that. If she didn't pay a parking fine, she'd end up in the High Court. That was the way life worked, Gracie thought grimly. It was fixed.

She closed her eyes for a few seconds and rested her forehead on the steering wheel. If only she could have a little sleep, she thought, before her presentation. A little snooze to rest her tired and cloudy brain. The plastic felt hot and sticky under her forehead and she could feel sweat running down the back of her neck. She could hear Jasper snoring away in his baby seat behind her. She'd dressed him in a little shirt with a bow tie and a waistcoat over his navy blue shorts, and he looked tiny and faintly ridiculous, like a little old man returned to babyhood. Gracie turned around and put her hand on his foot, giving it a squeeze. He didn't stir.

I really ought to be going over my notes, she thought wearily, turning around to look out at the lovely Victorian square, at the people passing by, living their busy lives, but instead, she found her mind turning to Elise and the view of her retreating down the driveway, this tiny little doll pushing a huge pram. There was something improvised about her, something that Mum, with her nose for such things, had picked up on — but there was something sad about her too, like that little white dog of hers, scrappy and a bit forlorn — perhaps she wasn't the monster that Gracie might have imagined her to be. Maybe she'd genuinely wanted to talk to her about Jane, and Gracie had turned on her with an anger that had shocked her. I'm a bad friend, Gracie thought, imagining Jane at home in Roscommon all by herself, with no friends to support her. I should have gone, she thought guiltily — what was I thinking. I'll call her later.

The knock on the window was so sudden that Gracie

jumped up, giving a little scream. She looked to her right to see Atiyah looking back in at her. Gracie managed to pull her mouth into a smile, pressing the button and letting the electric window slide down.

'Sorry, I didn't know you were asleep.' Atiyah's voice was soft, but she was eyeing Gracie as if she were a wild animal who'd stumbled out of the bush.

Do I look that bad? Gracie wondered. I thought I was keeping it all together. 'I'm not. I'm just resting so I can be fresh for the presentation.' Her eyelids felt sticky, as if they were glued together, and that headache was beginning again right over her left eye, a solid throbbing that made her wince.

'Are you OK?'

Fuck off, Gracie thought. You are not getting my job. 'I'm fine, thanks, Atiyah. Let's go up, and I can talk you through the slides.' Gracie reached down into the passenger footwell for her briefcase and laptop, then clambered out of the car, sticking out a hand to lock the doors behind her.

Atiyah gave one of her cryptic smiles. 'What?' Gracie snapped.

'Nothing,' Atiyah said. 'Nice car.'

'Thank you,' Gracie said, determined not to apologise for it. She'd worked hard precisely so that they could have a new-model Volvo, and not one of those awful Korean brands that looked smart but were really cheap.

They both walked up the stairs to the office and to

Gracie's old desk, which was now Atiyah's. 'Welcome back, Gracie,' Bernard, one of the graphic designers, said. Gracie gave him a vague wave. She couldn't get into chit-chat now: she needed to focus. With shaking fingers, she prised open her MacBook and pressed the start button. There was an awkward silence while they both watched it boot up.

'Nervous?' Atiyah asked.

'It's all under control,' Gracie lied. 'Now, slide one is a summary of the brand's positioning now and where the gaps are ...' As she talked, she found herself beginning to grow in confidence, flipping through the slides, sharing graphs on market share and growth projections. It'll be OK, she thought. I know what I'm doing.

'Great.' Atiyah nodded when Gracie had finished. 'That all looks very impressive.'

Gracie could tell that she'd surprised Atiyah. And there were you, thinking that I was some kind of an idiot with nappy brain, she thought smugly.

'Just wondering,' Atiyah continued, 'where are the implementation plans?'

'What implementation plans?' Gracie said.

'Toni gave them to you at the last brainstorm – do you not remember? She said they were crucial for Kitty-Kat. That they wanted to have a fully scaled model of how the roll-out process would work. They didn't want general stuff – they want to drill down to the specifics.'

Gracie felt herself go cold. Fuck. She had absolutely no memory of any implementation plans. She squeezed her eyes shut and pressed her fist into her forehead, desperately trying to remember what Toni had said to her at the last meeting. It all seemed to be shrouded in a kind of mist.

'Are you sure you're all right, Gracie? Only—'

'I'm fine!' Gracie barked. 'I'm just trying to think.'

Atiyah was silent for a few moments, but then gave a decisive sigh. 'We have five minutes. They must be somewhere on Circe's drive, so we'll cut and paste them in to the presentation. It's no big deal.'

The two of them stared at each other.

'You left them out,' Gracie said blankly.

'No, *you* did, Gracie,' Atiyah said crisply. 'Toni sent them to you from her iPhone, I remember.'

'Well, I didn't get it and, I must say, I find that very convenient,' Gracie said into the silence.

Atiyah gave her that laser-beam glare. 'What are you suggesting, Gracie?'

'I'm suggesting, as you put it, that you hobbled me so that you could come out on top, Atiyah. What were you planning to do — come to my rescue in the meeting, like you did the last time, Sir Galahad riding in on his steed?'

There was a long silence in the office as the clatter of busyness stopped. The two women glared at each other. Eventually, Atiyah said, 'I have no idea what you're talking about, Gracie. It was your job to put them in and you didn't. Blaming me won't change that. So, do you want to fix this, or not?'

'Fine,' Gracie said bleakly, sinking wearily into her chair.

'No need to apologise,' Atiyah muttered. 'I'll see if I can nab Circe's Mac. C'mon.' The two of them walked in silence to Circe's desk, Gracie following the slim, tall form of Atiyah, who looked amazing, she had to admit, in an olive jumpsuit. Gracie felt frumpy and middle-aged in her gloomy black.

They had to sneak past Toni's office, and then the two of them bolted for Circe's cubby-hole which was mercifully unoccupied, Atiyah flicking open Circe's Mac. Biting her lip for a second, she entered Circe's password. Seeing Gracie's look of alarm, she said, 'People are very transparent,' before bringing up the relevant file. 'Now, open your presentation and put the cursor on page twelve,' she ordered Gracie. Gracie bristled, but got on with it.

'Now,' Atiyah said confidently, pressing a button. 'I've emailed it to you, so you just have to cut and paste it in, then we'll go through it to make sure you're familiar with it.'

After a few frantic minutes during which it looked as if it wasn't going to work, a 'ping' on Gracie's laptop meant that suddenly it was there. She looked at the sheet, scanning the bullet points and the figures, the projected growth in market share for Kitty-Kat, wondering why she'd never seen this before or, worse, even thought to ask for what now seemed essential. How stupid of her.

'I owe you an apology, Atiyah. It was my mistake and I shouldn't have taken it out on you.'

Atiyah was busy typing and she didn't look around,

shrugging her shoulders as if Gracie's rudeness was what she'd expected. She slammed Circe's laptop closed. 'It's fixed now, so let's just get on with it. I'll take the current market projections and you do the future ones, OK?'

Gracie liked to do the current market projections because that way she could paint a picture of just how bad the client's situation was and, thus, how they could rescue it – but she wasn't exactly in a position to pick and choose. 'Fine.'

Atiyah turned to Gracie then, extending a hand, which Gracie took. Atiyah's handshake was firm and dry. 'Break a leg,' she said.

'Thanks, Atiyah,' Gracie said, eyes filling with tears. In response, Atiyah gave another one of her wry smiles. You just think I'm a spoiled rich bitch, Gracie thought miserably, adding to herself, You'd be right.

In spite of everything, the presentation was a big success, Atiyah and Gracie working in tandem to present the cold, hard facts and the lovely, warm solutions. Maurice, the MD of Kitty-Kat, a bluff man from County Longford with big red cheeks and an aversion to any kind of ad-world pretension, even took off the peaked cap he always wore, scratching his head and looking thoughtful, which Toni said was a good sign. When they'd finished, she'd given them a big thumbs-up before following Maurice out the door and taking his big, red farmer's hand in hers.

'I hope you're impressed,' she said softly, treating him to her most sincere body language, her perfume, like a cloud, around her. Maurice said nothing, but shook her hand so vigorously Gracie thought her twiggy arm might break.

'You are amazing!' Toni shrieked as she came back to the boardroom, pulling Gracie and Atiyah to her. Atiyah permitted herself a smile, but Gracie found that she just couldn't. She felt a wave of exhaustion break over her, so profound that she thought she might lie down right there and fall asleep. She tried to smile, but she knew it wasn't working by the look of alarm on Atiyah's face, the mouthed, 'Are you all right?' Gracie found the strength to nod.

Toni insisted on breaking out the champagne, filling glasses with expensive bubbly and holding them aloft. 'To you both — to my power team!' They clinked glasses. 'You two are out of this world,' Toni gushed, before her phone interrupted. 'Ooh, it's Maurice — already!' she said gleefully.

While Toni was on the phone, Atiyah quietly put her glass down on the corner of Toni's desk.

'Don't you drink?' Gracie asked.

Atiyah shook her head. 'Nope.'

'Is it, like, a religion thing?'

'What?'

'Well, Muslims don't drink, do they?'

'I'm a Methodist,' Atiyah said with a smile. 'I don't drink because I don't like the taste of the stuff.'

'Oh, sorry.'

Atiyah gave a short laugh in response – Gracie couldn't work out whether she was amused or not.

'Oh, yes, Maurice, I'd love to come down to Longford to the factory to see how Kitty-Kat is made,' Toni said, rolling her eyes to heaven at the girls. 'Absolutely, we'll firm something up next week. Bye-bye-bye,' she said as she hung up. Gracie was surprised Toni didn't blow the man kisses. 'That was Maurice. He says yours was the best presentation he's ever seen and that it's down to us and one other agency. But confidentially, I think the gig's ours!'

There was more high-fiving and sipping of champagne, and as she stood, clutching the glass in her sweaty hand, Gracie began to feel as if she wasn't there but was floating high above Toni and Atiyah, looking down at them both, discussing strategy as if it were nothing whatsoever to do with her. Come on, brain, she said sternly. Work.

'And we even managed without our mascot,' Toni was saying. 'I'm sure Maurice would have been utterly charmed with Jasper, and I want him to understand just how seriously we take family life at Cutlery … What?'

'Oh, Jesus,' Gracie said. 'Jesus. I forgot him.'

'Who?'

'My child,' Gracie barked, throwing the champagne glass on the floor, where it rolled over the expensive carpet, leaving a puddle of bubbles. She half-hobbled in her silly shoes to the door, then stopped and took them off, throwing them behind her, running down the cold granite steps in her bare feet, heart thumping in her ears.

'Hurry!' Atiyah called from behind her, as Gracie pulled open the front door, ran down the front steps and across the square. 'Please be all right. Please,' she said over and over again, like a mantra.

Then she saw the red bulk of a fire engine and the clamper's van parked in front of her Volvo. For a fleeting second, she wondered if they were about to clamp her, before she broke into a faster run.

When she got to the car, a burly firefighter was just taking Jasper into his arms through the mangled remains of the rear door, pulling at his clothes to remove them. Jasper looked peaceful, as if he was merely asleep, but a slight flush on his cheeks told her otherwise. She broke into the crowd gathered around him and attempted to pull him from the firefighter's arms. 'That's my baby! Give him back!' she wailed as an arm shot out, grabbing her by the elbow.

The garda was only about twenty, her tiny form bulked out by a huge stab-proof vest and a high-vis jacket. Her ginger hair had been pulled back into a severe bun and her mouth was set in a thin line. 'How long was he out there?'

'I don't know – maybe two hours?' Gracie said. 'I had a meeting and I went upstairs and I completely forgot. You see, the spreadsheet with the implementation stats was missing ...' Her voice trailed off as she realised how stupid she sounded. She turned her head and looked for Jasper. His little floppy body was being carried off to an ambulance. 'Please,' she begged the garda. 'I just need to see him.'

'You'll see him later,' she said, a little more kindly. 'He's being looked after. The best thing you can do is tell me honestly what happened.'

Gracie recounted the details, from arriving at the square to walking upstairs, the meeting and then the celebration. She told the garda everything, like she'd confess to a priest, hoping to cleanse her soul, but the garda simply nodded, making a series of notes in a black flip notebook.

'Will they take him off me?' Gracie said.

The garda gave a bleak smile. 'They only do that to junkies, love. The likes of you would have to do a lot more, believe me.'

Gracie had no idea what she meant by that, so she nodded and thanked the woman profusely. She had no clue what to do then, so she stood there, bare feet glued to the road, while the doors of the ambulance were closed and it drove away, lights flashing. I need to follow it, she thought. That's what I need to do. But I need keys to drive, she thought, and where will I find them? She looked up and the entire staff of Cutlery was on the front steps of the building, looking at her.

'Has anyone seen my keys?' she asked.

17

Elise

I make sure to get to the park early to bag us a seat because the Zumba class seems to have taken up residence on the grass again, even though it's not a nice day. It's the second week in September and for the first time in months it's grey and cloudy, a chilly breeze blowing through the park. The end of summer, I think gloomily, as I put Chloe's change bag onto the seat beside mine, pulling two other seats close in. It's only been just over two months, but it seems that everything has changed since I met the girls. On the outside, I still look like me, thank God. I still have my nice hair that cost me a fortune and the clothes that scream 'money', so I can keep up appearances. But inside? That's another matter altogether. I'm sure one of Lina's philosophers would have had something to say about it, but as far as plain old me is concerned, nothing is the same.

It's only been five days since our last meeting, but Jane's cryptic text didn't exactly leave us free to decline. *EGM tomorrow at the park. Please be there.* I've only seen her once since her dad's funeral and she seemed her usual quiet self, so this was a bit strong. She's not normally that bossy, I thought when I saw her text, that's Gracie's thing, so it must be something more important than the latest recipe for weaning foods. Honestly, Gracie thinks she can control everything, including how we raise our own children.

I'm praying that Lina turns up first because I really need to speak to her. She's hardly returned any of my texts and I'm dying to know how she got on with that TV guy. I think she's being a bit rude, after everything I did for her. It's not easy to tap someone's contacts for a favour — it puts Gray in an awkward position — so you'd think she'd throw me a bone and let me know how it went. I'm not about to ask Gray because we're still not speaking. I can't believe it, after seven years together, when we've never spent more than a night apart, he's sleeping in the spare room, where we store the junk, with the ironing board and the vacuum cleaner. He says I've changed, that I've gone somewhere he doesn't want to go, and I suppose he's right in some ways. He thinks it's all about new recipes and holiday ideas, about 'airs and graces', as he calls them, but that's not it at all. It's about finding the real me. I've been pretending for so long that I can hardly remember who that is. And now, I want to find out.

The Zumba class has just begun to shake its booty to 'Despacito' when Lina appears, shuffling down the path to the café. She looks distracted, and when she sees me, she doesn't return my wave. I suddenly feel very cold and alone.

'Hi,' she says. 'No sign of Jane yet?'

'No,' I say quietly.

'Right, I'll get a coffee while I'm waiting.' She doesn't offer to buy me one, but rummages in her purse for coins.

'I'll get them,' I say. 'Just keep an eye on Chloe, will you?'

She nods silently and sits down beside the Silver Cross while I go inside to order. My mouth is dry and my heart is fluttering in my chest. What have I done? I think as I order the coffees. Why isn't she speaking to me?

When I go back outside, a paper cup with cappuccino in each hand, she's staring into space as Justin Bieber and Daddy Yankee crank up the volume, and when I put the coffee down in front of her, she just gives a muttered, 'Thanks.'

We sip in silence for a bit, while I wonder what to say to break it. I try to come up with a roundabout way of asking, until I decide to just come straight out with it: 'Lina. Is there something wrong?'

Lina shakes her head but doesn't say anything and, quite honestly, I wish she'd cop on. We're not five any more. 'I'm just wondering how you got on with the TV producer. I texted you a few times and you didn't answer, so …'

She bites her lip and shakes her head.

'Ah, Lina,' I say. 'What happened? You were so excited about it all, really pumped — remember? And then you didn't reply to any of my texts, so I was left wondering—'

'Look, it went fine, OK?' Lina finally snaps.

'OK,' I say miserably. When she doesn't say anything further, I add, 'Please tell me. If you won't, I can't help.'

'Oh, I think you've done quite enough of that, Elise,' Lina says. 'Anyway, you'll be pleased to know that I got the gig.'

'Well, that's great! Why didn't you say so?' I say, wondering if I could risk a little hug, but her body language tells me not to even try.

'Because …' she begins, picking up the coffee stirrer and flipping it through her fingers, but then there's a cry of 'Girls!' and Jane comes running down the path. 'There you both are. I've been looking for you everywhere.'

'Well, we're here,' Lina says sharply.

Jane looks at me over the top of Lina's head, but I just shrug. Your guess is as good as mine, the gesture says. 'Oh, oh, well, good …' She seems flustered, turning around to look behind her, then looking back at me. 'I haven't got long. Mark's home early from work today, so I have to get the dinner on.'

'Jane,' I begin, 'how has everything been since your

dad ...' My voice trails off when I see that she isn't really listening. 'What is it, Jane? What's the matter?'

Jane says, 'It's awful, really awful,' and she bursts into tears.

'Oh, Jane,' Lina says, getting up out of her seat and putting an arm around her, pulling her gently to her and shushing her softly, ushering her into the empty seat at the table. 'What is it? You can tell me.' I notice that she doesn't say 'us'.

Jane's response is to sob a bit more, while Lina soothes her, giving her a tissue and a warm hug, while I sit there like a lemon, looking at them both. Finally, Jane blows her nose and sucks in a deep breath. 'It's about Jasper.'

'Is he OK?' I say.

She doesn't look at me, but at Lina. 'Oh, it's so awful ...'

'Jane, tell me what it is,' Lina says softly.

'He's in hospital, he's really sick. Gracie left him in the car and it was a baking hot afternoon and he ... he ...'

'You're not making much sense, love,' Lina says. 'How did Gracie leave him in the car?'

'She had a work meeting the day before yesterday – I remember she told me about it. Some big pitch to a new client and her boss really likes her to bring Jasper in, which I think is a bit strange, but anyway ... She forgot him and he was in the car for two hours in that heat. Oh, the poor little thing.'

'Oh, Jesus,' Lina says. Her face is white. 'Is he—?'

'He's very poorly. They've had to do an operation to help with the swelling in his brain.'

Lina puts a hand to her mouth. 'Christ. Can we go and see him? Which hospital is he in?'

Jane shakes her head. 'That's all I know. Gracie left me this message on my voicemail. I could hardly make sense of it. She was in hysterics, the poor thing.'

'Oh, Jesus,' Lina says again. 'I feel sick at the thought of it.'

'I know,' Jane says miserably.

I know what they are both thinking – what if it were me? What if I left my child in the back of my car in 26-degree heat for two hours. I could see them both visualising their own baby in the heat, temperature going through the roof, the child's blood pressure soaring ...

'Poor Gracie,' Jane says then. 'It could have happened to any one of us.'

'It could,' Lina echoes.

No it couldn't, I think. There's no way I'd leave Chloe like that, I know I wouldn't. She's the centre of my world. I close my eyes for a second and try to imagine myself getting out of my car, closing the door and walking off without her, but even the thought of it makes me shiver.

'She mustn't blame herself,' Jane is saying, when I tune back in. Lina nods in agreement.

Keep your mouth shut, Elise, I say to myself, don't say

a single bloody thing. But even as I think it, the words spill out of me in a hot gush. 'Hang on a minute,' I say. 'Gracie has to take some responsibility for this: she left her child in a roasting hot car for two hours to give a presentation at work, even though she's on maternity leave, and you say it could have happened to you? Really?'

Jane looks horrified, leaning back in her seat as if she doesn't want to sit too close to me. 'Well,' she says, glancing quickly at Lina, 'it probably wouldn't have happened in exactly the same way because I haven't driven in a while, but something else could have happened. I could have dropped something on Owen or he could have been scalded or put his hand on something hot ... Accidents happen, Elise.'

I wish to God that I could take back the words, but the genie's out of the bottle now. I've got no choice but to plough on. 'I know for a fact that there is no way I'd leave Chloe in the back of a car for five minutes, not to mind two hours. I know I wouldn't because I'm a responsible parent.'

'And Gracie isn't? So good to hear you taking the high moral ground, Elise,' Lina barks.

Well, that stings, from Lina of all people. I'm reminded of the way everyone in work used to say that I had foot-in-mouth disease, but maybe that's the price I have to pay for speaking my truth, for being fully myself. Still, I try to soften my words. 'Look, Lina, I'm sure Gracie didn't set out to injure her child. She didn't get up in the morning and think, "Oh, I'm going to try to kill my baby today," of course she didn't, but the long and short of it is that's exactly what's happened, because she wasn't thinking about Jasper: she was thinking about herself. When you have a child, you put them first, as simple as that. That's motherhood.'

There is a long silence, broken by another blast of music from the bloody Zumba class. I look at Jane, who is biting her lip and fiddling with the strap on Owen's pram, and then I look at Lina, who is staring into the distance, chin set, a tear running down her cheek. I want to get up and hug her, to wipe the tear away, but I know that she won't let me. She probably hates me now — but I know I'm right. Gracie has been negligent, it's as simple as that. I know it's not polite to say it in these circles, but it's the truth.

I watch Lina now, willing her to see things from my point of view, and I'm relieved when I notice that the expression on her face is changing. It looks as if she's making her mind up about something. Eventually, she sighs heavily. 'Jane, don't you think Gracie has been very distracted lately? She has too much on her plate and I'd say she took her eye off the ball for a second—'

'That's all it takes,' I add, thanking God that Lina agrees with me.

'That's all it takes,' she repeats.

'It could happen to any of us, Lina,' Jane says, eyes wide. 'You must know that.'

Lina shifts uncomfortably in her seat. 'Well, yes, theoretically, it could happen to any of us ...' Her voice trails off as she watches Jane carefully.

'What are you suggesting, Lina?' Jane says. She's speaking in her usual mousy manner, but I can tell that there's steel underneath. I wonder if Lina will have the nerve to speak her mind.

'Nothing,' Lina says quietly. 'I'm suggesting nothing.' Oh, you coward, I think, leaving it all to me.

'Good,' Jane says firmly.

'Look, it's about putting the baby first,' I say, looking at them both. 'You choose to put Owen first, Jane, and Lina, you choose to put Tommy first, as I put Chloe first. And because we've made that choice, we are just that tiny bit more careful, that bit more vigilant—'

At this, Jane gets up from her seat, face set. She checks over Owen's parasol and puts her handbag under his pram.

'Jane?' Lina says, putting a hand on her arm. Jane shoves it away with a violence I find really surprising. 'I'm going home. I'll text you both to let you know how Gracie is.'

'Jane, hang on, we're not judging Gracie. We all know how hard it can be,' I say.

'Aren't you?' Jane says quietly. 'Really? Because I think that's precisely what you're doing, both of you.'

'Look,' I say, 'we have every sympathy for Gracie and we'll be praying that Jasper pulls through – but as far as I can see, she's changed over the past couple of months. She's working, for a start, even though she's on maternity leave and Jasper's barely six months old, so that tells you something about her priorities ...' My voice trails away as I catch the expression on Jane's face, a kind of tightness that I find frightening.

When she speaks, her voice is barely above a whisper. 'Well, you'd better hope that you never slip, Elise. That you never put a foot wrong as a mother, never make a bad choice or a poor decision or a split-second mistake, because when you do — and it *will* happen, believe me, because we are all human — maybe then you'll understand. And in the meantime, enjoy the view from your lofty perch — it sure must be lonely up there.' And with that, she shoves the changing bag under the buggy and undoes the brake, then she turns on her heel and walks back up the path to the park gates, pushing Owen in front of her, back straight. The mouse that roared, I think.

It's really cold now, and I'm desperate to leave, to go home and cuddle up on the sofa with Chloe and watch TV, but I know that I can't just walk off and leave Lina like this. Not when she needs me. Instead, I lift Chloe gently out of her buggy and put her on my knee, holding her soft little body against mine. She reaches out a hand and I have to move the coffee cup out of her way so she doesn't up-end it on herself. The action makes me suddenly aware of how quickly an accident could happen, and for a second, I feel bad about what I said to Jane.

But then I think, no, I'm right. It's a question of priorities, and when you have a baby, they need to change. It's as simple as that. But the thought makes me emotional all of a sudden, and the tears just seem to spring to my eyes. I rummage in my jacket, giving a little sniff, burying my nose in the scrap of white tissue when I find it. And once I've started, I can't stop. The tears are like a waterfall, pouring out of me. I don't really know why I'm crying – for Jasper, fighting for his life in his little hospital bed, or for myself and everything that's changed in the past year? I've gained so much with little Chloe in my life, but I've lost, too. I've lost the woman I was, and I've lost Gray – or at least, I've lost the way we were together. I know I'll never be the same person, and meeting the girls just made that clearer to me, even though I've just risked their friendship to tell the truth as I see it.

'I'm sorry, I didn't mean to sound judgemental,' I sniff. 'I feel terrible for Gracie, I really do. I should have kept my big mouth shut,' I say sadly.

Lina looks as if she's making her mind up about something, then she says, 'Look, I agree with you. You can have all the au pairs you want, or the cleaners or whatever, but at the end of the day, it's just you and the baby, and there's no getting away from that. Things change when you give birth and you have to change with them. Or else ...'

'Exactly,' I say. 'So why didn't you say it to Jane then?'

'Oh, for God's sake, Elise,' Lina splutters. 'Are you

mad? Gracie's child is in the hospital – now is not the time for judgement.'

'But you agree with me,' I begin. 'Doesn't that make you a hypocrite?'

Lina gives me a long, cold stare, before nodding. 'Yes, it does, Elise, you're right.' She reaches into her handbag and takes out her phone, looks at it, then says, 'Listen, I have to go.'

I see my chance. 'Lina … Can I ask you something?'

'If it's about the audition, it's not a good time, Elise,' she says, sitting back in her chair, arms folded.

'But—'

'Listen, Gracie's *baby* is in hospital – he might die – and you're bugging me about a disastrous audition, which, frankly, I couldn't care less about now. Please, Elise, a bit of perspective.'

I'm absolutely gobsmacked. This is the gratitude I get – from Lina, of all people. I thought we were friends. Have I misread the situation again? I can't help it, I start blubbing once more, tears spilling over my eyelashes and rolling down my cheeks.

Lina tuts when she sees me and shakes her head, and it's as if she's driven a knife into my chest. I get up with as much dignity as I can muster, wiping my eyes with the backs of my hands, putting my bags and Chloe's things into the basket of her pram. She looks so pretty in her lovely pink straw bonnet, with her long eyelashes stroking the top of her cheeks as she looks down at the little toy in her hands.

My Chloe. What would I do without you? I think. You're the only thing I have left.

'I think I'd better be going,' I say.

She doesn't reply, and it's all I can do not to give her a piece of my mind, but even when I've been hurt so badly, I can't hurt her back. I am not that kind of person.

18

Jane

Jane spent half the journey home fuming about Elise
and the other half wondering about Gracie — about how
she was coping. She couldn't believe the judgemental
crap Elise had come out with at the café — not that Jane was
all that surprised. Elise had always had that capacity. But
Lina? Oh, she'd been careful not to say anything directly,
but Jane *knew*. Turned out the Earth Mother wasn't so 'live
and let live' after all.

Jane felt betrayed. Whatever Lina might privately think,
Jane had expected her to back her up against the kind of
bile that Elise had expressed. It was the sort of thing she'd
hear on a phone-in radio show, late at night, when no one

was listening: the self-righteous of the land would come out of their lairs and declare war on mothers. And there she'd been, beginning to warm to the woman: she was funny and fresh and Jane had enjoyed her energy and zest, the way she wasn't afraid to call a spade a spade. And she'd been kind, Jane had to admit, sending that card, which was more than the others had done; and they'd had that moment in Brittas, when Jane had told her more than she should have. At the thought of it, she felt herself grow hot. Really, Elise was the worst kind of woman — one who passed judgement on other women. Life was tough enough without that kind of behaviour.

When Jane thought of Elise, she was surprised at the violence she felt inside, a kind of tightness in her stomach, a fizzing in her head. She found herself clenching her fists and she looked down at them in amazement as she understood the intensity of her anger with Elise. She'd thought that all her feelings had been totally and successfully shut down. She'd had to shut them down, after what had happened with Tom. Growing up, she'd had to become an expert at displaying nothing of what she felt inside, while thinking all kinds of things, but then Tom had come along and she'd been able to find some expression for everything that was inside of her. Maybe too much expression, which is probably how she'd ended up in St Dympna's.

But Gracie ... When she thought of what her friend must be going through, Jane had to stop in her tracks. She took out her phone and went to call Gracie back, but then put it back in her bag. She had no idea what she'd say. Gracie must be torturing herself because she held herself to such impossibly high standards. Of all the people for this to happen to, Jane thought. Elise and Lina were completely wrong about Gracie. 'They make me sick, both of them,' Jane said to herself. She sucked in a deep breath and took the phone out of her bag again. She punched in Gracie's number and it rang and rang, then went to voicemail, Gracie's crisp, cheery voice inviting her to leave a message. Jane didn't know what to say, so she cut the call, biting her lip. She pushed the buggy on towards home, imagining Gracie sitting in some awful waiting room, drinking terrible coffee and blaming herself. She needed to talk to her – to tell her that it would be OK and that she would be there for her, just as Gracie had been there for Jane when she'd needed it. Eventually, as she turned in to the road where she lived, her heart sinking as she walked slowly towards the house and to another evening spent sitting silently across the table from her husband, she remembered that she had Jake's number on her phone. Before she could talk herself out of it, she rang.

'Hello?' Jake's voice sounded muffled, as if he had his hand over the phone, and Jane could hear a tannoy in the background. She hesitated, wondering what on earth she was going to say.

'Jake – it's Jane. I'm sorry to ring like this—'

'Jane!' he said, as if he'd been waiting for her call all day. 'You're so good to call.'

'Oh,' Jane said, taken aback. She'd never thought someone would be delighted to get a phone call from her. 'I was just wondering how Gracie was ... how you both are.'

'Oh, God,' he said, and for a second, Jane thought he might be about to cry. She wasn't sure she knew what to do about a man crying. 'Gracie's eating herself up, as you can imagine,' he said, his voice wavering.

'Is Jasper ... will he be OK?'

'They took him away, Jane, to operate on him.'

Now, Jake was crying, and Jane found herself soothing him, murmuring that Jasper was in the best hands and that she was sure he'd pull through, as Jake's snuffles subsided. She was surprised when he stopped crying – that her words seemed to be having some effect. 'Listen,' she continued, 'do you think it would be OK if I visited? Would Gracie find that helpful?' Even as she spoke, her mind began to whirr as she wondered how she'd explain it to Mark. Maybe if she told him after she put the dinner on the table, he might be a bit more mollified, and he had been slightly more cheerful of late. Must be the stupid bloody promotion, Jane thought to herself. And he'd taken to drinking wine with his dinner, which she didn't know what to make of. Sometimes she had a vision of herself adding something to it, one of the sleeping tablets her doctor had given her last year, when she'd had a bout of insomnia. But she worried then that she might end up killing him, and then she worried that this might not bother her very much.

'God, Jane, would you?' Jake was saying. 'I've no idea

what to say to Gracie because she thinks I'm judging her, no matter what I do or say, and I'm not. It could have happened to me. Why the hell didn't I see how much pressure she was under?'

'I'll come as quickly as I can,' Jane said. She'd arrived at her garden gate now, and as she assured Jake that she'd be there within the hour, she scanned the pretty cream-coloured facade of the house, the purple wisteria that had come into bloom over the front door, and she imagined herself being sucked through the brightly painted door into the darkness inside. She got that sudden clenching feeling in her guts and she had to close her eyes for a second. When she opened them, Mark was standing there on the garden path, his body a rigid coil of impatience. Jane stifled a scream. 'Jake, I have to go. I'll call you when I'm setting out,' Jane said in her most businesslike manner, disconnecting the call.

'Who was that?'

'Jake, Gracie's partner. Their baby had an accident — he's in hospital.'

But Mark didn't appear to hear, striding to the front door, leaving it open behind him as he went inside. Jane followed into the thick darkness, taking her sandals off, her feet unsteady on the wooden floors. She knew he could be waiting anywhere.

And he was, reaching out from behind the kitchen door and grabbing her arm, twisting it behind her back so hard she let out a cry.

'We have guests in an hour and we've nothing to feed them.'

'What guests?' she managed, even though the burning pain made her feel that her shoulder would be ripped from its socket.

'Deirdre and James from my office. And they expect to be fed a decent meal. My partnership depends on it.'

'But you didn't tell me, and I was going to visit Gracie ...' Jane's voice trailed off as he released her for a second, pulling his wallet out of his back pocket. 'How was I to know that they'd bloody ambush me. That Deirdre is some bitch, trying to catch me out like this, inviting herself around for a "casual supper",' he ranted. 'I knew she never liked me.' He pulled two twenty-euro notes out of his wallet. 'Go and get something and make it quick.'

'No,' Jane said.

'I don't think you heard me.' He grabbed Jane by the collar of her T-shirt and pulled her towards him, until his face was inches away from hers. His eyes were black and his face was puce with rage.

I mustn't waver, Jane thought. I mustn't give in. 'I said no. I want to see Gracie. Jasper might die — it's very serious.'

'And you don't think my bloody dinner is serious? This is make or break, Jane, and you are not going to fuck it up.'

'Look, you're just stressed. I'll order in from The Butler's Pantry and it'll be great. Please, Mark, I can't face making a three-course meal now ...'

She felt the full force of his weight behind her now, pushing her into the kitchen counter so that she hit it hard, folding in two over it. She rested her head on the cool granite for a second, but regretted it instantly when her head was lifted up by her hair, then slammed down on it over and over again. With each slam, Mark repeated, 'You, will, not, fuck, up, my, career ...' She could hear Owen roaring in the background and she knew he needed her, but she didn't have the strength. She couldn't push back, so she just let her cheek be smashed down until she felt it grow spongy and soft, and she tasted blood in her mouth from where she'd bitten her tongue.

'Clean yourself up. You have ten minutes, then get to work. You can use this to buy a decent bottle of champagne.' The money was thrown down on the counter, where Jane could see it out of her good eye. 'Oh, and don't set foot in the living room in that state.'

Jane remained still until she was sure he'd left, then tried to stand. It was hard. Her face felt like an inflated balloon and she could feel a sharp throbbing on her cheekbone, which she thought might be broken — but somehow, her brain seemed to be clear. Maybe it was adrenaline, but she found that, even though she couldn't open one eye, she could at least think. What would she do? If she didn't look busy, he'd kill her. She went to the freezer and took out a piece of meat that looked about right. It'd never defrost in time, but they wouldn't know until it was too late. She banged pots and pans in the kitchen, hobbling around, her vision clouded with pain, until she heard their guests arrive and Mark's over-cheery tone as he greeted them.

Then she had an idea. She opened the kitchen door, carefully avoiding the hall mirror, so she wouldn't have to see herself — it was too late for that now — and she walked across the hall to the living room. Time to introduce myself, she thought — the little wife.

As she walked in, she could see Mark fixing his habitual gin and tonic, three glasses in front of him, each filled with two ice cubes. He had the measure in his hand and was about to pour, talking in a voice she didn't recognise, an eager, reedy chatter, about some case. He sounded worried, insecure, and Jane felt her heart lift.

'Oh, my God,' the woman, who'd been perched on the sofa, said when she saw Jane. Her eyes were round with horror and her mouth formed an 'o'. She edged a little closer to her colleague, a man in a wide-boy pinstripe suit.

Mark turned around, his expression flicking from rage to concern in a second. 'My goodness, darling, what happened?'

Jane tried to smile, but realised that if she did, blood would pour out of her mouth, so instead, she just nodded to the woman, in her severe black trouser suit, and the man with his slicked-back hair, taking in the looks of terror on their faces. She reached out a hand and shook the woman's, which felt clammy, and then the man's, then attempted to speak: 'I tripped on the front doorstep earlier. I was trying to put out the bins.'

The silence seemed to stretch into eternity, the man and the woman looking first at Jane, then at Mark, clearly wondering what they'd stepped into. 'I think maybe we should go ...' the man began.

'Not at all,' Mark said, walking over to Jane, putting an arm around her shoulder. Jane thought that she might throw up, her whole body tensing as he looked at her with fake concern. 'Jane, I'll be out in a second to have a look at that, don't you worry. I'll sort it out.'

I'll bet you will, Jane thought, a feeling of panic suddenly gripping her at the thought of the price she'd have to pay for showing him up. How long have I got? she wondered. One minute, two? She calculated the distance between the kitchen and the front door — about twenty feet, she reckoned — and wondered if she could cover it in time. She'd have to hunch down on the front path, so they wouldn't see her from the living room, and then what? She'd have to make it to the main road and flag a taxi. Nope, she thought, there was no way.

'It's fine,' Jane said blankly. 'Dinner will be in ten minutes,' she added, with what she hoped was a smile. They looked at her in alarm, so God knows how that had come out, but it would have to do. 'Darling,' she said to Mark, 'make our guests comfortable and I'll be back in a sec.' And, without waiting for an answer, she turned on her heel and went into the kitchen.

The pain was now a hot throbbing from her jaw to her eye socket, as if someone was jabbing the side of her face with a poker, but she knew that she had to move – she only had a few minutes. She put the frozen meat into the oven, turning the gas up to nine, so that it would char on the outside and look cooked and the reassuring smell would waft into the living room, a sign that all was well. Then she thought, taxi, but how will I get one? I could hail one from the street, she thought doubtfully. Suddenly, she caught sight of Mark's mobile on the counter. It must be a sign, she thought, because he's normally never without it. She picked it up, ignoring the fingerprint ID request and tapped in the password – his birthday, predictably enough – then located the taxi app, realising that Jarshid and his Opel Zafira were one minute away. The rest happened in a blur, as she saw herself grabbing the forty euro Mark had thrown at her off the counter, pulling Owen out of his baby seat, where he'd been gnawing on a rice cake, so quickly he wailed in surprise, then walking out of the front door in her bare feet, not even bothering to hide her departure. If he caught her, there was no way he'd risk a showdown. It was her only chance.

She saw the silver car turn in to the road and she ran towards it, hand in the air.

'Jane!' Mark's voice boomed from behind her and she let out a little scream, but she kept on running, feet slapping off the pavement, Owen bouncing up and down on her hip, until she yanked the door of the car open and jumped inside, realising, as she did, that the only two things she had in the world were Owen and forty quid.

'Would you be able to turn around – quickly?' she asked Jarshid as she saw Mark walking towards the car, face like thunder. He's going to kill me, Jane thought, unless we get a bloody move on. To his credit, Jarshid just nodded and, after he'd wisely pressed the central-locking button, did a very quick three-point turn, roaring off up the road. Jane didn't look around. She knew that she'd never set foot in that house again. Not if she wanted to live.

Jarshid said not a single word all the way to the hospital and Jane was glad about that. No chit-chat about the state of the country and the shysters in government, just blissful silence. She rolled down the window and let the early autumn air fill the back seat of the car. Owen, on her knee, gave a gurgle of delight as the wind whipped his hair up around his head. So you're happy too, she thought. No wonder. Her heart squeezed as she thought of what it must have been like for him, seeing and not understanding.

Do it for him, she thought to herself. Do it for your son.

When they pulled up outside the hospital, a long, low modern building surrounded by car parks crammed with cars, Jarshid refused to take the fare until Jane explained that it was on her husband's account. 'Eighty euro,' he said, the flicker of a smile on his face.

'Don't forget the tip,' Jane said.

Then he clambered out of his seat and opened the back

door for her, holding Owen while she stepped out, her feet
tender on the hard tarmac. As he placed Owen back into her
arms, he gave a short nod and handed her a card. 'Jarshid
Marwani' it said, followed by a mobile phone number.
'Call me when you are finished,' he said solemnly, 'and I
will take you where you need to go.'

'Thanks,' Jane managed through her swollen mouth.
'I'm actually visiting a friend,' she said unnecessarily,
before repeating, 'Thanks very much.'

She found Gracie and Jake on the first floor, in a gloomy
little space beside the ICU. Gracie was lying across the red
plastic chairs, her head on Jake's lap, and Jake was staring
into space. Opposite them, a woman was attempting to
corral her over-active toddler, handing him individual
crisps from a bag. When Jake saw Jane, his face lit up —
before he got a closer look at her. Jane remembered the
well-dressed woman in her living room, and the look of
panic on her face at the realisation that she'd got herself
into something for which no amount of crisp dressing or
impressive legal files had prepared her. Jane wondered if
they were tucking into the burned-frozen joint — before
realising that she couldn't care less.

'Jane, are you … is everything all right?'

'Of course,' Jane said. 'I just had a bit of an accident in
the car, that's all.' Another lie, because Mark had never let
her drive, but she knew that she'd tell Jake the truth later,

when he was able for it. She couldn't unload on him now, not like this.

But he surprised her. 'Ah, Jane,' Jake said softly, as she sat down beside him. 'There's no need.'

'No need for what?' Jane said quietly, finding herself resting against him, feeling his warm steadiness beside her. He didn't add anything, and because he just waited, she found herself telling him the whole story, the words pouring out of her as Owen sat in front of them on the floor, his back resting against her knee. He was bashing one of the wooden toys provided and grabbing a crisp from the toddler, who wailed in outrage. Owen's answer was to giggle and shove the crisp into his mouth. Jane knew that he might choke on it, but she found she didn't have the energy to remove it, so she watched him push it around his mouth, his face brightening as he registered its deliciousness.

In an urgent whisper, not wanting to wake Gracie, Jane told Jake everything, from the first time it had happened to that awful scene in the living room. 'I normalised it, can you believe it,' she said. 'I just explained it away, but when I saw the look on their faces, I realised just how far it had gone and that it wasn't normal at all ...'

His answer was just to nod and to give her arm a gentle squeeze. 'Will you listen to me,' Jane said with what she hoped was a smile. 'After everything you've been through, here I am—'

'It's fine. We're all in it together,' Jake said softly. 'All in this big mess,' he added with a rueful laugh. 'Honestly, look at us,' he said. Gracie shifted on his lap, and her eyes opened. Then Jane saw it, the brief, blank look and the pain that came after as she remembered.

She sat up, eyes scanning Jake's face for any signs of disaster. Then she saw Jane. 'Jane, oh, Jane,' she said, getting up and going to her friend, pulling her into a hug and collapsing into sobs.

'Ah, Gracie, love,' Jane said, over and over again, stroking her friend's back and smoothing down her ponytail. 'It's going to be OK.'

'Is it?' Gracie said, pulling back from her. 'Is it really?'

'Yes, in time,' Jane said.

Gracie shook her head. 'I wish I could believe you,' she said tightly. 'You know, I think he might be better off with somebody else. Someone who can give him what he needs.'

Jake pulled her towards him. 'Gracie, we're not thinking like that right now. We are just focusing on the next minute, and then the one after that. One minute at a time.'

'But the minutes are so long!' Gracie wailed.

'They seem like that now,' Jane said softly, 'but that's all we have. Hang in there, hmm?' and she stroked Gracie's hair again. Gracie nodded softly, sitting down on the plastic chair again and staring into space for a few moments. Jake and Jane exchanged a look, and then Gracie said, 'What happened to your face?'

'It's a long story,' Jane said. 'For another time.'

*

Like everyone else, the nurse was so kind, asking a mousy-looking girl in blue scrubs to take Owen while she saw to Jane. 'You'll need an X-ray,' she said, examining Jane's cheekbone, pressing it gently, which made Jane stifle a scream. 'But first, we need to record everything.'

'Record what?'

'Your injuries. So you can ... take things forward in due course.'

Jane's heart squeezed. 'Oh, no ... it was just an accident—' she began, but then she thought, Who on earth am I kidding? 'Thanks,' she said, as the nurse helped her into a thin cotton robe and steered her towards the X-ray department. 'I didn't have an accident,' she said, as she was pushed along the corridor in a hospital wheelchair. 'My husband did this to me.'

'I know,' the nurse said softly, putting a hand on Jane's shoulder.

The garda was nice too, a young girl, clearly out of her depth but determined to do the right thing, pressing her lips together and opening her notebook, a look of concentration on her face. Jane felt a bit sorry for her, fresh out of Templemore, faced with the terrible things people did to each other. She wondered if that made her believe that the world was an awful place, but she could see by the eager look on the girl's face that she hadn't gone down that road just yet.

Jane wanted to save her from the worst of it, so she began by skirting around the subject, omitting key details, until the girl sat up straight and cleared her throat. 'Jane. This will only work if you tell me the truth.'

'The truth,' Jane repeated.

'That's right.' The girl's gaze was steady and Jane could see now that she was made of steelier stuff than she'd thought. She cleared her throat and began.

When she'd finished, she felt hollowed out. She'd needed to sit in the wheelchair again and be pushed back along the corridor to where Gracie and Jake were still slumped on the red plastic chairs. 'They've given her a sedative,' Jake said quietly, nodding at Gracie, who was curled up on the bench, snoring softly.

Jane thought of the painkillers the nurse had insisted she take home with her. 'You'll be in pain later,' she'd said.

'Worse than this?' Jane had attempted a joke, and the nurse gave a brief smile. 'Take the tablets, Jane, and let yourself rest.'

She couldn't, of course, with Owen to listen out for. 'That's good,' she said to Jake. 'Any news yet?'

Jake shook his head.

'I hate to ask at a time like this, Jake, but is there any chance ...? You see, I've nowhere else to go.'

Jake rolled his eyes to heaven, and for a second, Jane thought that he was annoyed with her, but then he said, 'Jeez, Jane, why do you even ask? The keys are under the aloe vera plant on the front porch. Run yourself a bath and have a drink. God, that sounds like I think all you need is a bit of a pampering session ... sorry.'

'Don't be silly, Jake. Thanks.' More thanks for more kindness. How would she ever repay it?

Jake's hair was musty when Jane went to hug him, the odour of anxiety and stress. 'I can stay ...'

'You can*not*. You can go home and rest and I'll call you when there's news.'

So, she did. She called Jarshid, and, true to his word, he came to collect her and took her through the silent night-time streets to the sea.

19

Lina

Lina had watched Elise's tiny frame push the huge, vulgar pram up the hill from the park, like a tortoise carrying its shell on its back. She looked burdened, Lina had thought guiltily, but not guiltily enough to catch up with her. Instead, she just let Elise keep going, to nurse her self-righteousness to herself — because she kind of hated her.

Now, she soaked Tommy's new bottle in boiling water — they'd taken to it with an enthusiasm that Lina had found insulting, until she realised that this meant that Mama could feed them, leaving Lina a bit of time to think. Once upon a time, she'd have used this time to write, to practise her best lines out loud, laughing away at herself, but now, she couldn't see the point. The thing is, she thought as she cleaned the bottle scrupulously with a bottle brush, she didn't hate Elise because of Graham McSween, which Lina knew wasn't actually Elise's fault; besides, she was far too busy hating herself for her own stupidity, for the way she'd sold out every other woman who'd be faced with that ... that animal. No, she hated Elise for saying what she herself was thinking about Gracie and poor Jasper. She'd let Elise be her mouthpiece, but they were both judging Gracie, standing over her and finding fault – when, really, it could have been any of them. Was she a better mum than Gracie because she walked around with Tommy clamped to her bosom; because she proclaimed to all and sundry that she was raising Tommy to be a person, not a woman or a man? Gee whizz, she thought, top marks for me. She turned the bottle upside down on a clean piece of kitchen paper to dry. I've discovered that, basically, I'm not a very nice person, she thought sadly to herself, and even though it's not fair, I can't help blaming Elise.

She went to see what Mama was doing because there was deafening silence from the living room. Mama was worse than Tommy in that way: silence usually meant that she was up to something. Now, she was tapping away at Lina's laptop, reading glasses halfway down her nose. 'What are you doing?' Lina said.

'Nothing,' her mother replied, slamming the laptop shut. 'Just looking at clothing online. I think I will order you a nice dress,' she said, taking her glasses off and smiling at her daughter.

'There's no need—' Lina began.

'Let me cheer you up, even if it's only with something silly,' her mother said, extending an arm to pull Lina closer. 'If I can't do that, what kind of mother am I?' And she gave a small smile.

'A good mother,' Lina said, squeezing her mother tightly, wondering how it was that she'd never seen this. Possibly because she'd been too busy fighting with her, trying to pull out of her orbit, the only one she'd ever known, to establish herself as her own person, someone who didn't need anybody else.

'Mama?'

'Yes, *mein Liebling*?'

'Who was my dad?'

Mama took her glasses off very slowly, putting them gently down on the table. 'Why do you want to know now, after all this time?'

'Because of Tommy, I suppose,' Lina said. 'Because I'm beginning to realise in a way I didn't before that dads matter. The fact that it took that git to show me is neither here nor there,' she said dryly. When her mother looked at her, mystified, she added, 'When I see Seamus, I realise that there is no connection whatsoever between him and Graham McSween, that all men aren't alike.'

'Ah,' her mother said with a small smile. 'I never said

that men were the enemy, Lina. I just didn't feel we needed one in our lives, that's all.'

'Yes, but what about Simon? He was in our lives, wasn't he? He chopped wood for us and got the mower going that time—'

'All of which were things we could have done ourselves,' her mother said firmly. 'I just chose to let Simon help us because he really wanted to. Surely you can't be saying that women aren't able to chop wood and fix lawnmowers?' She shook her head, laughing.

'It's not that simple, though, is it?' Lina said. 'It's not a question of men can do this and women can do that, or men are all beasts and women are all saints.'

'No, of course it isn't, but that's not what angers me, Lina. What angers me is the structure that exists that will allow men like that McSween to do what they do. To use their power to bully and intimidate, and make women feel that it's all their fault. Which is what you have done, my pet. You have done nothing wrong, nothing, and yet, you have fallen for his tricks and we must stop him, for the sake of all the other women who will come after you.'

'Oh, Mama,' Lina said. 'I don't think I have the courage. I just want to forget it all happened and move on, I really do.' And, she thought miserably, I want to forget my own dismal role in the event, my culpability. I haven't shared it with you, Mama, because I'm too ashamed.

'But you can't. What about the next girl who comes up

from the arse end of nowhere and doesn't understand what she's being asked to do? Sometimes we owe it to others to rise above ourselves and to fight,' her mother said, banging her fist on the table.

'The arse end of nowhere' — the expression, repeated with her mother's German accent, made Lina want to laugh, and yet, she knew that what her mother was saying was true. She just wasn't ready yet. 'Let me think about it. Besides, you changed the subject,' she said.

Her mother shrugged. 'I know. It's a long story, as the Irish say. I need a little time. Can you give me that?'

Why? Lina wanted to say. What's so bloody mysterious — he's hardly James Bond, is he? But one look at her mother's face told her to leave it alone, for the time being anyway.

'Fine,' she said shortly. 'I'll get the dinner on.'

'Oh, not for me, my dear,' her mother said. 'I'm going to play bridge with Zaynab — you know, Mrs Abdallah. She's such a cardshark, you wouldn't believe. She's been trying to teach this silly woman here how to play, even though she knows I'm a lost cause.' She turned her hands upwards in a 'what can you do?' gesture.

'You've got your mojo back.' Lina smiled, thinking of the thin, forlorn creature who'd turned up at her door a few weeks before, with her limp and her ratty hair. Now, Mama looked pinker, her hair a soft puff around her head. After all those years of doing everything for yourself, you've finally learned, Lina thought, that you need other people.

'*Ich verstehe nicht*,' her mother replied.

'I'll bet you don't understand,' Lina laughed, 'when you feel like it.'

Her mother smiled happily. 'So, what will you do?' she asked. 'You can come with me to play bridge, but you will find it very dull ...'

'God, no,' Lina said. 'I'll leave you to it. It's a lovely evening. I'm going for a walk down the canal.'

'Just you and Tommy?'

'Maybe.' Lina shrugged. 'Why?'

'Oh, no reason,' her mother said, smiling.

A few nights before, Lina had asked Seamus if he fancied a walk with herself and Tommy, to make the most of the still-mild September. After a couple of cloudy days it was warm and dry again and the crowds still lined the canal, making the most of the Indian summer, spilling over onto the cycle lane, cans of beer and picnic sets beside them. Lina found that she liked the energy, the roar of chatter in different languages buoying her up, making her feel that she was part of something larger than just her own small world. It soothed her and Seamus was easy company, walking along beside her in his board shorts and flip-flops, content to just chat, filling her in with stories about the office and so on. He was also a good listener, and she'd told him about what had happened to Jasper, including her own rush to judgement, enjoying the lightness that came with unburdening herself. It was only ten days ago, but it felt like a lifetime. She'd got a text from Jane to say that Jasper was on the mend, but its frosty tone didn't invite her to reply – and she didn't have the nerve to ring Gracie. What's more, the Tuesday meetings had fizzled out. She missed the girls, she realised. Even Elise. She'd taken all of their friendships for granted, thinking that she was better than them. She sure as hell wasn't.

She'd noticed that Seamus hadn't asked her about access to Tommy in a little while and she was grateful for that, not to have to fight him on that front, but she did let him carry her in the sling, Tommy turned forward so that she could see the world, legs kicking with excitement. Lina knew that it looked like they were a family, but she began to wonder if it really mattered how things looked from the outside, when how they actually were could be so different.

Since that first outing, they'd walked the canal every evening, all the way down to Grand Canal Dock, where they'd sit by the water and watch the kids jumping in and emerging again, hair plastered to their faces, trotting across the cobblestones to the end of the queue to dive bomb in once more. Tonight, two boys turned up, pushing their bicycles, and after they'd had a swim, they clambered back on, dripping wet, to cycle home, not even a towel between them.

'Isn't it great to be that free?' Seamus said, handing Lina the milky coffee he'd bought at the overpriced deli.

'Sometimes, I wish I could join them.'

'Well, why can't you? You've got the shorts for it.' She laughed, nodding at his blue shorts with their flamingo pattern. 'And you'd dry off on the way home, so what's stopping you?'

'Ah, I'm a grown-up,' Seamus said, sipping his coffee.

'Well, even grown-ups need to play,' Lina said.

'Hah.' He took a sip of his coffee and then said quietly, 'I hate it.'

'Hate what?'

'Everything,' Seamus said. 'My life. I don't know what I was expecting from Download, but it sure wasn't the job I'm doing now, although I was thrilled to get it at the time. Can you imagine? I was grateful for the opportunity to trawl through every kind of depravity you can imagine. Kittens being cooked in microwaves? That's only the tip of the iceberg.'

Lina felt a sudden rush of empathy for Seamus, who sat, day after day, in a big pool of people at Download doing what he did. From the outside, it looked like fun: all pool tables and throwing American footballs across the office, but it didn't really bear much scrutiny. When it came down to it, was there all that much difference between places like Download and the factories and mills she and Seamus would have worked in had they been born in another time? Lina doubted it. And she'd thought her comedy, her writing, was setting her free, making her better than Seamus — but she'd been wrong. 'What would you do if you didn't have to wear the suit, so to speak?'

'Oh, I don't know.' There was a long pause. 'I'm really into birdwatching.'

'Birdwatching?' Lina couldn't believe her ears. 'You're a twitcher, a warbler, a shag?'

'I've heard it all before,' Seamus said, smiling. His face was usually so earnest and serious that when he smiled it became something open and lovely. 'Well, really, I'm into nature and stuff. I'd like to do guiding and foraging, that kind of thing. I have training, believe it or not, and I know where the good stuff is. But there isn't too much foraging to be done in Rathmines — at least not of the plant variety — and the depravity business pays well, which it'd want to.'

'What kind of things do you forage?'

'Oh, anything. It depends on the season: wild garlic in spring, mushrooms in autumn. I'm very good on sea vegetables, as it happens.'

'I'd like to try that,' Lina said wistfully. She could just see herself in one of those aprons with big pockets, trawling along a beach in Connemara, picking up mermaid's purses or samphire.

'Well, I'll take you. We can just go up to the woods in Wicklow — the mushrooms are amazing; all kinds of varieties.'

'I won't come down with some terrible case of poisoning, will I, that eats my brain and shuts down my entire nervous system?' Lina joked.

'I know what I'm doing,' Seamus said. 'My dad used to take me out every weekend in the autumn and we'd forage and cook, and I learned how to pick the best and leave the dangerous ones. It takes a bit of practice, but I'm good at it now – honest.'

'It sounds as if it's your passion.'

'If you want to be millennial about it,' Seamus said, taking a sip of his drink. Lina watched him as he drank, the slow bob of his Adam's apple as the coffee went down. I didn't know that about you, she thought. There's a whole side to you I never even realised existed. Probably because I never asked.

'So what are you going to do about it – just let your dreams wither?' Lina knew that she was talking about herself, really, but it was easier to ask Seamus, to deflect, because she didn't want to think what she might do next. Where she'd go from here. The only way seemed down. Back to Download after her maternity leave, to more chat about box sets and holidays, to the sense of life just drifting by.

He sat back, looking surprised. 'Well, I wouldn't put it like that. I'm being practical, putting reality first. As I said, depravity pays – and I'm a family man now,' he added quietly. 'I have responsibilities.'

'At least, that's what you tell yourself,' Lina said, thinking of the weekly money that Seamus had insisted on paying into her post office account and which she'd told him sharply would only be spent on Tommy. 'What's to stop you guiding or whatever, really? You could live on half the money you do here in the arse end of nowhere, which I presume is where guiding happens, unless you're planning to guide people around the discarded pizza and chicken boxes of the neighbourhood.'

Seamus leaned back on the bench, a look of indignation on his face. 'I'm sorry, but if I want to support my daughter by looking at the awful things humans do for the rest of my life, I bloody well will.' His face was flushed now and a crease had appeared between his eyebrows. Gone was the open, placid look he normally had.

'I didn't ask you to support them,' Lina barked. 'We were managing just fine, you know.'

'Well, excuse me for being an adult,' he snapped, lifting his coffee to his mouth, taking a big sip and putting it down on the bench with a thump. Then he said softly, 'How did we end up like this?'

'Like what?' Lina snapped.

'You know, rowing. It was all going so well.'

'I don't know,' Lina said sadly. 'Do you think it's because maybe we're both in limbo?'

'I'd say that'd be it all right,' Seamus said. The two of them said nothing for a while, and Lina wondered again if this was why they'd found each other, both of them bobbing along in the slipstream, unsure of who they were or where they were going.

'So, what are you going to do about that guy?' Seamus asked suddenly.

Lina crossed her arms defensively. 'Nothing.'

He didn't say anything, and she looked at him out of the corner of her eye, while watching a boy run and jump, doing a twist in mid-air for good measure, before hitting the water with a big splash.

'What?'

'I didn't say a word,' he replied.

'Look, this kind of thing is par for the course in this business and there's nothing I can do about it, Seamus. I've tried explaining it — it's not like Download, where there are rules and procedures. In this world, there are no rules — you get what you want by chance or by luck, or ...' She hesitated as she thought of the other, less savoury options.

'Right,' he said noncommittally. 'So you're going to take the gig?'

Lina sighed. 'I don't know. He's offered me a slot, but I haven't decided yet, but I feel that I don't have a choice. I go along with him and I get my shot — although God knows what he'd be like if we actually made the bloody films — I make a big song and dance about it and I'm toast. Career over. End of.' She made a chopping motion with her hand.

'Hang on, does it have to be either/or?' Seamus said.

'Either/or what? I don't follow,' Lina said.

'Well, surely in this day and age, you can do it yourself. Make your own show.'

'Ah, Seamus, it's not as straightforward as that. You need a crew to film and a script and so on.'

'And you can't find that anywhere else except with that tit? No one else in the whole world possesses a camera or sound equipment or whatever?'

'It's not that, Seamus. Digital is the new platform for people like me, but it's the contacts Graham McSween has — he can talk you up, get your stuff into the hands of the right people. And, can I just remind you, I have emptied a Guinness into Mack McCarthy's lap, so he won't exactly be well disposed towards me.' As Lina said this, she had a sudden vision of Abbie, with her guileless act and her silly T-shirts, the gatekeeper, the enabler. You'd never know it, but people could surprise you in all kinds of ways, Lina thought sadly. That includes me, she added to herself, thinking of Conor Creighton. Gracie had been right — definitely not sisterly.

'Correct me if I'm wrong, but is there not such a thing as YouTube, and did Ed Sheeran not make his name by just uploading his stuff? He doesn't seem to be doing too badly.'

'Hmm,' Lina said, unable to think of a response to this.

'Hmm, what?' Seamus said. 'What is there to think about? Look, Jason in work has a camera — he makes corporate videos in his spare time — and Magda will let us have the boardroom, I'm sure. We'll record and upload and next thing you'll be the new Joan Rivers.'

'No one can be Joan Rivers,' Lina said, smiling. 'Only Joan Rivers.'

'Well, Sarah Silverman or Amy Schumer — take your pick.'

'I'll think about it,' Lina said, her mind already beginning to whirr. The truth was, what Graham McSween had done had left a gaping hole where her confidence should be. She'd gone over and over that afternoon in her mind, wondering if she could have done something different; if she could have just fled, or stood up to him, told him to go fuck himself — anything but say, 'Yes, please, Graham. Remove my clothing and fondle me. I don't mind.'

As if Seamus had read her mind, he said, 'Don't let what Graham McSween did to you stop you, Lina. That's not you — that's not the Lina I know and love. The Lina I know and love would run up and down O'Connell Street with a banner in her hand denouncing the little shit.'

Lina shrugged. 'I'm not the Lina you know at the moment. I'm tired, Seamus, and I feel ashamed that I just crumbled like that.' She avoided repeating the word 'love' because she didn't know if he really meant it.

'You were alone and vulnerable and he took advantage of you. That's what he does. And he's responsible for his behaviour, not you. You're the victim here.'

'I know,' Lina said sadly. She risked a little lean against Seamus, resting her head against his shoulder. 'Thanks.'

They watched the kids swimming for a bit, then Lina said, 'Seamus, I think I owe you an apology.'

'Oh, yeah?' Seamus said, careful not to look at her.

'I didn't take your feelings into consideration, you know, with Tommy. I didn't even think about it. I just kind of—'

'Used me?' Seamus offered.

Lina blushed. 'Well, yes. I didn't take you seriously and I could blame my upbringing or my mother, but really, it was my decision. I wanted what I wanted and I didn't think about you. I'm truly sorry, Seamus. I hope … I hope that maybe you might like to be a part of her life now.' When he looked stunned, she added, 'Look, I'm not suggesting that we move in together – just that we formalise the arrangement.'

'I'd like that,' Seamus said. 'Maybe you could write while I look after her or something?'

'I'm never writing again,' Lina said morosely. 'I am so over comedy.'

He put an arm around her shoulder and gave a brief squeeze, before carefully removing it. 'You're the funniest person I know. And you have something to say. You'll find your way. I know you will. Persevere, Lina. That's what my dad said – that's all you really have to do in this life.'

'Well, thanks, Dalai Lama, for that piece of wisdom,' Lina said.

'You're welcome. And when you're ready, do another woman a favour and report him – will you?'

'I'll try,' Lina lied. 'And now,' she said, getting up from

the bench and taking their cups to the bin to dispose of them, 'there's only one thing left to do.'

'What's that?' he asked.

'C'mon,' Lina said, walking over to the gang of kids.

'Ah, no way.'

'Way.' Lina laughed. 'C'mon, give me Tommy. I don't think she needs to learn to swim just yet.' Reluctantly, Seamus removed the sling — quite an operation — and handed Tommy to her mother. The kids gathered around Seamus chanting, 'Get them off,' as he removed his T-shirt and flip-flops; they let out a roar of applause as he ran towards the edge of the dock, hesitating for a fraction of a second before holding his nose and taking a flying leap into the water. Lina peered over the edge, at the white splash of foam rising to the top, and then he was there, fists aloft. 'Woohoo!'

It's good to be a child again, Lina thought, even if it's just for a little while. She clapped and hooted with the rest of them as Seamus lay back in the water, floating, squirting not-very-clean water out of his mouth.

'Your turn, missus,' a voice said beside her. Lina turned to see a teenage girl, shivering, beside her, her skin blue, water dripping onto the cobblestones.

'Ah, no,' Lina said. 'I have the baby to mind — and I'm not exactly dressed for it.'

'Do you not have underwear under that dress of yours?' the girl said cheekily.

'I do, but not the kind I want the world to see.' Lina laughed.

'Ah, c'mon. YOLO.'

'YOLO — will you listen to yourself?' Lina guffawed.

'Well, it's true,' the girl said, reaching out her arms to take Tommy, who looked slightly alarmed to be handed to a stranger, staring at the girl as if she were an alien. When the girl put Tommy on to her damp hip, she spoke to her as if she were entirely used to babies and Lina wondered how much mammying she'd done already in her young life. More than the boys, that was for sure, she thought, wondering if some things would ever truly change.

'C'mon in, the water's lovely!' came Seamus's voice from below.

'Right,' Lina said, whipping off her summer dress before she could talk herself out of it, slipping her feet out of her ancient trainers and walking towards the edge of the dock. It suddenly seemed very high, and the water below very far away, but as the applause gathered, she took a few steps back, then ran forward, lifting high into the air, before landing in the water with a huge splash. From below, she looked up at the surface, to where Seamus was floating, and she swam up to join him.

Later, when they got home, skin damp from the cold water, she invited Seamus up to the flat. 'I think I have a spare pair of shorts,' she said. 'You'll catch a cold if you don't change out of them.' He didn't point out that she sounded like his mother, which was kind of him, following her up the stairs, with its threadbare maroon carpet, waiting patiently while she fumbled with the keys, her hands still cold from her impromptu swim.

'We're home!' she shouted into the living room.

'In here,' her mother's reedy voice answered. When Lina opened the door, her mother was sitting on the sofa, and beside her was a figure in a navy blue sweatshirt. They were leaning towards each other and they seemed to be looking down at something. Lina recognised that shape, she thought, she'd seen him every day before leaving for Dublin. At the sight of his head of light-brown hair, bald patch at the crown, her heart lifted. She crept over and put an arm around each of them, just as she'd done when she was a teenager and she placed a kiss on the man's cheek.

'Hi, Simon,' she said, as if she'd seen him only yesterday and not three long years before.

'Ah, Lina, I was hoping I wouldn't miss you,' Simon said, turning to return her kiss. 'I have to see this fine baby of yours.' He turned to see Seamus hovering there, Tommy peering out at them from her favourite perch in the sling.

'This is Seamus,' Lina said. 'Tommy's dad.'

Seamus got up to shake hands and the two men did a man-dance, where they both shuffled around, looking a bit embarrassed, making small talk about the weather, while Lina admired what her mother and Simon had been looking at: a photo of her, aged ten, in one of Simon's apple trees, his Collie, Scooter, standing at the bottom. 'Do you know,' Mama said. 'I never really realised what I had, right where I was. I never appreciated it until it was too late.' Her pale eyes filled with tears.

'Mama, don't say that,' Lina said, giving her mother a hug. 'It's never too late,' she added, turning to look at Simon, then back at Mama. The two of them laughed, and when Simon said he'd better be off, Lina replied that she wouldn't hear of it. 'You can sleep on the sofa,' she said. 'And we can catch up in the morning.' Adding, to herself, and you can tell me why you're here.

'Lina, why don't you stay in mine?' Seamus offered. 'You can take the spare room,' he added, in response to her sharp look.

She shrugged and looked at her mother and Simon, two guilty children waiting to be punished. 'We'll leave you to it,' Lina told them, and they had the grace to look a bit sheepish. 'Don't get up to mischief.' Her mother said something rude in German in reply.

'Who's that guy?' Seamus asked when they were going back downstairs. 'He seems to know a lot about apples.'

'He's a fruit farmer' Lina said. 'And he's my dad, or as good as,' she added, thinking how funny it was that she now had two men in her life, and it really wasn't that bad. She might even get used to it. Not that she *needed* either of them, she mused.

'He likes your mum anyway,' Seamus said. 'I can see you

The Start of Summer

take after her,' he added, letting that remark hang in the air as he held the door to the street open for her.

'There's no need,' Lina snapped. 'It's sexist.'

'Right,' Seamus said, standing back to let Lina out first.

'Oh, for God's sake,' she laughed, going out onto the busy street.

20

Gracie

She felt that she didn't really deserve Jasper coming back to her. In the days that followed, she'd found herself obsessively scrolling through online stories of parents who'd done exactly the same thing as she had: mums and dads who'd driven to work and forgotten to drop their babies off at crèche, leaving them in boiling hot cars for the whole day, and with each story, she kept hoping that the outcome would be different.

How could it be? she wondered. How did parents just forget the most important thing in their lives like that? The answer was that it was surprisingly easy — terrifyingly easy. Some professor had written a report on it, saying that it wasn't the parents' fault: that their brains were wired to do certain things in certain ways, and so they could easily forget something that was out of the ordinary. Like your child, Gracie had thought miserably; like another human being. It was nice of the professor, she thought — but unnecessary in her case. The blame was all hers.

That was why she'd accepted all of it — from the frosty silence of the medical team looking after Jasper; to the agency nurse telling her that he should be taken off her, that 'women like her' didn't deserve to be mothers; to the garda who'd appeared to take her statement, lips pursed as Gracie had told him everything. 'It sounds bad, doesn't it?' she'd said quietly to the man.

'It does,' he'd responded bluntly.

Bring it on, she'd thought, catching sight of the evening newspaper in the hospital waiting room, the lurid headline screaming, 'WHO WOULD DO THIS TO AN INNOCENT CHILD?'

Me, that's who, Gracie thought.

'It'll pass,' Jake had told her. 'They'll move on to another vehicle for their outrage.' Jake, who hadn't uttered one word of reproach from the moment he'd found out. Not one word. He'd held her in his arms in the overheated waiting room and the only thing he'd said was, 'It could have happened to me.'

'Yes, but it didn't,' Gracie had wailed. '*I* did it, Jake. I tried to kill him ...' She'd screamed so loudly then that the others in the waiting room, the little knots of mums and dads with children with flushed cheeks and seal-like coughs, with bandages on gashes, had fallen into complete silence. They'd had to sedate her then, hurrying her out of the waiting room to a small, dismal spot with plastic chairs and a single, forlorn potted plant. This must be where they tell the parents that their child has died, Gracie had thought. Imagine. In this dreadful place. Maybe that's what they were doing: preparing her for the worst. The last thing she'd heard, before she'd been knocked on the head with a cocktail of opiates, was Jake saying, 'You didn't kill him, Gracie. He's still alive. Hang onto that.'

And so, she had, even as she blamed herself, the accusations going round and round in her brain, action replays in which she got out of the car and then turned and walked to the rear door and took Jasper out, holding his soft little body to hers in his little-old-man outfit. She dreamt this so often that she was almost convinced that it was real. Only when she'd woken up from her drugged sleep, after the first five blissful seconds of ignorance, did all of the awful reality come back to her.

Mum and Dad had been the worst, which Gracie thought was ironic. They'd arrived when Jasper was in surgery, ahead of which the consultant had explained what they would be doing in excruciating detail — how they'd cut a hole in Jasper's skull, 'a decompressive craniectomy', which, she'd explained, would relieve the swelling and 'hopefully' restore normal oxygen levels.

'Hopefully?' Jake had said.

'Yes, hopefully,' the consultant had replied sternly. 'Only time will tell.'

Gracie's mother had burst through the door in her gardening gear, old trousers that used to belong to Dad tied around her waist with a belt, hiking boots on her feet. She'd stood in front of Gracie for a few moments, biting her lip.

'He's in surgery, Dervla,' Jake had said quietly.

'Surgery?' Dad had said, standing there in his cycling gear. He'd become a middle-aged man in Lycra recently, and no amount of jokes about Mamils seemed to put him off. 'What does he need surgery for?'

'There's some swelling,' Jake had said diplomatically.

Mum had nodded and sat on the edge of a red plastic seat, perched there like an anxious bird. 'So, how long before we know if he's out of the woods?'

'Twenty-four hours,' Jake had said.

'Oh,' Mum had said, reduced to silence. Gracie's dad had started an agitated pacing of the corridor. 'Alan, maybe you could sit down,' Jake had suggested.

Reluctantly, Alan had sat beside his wife, picking up the paper that had been placed on the waiting room table, noticing the headline, then putting it back down again, opting for an ancient copy of *Cricketing Monthly* instead.

There had been silence in the room, while Gracie had drifted in and out of sleep. She'd been half-lying on top of Jake, and every so often, he'd shift a little. 'I'm sorry,' she'd murmur. 'I'll sit up.'

Alison Walsh

'Rest,' he'd insist, pulling her gently back to sleep once more. Gracie had felt as if she were under water, a world where sound was muffled and where her limbs felt heavy, her breath bubbling into the blue.

Then Gracie's mother's voice had burst into the silence. 'I told you not to go back to work, Gracie. I don't know what you were thinking bringing Jasper in. Could you not have left him to that Chinese girl of yours? Isn't that what you pay her for?'

'Now is not the time, Dervla,' Jake had said.

'Well, when is the time? When the poor child's dead and gone?'

'Dervla, pet, let's stay calm,' Dad had said. 'What matters now is that Jasper recovers and we can deal with the rest later.'

'What's the rest?' Gracie had felt herself coming up from the deep, eyes opening into the harsh glare of the waiting room.

'It's nothing,' Dad had said soothingly. 'We can talk about it when we're all in a better place.'

'Talk about what?' Suddenly Gracie had been alert, sitting up in the chair, hair prickling on her scalp.

'We think Jasper should come to us for a bit,' Mum had said. 'It might be for the best.'

'You have got to be joking,' Gracie had said. 'All those months when you could have helped and the two of you did fuck-all—'

Then she had heard Jake interrupt, 'It's lovely of you to

416

offer, but I don't think you'd find the time, Dervla, what with the bridge and the choir and the flower arranging ...'

'Nothing's more important than my grandson,' Mum had said defensively.

And when exactly did you decide that? Gracie had thought bitterly.

Jake had given her a warning squeeze. 'You're too good, Dervla, but I'm taking some time out to help Gracie, so you've no need to worry on that score.'

'Have you not been on a year's timeout already?' Dad had muttered from behind his magazine.

'I've been working on website development, Alan, but point taken,' Jake had said equally. 'I'll be at home from now on.'

'You will?' Gracie had said.

'I will,' Jake had replied.

'But what about Deadpool ... Deadwood, or whatever?'

'Some things are more important,' he'd told her, 'like Jasper. And now,' he'd said, pushing Gracie gently to one side and getting up. 'Thank you for coming, Dervla, Alan.' He offered his hand to each of them in turn. 'It was good of you both, but there's no need for you to stay. We'll give you a call as soon as we have news.'

'Well, that's nice,' Mum had said sarcastically, but she'd actually looked relieved, Gracie had thought, wondering which one of them had come up with the bright idea that they should insist on taking over the care of their grandson. They probably thought they had to: they didn't want to have their reputations ruined by their younger daughter, after all. They'd want everyone to know that they were stepping in, taking action when needed — now they'd been let off the hook with a clear conscience.

'Don't mind them,' Jake had said when they'd left.

'I don't think I have the energy,' Gracie had replied. 'Jake?'

'Yes, love?'

'Why don't you blame me? Everyone else does.' She'd rested her head against his chest again, feeling the rhythmic swish of the blood pumping in his heart, the steady *thump-thump* of his heartbeat.

'We're in this together, Gracie. We always have been. If I had copped on sooner and thought to help, it ...'

'It might never have happened,' Gracie had finished for him.

'No,' Jake had said carefully. 'I don't mean it like that. It could just as easily have happened to me. I could have left him outside the supermarket or the recycling centre or anywhere — the two of us are responsible for him, Gracie, not just me or you. So we both left him outside Cutlery — that's the way I look at it, anyway.'

Except you didn't, Gracie thought now as she placed Jasper gently onto the changing table, taking care to put a clean towel under his bandaged head. The consultant had told her what to watch out for, the signs of possible brain damage — but so far, the only visible sign of his ordeal was a row of ugly staples from his ear to his left eyebrow. The scar would never really fade, even when his hair grew back — maybe he'd want to do something about that in the future, but until then, it would serve as a reminder to her of how close she'd come to losing him. She wondered how she'd answer his questions about it when he got older: how she'd explain what she'd done, even though she loved him more than anything.

She undid the snaps on his vest and removed his nappy, whereupon an arc of wee shot over his head and hit the black-and-white portrait she'd had taken of them when Jasper was two weeks old. It was one of those studio shots, she and Jake kneeling on the floor, Jasper propped up between them in her old christening gown. They looked fake, the bright smiles pinned on their faces to hide the fact that their world had been blown apart, that Jasper's arrival was a depth charge into their fragile romance. Why do people hide that kind of stuff, Gracie thought, the mess of life? Why do they pretend everything's just fantastic?

It seemed somehow fitting that Jasper wee on all three of them, and for the first time since they'd taken him home from hospital, ten days before, Gracie laughed. 'You silly boy,' she said, poking his soft tummy gently with her finger. He gurgled with delight, so she poked again and he laughed hysterically. 'It's easy to make you laugh,' she said gently. His response was another cackle.

'Everything OK?' Jake stuck his head around the door

of the nursery. He was trying not to look too eager, too keen to take Jasper off her hands. He wouldn't have been able to do so anyway because Gracie wouldn't let her son out of her sight. The social worker at the hospital had said she'd be like this for a while, but that slowly, she'd learn to let go. Gracie doubted it. She'd been given a second chance and there was no way she was going to mess it up this time, in spite of what Felicity said.

Felicity, the social worker, was what she'd ended up with after everything, and while Gracie was mortified to find herself needing supervision, and by a twenty-four-year-old from Mullingar with flat black shoes and a sensible middle parting, she'd accepted it as the very small price she'd have to pay for her negligence. She knew that the garda at the scene had been right: if she'd been a 'junkie', as she'd put it, Gracie doubted very much she'd be looking at Jasper now, safe in her arms. He'd have been carted off to some lovely middle-class couple who could 'give him what he needed', as the jargon put it. An irony, Gracie thought, and no, it wasn't fair, but then life wasn't fair. That was one of Dad's favourite sayings – and he was right, she thought now, telling Jake that she was absolutely fine. 'Go and put the lunch on,' she said, 'will you?'

Sunny had gone, thankfully, to the Mackintoshes down the road. Jen Mackintosh had five boys, all of them wild animals, so that'd keep Sunny busy. Ironically, it was easier to get things done without her around. She'd been in the way, Gracie realised as she carried Jasper carefully down the stairs: with Sunny there, there had been no need to work out how two would become three.

Jane had gone too, just the previous week, piling herself and Owen and all their stuff into a taxi and heading off to house share with one of the teachers from the school she used to teach in. She missed Jane, Gracie realised — her steadiness and her dry sense of humour, which she'd managed to retain in spite of everything. And Jane had grit: she was pressing charges against Mark, and even though he had his big law firm behind him, Gracie had a feeling that Jane would win out.

Now, Gracie supposed, she and Jake were at least giving it a shot, which was probably good because, she realised as she sat down at the kitchen table and accepted the bowl Jake put in front of her, they'd known each other for a grand total of a year and a half. Some people hadn't even moved in together at that stage, and yet, here they were, parents, in a grown-up house, living a grown-up life, whatever that was.

'Oh, this is nice,' Gracie said now, seeing what was in her bowl: a coriander-scented broth with slices of chicken, noodles and veg.

'It's ramen — I've been experimenting,' Jake said.

'Well, it looks delicious,' Gracie replied, picking up the wooden paddle that was her soup spoon, looking at it carefully.

'I'm trying out a few new things,' Jake said. 'I used to be quite the cook for a while, but then other things got in the way. And before you say it,' he said, as Gracie's head shot up, 'I don't mean you or Jasper. I mean the idea I had for myself as a thrusting businessman.'

'I thought Deadwood was a good idea,' Gracie said. 'I looked up a few other channels and they weren't doing horror, so it's a niche ...'

'Yes.' Jake smiled, slurping up his soup. 'By the way, you're supposed to slurp,' he added when Gracie gave him a look. 'It oxygenates the soup and makes it taste fresher.'

Gracie snorted with laughter and then Jake did too, and before they knew it, they were both laughing away, their voices sounding loud in the house, which had been so silent for the past ten days. Gracie put a hand over her mouth then, guiltily. She shouldn't be laughing like that when she didn't deserve it, but sometimes it was hard not to: her earlier depression had turned to a form of elation, a gleeful almost-hysteria, like someone released from a long jail sentence. For the first time since Jasper was born, absolutely nothing filled her days. No organisation of household tasks that didn't need organising, no harrying of Jake or making silly muffins to show everyone that she was still in control — and life seemed to go on nonetheless without her grimly steering it from the engine room.

And no work! Gracie thought she'd miss it, but she didn't, which was probably just as well. Toni had sent a giant bouquet of flowers, a little card pinned to the side. 'Get Well Soon!' along with a picture of a teddy bear with a bandage over its eye. Gracie hadn't known what to make of it, but then, she supposed, Toni didn't either. It was nice anyway.

'Gracie, I have something to ask you,' Jake said then. 'On the subject of Deadkill …'

'Sorry, yes, Deadkill,' Gracie corrected herself.

'I'm going to let the other two lads handle it for a while.'

'Why? It's an opportunity you don't want to let slip,' Gracie began, 'that industry moves so fast and everything. I can help, if you like.'

He interrupted her. 'It's not for me. I think I was trying to prove myself after losing my job, but what I really want is to be at home.'

'What do you mean — you *are* at home,' Gracie said carefully, spooning noodles into her mouth. God, this stuff was nice.

'I mean home, home. As a stay-at-home dad, whatever you want to call it.'

'Oh,' Gracie said. 'Oh.'

'Gracie, you need to work,' he said softly. 'You need it like oxygen — it's who you are. And what happened at Cutlery won't happen again, so for God's sake let yourself off the hook.'

Gracie shook her head adamantly. 'Nope. Never. It's a small price to pay, don't you think?' Gracie looked down at her soup, which suddenly didn't seem that appetising any more. She pushed it away from her. 'I'm sorry. I just don't seem to be hungry.'

'It's OK,' he said, coming over to her and letting her

rest her head against him. 'It's too soon. I'm sorry.'

It *is* too soon, Gracie thought, as she tidied up Jasper's little chest of drawers later, her son sitting on the floor beside her, propped up in that awful V-cushion she'd bought when she was breastfeeding, with its horrible pattern of bunny rabbits. A tiger baring its teeth, ready to pounce, would have been more appropriate as a metaphor, she thought, as she handed Jasper another little tie-vest to fold, watching as he grabbed it in his hand and tossed it gleefully onto the floor.

Then the doorbell rang. It hadn't in so long that at first Gracie didn't register it, continuing to fold pairs of little blue socks, but then it rang again. 'Oh,' she said to Jasper, 'let's see who it is, will we?'

As she walked downstairs, Jasper propped carefully on her hip, she tried to peer through the glass panels at either side of the front door, remembering that her last surprise visitor had been Elise, whom she firmly hoped never to hear from again. Cautiously, she opened the door.

'I thought if I phoned first, you'd put me off.' Atiyah was standing on the doorstep, looking not like her usual self in a pair of lemon-yellow shorts and a stripy yellow and white T-shirt. She looked more relaxed, Gracie realised, without her work uniform, her lovely hair normally pulled into a tight braid, now softly natural around her face. 'Here,' she added, 'I brought you supper.'

'Oh, thanks,' Gracie said, reaching out to take the two large plastic lunchboxes, before realising that Jasper made it difficult. 'C'mon in,' she said, ushering Atiyah into the kitchen, where she put down the lunchboxes.

'It's jollof rice, Mum's speciality — she thought you might like it. She says it'll cure any heartache, and it's true.' Atiyah smiled, taking off her little backpack and looking around.

'Sit down,' Gracie said, going over to the giant sofa and removing the bundle of papers and Jake's day-old nachos from the grey felt cushions. 'Sorry, we're still in a bit of a heap.'

Atiyah waved a hand in dismissal. 'Beats my place,' she said. 'Try sharing with four camogie queens from Kerry and you'll soon learn about mess.' She laughed.

Gracie smiled politely and inched onto the easy chair opposite Atiyah. She held Jasper to her closely, patting his little fat thigh.

'I wanted to see how you were,' Atiyah said finally. 'I'm sorry I didn't call or text before now. I didn't know what to say, to be honest. I wanted to see you face to face.'

Gracie braced herself for the diatribe: she'd got used to them during the brief notoriety she'd enjoyed, her two-day sojourn as the focus of rage on social media, before the herd galloped on to judge someone else and find them equally wanting. 'You see,' Atiyah said, hands working the strap of her backpack, 'I feel I owe you a huge apology.'

'Why?' Gracie said, baffled.

'I feel that I let you down. We all did, and I am so sorry about that.'

'What do you mean?'

'Oh, the fact that we took a new mum from her baby and made her work her ass off for weeks on end for nothing, except the vague promise of her job back – which was actually her entitlement, not an optional extra – and we blame her for what happened then. Nice. It's really opened my eyes, let me tell you,' she said with a small smile. 'So much for all that family-friendly BS Toni comes out with. When it comes down to it, she's as bad as the men – honest.'

'Well, it's tougher for women,' Gracie said kindly. 'To succeed in that world, you have to prove your balls are bigger than theirs.'

Atiyah shook her head. 'Nope. No, you don't. You have to prove that you have fresh ideas and that you can make them work. That's all. It's as simple as that. Or it should be.' She picked away at a loose thread on the sofa and Gracie suppressed the urge to tell her to stop – she'd make a big ladder in it if she didn't. 'It's some world where your duty to the human race comes second to bloody cat food,' Atiyah said. 'Anyway, I told Toni to go and stuff her job – *your* job, which she offered me while you were in hospital, by the way. And I'm saying this not to make you feel worse, but just to make you understand what you were up against,' and she rolled her eyes to heaven.

'Well, thanks,' Gracie said. 'But there was no need. I don't think I'll be going back to Cutlery somehow.'

'You should,' Atiyah said. 'That's the only way Toni will learn. You go back and dare her not to give you back your job, then you sit there until a time of your choosing, before you tell her to fuck the hell off. Your terms.'

'Ah, no, Atiyah. I couldn't face her. I couldn't face anyone in that place,' Gracie said, a flashback to them all standing on the steps, mouths open, filling her mind. 'But thanks for your support. You should take the job, you know. Get the experience then take it elsewhere in a few months' time.'

'Well, that's what I was thinking, actually,' Atiyah said.

'What?'

'I was hoping that maybe you and I might do something,' Atiyah said. 'I think we could poach Kitty-Kat from Toni — in fact, nothing would give me greater pleasure. That Maurice fellow has taken a real shine to me.' She giggled. 'Sexist pig — but he's a rich sexist pig, so that makes life a bit easier. Says he likes my energy — he actually said my "ju-ju",' and she exploded with laughter.

Gracie couldn't help letting a small giggle escape, before admitting, 'I wasn't a lot better, Atiyah. I'm sorry, if that's any good.'

Atiyah shrugged. 'Look, I'm used to it, and if we work together, you'll get an education.' She smiled.

'I need it,' Gracie admitted. 'But let me think about it, OK? It's a bit soon.'

'Of course,' Atiyah said. 'I'll keep Maurice's account warm in the meantime,' and they both exchanged a smile.

Atiyah refused all refreshment, prising Jasper from Gracie's grip for a few minutes to put him on her knee and play 'Incy-Wincy Spider', which made him laugh hysterically, and then she said, 'Well, I'll be off.'

Gracie didn't bother to say the usual stuff, the 'won't you at least have a coffee', the foisting of biscuits — homemade, of course — on the house guest. She couldn't really be bothered with that kind of thing at the moment, whatever Mum would have to say about her lack of manners — and actually it didn't matter. A lot of things no longer mattered, she realised, including standards. Standards had been the cause of so much trouble: it was time to ditch them for a while.

'Don't be a stranger,' Atiyah said, standing on the doorstep.

'I won't — anyway, I have to give you back your lunchboxes,' Gracie said. 'Will you thank your mum for me? People have been so kind.' She pushed the lump down in her throat. 'I'm sorry, I just wasn't expecting it. I don't feel I deserve it.'

Atiyah nodded. 'I know.' Then she pulled Gracie into a tight hug. 'But it'll get better. One day at a time, eh?' And she reached out and gave Jasper a gentle pinch on the cheek, blowing a loud raspberry, which he seemed to find very amusing. 'It's a cliché, but it's true.'

Gracie didn't know how Atiyah had come to learn this, but she'd ask her soon, she thought, as she and Jasper stood on the doorstep, waving at her.

*

Jake spent the next couple of weeks quietly showing her how he could make it work, this new life of theirs. He had even done a spreadsheet, with little boxes showing her how much money they could save by taking in a lodger or by renting this place out and moving somewhere smaller, how much of an income stream they might get from Deadkill, even with his reduced role in the business. 'It's still my creation, so if it takes off, there'll be money from that ...'

'You have it all worked out,' Gracie said. 'But where does that leave me?' She thought of Atiyah and of Maurice with his slicked-back hair pressed to his greasy head. She could certainly work with Atiyah, but could she work with him – would she want to?

'It leaves you wherever you want to be,' Jake said, kissing her on the top of her head and leaving her in front of the laptop, wandering off to take a lemon-and-raspberry tray bake out of the oven. He'd made it for the mother-and-baby group at the church hall, proclaiming himself delighted to be the only father-and-baby, prising Jasper out of Gracie's hands every Tuesday morning and heading off, just the two of them. Gracie felt empty then, her arms light without the weight of Jasper in them, but she managed to quell her anxiety about him, knowing that she'd have to get into the habit eventually. She sat on the sofa for the couple of hours they were gone, reading, of all things. She hadn't read a book in years. She'd forgotten that words could be so enjoyable, as she ploughed her way through the summer's thrillers, people killing each other every second page, blood spatter and brain matter scattered over every chapter. The funny thing was, they weren't that disturbing, which Gracie thought probably said a lot about her mental state.

She left Toni until she was feeling a bit better, six weeks later. She walked into town this time, memories of that last crawl along the baking streets too fresh in her mind. It was much cooler now, in October, and Gracie found that she was almost enjoying herself as she followed the path along the river, with the dog walkers and the young mums like her, then around the flying-saucer shape of the stadium, until she turned right towards town. She'd left Jasper with Jake, knowing that he'd be safe.

Tracey at reception nearly fainted when she appeared, eyes widening as Gracie waved. 'Will I call up to her?' she said as Gracie wafted by.

'No need,' Gracie said. 'I'd like to maintain the element of surprise.'

'Right,' Tracey said quietly. Gracie felt like giving her the finger but decided dignity was the better option. She walked slowly up the wooden stairs, knowing that Tracey would have rung Toni anyway, and sure enough, when she got to the first floor, there was Circe, in one of her 1950s summer dresses, hair tied up in bunches. 'Gracieeeee!' she said. 'What a surprise.' She didn't move to hug Gracie and

Gracie was glad about that, because then she'd have had to deck Circe, and she didn't want to unless she had to.

'Not a good one, I'd say,' Gracie replied, smiling.

Circe giggled nervously. 'Toni's just finishing a meeting. Do you mind waiting?'

'Not at all.' Gracie smiled warmly. 'I have all the time in the world.'

'Well, that's nice,' Circe said. 'Coffee, tea, soft drink?'

'Water would be good.'

'Sure,' Circe said, wandering off to the water fountain, leaving Gracie on the squashy guests' sofa outside Toni's door. How many times had she waited here, Gracie thought, to worship at the altar? But then, she'd learned a lot at Cutlery: she had to give Toni that. She'd been allowed to make her own decisions, to make mistakes and to learn, all of which she'd be glad to take with her somewhere else. Because she would be going somewhere else. That's what happened when someone broke your trust, as Toni had broken hers.

She waited for almost an hour, until she was beginning to think that Toni wasn't going to face her, but then the door opened and there she was, this tiny little reed of a woman with her helmet of greenish-auburn hair, her stick-like legs, her uniform of cashmere knit and skirt. 'Gracie,' she said softly, opening her arms.

No way, Gracie thought, standing up. We are *not* hugging. She waited until Toni's arms dropped and then she said, 'Thanks for seeing me, Toni.'

'And why on earth wouldn't I see the best marketing executive I've ever had,' Toni said, tilting her head to one side, like a bird. 'My door is always open, Gracie. I hope you know that.'

'Thanks,' Gracie said, sweeping past her into her office, where she sat on the silly red cube, waiting for Toni to busy herself pouring a glass of water, sipping it slowly, obviously playing for time. Gracie knew that Toni wouldn't mention Jasper, the elephant in the room — she wouldn't have the balls — but she still waited. You go first, she thought, as Toni perched nervously on her desk.

'So ...' Toni said. 'Gracie, how *are* you?' Her face was a picture of concern.

'Honestly? In bits.' She looked at Toni, and when the other woman didn't respond, she added, 'Have you ever endangered someone's life? Really? Done something that could result in harm to another human being?'

'No,' Toni said quietly.

'Well, I have,' Gracie said. 'And it turns out that it really is the worst thing that can ever happen to you.'

'Yes,' Toni whispered. 'I can imagine.'

'Can you?' Gracie barked. 'I know that I'll lose people in life: my parents will die, I'll grow old, maybe I'll get sick, maybe I'll get knocked down by the 46A bus — but none of it will match up to what happened to Jasper. What I did to him. And no amount of people telling me it wasn't my fault will make a jot of difference because it *was* my fault. One hundred per cent. And I have to live with that for the rest of my life. And you know what? I'm glad about it. I'm glad I'll have to live with that guilt: it'll keep me human. You know that cheesy expression "What doesn't kill you will make you stronger"? Bullshit. It's weakness that really matters, Toni, not strength, as it turns out. I'm not strong any more. I'm fallible and guilty and weak, and hopefully it'll make me a slightly better person.'

When she'd finished her speech, she just sat there, in shock. Who had said those words — was it really her? The terrified look on Toni's face told Gracie that it was, and she was glad because she felt as if they were the truest words she'd spoken in a long time.

'Thank you for sharing that with me, Gracie,' Toni said. 'I'm humbled by your honesty.'

'Ah, will you fuck off,' Gracie replied. 'Try treating your employees with genuine respect for a change, instead of spouting meaningless drivel. All that bloody hugging when you didn't have the manners to leave me alone while I was on my maternity leave. I gave you everything — my loyalty, my effort, my energy. I gave you the best year of my life and what did I get in return?'

'I don't know,' Toni whispered.

'I got what I deserved.' Gracie said this quietly, getting up off the tiny pouffy nonsense of a chair and putting her bag on her shoulder. She turned to Toni then. 'I could fight you, Toni, to come back to this place, but I won't. I won't embarrass you. A year's salary and you'll never have to see me again.'

'Done,' Toni said, with an alacrity Gracie found almost amusing. She extended a hand and when Toni put her tiny little fingers in hers, Gracie gave a good, hard squeeze.

Not exactly one for the sisterhood, Gracie thought as she left Toni's office. Nothing would change while women like her took deals, accepted less than their due because they'd had the temerity to have a baby, but the fight wasn't in her. Not now and possibly not ever, and she suspected that she wasn't alone in this – that lots of women had walked out of offices like Cutlery's every day, never to return, beaten by the system, beaten by empty words about equality and parity which, when it came down to it, meant nothing. She walked slowly down the stairs for the last time, watching everyone in their little cubicles beavering away, giving their best for Toni and the team. For what? she wondered. Another little hug? A silly mug with your name on it or a gift voucher in place of a pay rise? It was all meaningless – but then, I'm hardly the first person to work that out, she thought ruefully.

When she got to the bottom of the stairs, Gar was standing there in his red Cork jersey, looking nervous. 'Gar!' Gracie pulled him into a hug, a genuine one, and as she pressed herself to his flabby body, he murmured in her ear, 'I'm so sorry, Gracie, girl. It's shit what happened to you. Absolute shit.'

Gracie held him at arm's length. 'It's fine, Gar. I have Jasper and that's all that matters.'

His eyes filled with tears, and he shook his head sadly. 'Ah, dear,' he said. 'Dear, oh dear.'

'Gar, don't be sad, please?'

He gave a sniff then whipped out the hand he'd been hiding behind his back. In it was a portrait of Jasper in a cute little ceramic frame. In the photo he was wearing his miniature Cork jersey, stripes of red across his face, and he looked so happy, so full of life, his hand reaching out towards the photographer. My son, Gracie thought.

'Thanks, Gar. I think that's the nicest present I've ever got,' Gracie said. 'Another hug?'

'Ah, go on, so,' he said.

This time, they did the man-clap manoeuvre, both of them slapping each other on the back, and then Gracie stood back, the little picture in her hand.' So, see you round.'

'Yah, girl, you will,' Gar said quietly. 'Better be going back. Nose to the grindstone and all that.'

'Take care, Gar,' Gracie said, and then she turned, walking past Tracey again, this time flipping the bird with gusto, and out onto the sunlit street.

21

Elise

I never thought I'd find myself in Gracie's lovely car again, watching the sea go by as we drive to Brittas Bay – but here I am! I thought the girls would never speak to me again after that afternoon in the park, but two days ago, Jane rang. I was on the sofa, where I usually am these days, eating from a tin of those nice butter biscuits that Gray's ma brought the last time she visited. I keep telling Maeve not to bring anything, but she never comes empty-handed, God love her.

To be honest, eating's the only thing that's kept me going over the past couple of months. That, and walking Chloe. Every morning, we take a long walk, making sure to avoid the park and instead going along the river, Chloe sitting up in her new lightweight buggy, that feels so easy to push after that juggernaut of a Silver Cross, Poppy trotting along beside me. I have to keep Poppy on a tight lead because she's been lunging at people all the time recently — well, she's actually been lunging at old men, and specifically the ones who wear those awful red corduroys. She has taste, that dog.

The walk takes me at least two hours, so plenty of time to think everything through. 'Make up your mind, Elise,' Gray said to me when we had our heart-to-heart a few days after Jasper's accident. 'And I'll be waiting.' It was good of him, but then Gray's one of the best.

It was actually Jasper who brought things to a head between Gray and me, the poor mite. I'd come home from the park, ranting and raving about Gracie and what a careless mother she was, how I'd never let that kind of thing happen to Chloe and so on, banging pots on the stove and opening and shutting cupboards with a clatter. Gray let me go on until I ran out of steam and then he said, 'Elise. What's wrong?'

'What do you mean "what's wrong"?' I said. 'I would have thought it was bloody obvious.'

I was standing with the Le Creuset in my hand, like a weapon, and he came and gently took it off me. 'Sit down,' he said. 'Now, what has you like this, Elise? Tell me. We've always been able to talk.'

'Oh, I don't know,' I said sadly. 'I just feel so terrible

for Jasper and maybe I feel a bit bad about judging Gracie because it could so easily happen to me, even though I think she must have been out of her mind—'

'The truth, Elise,' Gray said softly. 'Tell me the truth.'

'It *is* the truth!' I said indignantly. 'Gracie's child nearly died, so I think I have the right to be upset about it!'

Gray just shrugged then and said absolutely nothing while I cooked our dinner in silence, and we both sat in front of the telly to eat — standards have slipped in our house recently, I can tell you. As I ate the steamed chicken, pretending to watch some travel show, my mind was racing. A film of the summer was playing in my head: the freedom of Brittas Bay, the golden afternoons in the park, the four of us sharing secrets and really confiding in each other. And I'd gone and ruined it all with my big mouth. I hadn't been able to keep my own judgemental thoughts to myself.

'Gray,' I said. 'I need to tell you something.'

He turned to me then and said, 'Good.'

I have no idea how he knew, but he just knew. The big secret that I've been holding inside for all these years isn't really a secret at all. I wonder how many other people know. Do I have it tattooed on my forehead?

'You know I love you,' he said, as the TV murmured in the background. 'I always will. But I also know that honesty makes a relationship, babe, and if we can't be honest with each other, we have nothing. Nada.' He looked at me with those gorgeous baby blues of his and I knew it was time. But could I say it? I couldn't just get my mouth to open and tell Gray the truth. Instead, I just sat there, like a complete eejit. Where's my 'foot-in-mouth' disease when I bloody need it, I thought.

Eventually, he said it for me. 'Do you like women?'

'I think so,' I reply. 'More than like them, really,' I added in a near-whisper, thinking of Fiona and her lovely softness, of Lina's tanned skin. What a fool I am, I thought, to have lied to myself — and Gray — like that.

His face crumpled, and he looked as if he was going to cry, my big, brave man. I didn't know what to do, so I reached out to give him a hug, but he pushed me away.

'Gray, I'm sorry ...' I began. 'I'm not doing it on purpose. It's just who I am. I didn't mean to hoodwink you when we got married, it's not like that. It was just that I never admitted to myself until now who I really was. I thought that if I tried really hard, I could live normally—'

He cut me off. 'There's nothing abnormal about it, Elise, and there's nothing whatsoever wrong with being gay. I just wish you'd been honest with me. That you didn't make me fall in love with you first.' His voice broke then and the tears poured down his lovely face. My heart plummeted.

'I fell in love with you too,' I said. 'It's the truth.' It *is* the truth — Gray means everything to me, just not in that special way, a way that feels so obvious to me now that I can't believe I never really saw it. 'How could I tell you, when I couldn't be honest with myself?' I added. I didn't tell him about Fiona and about Ma calling me a freak — what was the point? I'd done enough damage.

He shrugged then and sniffed, accepting the balled-up bit of tissue I held out to him. 'I'm going to sleep in the spare room.'

'Ah, Gray, don't do that,' I said. 'Please. I need you. I can't be without you.' I knew that I sounded desperate — and I felt desperate — but I love Gray as my best friend and as Chloe's dad. I'll always love him. No other person in the world knows me as he does.

'We both have some thinking to do, love. I'm not sure I can live like this — that's the truth,' he added when he saw my stricken look. 'Work out what it is you want and then we'll talk,' he said.

What *I* want — God, where do I even start? I've always gone along with what other people wanted. I've just wombled along, agreeing with what they suggested, allowing them to take the lead. Maybe that's why I feel so lonely sometimes, because I don't have the nerve to do what *I* want to do. And I keep putting my foot in it, which definitely doesn't help. Honestly, there should be a course in this kind of thing — but if there was, I'd probably fail it anyway.

Gray said he'd stay in the spare room while we were 'working things out', but I said no. I haven't suddenly developed an allergy to the man, and besides, I'd really missed his warmth in the bed beside me, the sense that there's no other person in the world who knows me better than he does. After I'd made that decision, I sat down to write to the girls, to each of them in turn. I didn't have their postal addresses, so I cut and pasted the message from my laptop to my phone messaging. I can't type big long messages on my phone with these acrylic nails anyway: they're a bloody nuisance — and they cost a fortune.

I started with Gracie and I told her exactly what I'd said at the park: how I'd blamed her and how sorry I was for doing it, which I am. I didn't leave anything out because I wanted to tell her the full truth and leave it up to her whether or not to forgive me. I know that I'm a good mum, but so is Gracie: she just had a lot more to deal with than I did. Then I wrote to Lina and I told her that I was really sorry that git had groped her and that I'd gladly kneecap him — all she had to do was say the word. I didn't mention the crush I'd had on her because I know that's what it is and that it's not going anywhere. It might with someone else, but not with Lina, even if I'm completely mortified to have behaved like a lovesick teenager. Finally, I wrote to Jane, and I cried as I told her how ashamed I'd felt that I'd done nothing to help her when she'd needed it. 'I'm sorry I failed you as a friend,' I wrote. 'When all you did was be mine.' Which is true. Of all the girls, Jane was the one who had truly accepted me, warts and all. And all I did was find fault with her in the silliest ways.

I sent the messages and I waited. And then, silence. Well, that's it, I thought. Game over. At least I'd done the right thing this time. So when Jane rang, two weeks later, I couldn't believe it at first. I can remember picking up my phone and seeing a thumbnail of her face appearing on the screen. I stared at it for ages before I pressed Accept.

'Jane?'

'Hi, Elise,' Jane said. Her voice was soft, as usual, but there was something else there too. Something firmer, more definite.

'Long time, no speak,' I said, cursing myself for my inability to say something more witty or intelligent.

'Aha, that's true,' Jane said, letting that fact hang in the air.

'How is ... everyone?' I said carefully.

'We're all fine,' she said. 'We're doing well.'

'Great,' I said. I was about to launch into twenty questions, but then I told myself to shut the hell up. I just waited.

'So, listen, I'm calling because we're going to Brittas Bay on Saturday. We thought you might like to come. The last weekend in autumn, that kind of thing. It's supposed to be a full stop to the summer, but it's really for Gracie. She needs our support.'

'I don't know, Jane ...' Sending them letters was all well and good, but facing them in person was more than I could manage, I thought.

'Please?'

*

I had to ask Gray — not because I need his permission, but because I know that he blames the girls, even though I told him that it wasn't their fault that I'd changed. They may have been the catalysts, but somewhere deep down, I expect that I wanted it. I wanted to be me.

Gray was in the home gym, using one of those rowing machines that look like pure hell, his face red with effort as he pulled himself back and forth. When he saw me, though, he stopped, draping a towel across his neck, wiping his face with a corner. 'Hi, babe.' He gave me that smile that could always melt my heart.

I told him about Jane's invitation, waiting for the backlash, for the fight that would follow. But instead he just said, 'Go'.

'But what about us?'

'Look, we haven't been speaking for the last few weeks and we've been sitting a few feet away from each other. I can't think that fifty miles will make much of a difference.'

'Oh,' I said. 'Right, then.' Then we both looked at each other and laughed.

Jane is driving because Gracie can't. She hasn't been able to since that day with Jasper, which is terrible, really. She has a complete phobia about driving now, and when they pull up outside mine, her face is white and she's gripping the handle of Jasper's little car seat. Her eyes are locked on him, as if she is a lioness, eyes fixed on her cub. Lina sits beside her, the hypocrite – I have to call a spade a spade, even if only in my mind, which is progress – while I sit in the front with Jane. I'm relieved that I don't have to sit beside Gracie, because I just can't face her yet.

I'm wondering what Jane and I will find to talk about for a whole hour, but honestly, she never draws breath, keeping up a stream of chatter all the way down, asking me what my plans are for the future. 'I'm going back to work soon,' she says cheerfully. 'And I'm going to retrain as a drama teacher. I tell you, I can't wait. I know that motherhood is amazing and all that, but I found it so lonely. And besides, I need the money now that I'm a single parent.'

Now's my chance. I take a deep breath. 'Jane, I'm sorry, I should have done something,' I begin, but she lifts a hand to stop me. 'Please, Elise. There's no need. You sent me that lovely message anyway, and I appreciated that.'

'Thanks,' I say. 'I meant it.'

'I know.' She smiles. 'You've never said anything you don't mean, Elise.' I open my mouth to protest, but then I see that she's joking and so we both laugh. 'Do you know, Lina's mum wanted to post photos of me online?'

'She did? Why?'

'As a warning to other women about domestic violence. She has a point, but I told her that I'm not on a crusade. Shouting about it in public won't make what he did go away, or make him less of a danger. Putting him in jail will.'

Lina's mum has a big anti-sexism social media campaign on the go. Honestly, the woman is seventy and yet she's taken to it like a duck to water, posting all kinds of things about 'structural inequality', whatever that is. Now, Lina is going on some kind of march along with 'women in the media' to denounce sexism and double standards. It's a good idea and I'm hoping she'll ask me along: mind you, she won't be getting me to wear one of those awful hearts her mother's knitted. They look like shredded wheat. So ugly.

'So, you're going to press charges, then?'

'I am,' Jane says. 'Even if he walks, I'll still know that I did something about him. The thing is, he's so bloody plausible. When I met him first, I loved the sense that he was in control — I thought it was romantic, can you believe it? Opening doors, ordering for me, buying clothes for me ... I was so naive.' She shrugs. 'I can't guarantee that he won't do it again with another woman, but at least, if he tries, I'll know that I've done everything possible to stop him.'

'Good for you, Jane,' I say.

'What about you? Any plans?' Jane asks me.

Oh, God, I think. For the first time in my life, I haven't a clue. 'I'm not sure what I'll be doing,' I say vaguely. 'I'd love to have another — Chloe needs a brother or sister. In fact, I'd like a football team!'

I would like a football team, it's the truth. I love Chloe and I love babies, so bring it on, but where Gray will fit into my life, I'm not sure. I'd be lying if I said otherwise.

'I'm not sure Gray and I will stay together,' I say quietly. 'I love him, but I need time to be myself.'

There's a slight pause before Jane says, 'Oh, I'm sorry to hear that. I thought he was one of the good ones.' She gives that cryptic Jane smile. I'm about to agree, when she adds, 'I think Owen will be an only child.' That's kind of sad, I think, but then, after what she's been through, I can hardly blame her.

We pull up outside Gracie's magnificent 'van' in the gloom. It sure looks different under a grey sky in late October! The little plants on the sun deck are drooping and dusty, the sea is a kind of steely grey – and the resort is deserted. You can practically see the tumbleweed.

'Here we are!' Jane says in her best jolly-hockey-sticks voice. There is a long silence and my heart sinks. Uh-oh – this is going to be a long weekend.

Then Lina pipes up. 'Great! Let's get the barbecue on and the cocktails brewing.'

Gracie looks as if she'll fade away with misery, but she lets Jane open the door and help her and Jasper out of the car. She stands on the deck for a long time, staring at the sea, Jasper's seat beside her. Jane goes to lift him into the kitchen, but she says, 'Please, leave him. I'll look after him.'

'Of course,' Jane says, leading her to the lovely cream outdoor sofas, now covered with a grey tarpaulin. She unzips it and pulls it off and settles Gracie down on one of the cushions, running into the kitchen and coming back with a bright-yellow throw which she tucks around her, placing Jasper right at her feet.

We troop into the kitchen then and look through the French windows at Gracie, sitting immobile outside.

'I'm not sure this was such a good idea,' Lina murmurs, putting the contents of the supermarket bags into the cupboards and fridge, placing a bottle of champagne on the counter and looking at it as if it's dangerous. Then she shrugs. 'Oh, well, we might as well drink — it can't make matters worse.' She goes to the cupboard and takes down four glasses, then undoes the wire on top of the bottle and pushes the cork, so it shoots out with a loud 'pop'. 'Ah, yes,' she says happily, filling four glasses before bringing one outside and handing it to Gracie, who looks as if she is being given an unexploded missile, not a flute of champagne. I can see her shaking her head and Lina persisting, before putting it gently down on the table in front of her.

I offer Jane a glass. 'Oh, I don't know,' she says. 'Remember what I was like the last time?'

'It was funny in an awful way.' I smile.

'I'm sure it was,' she agrees, taking a glass from me and disappearing into the biggest bedroom, from where her voice drifts out. 'I'll get this room ready for Gracie, OK? I'm sure you girls won't mind giving her the nicest one.'

'Of course not,' I say, taking a long swig of the champagne, feeling the bubbles shoot up my nose. It gets stuck in my throat then, and I start coughing and coughing

Alison Walsh

until I have to get a glass of water to wash it down. 'I'm out of practice,' I say.

'I'm sure you'll get the hang of it again,' Jane says, emerging from the bedroom, a smile on her face. She fills our glasses once more. 'Time for some training,' she says. Honestly, she's a bit of a surprise, is Jane.

Because Gracie isn't in charge, dinner is supermarket burgers and cheap buns, but they sure taste good. Sometimes simple, dirty food is all you need. We sit outside after, even though it's bloody freezing. At first, we talk around things, with silly small talk about the weather and how quiet everything is after the summer. We are all circling the elephant in the room, of course. Not just what happened with Gracie, but everything that went on this summer for all of us. I have no idea how I'll break it to them, my other news. How do you do these things? I haven't a clue — but maybe they'll be like Gray and say they already know, seeing as I have a beacon flashing above my head with 'I AM GAY' on it. It seems important that I tell them, though: it's my first step in living my new life, in being truly myself. And then there's what I'd said about Gracie behind her back. I'm waiting for my chance to get it all out in the open. It's the only way. But I'll need a few more glasses of bubbly first.

Gracie is looking a bit more cheerful. She takes a small sip of her champagne. 'Hmm, nice. I'd forgotten champagne tasted so yummy.'

The others laugh. 'Better drink some more of it then to remind ourselves,' Jane says, leaping up and going into the kitchen, returning with another ice-cold bottle in her hand, streaks of moisture running down the green glass. 'Ta-dah,' she says, putting a tea towel over the cork and pulling it gently so that it opens with a soft *thunk*.

'I like your technique,' Lina says.

'Why, thank you. I worked in a hotel in Limerick for a summer and we did lots of weddings. That's where I picked it up. I'm a dab hand at using a fish-knife and laying the correct place settings.' She gives a little giggle. 'All essential life skills.'

'I worked in a chicken factory in Enniscorthy once,' Lina says, holding out her glass, letting Jane fill it almost to the top. 'I can truthfully say that it was the worst job I've ever done: it was a really hot summer, but it was refrigerated inside, so we all had to sit in parkas, plucking chickens. Twelve an hour, or we'd get fined.'

'I had a modelling job once,' I say. 'I had to get a spray tan and stand on O'Connell Street in a bikini in November selling packet soup.'

'Oh, that's a good one,' Jane says, then they all start lobbing in crap jobs: rodent exterminator, armpit-sniffer for deodorants, sewer cleaner and so on. I don't know why they think they're so funny: my eldest brother, Paddy, drives a septic tank truck — at least, that's what he was doing when I last heard from him. Maybe I'll give him a shout, tell him the news that comes as no surprise to anyone except me. I miss Paddy.

'That's nothing,' Gracie says. 'I worked at a rock festival once, cleaning the toilets. The deal was, I could go to any of the gigs I wanted, as long as I did an hour's cleaning morning and evening. I have never seen anything like it.' She shakes her head. 'I actually took photos of me posing beside them to show my friends.' She laughs. 'Hang on,' and she rummages in her handbag. 'I have one in here, I think.' She takes out her wallet and leafs through the contents, emerging with a dog-eared photo. 'Ready?'

'I've just eaten,' Jane says, taking it gingerly between thumb and forefinger. She looks at it and clamps a hand over her mouth. 'Oh, that's gross.'

'Here, let's see,' Lina says, guffawing when she takes the photo and looks at it. 'That is totally disgusting.'

'I know,' Gracie says. 'I keep it in here as a reminder that, no matter how bad things may seem, they are not on a par with this.' There is a moment's silence, to which she adds, 'Well, until now, anyway.'

I see my chance and open my mouth to say something, but Jane gets there first, putting an arm around Gracie and giving her shoulder a squeeze. 'Well, here's to things getting better,' and the three hold their glasses aloft. 'C'mon, Elise,' Jane says, inviting me to join them.

'Ah, no,' I say quietly. 'I can't.'

'Why not?' Lina says.

'You all know why not.' I debate whether or not to name

it, my betrayal, before deciding that I should know better by now. These women would never do anything as vulgar as air their dirty laundry in public. If I've learned anything this summer, it's that.

Then Gracie speaks. 'I don't know what you're talking about, Elise. If it's the lovely letter you sent me, I should have thanked you earlier. I really appreciated it.'

Forgiveness. There it is, staring me in the face. I have to decide whether to grab it or to let it go. To continue on my lonely road or to accept the mistakes I've made and the olive branch that's being extended to me. To understand that friendship — real friendship — is full of moments like this. I play for time, getting up and going to the little bar, lifting the bottle up and pouring the last drop into my glass. And then I go and sit back down beside Jane. She's wrapped in a blanket and she lifts a corner of it and flips it over my knees, winking at me. 'We'll keep each other warm.'

I lift my glass then, and I say, 'A toast. To a summer we'll never forget.'

'God, you can say that again,' Lina says, and we all laugh quietly in spite of ourselves.

We sit there for a while longer, in the pitch darkness of late October, until it gets too cold, and Jane says she'll boil the kettle for hot water bottles and she wanders off to the kitchen, followed by Gracie, who wants to check on Jasper, for the hundredth time. Now, it's just Lina and me, the two of us facing each other on the lovely squashy sofa. Lina takes a sip from her champagne and looks thoughtful. I want to ask her about her woman-only comedy show that her mother's been shouting about all over Twitter, and whether she might invite me to come along, but instead, she says, 'Listen, how's the swimming going?'

'Badly,' I reply. 'I haven't been in since the last time we were here.' Adding to myself, the time I fell for you, like a hormonal teenager, and my life was turned upside down.

'Well, we'll have to fix that,' she says. 'You will not leave Brittas Bay this time without being able to swim. Deal?'

'Deal,' I reply, looking warily at the gloomy water. She laughs and reaches over to me, giving me a hug, then gets up and says, 'Right. If we're getting up early for our lesson, I'd better turn in. Don't stay up too late.'

'I won't,' I say. 'I just want to sit here for a little bit longer.' And so I do, sipping my champagne and thinking of the girls, asleep in their beds, and our babies and how lucky we are to have each other. My friends.

Acknowledgements

To Colm for being there this year, and all of the other years, and for wisely ignoring what he needs to ignore. To my children, Eoin, Niamh and Cian for being themselves. To my sister, Caitriona, with whom I laughed last year as I haven't in twenty years, and to the lovely Dannan and Sadhbh. To the wider Walsh and O'Gaora clans, my thanks, particularly to Annette — and a big cheer for Cliona, embarking on her own new journey with Rory.

Thanks to my agent, Marianne Gunn O'Connor, and to the ever-patient Patrick Lynch. Joanna Smyth at Hachette Ireland made this novel much better, and I'm grateful to her for her careful reading and for shared laughs. Also, to Ciara Doorley, Breda Purdue, Jim Binchy, Ciara Considine, Bernard Hoban, Siobhan Tierney and Ruth Shern, as well as to Elaine Egan. A special thank you to Susan Feldstein for her tact and patience and excellent suggestions. Thanks again to Emma Dunne for her eagle eye at the copy-editing stage. Thanks to my 'favourite cousin', Kate Walsh-Mutlu for translation help and to Louise Williams for her insights.

To my friends Nerea Lerchundi and Eleanor Kennedy, for shared chat and laughter, and for regular check-ups, to Veronique O'Leary for so much practical help, to Sara Morris and David Silke for support and inspiration, and to Enda Wyley for her good humour and fun. To the Dog Walkers: Therese and Therese, Rita, Patricia, Grainne, Louise, Cale and Eileen, for all those coffees and walks in the park and for channelling their inner Midge! Most of all, to the staff at St Vincent's University and Private Hospitals and St Luke's hospital, for the wonderful work they do.